SHIVERS

EDITED BY RICHARD CHIZMAR

CEMETERY DANCE PUBLICATIONS

Baltimore
❖ 2002 ❖

SHIVERS
Copyright © 2002 by Cemetery Dance Publications

Cemetery Dance Publications 2002
ISBN: 1-58767-063-1

All persons in this book are fictitious, and any resemblance that may seem to exist to actual persons living or dead is purely coincidental. This is a work of fiction.

Dust Jacket Art: © 2002 by Gail Cross
Dust Jacket Design: Gail Cross
Typesetting and Design: David G. Barnett
Printed in the United States of America

Cemetery Dance Publications
P.O. Box 943
Abingdon, MD 21009
http://www.cemeterydance.com

10 9 8 7 6 5 4 3 2 1

Second Printing

Fodder

Brian Keene
and Tim Lebbon

'What passing-bells for these who dies as cattle?'
—Wilfred Owen

The sun was already scorching, yet Private William Potter's watch showed only nine o'clock. The straps of his knapsack chafed his skin as he walked. He tried to ignore the protests from his aching muscles, but his blistered feet were balls of flame, and his neck was burned lobster-red. He had never felt so exhausted.

The remaining men of the British 3rd Infantry shuffled southward. Swirling clouds of dust, kicked up by their boots, marked their passage along the road towards Argonne. Around them, the beet fields had come to life with the buzzing chatter of insects and the birds' morning chorus, interrupted only by muffled booms from the front; intermittent, yet always present. The sounds of battle were drawing closer with every step.

William blinked the sweat from his eyes and listened to the symphony around him, losing himself in the strange beauty of the moment. The strings and brass of the remaining wildlife accompanied the angry percussion of man. A new poem began to suggest itself to him then, and he longed for a sheet of paper and a pen to write it down. He was away pondering the first line when he slammed into Liggett.

"You Bollocks," the irate Corporal spat in his thick Cockney accent, "why don't you watch where yer going?"

"Sorry Liggett," William mumbled apologetically. "I was listening to the birds."

"Oh yeah, listening to the birds, were you? Walking around with

7

your bloody head in the clouds more like." He stopped to rescue his dropped cigarette from the dirt.

"He's right, William," laughed Winston. "Keep going like you are, you'll float above this mess one day."

"Leave him be," Morris said, coming to his friend's defense. "You can laugh all you want now, but William will have the last laugh when he writes a book about all of this."

"Not if he gets his head blown off first," Liggett mumbled, "and that's exactly what'll happen if he don't join the rest of us back down here on earth." His mood did not improve when he found the cigarette in a small, brown puddle. "Look at this," he gasped. "The only bit of water on this whole bleeding road, and Potter makes me drop my last ciggie in it!"

"Can we have a break, Crown Sergeant?" Winston called out to the large man ahead of him.

Crown Sergeant Sterling paused and looked back at the four men. "I suppose you lads will be wanting tea next then?"

"No, Crown Sergeant, it's just that we haven't stopped since..." Winston's voice trailed off, lost in the warbling of the birds.

William closed his eyes and unbidden images of the last battle flooded in, the horrors of close-quarter bayonet fighting, the brutal, terrified expressions on their enemies' faces that meant *It's you or me.* Hideous memories of how Dunhill and the others had died.

Sterling softened. The past was haunting him as well.

"I guess we could all do with a break," he said quietly. "Right then! We'll rest here and carry on just before sunset. Should be there within another couple of hours."

Gratefully the exhausted men unslung their knapsacks, rested their rifles upright to keep them clean and sank to the ground. William felt his muscles knotting into cramps, and he spent long minutes stretching the pain away. He did not mind the cramps. He could deal with them. There were far worse pains he had seen other people suffering, indignities visited upon them by murderous Man...

"What will we do when we reach the forest, Crown Sergeant," Morris asked.

The big man drank deeply from his canteen before answering. "Find out if any of the other lads made it out alive," he answered grimly. "See if we're the lot of it. If so, we'll fall in with the French and the Yanks until we reach the Hindenburg line. The Yanks are sure to have a radio. I'll get advisement from headquarters on what we're to do."

"If it's all the same to you, Crown Sergeant," Winston joked, "I'll just walk on to London. I've seen enough to the Hun and I'd like to hear a bit more about this Chaplin fellow."

"That's very noble of you, Private," Sterling said with a humorless grin. "But I'm guessing you'll stay with the rest of us."

"Who is this Chaplin bloke anyhow?" asked Morris. "I heard some boys from the Royal Fifth speaking of him as well."

"A politician, I should guess," Liggett said. "One of the bastards..."

They chatted, bantered, avoiding any subject close enough to remind them of the war. William tuned them out because he so liked to watch, to see the way their eyes changed when they spoke of home, to sense the relaxation settling into their bones when they could forget the fight, even for a moment. Fighting men, he thought, were as close to the basis of the human animal as could be. Every emotion was emphasized, every thought clear, the fear and the hope and the dread actually *felt*, not just thought.

"Penny for your thoughts, William," Morris said.

William started, realized he had been drifting away, although to where he had no idea.

"I'm not sure I could articulate them properly," he said, pausing to think for a moment. He was aware that the others were silent now, watching him. "Have you noticed the birds and the insects all around us?"

"I hadn't given it much thought," Morris admitted, fishing through his knapsack.

"There's a war going on all over, happening in their very home, yet they stay. They adapt. They sing along with the sounds of the artillery. Remember when we saw the tanks?"

Morris nodded. Then he frowned.

William wondered if they were remembering the same thing.

There had been more of them then, of course. They'd been farther north, securing a bridge to provide safe passage for the armored column. It was the first time any of them had actually seen the new form of weaponry. The tanks had been slow, ponderous things. Even Crown Sergeant Sterling, a career soldier, marveled at the sheer destructive force the machines bespoke.

As the column had rolled safely across the bridge and chewed its way through a field on the other side, a herd of deer stood watching from the treeline.

"Those deer adapted as well," William said to the seated men. "Something new had entered their home and they investigated, then dismissed it. The sound of artillery echoes off the hills, and the birds become accustomed to it so quickly. I was just wondering…how does nature accept the changes?" He shook his head. "How long before it *refuses* to accept them?"

He kicked at the dirt under his feet, and wondered whether it was the dust of dead men.

"And just look at the new ways we've devised to kill each other: the machine-gun; the tank; poison gas! The press calls this the war to end all wars. We hurtle toward our date with destiny, our date with the future. Yet what do we really know of the world we live on? What mysteries of nature have eluded our grasp? What do we truly know of this planet's inhabitants? I wonder what other creatures have adapted to this chaos…creatures we don't even know about yet. After all, this is their home too. We're the intruders here. We're the murderers."

"Well, that may be," Morris replied, "but it's not very well our choice." He fished around in his rucksack and pulled out a faded photograph. A young woman stared back at him. He sighed deeply.

"You miss her," William stated.

"Oh aye, I miss her terribly," Morris whispered. "But it's more than that."

"What?"

The men were silent, none of them looking at Morris, all of them waiting to hear what he had to say.

"I'm sure I'll never see her again."

«« —»»

There was something wet and red in the middle of the trench. William stepped over it as he ran. Behind him, Brown was still screaming.

Dunhill was holding something ropy and glistening. As William raced toward him Dunhill held up his cupped hands in a plea for help, and the shining strands spilled out into the mud.

William knelt to help him, the mud squelching around his knees. Desperately, he grabbed at the soldier's innards, clawing his hands as they slipped through his fingers and into the dirt.

He scraped at the mud. A pair of yellow eyes stared up at him. They blinked.

"*Everything* has adapted, William," Dunhill spat, a crimson froth forming on his mouth. "Known, and not yet known."

Morris careened around the corner then, running at the two men squatting in the muck. Behind him came the Hun, bayonets gleaming in the moonlight.

"William!" Morris screamed as a blade sprouted from his chest. "Are you writing this down?"

The Germans trampled over him, bearing down on William. The eyes in the mud blinked again, then narrowed. William struggled to rise and two gnarled hands burst from the earth, grasping his shoulders in a fierce grip.

"William!"

He opened his eyes with a gasp. Morris was shaking him.

"Come on then, time to get up. Something's happening."

"I was dreaming," William said breathlessly, looking around in confusion. "Dunhill…"

"I dreamed about him too," Morris said, nodding his head sadly. "I imagine we'll dream it forever."

"No," William insisted, "this wasn't just the battle, not just what happened to Dunhill. There was something in the earth."

"Look lively lads," Sterling hissed. "We've got company."

A thick fog had descended over the countryside, obscuring the beet fields and the road in front of them. William glanced at his watch. It was nearly sundown. Already the gloom was pervasive; the mist swallowing what little sunlight was left.

Something was coming toward them.

"Off the road," Sterling commanded in a harsh whisper.

They scrabbled into the bushes as the disembodied sounds of many booted feet approached.

"Bloody hell," Liggett muttered, "if it's a fight they want, we'll give it to them."

"Quiet," Morris whispered.

Out of the fog a column of men appeared. French infantry. A slackness pervaded their tattered ranks. The soldiers looked exhausted, covered with dust and dripping with sweat. Gloomy and silent, the procession passed by their hiding place.

Sterling called out a challenge and the ranks halted. They stared at the soldiers in the ditch, showing no hint of surprise. In halting French, Winston conversed with them. Then they shuffled onward.

"What news?" Sterling asked him.

"I'm not sure, Crown Sergeant," Winston replied, a look of confusion on his face. "Apparently, a major offensive is about to begin in the Argonne trenches. But they're not participating. They're leaving this area."

"Deserting," Liggett snapped. "How do you like that?"

"No," Winston countered, "that's what doesn't make sense. They said that they just had an encounter in a village up the road here. I couldn't understand it though. My French is lacking. Something about the dead in the ground."

"What do we do, Crown Sergeant?" William asked.

Sterling shrugged. Shouldered his knapsack. Slapped a fat fly from his cheek. "We move on."

Edging along the fog enshrouded road, they encountered the sad dregs of a fleeing army. Soldiers and civilians passed by in disorder and panic; women carrying children in their arms and pushing them in small carriages; young girls in their Sunday best; boys and old men hefting all sorts of pointless artifacts of their safe life before the war. Soldiers slumped on peasant carts, gazing at nothing.

An infantryman galloped by on an officer's horse. Spying them, he dismounted and threw his arms around the animal's neck. He gasped something in French and then dashed off into the fields.

"What did he say," asked Liggett.

"He thanked it for saving his life," Winston replied.

"That's an officer's horse," Sterling observed. "The fellow fled on his captain's horse!"

Another soldier paused to speak to them.

"Ask him why it is he doesn't have a rifle, knapsack, or equipment," Sterling told Winston.

Winston listened to the soldier's reply and then translated. "He says he lost them swimming across the Meuse."

"Bollocks," Liggett replied critically. "His clothes are dry! Here we are, fighting for their country, and they flee like schoolchildren!"

Darkness encircled them like a steel trap as they approached the village. The procession had trickled down to a few stragglers, the last of whom approached them through the dispersing mist. He bore the rank of officer and greeted them in English.

"Where are you going," Sterling inquired. "We're on our way to the Argonne forest. Do you know what's happening there?"

"I wish only to be away from this cursed ground," the Frenchman replied.

"But sir," Sterling said, fighting hard to hide his exasperation, "why have you left your unit?"

"I am a company commander," be stated proudly. Then he cast his eyes to the ground. "And my company's only survivor."

"But what the hell happened?" shouted Sterling.

"I can speak no more of this place. Let me by!"

The Frenchman brushed past them and William caught a brief glimpse of the tears streaking his grimy face. Then he vanished into the dark along with everyone else.

Face set with steely determination, Crown Sergeant Sterling motioned them onward. With the sounds of the battle drawing closer —the noise of death seemed to be carried further by the night—they entered the village.

Nothing remained save for a few crumbling walls. The five men walked slowly, rifles at the ready, their hearts hammering with fear. The road was paved with rubbish: linens and undergarments; litters of clothing; letters; burst mattresses and eiderdowns; fragments of furniture and shattered pottery.

And the dead lay everywhere.

Retching, William stumbled across five corpses in a tattered heap, all of them children, all of them hugging each other for comfort in death. Farther along lay a young mother and her two daughters, all dressed in their Sunday best, their faces forever frozen in an horrific visage.

Morris placed a comforting hand on William's shoulder as the young man heaved into the dust.

"What do you think happened here?" William rasped.

"I don't know. They don't seem burned or shot. Yet most have been—" The private's answer was cut short by a piercing squeal from behind a ruined building, followed by a guttural grunt.

William jumped to his feet and dashed after Morris and Sterling.

Another squeal ended abruptly as a rifle echoed in the darkness.

They rounded the corner and halted in shock. In what had once been a courtyard, bodies had been stacked like cordwood, limbs flung out in deathly abandon. Pigs wandered through the pickings, feasting on human flesh.

Winston sighted and squeezed the trigger. A second bloated beast sagged to the ground, ignored by its brethren. Liggett was frantically reloading, his efforts punctuated with more swearing.

"Stand down," ordered Sterling. "If there're snipers about, you'll bring them down on our heads!"

Liggett cursed again and brought the rifle up to his shoulder, drawing a bead on the nearest swine.

"Stand down Corporal! That's an order, Liggett!"

The shaken Corporal looked at them, and in the moonlight William noticed the tears of rage and bewilderment that streaked the dust on his face.

"This isn't right," Winston exclaimed. "It's not natural!"

Sterling stepped forward to survey the makeshift abattoir. "I spent twenty years on the farm, lads," he said quietly. "And I never saw pigs do this. They'll eat most things, but…"

"Crown Sergeant," called Morris. "Come and look at this!"

He was standing before a small mound of dirt. The men approached, wondering what new horror was about to be revealed. Slowly, they took their places next to Morris.

In the ground before them was a gaping hole. The yawning entrance led down into the earth, disappearing from sight. A peculiar smell wafted from the chasm. It reminded William of pig iron and summer storms.

"What do you make of this, then?"

"Artillery," Winston answered, the word almost forming a question. "The Germans must have shelled the village."

"No," Sterling countered, "this was no explosion, we can all see that. This was dug. See that dirt? This tunnel was made from beneath the ground, not from above."

"Well then what in bloody hell was it," Liggett stammered.

"Something else. I don't know what."

"Perhaps the Germans have some new tunneling machine," William offered.

"There you go, thinking you're bleeding Jules Verne again," growled Liggett. "Pull your head out of yer arse, William!"

"Leave him alone," Morris retorted and stepped toward the surly Corporal.

"Enough!" shouted Sterling, his voice echoing in the silent streets. "The Devil take you all, that's enough! Whatever made this hole, whatever atrocity occurred in this village, we won't solve anything by standing here. Let's move on!"

Shaken, they departed from the village, stepping gingerly over the scattered corpses. The road wound on, cresting a hilltop a few kilometers away. Stealthily, they crept over the hill and looked down upon the valley of the Argonne Forest.

Away in the distance, the trees stood silent watch over the battlefield. The valley was a labyrinth of trenches, both German and Allied. To William, it looked as if ants had burrowed through the vast field, leaving no acre untouched. Ghostly fires dotted the landscape, as soldiers from both sides huddled in the mud while darkness closed upon them.

A maze of barbed wire surrounded the trenches, and they picked their way carefully through it.

William was struck by the silence engulfing the valley. During a battle, when the heavy field guns, rifles, and machine guns were all booming at the same time, the noise was so tremendous that it seemed beyond the limits of human endurance. Amidst a storm of steel and fire, the riot of battle would change in character, volume and tempo; rising and falling with alternating diminuendo and crescendo in both a hurrying and slackening pace. Relentless, the deafening volley of reports had always sounded to William like the clattering of a clumsy and lumbering wagon, jolting heavily over the frozen ruts of a rough country lane. Sometimes it reminded him of the brisk hammering of thousands of carpenters and riveters. Or it could have been the rumbling of hundreds of heavy-goods trains, thundering and bumping over uneven points in the line and meeting head on in a hideous collision.

But even more awful than that hellish cacophony were the sudden and unexpected silences, which made William hold his breath and wait for the storm to start again.

It was this silence that greeted them as they entered the trench system. And William finally gasped a new breath, because the barrage had truly halted. For a time, at least.

The ground was a heavy, impermeable clay that had been gouged and displaced in a series of tunnels and ditches. Thick mud puddles filled every hole and depression, forming a sticky mire for them to flounder through.

"Halt," called a voice from the darkness. "Who goes there?"

Sterling brought up a hand, stopping them as they slogged through the water. "Who do you think? The bloody Red Baron?"

"I've got to ask. Wh-who goes there?"

William could just make out the young private who had issued the challenge, a skinny chap barely old enough to shave, with a uniform caked onto his body like a second skin. His eyes seemed far too big for his face. His rifle was shaking, the butt clinking against the lad's belt buckle.

"We're from the 3rd," Sterling said. "Any good down here?"

"Good," the boy said blankly. "Don't be daft. How could anything be good?"

William frowned. He had seen many strange things during his last four months in France, but the private's nonchalance when addressing the Crown Sergeant was something new and unsettling.

The boy lowered his rifle and slumped back against the side of the trench. He seemed to merge with the ground, such was his grubby appearance. William wondered if he'd ever move again, or would he be sucked into the trench wall, subsumed into the churned mud of the battlefield like so many of his mates?

Sometimes, they left dead men on the edge of the trench because they absorbed more bullets.

"Come on you lot," Sterling said. "Let's get some grub inside us, then I'd better track down someone in charge."

The young soldier began to laugh. It was a sickly sound, like gritty oil being poured through a sieve; more a hiss than a chuckle. "In charge," he said. "In bloody charge!" He laughed again, but never once looked at William or his friends. He stared through them and beyond, as if he were talking to someone else entirely. As they shrugged past him, his laughter broke into a rapid volley of violent sneezes.

They slopped through the trench, up to their knees in muddy water most of the time, feces or rotten food floating on its soupy surface. William closed his eyes for a few seconds every now and then, navigating by sound alone, and tried to imagine the summery meadow back home. He could find the smells of flowers and the sounds of birds, the feel of grass beneath his hands and the sense of one of the girls from the village sitting primly by his side ... but he could not see it. Even when he tried to make-believe, he could not see it.

Still, he had to try. Anything was better than this. Even despair was better than this hell beyond despair.

Again his mind drifted back to the previous battle. He thought of the wounded soldier left out in no-man's land because it gave the enemy snipers something to shoot at. Dunhill.

"This'll do," Sterling said from somewhere up ahead.

William opened his eyes. The Sergeant had paused in a much wider area of trench, two further burrows running away left and right. Straight ahead, a depression had been carved from the earth and covered with roughly chopped branches and shattered tree trunks. It was flooded but there were seats gouged into the walls, an unopened crate of rations, and a dead soldier bobbing facedown in the water.

No one liked to touch a dead man. Some thought death was catching, like bad luck or a cold.

"I'm not going in there, with him like that," Liggett said. "Someone should bury the poor sod."

"Go on then," Winston mumbled, just loud enough for the others to hear.

"You do it," Liggett said. "You and Morris drag him out of there and—"

"No way I'm touching him!" A cigarette dropped from Morris's lips as he spoke.

"Just stop it," William sighed, shaking his head. He felt like crying. He often felt like crying, and when he thought it would really help, he did. When it was dark mostly, the night lit only by the intermittent flashes of the guns. It was yet another thing he envied the animals; they would never have cause to despair at the savagery of their own race.

He pushed past the bickering men, glanced at Sterling, and then stepped into the depression in the earth. The soldier was very heavy, weighted down with water, his rifle strap still tangled around one arm—

"Oh Christ!" William gasped as the body flipped over.

The dead soldier had no face.

There was a hint of eye cavities, a hole in his head where his nose should be, but all other features had been destroyed.

William closed his eyes and tried to dream of the meadow as he dragged the body into the trench. He left it against the sidewall. And he could sense everything of home apart from what it looked like.

«« — »»

"What did that?" Sterling whispered later.

William glanced at his Sergeant, unable to find an answer, unwilling to look.

Sterling's gaze did not falter. "That dead chap over there. What did it to him?"

"A shell. A bullet. I don't know." William shrugged. "Perhaps he blew his own head off."

"You know what I mean, Potter. I've seen enough dead men, so have you. His face was taken off after he died."

Yes, thought William, *I had thought that. I've tried to forget it, but it is what I thought at first.* He wished he could lose the memory of the man's ruined face as easily as he had mislaid the image of home.

"Rats," he said quietly.

And then the first barrage of the night began.

«« — »»

The walls of the trench were shaking. Not just vibrating, but actually *moving*, shedding clumps of dirt as if there were something inside trying to break out. Shells staggered the trenches, some of them striking home in sickening explosions of water and smoke and flesh.

The sky was blinking at them with each burst of energy, clouds gray against the night, moon barely peering out at the slaughter its erstwhile worshippers were committing. While down here Man was busy racing to his death, in the heavens time was frozen.

William ran through the trenches. Flowering eruptions of mud splashed the landscape, the ground shook, water sloshed around his feet, men shouted, men screamed, shells screamed, Morris shouted at him: "It's all over now, William! The poem's ending now!"

William reached a section of trench that had been blown to smithereens. It looked like a giant hand had scooped up a thousand tons of mud, men, weapons, timber and water, then flung them back at the ground. He saw the bottom half of a body protruding from a bank of earth…its feet were shaking, trouser legs rippling and ripping as something pulled it further in.

Then he was out of the trenches and into no-man's land, and everything was being destroyed. In a swirl of colors—apple blossom and setting sun and poppy red—he caught a glimpse of rolling hillsides of gorse and grass. He could smell the loamy scent of moorland in the air, taste summer on the breeze, see sheep boiling the hills higher up…and the artillery barrage blew it all apart.

Something grabbed his feet and he looked down.

There was a girl wrapping herself around his lower legs, working herself tight like a snake. He could not recall her name, but he knew that she worked in the baker's shop back home. He thought that perhaps he had loved her at one time.

She looked up at him. "Come home, my darling, my sweet. Come back to the valley. We so need a poet." But then the ground broke apart as another shell struck home, and the girl vanished into mud, and the night was completely dark at last.

≪≪—≫≫

There were explosions and shrieks, but they were muffled. Something had a hand clamped across his mouth and nostrils, over his ears, arm pressing into his throat and choking off the scream he was desperate to vent. He sucked in a difficult breath and smelled mud and rot and age. Filthy water seeped into his mouth and trickled down his throat, like an icy finger tracing his lifeline straight to his heart.

He wondered how long he had been buried down here. Sometimes a barrage would seem to go on forever, so it could be anything from seconds to days. He hurt all over, but he could still shift his limbs, he could still *feel* the hurt. That was a good sign, at least.

He pushed his arms and legs, shoved out from where he was curled up like a sleeping baby, trying to distinguish up from down. Fresh air suddenly washed across his face, a cool night kiss tainted with a tang of smoke and its constant companion, death. William pushed some more, heaving with his shoulders, dragging himself from beneath the showering of mud and into the waterlogged trench.

He could not help rolling into the water. He closed his eyes and held his breath, stood quickly, shaking off the rancid mess like a wet dog.

Confusion settled upon him. Where the hell was he? Where were the others, just what had happened?

And then he saw.

Liggett had never been a polite man, but now his arrogant self was spread around the remains of the trench. There were bits and pieces here and there, but it was his head that William recognized, face reddened by blast-heat but still undeniably Liggett. Whatever blood had leaked from him had been consumed by the earth. Here, everything was a constant shade of dirt.

A line of inhuman creatures walked across the shattered horizon. Humped, slow-moving, paying hardly any attention to the massive conflict around them…and then William saw that they were medics evacuating no-man's land of the injured and dead. It took him only seconds to identify them, but in that time his imagination had given them glowing red eyes and a lumbering, hippopotamus gait.

He shook his head, looked back down at Liggett. He tried to imagine the dead corporal blinking, his severed arm waving. Grotesque and insensitive, perhaps, but sometimes the craziest notions kept William alive. Thinking about odd things meant, ironically, that he could forget about a whole lot more.

"Potter!" someone shouted.

William ducked as a new volley of shells fell a hundred yards away, then the voice called out again.

"Potter! Over here!"

He tried discerning which direction the voice was coming from, then made his way along the ruined trench. Mud sucked at him, the collapsed walls loose and moist. The night was almost permanently lit now by a flurry of flares. One of the sides must be charging across no-man's land in the wake of the barrage…and sure enough, the cackle of machine-gun fire commenced out of sight, mowing down soldiers in hysterical patterns.

William kept low. Above the background roar of the battlefield he heard the bee-buzz of bullets tearing the air overhead. And above even that, the cries of already-forgotten men falling into freshly-blown graves.

"Potter!"

It was Winston. He was huddled at a junction of two trenches, hunched down like a beggar-boy on a London street. Something stirred at his feet, a shape whipping back and forth in the wet mud like a landed fish.

"It's Crown Sergeant Sterling. We were running for help after the shell fell, we'd lost you and Liggett—"

"Ligget's dead."

"Oh." Winston paused briefly, but death was no surprise. He went on: "We only got this far. The tail end of that first volley caught us here, and…look. Look, Potter!"

Those last words were cried, not spoken, and in the monotone of the flare light Potter could see Winston's eyes. They glittered, but there were no tears. And then he looked at where Winston was pointing.

Sterling was stuck up to his waist in a hole in the trench bottom. Water swilled around his chest. His eyes bulged from his face, his arms skitted across the surface of the water as he twisted…or was twisted by something, because he was dead. He was as dead as anyone William had seen, his throat was gone, the front of his uniform was glistening a different wetness to the rest of the place, a rich syrupy mess in the sodium glare of flares.

"What the hell…"

"I've tried to pull him out, but he won't budge."

"He's dead," William said.

"No, no, he can't be, he's trying to get out. Look, if we grab an arm each—"

"He's dead!" William frowned, closed his eyes and strove for home. Even trying to do so calmed him, though the image was as elusive as ever. He supposed it could be worse. It could be that he *was* able to think of the valley where he was born, like imagining the purity of Heaven in a never-ending Hell. Small mercy.

A shape leapt across the trench.

Another, merely a shadow blocking out the star- and flare-light, following the first into no-man's land.

"Winston!" William hissed.

"I dropped my rifle," Winston gasped, voice barely audible now that a new barrage had begun to shake the ground.

This time, William thought the shells were aimed in a different direction. Something felt different; not better, just different. A new kind of promised pain.

"Me too. Get down, and—"

Something else leapt, hit the wall of the trench and slithered down into murky water.

William froze. The soldier was yards from him, struggling to bring his rifle to bear, whining deep down in his throat like a dreaming dog. His nose was running, his mouth slack and dribbling dark saliva onto his tunic. He sneezed.

"Wait, who are you?" William said, more to establish a language than anything else.

"What are you?" the man shouted.

"William Potter, 3rd Infantry."

The man laughed and lowered his rifle. "You'd best follow me then, or they'll get you too."

"Is there an offensive? Are we storming the Hun's trenches? In the night, with a barrage still underway?"

The man shook his head and slumped back against the rough earth, letting its slickness lower him into a sitting position. All the time he talked he looked back the way he had come. And he kept his rifle pointed that way, too…back at their own lines.

"Who cares about the Hun," he said. "Who fucking cares? And the barrage? We're not shelling the enemy, you fool. We've turned the guns around to—"

Winston screamed. It was a sudden, irrational exhalation of terror and pain, heartfelt and automatic. By the time William had spun around, his friend was already splashing on his stomach in the bottom of the trench, hands and feet throwing up fans of dirty water. He hadn't been hit by a bullet or shrapnel; whatever had struck him down was still happening, still whipping his body back and forth.

"Winston!" William shouted.

"Don't bother," the soldier said, his voice high-pitched and insane, and he fired his rifle along the trench at Winston.

William took one step to tackle him, and then something else happened. He felt it first, a vibration more frequent and intense than the regular *thud* of explosive shockwaves. This was machines churning underground, or something rolling over. He paused and looked along the trench…and the knee-high water began to swill and flow, down into several holes that had opened beneath their feet.

William leapt at the trench wall and grabbed hold of something hanging down from above. He looked up into the blank eyes of a dead soldier, his extended arm William's lifeline, his hand cold and hard.

Looking back down he saw Sterling disappear underground with a squelch, and Winston drifting to one of the holes and remaining there, half in, half out, filthy water flowing by him.

In seconds, the trench had emptied of water. Six inches of mud was all that remained; that and humped bodies here and there, rotting, disintegrating already. There were also the pits, each of them steaming and spitting sprays of water into the illuminated night.

He recalled the holes they had seen in the decimated village…and the smell that had come from them.

This tunnel was made from beneath, Sterling had said. Well, now the Sergeant knew just where they led.

William hauled himself out of the trench before he could see what emerged from the holes.

Once on top, he lay flat out and searched for the soldier who'd fallen in moments before. But the madman was already dodging his way into the murk of no-man's land, rifle thrown away, arms held wide as if craving a liberating spray of bullets across his chest.

William thought to call after him but knew it would do no good. He was mad. Everyone was mad. Maybe there was a poem there some-where, but who would be left to read it? Madmen? He laughed, and the sound of his own lunatic giggle perturbed him greatly.

More men came from behind, scrambling over the trench, some of them falling in and never reappearing. There were noises from down there now, shouts and shots and the sound of flesh finding its doom.

Ahead of him, certain death under a hail of enemy fire.

Behind him, dead friends and dying men, dying in ways he could not properly describe or even imagine. From the sounds drifting from the trench…the terrible screams suddenly cut off, the crunching of bones being snapped and pulled apart…his choice had already been made.

It was war, after all.

William stood and ran into a storm of lead.

«« — »»

Liggett was following him. His various dismembered parts skipped and dodged shattered tree trunks and fallen bodies. One remaining arm hauled his torso through the mud, and his head moved by rolling itself forward. Its mouth was wide open, trying to scream, but it had no neck or throat.

"Help me!" Liggett croaked nonetheless.

William slowed to a halt. Bullets whipped the air around him, slamming into bodies and sending them toppling down to add to the muck. He was in what had once been a forest. Now it was merely another part of the mud, with strangely contorted stumps seeking their lost heads.

"Help!" Liggett rasped as the first of his parts dashed past William.

Dreaming. He had to be dreaming. He could smell home here, not war and death. He could taste honey on the air, not cordite and blood and smoke.

He looked back from where Liggett had fled.

Dreaming.

Strange shapes lumbered from the smoke, slopping through the mud but unhindered by it. Indeed, these things seemed to flow with the filth, not struggle against it. They looked like the stretcher-bearers he had seen earlier, but as they approached he saw that there was no likeness there. None at all.

Dreaming...please God, let me be dreaming.

The demons had yellow eyes.

《《——》》

William came to in a flooded shell hole. At first he thought he was alone, but then he saw the dead men keeping his night company. He lay in a horrible mire of flesh and blood.

He shuddered, a tortured sigh escaping his cracked lips. The battle continued around him, but now the fighting was more scattered. In the midst of the tumult, he could hear the steady *tac-tac-tac* of the German machine guns, spreading death precisely and methodically. William reflected on how the emotions of the man behind the weapon never hindered its evil effects. The machine gun was new to this world, yet it could have been created and directed by some ancient, scheming spirit of destruction.

Grabbing a rifle from the clutches of a corpse, he peered cautiously over the edge of the crater. The dream lingered with him, the glint from the creatures' yellow eyes as they lumbered toward him like misshapen men...

He was in the middle of no-man's land.

SHIVERS

And something was charging his position.

Screaming, William pulled the trigger and was greeted with an empty click.

The thing drew closer, it's harsh and ragged breath echoing in the darkness. Ducking back down William flailed in the water, searching wildly for another weapon. His hand closed on something round and he brought it up to the surface—he had to, he could not help himself—and an eyeball stared back at him from his glistening palm.

He screamed again.

The shriek was answered from above.

The thing towered over the shell hole, darkness enshrouding its body like a blanket. William scuttled backward like a crab as a guttural laugh mocked him. The thing cocked its head, surveying him calmly.

It's a man...it's a man...it's got to be a man...!

A flare popped half a mile away, throwing a sheen of sickly light over the scene.

Its body was pale and bloated, the skin mottled like melted cheese or wax. The creature bent at the knees and leapt, landing in the hole but not sinking into the mud. It snarled at him. Its fetid breath fogged the air between them.

It was not a German. It was not a man. Men didn't have yellow eyes. Or tusks.

Scampering up the slope, William fled across the field with the howls of the creature nipping at his heels. He risked a glance to see if it was gaining. Blessed relief washed over him when he noticed that the thing hadn't left the hole.

He heard the ripping sounds, and the chewing. It was feeding.

He turned and ran into the night. The air exploded and burned around him as he dashed across the field and back into the labyrinthine trenches. Leaping over a sandbagged parapet, he saw hunched forms moving in the darkness below. He jumped another trench, missing his mark and clawing wildly at barbed wire as he slid down.

A cluster of German and French troops struggled against one another, not in battle, but in flight. Even as he watched the mud erupted before them, spewing earth and water skyward. William turned and ran before he could see what had caused it.

The earth was giving up its secrets.

The trench crossed another, then another, and soon he was lost in the intersections. The Argonne battlefield was a cacophony of hellish sound now, gunfire and explosions punctuated by cries of agony and other, less human exhortations.

Above him, out in front of the barbed wire, a man was being torn apart. The attacker ripped the victim's arm from its socket. Brandishing the bloody trophy like a club, he began to beat the other man mercilessly. He sank into the mud, raised his remaining arm in a feeble attempt to ward off the blows.

The victor *squealed* in delight.

William continued moving, never willing to stop, always fearing that to halt would be to give in…give in to whatever had taken possession of this battlefield.

He reached an empty portion of the trenches and slowed for a moment, gasping for breath. The sounds continued from all around him. The air was heavy with the stench they had first encountered in the village.

Around a dogleg in the trench, footsteps approached.

William looked to his left and saw a thick, yellowish-green cloud veiling the night sky. He wondered if the forest and trenches were on fire. Perhaps that would be good. Maybe flame would purge this place of all its ills, both manmade and…other.

The footsteps grew closer, falling faster.

Dizzy, William struggled to remain standing. His throat burned as pain lanced into his chest. His eyes watered. Breathing became difficult…and then impossible. He spat blood; crimson frothed on his agonized lips.

Something raced at him along the trench.

"William!" It growled his name, voice horribly distorted, inhuman.

Then he saw that the thing was Morris, a wound on his scalp bleeding freely and matched by a gash in his side.

"William!" his friend screamed again through his mask, and then he was there, catching him as he fell.

"Morris…" he coughed. "Hurts."

"Gas. They've gassed the trenches. Come on, we've got to keep moving."

"The Sergeant…Winston…Liggett…they're dead," William spat.

"We're all dead, William," Morris answered as he dragged him through the mud, away from the cloud.

Through the haze, William saw that his friend's hair had turned white.

And then he knew no more.

«« —»»

SHIVERS

The grass in the meadow was cool. Beads of dew still clung to the green blades. Wetness also coated William's face as he sobbed quietly, his knees drawn up to his head and his notebook discarded beside him.

"Why do you cry, William?"

The voice startled him. He looked up and saw beauty.

It was the girl from the baker's, her head surrounded by an aura from the bright sun. Light gleamed from her golden tresses as she sat next to him. He remembered her name now. Clarice. She was...had been...his girlfriend. How could he have forgotten?

Slowly, as if surfacing from a dream, it was all starting to come back. He knew why he was crying. He'd had this conversation before.

"My father is butchering Onyx today," he said quietly as she took his hand. "I know he's only a silly cow, but..."

"You've grown fond of him," Clarice finished.

"Well, yes," William agreed. "I've looked after him since he was a calf. I can understand why father must do it, but it all seems so bloody unfair. Onyx has lived his life, day after day, never knowing why he really existed: for food. What kind of fate is that?"

"That is simply the way of things, my love," she answered softly. "There's too much of the poet in you. He's just a cow. We raise cattle to eat. That's why they exist."

"Is that the only reason?" William retorted. "Aren't they intelligent creatures, living things? Maybe they have hopes and dreams? How would you feel if you lived your life only to end up on someone's supper table? It's not fair, Clarice. Onyx is nothing more than fodder."

"Maybe we all are, William," she stated simply. "Come, would you like to see your home?"

"Yes!" William cried. "I'd like that very much. I can't seem to remember it properly at all."

They walked hand in hand through the pasture, the roof of the farmhouse looming just over the hill. They passed through a grazing herd of Holsteins.

"Mind the dung," William warned her, stepping lightly.

Then he stopped, terror rooting him to the spot.

A monstrous bull gazed at him with Sterling's face. "We're all fodder, lad," said the Crown Sergeant, slowly chewing his cud, a bulbous wound opening in his side.

"That's right, William," echoed Winston, his teats swollen with milk as he tore ravenously at a patch of grass. "It's the way things work. We exist to provide sustenance to the planet."

"We're germs," Liggett mooed through a splitting throat.

"I don't understand," William gasped.

"Perhaps you are not meant to," said a voice from behind him. Clarice had vanished. William turned and saw Morris, buried up to his waist in the soft earth of the meadow.

"The earth still has secrets, William," he said gravely, sinking deeper into the loam. "Buried forever and never meant to be seen. Not by us."

"Come, William," his father cried from over the hill. "Bring the cattle. It's time for the slaughter."

Liggett, Winston and Sergeant Sterling began to snort in agony. Then William was sinking into the earth as well, struggling desperately as he watched the tufts of Morris's hair sink below.

It's a dream, I know it's a dream because his hair turned white back at the front.

William opened his mouth to scream and the earth rushed in. Above him, the slaughter began anew.

«« — »»

He tried to scream again, but his mouth was still blocked. Something long and cold was stuck in his throat. It was connected to…

He gagged, grasping the thing and pulling the cadaverous fingers from his mouth. Gasping for breath, he panicked when he found he couldn't move. He turned his head to the right and Morris's glazed eyes stared back at him, unblinking and filled with blood. A warm and sticky fluid dripped onto his forehead. Something heavy lay on top of him.

Bodies, he realized. He was buried beneath bodies. Muck and water covered most of his form, leaving his shoulders and head above, but the night was hidden from view. The echoes of the artillery blast still ricocheted through his mind, even though it could have been minutes or hours ago.

Something landed nearby with a heavy splash and a grunt, and then, for a few brief moments, there was silence. William held his breath and strained to hear or see, but his world had contracted to this; a claustrophobic stench of fresh blood and turned earth, and a cloying darkness caused by the shadows of the dead. He whispered Clarice's name—and then something started ripping and tearing at the bodies around him.

It's time for the slaughter, he heard his father say again.

Something stopped him from crying out. At the time he thought he was being calm and cautious, but later—when he was walking across

27

a shattered, silent landscape with only the dead and unwanted as company—he realized that it was outright terror.

He was frozen stiff by fear.

Animal sounds of feeding, the snap of bones, wet sucks as bodies were hauled from the mud...whole or in pieces...gulping and retching. And in the background there was still gunfire, still the occasional thud of an artillery shell finding a home somewhere, but it no longer had the sound of a full-blown battle. Now, it was more like a skirmish.

Soon, with the sounds seeming to grow nearer as the thing ate its way down to him, the gunfire ceased altogether.

But the fighting continued. William heard shouts and screams, feet splashing through water and mud, bodies hitting the ground. At one point, he heard the Lord's Prayer chanted frantically in German. A horrific squeal sent him into a shiver. He clenched his fists and bit down on his lip, tasting blood, desperate to remain still lest the gorging thing sensed him down here.

He realised that he could see it, now. The body above him shifted and jerked as mouthfuls were taken from it. It's head snapped back and crunched into William's nose. His eyes watered, his face caught fire, but he remained still. He should be playing dead, he knew, holding a breath, narrowing his eyes so that light could not glint from the moisture there...but he could not close his eyes because he could see the thing, and the horror of it forbade him any solace.

Its mouth was the worst because it was surrounded by flecks of blood and clots of meat. The pale snouted nose leaked copiously over its fleshy lips and chin, diluting dead men's blood and sending it spraying into the air every time the thing moved its blocky jaws. A second before William finally managed to close his eyes, it sneezed.

Retreating into his own mind—trying to escape, to find beauty in his memories—William felt the warmth of alien fluid spatter across his face and run, slowly, down over his split lips.

He imagined blood gushing from a slaughtered bull's throat.

He tasted the vile mucous of the creature, the salty blood of the dead men, and the alkaline fear that was his own.

《《—》》

Daylight woke him. If the corpse had still lain atop him, he may well have remained there until his own body weakened and died, cosseted within his own strange dreams. But the dead soldier had been ripped up and scattered. The sun found William's face and gave him back his life.

He struggled from the loose earth and the body parts that surrounded him, trying not to look too closely. His hands found some horrendous things as he tried to haul himself upright. They were all cold.

An eerie silence hung over the battlefield. There were no whistles or whispers, no crackle of gunfire, no shouting or groaning or screaming from no-man's land. There was not even a breeze to rustle by his ears. Nothing. And as William dragged himself from the collapsed trench that had so nearly been his grave, he saw why.

Everyone was dead.

Never had he seen human destruction on this scale. The landscape around him was carpeted with corpses, piled two or three deep in places, all of them mutilated and tattered by whatever had killed them. Both armies must have abandoned their trenches to fight in the open...but fight whom? Not each other, he knew that. He had heard tales about the Hun, seen caricatures of them before he came to war, but the ones he had seen since then...the ones he had killed...had all looked exactly like him.

The things doing the killing last night were not even human.

William picked his way between corpses, but it soon became too much to look down all the time. So he strode, arms swinging, every fourth or fifth step finding something soft to walk on. He closed his eyes for minutes at a time, mindless of the danger of flooded shell-holes or barbed wire. He had faced much, much worse.

On the backs of his eyelids he saw perfection, beauty, Utopia: the valley back home that could not possibly be as wonderful and innocent as he saw it now, but in his mind's eye it was still the ultimate aim for his poor wandering self. He could smell it and taste it, and he could see it as well, every detail clear and defined, every rolling field—

He wondered what might live beneath his father's farm.

He had to get back to his lines, warn them, tell them there was something here worse than the Hun. He had seen and heard thousands die, but he could save many more if he hurried. There was so little time. It was midday already. He did not want to be out here after dark.

William sneezed twice and spat out a great clot of mucus. A parliament of rooks feeding on a horse's bloated corpse took to the air.

He wiped his nose with a muddy sleeve. His head had begun to throb and his joints were stiffening with every step.

Damn. After all this, he was coming down with the 'flu.

Ice Box

Jay Bonansinga

I awaken to the cool, dry-husk sound of tree branches scraping the window screen next to me, and the disorienting waltz of shadows across the cracked plaster ceiling above me. I was dreaming a moment ago—an awful night terror—something about a mortician with a chainsaw carving a statue of my little brother out of a block of ice.

The same vague, recurring dream I've been suffering since little Aaron's death nearly thirty years ago.

I lie in the tangled bedding for a moment, my heart thumping, my senses reorienting themselves to my surroundings. I can still smell the cloying, stale aromas of my recently deceased mother—Minute-Rub and Prince Machiabelli. It's freezing in here. Did somebody leave a window open? Eyes adjusting to the darkness, I glance across the floor and take in the cheap, shopworn Colonial furniture of my mom's old second-floor bedroom, the yellowed doilies, the fossilized bowls of potpourri, and the Hummel figurines of ice skaters.

I rub my eyes and sit up against the creaking mahogany headboard. The bedroom door is slightly ajar, and I can see a portion of the moonlit hallway. The silver light paints the threadbare carpet runner like a thin layer of frost. Somewhere, in another part of the empty house, beneath the tomb-like silence, there's a faint, guttural humming noise.

What in God's name am I doing here, alone and disoriented, an overweight, middle-aged college professor in worn flannel jammies and receding hairline? Teacher of such time-wasters as "The Nineteenth Century American Gothic" and "The Semeiotics of Guilt in the Stories of Nathaniel Hawthorne"? On *this* of all nights—the infamous Hallowed Eve of soaped windows, flickering jack-o-lanterns and distant giggling children trundling from porch to porch. Ostensibly: I'm here to tie up the loose strings after mom's funeral—her estate was a disaster, her will outdated and her assets woefully under insured. But I suspect I'm here for another purpose altogether. I suspect I'm here to work through something painful and unresolved.

Eons ago, I cowered in this old pile of brick and tarnished copper during the hours after my brother Aaron had turned up dead. I was only twelve, but the loss aged me beyond my years. I think it was *I* who suggested going to that dump in the first place on that chilly October day. It was such a lurid, ironic way for my brother to die: only six years old, accidentally suffocating in a discarded Kenmore freezer in the North Park landfill. It was as though my brother had suffered death-by-urban-legend. But the fact is, kids *do* die in such ways. Kids *do* put their eyes out with sticks. Kids *do* stick their fingers in electrical outlets.

And my brother Aaron *did* die by getting locked inside an abandoned refrigerator.

I remember mom calling it an ice box. She always used anachronistic words like that. She called the highway the "hard road," and she called the car's gas pedal "the foot feed." And when my brother died, she told the newspapers that her precious little angel had met his maker inside an "ice box."

I manage to swing my legs over the side of the bed, sitting there for a moment, shivering, listening to that infernal humming noise— whatever the hell it is—resonating up through the floorboards from somewhere downstairs. The hardwood is icy on the soles of my bare feet.

I get up, pad across the room to the chair by the dresser, grab my robe, pull it on, and slip my feet into a pair of moccasins.

The furnace cycles on suddenly, the air wafting out of the vent in the corner. It sounds like a ghostly voice whispering, "*C'monnnnn, c'monnnnn*— (tick, tick, tick) —*c'monnnn-c'monnnn-c'monnn.*" I've been hearing that dead whisper like a fever throbbing in my brain all night. *C'monnnnn-c'monnnnnnnnn-c'monnnnnn*—"

Girding myself, I make my way out the door and down the hall to the staircase.

The house is a typical turn-of-the-century Evanstonian two-story: Narrow hallways, low-hanging ceilings, painted-over moldings with bulls eye cornices and windows that perpetually stick. Halfway down the staircase, I start to smell the gelid odors of freezer-burned food. In her final years, Mom was a shut-in. Legs ravaged with rheumatoid arthritis, Alzheimers disease stealing her awareness, she spent most of her last days wrapped in blankets, staring at game shows, drooling on herself. She rarely set foot in the kitchen. Barely used her fridge. So why am I smelling frozen ground beef right now?

By the time I reach the bottom of the stairs, I'm dizzy with contrary emotions, the icebound stink engulfing me. On the one hand, I'm reeling with nostalgia for the old days, and my mom's depression-era cooking: Chili made with Campbell's soup and hamburger, tuna wiggle casserole and pickled pigs feet with Plotchman's mustard. On the other hand, my stomach is clenching suddenly, an inexplicable revulsion washing over me. The odor is evocative of dead flesh petrified in a deep-freeze—slabs of meat frozen for years—a grey, desiccated, rotten smell.

The furnace cycles off with a sigh, and the funereal silence returns to the house like a vice pressing on my skull. Once again, there's only the humming noise. My heart races. I force my legs to move, to lumber forward through this fragrant crypt of a house, down the hallway, through the doorway, and into the deserted kitchen—into the pale light.

There's nothing there. The humming noise is coming from somewhere else. The kitchen is empty and silent, and even the light is coming from somewhere else, another doorway. Eyes quickly scanning the room, I see the oil-cloth covered table and the old formica counters where Mom once made us peanut butter and marshmallow fluff sandwiches. That was when little Aaron was still alive. He used to love chewing ice cubes made from Kool-Aid, and he would make a horrible racket, chewing that red ice, then grinning with pink-stained teeth. So full of life and promise back then. The grief is still with me, a dull ache in the pit of my stomach.

The furnace cycles back on, the stagnant warmth rushing out of the vents. *"C'monnnn, c'monnnn, c'monnnnnnn—!"*

My gaze falls on another doorway in the northeast corner of the kitchen. The milky light is emanating from this door—the door to the cellar—and it sends a feathery shiver up my spine. Incandescent lightbulbs have a certain color temperature that's very familiar. The light is yellow, warm. Fluorescent light is cooler, bluer. But *this* light—this light coming from the basement stairs—is boreal. Like a nimbus of magnesium reflecting off an iceberg.

—C'monnnnnn—

Somehow, someway, with great effort, I reluctantly urge myself across the cold linoleum. I pause at the top of the stairs and summon whatever courage this old professor has left in his degenerate, booze-sodden bones. I know what the humming noise is now, and yet—and *yet*—I am compelled to walk down the rickety wooden steps into that arctic light.

I begin to descend—into the white nebula of light—each unsteady foot-fall making a ragged creaking noise, as though the ancient wooden risers are about to collapse. The smell of mildew, roots, and pickled vegetables are engulfing me. The humming is so loud now I feel it in my bones, vibrating my fillings.

I reach the bottom of the steps and stand there on the cold, painted concrete floor, blinking, squinting at the light. The basement looks like a near-death experience, a cone of alabaster vapor swirling in languid slow motion around a brighter center. I can't move. The soles of my feet are glued to the icy cement. There's an electric tingling in the base of my neck. The guttural, pipe-organ humming is vibrating the floor, emanating from the nucleus of white vapor.

Then, almost as if on cue, the light shrinks suddenly, collapsing in on itself—

—and there's a metallic thud, a sort of familiar clunk that sounds like a car door closing. It makes me jump, and I stagger backwards against the plywood banister, nearly falling. The cellar is plunged into silence and darkness, the humming noise gone, the light extinguished. And I stand there for a moment, swallowing hard, my heart galloping, my flesh crawling.

It takes a few moments for my eyes to adjust. A few moments before I can make out this huge *thing* shoved against the far wall next to the furnace—the source of all the light and noise. It was the *lid*, the thing's top lid, that had fallen shut a moment ago, cutting off all the light and humming noise.

Terror squeezes my chest, the source of the noise materializing in the gloom before me. My traumatized brain fumbles for explanations: Am I still dreaming? Did Mom have one of these in her cellar all these years? No, no, no, absolutely not. These contraptions were far too expensive for my "frugal-to-a-fault" mother, and besides, besides—*besides!*—I would have remembered. I was a resident of this house for eighteen years, I would have certainly remembered.

I gape at the horrible monolith.

It's the same one. *Impossible.* But there it is, shoved against the exposed brick next to the cobweb-clogged ducts of the furnace. I can see it clearly now. The vapor is gone, and I can see the chipped, painted steel hull, the pocks of rust, the tarnished latch. I can see the broken trademark hanging off one corner, the K missing: *ENMORE.*

I take a step toward the freezer, the floor like ice on the soles of my moccasins. In my imagination I see myself opening the lid, revealing the withered corpse of my little brother, blackened from decay, the rotted flesh of his face pulled away from a tiny rictus of a smile. It wasn't my fault. I wasn't even there when he died so many Halloweens ago.

—*c'monnnnnn*—

I take another step. I imagine opening the thing and seeing my mother lying in her coffin, her gnarled hands folded across her chest. It wasn't my fault she died alone. I was busy dealing with a divorce, and a hostile tenure committee at school, and a life spinning out of control.

—*c'monnnnnnn*—

I approach the ice box. My scalp is prickling. My eyes burning. Tears of grief are very similar to tears of absolute terror—they both scald.

—*c'monnnnnnn*—

It takes a great deal of inertia just to get my arm to move, my hand to grip the cold latch-handle.

I open the freezer and look inside.

The tiny bunk-bed is freshly made, the stuffed animals and Dr. Seuss books right where they usually lay, and I recognize the Roy Rogers bed spread—even after all these years, even in the darkness of the cellar—the stitched rendering of Trigger missing a chunk of its yellow-yarn tail. It's my brother Aaron's bunk, the same one that once lay directly below mine. *I* was the older brother, so, of course, *I* got the top bunk. But sometimes, when the night raged with lightning, or the wee hours of Halloween stretched interminably, I got scared, and Aaron would whisper, *C'mon, Ritchie, c'mon down, you can sleep with me, I'm scared too, c'mon, c'mon*—

It takes a little doing, but I swing my right leg up, position my body sideways, then slide into the freezer. I land on my back. The blankets and stuffed animals are gone. I feel the cold shelf of metal beneath me, and smell putrefied food. My breath catches in my throat.

A tiny, frozen ghost is whispering in my ear. "You were the one, Ritchie," he whispers. "You were the one who slammed the lid shut."

Above me—before I even have a chance to scream—something moves.

WHAMMM!

SHIVERS

The lid slams down upon the freezer, the pitch black punching me in the face.

All at once I'm gasping for breath. There's no air—THERE'S NO AIR! And my lungs are a maelstrom, my ragged fingernails clawing at the air. Again I try to scream, but my body is paralyzed, and my brain is a flickering Nickelodeon of memories unfolding in a single instant: *memories of running through the darkness of a deserted landfill, heart about to explode, tears stinging in the wind, Halloween night 1966, dressed up as a pirate, the black grease paint itching under my nose, the dead leaves swirling, a bone white moon looking down at me like a frozen face, judging me, the face of God, I was the one, I was the one who slammed the lid and ran...I did it because my brother got all the attention...and mom loved him the best...I was the one...I did it...I locked my brother in that freezer...suffocating...suffocating...alone... in the dark....*

...all alone.

«« — »»

(EDITOR'S NOTE: In the Cook County Medical Examiner's report— dated November 1, 2000, 1532 hours—there is a description of the Judson house death scene. There is a meticulous rendering—in full detail—of the basement, including the cast iron sinks and the thirty-five year old Carrier furnace. But there is no mention of a horizontal freezer. The only unexplained detail in an otherwise routine death-by-heart-attack is the notation of an unidentified impression discoloring the decedent's lower back, an apparent abrasion consistent with what is commonly known as freezer burn.)

The Hand of Glory

Simon Clark

Oh, Hand Of Glory,
Shed thy light,
Direct us to our spoil tonight.
(From *The Burglar's Psalm*, circa 1800)

He began screaming an hour ago. I'm shutting it out. I'm going to write this down...

Clayton was the idiot. Not me. He was pissed because there was nothing worth taking from that poxy little house at the end of Church Lane; the weird one that leans so far out over the harbor wall you could sit in the kitchen window and dangle your feet above the sea. He busted the TV screen with his foot—*POW!*—it went off like a bomb and filled the house with smoke. Then he wrecked the place up a bit. He got all lusty about it. His shaved head sweated so much it shone like a glass ball. While that big gorilla face of his got so screwed up the crucifix tattoo between his eyes disappeared into a fold of frowning skin. It was when he kicked the bathroom to crud that he found a shoebox behind the bath panel.

That was going to be our lucky break. A box hidden under a bath? That had to be something special, didn't it? You don't go to all that trouble to hide your favorite pair of Nikes, do you?

So chuckling away like B movie villains we quit the house by the same window we'd come in through and carried the box back home— if you can call a poxy trailer by the river home. There, the branches of a bony old tree beat the roof with all the berserk rhythm of a drummer who's burned out his brain on crack-cocaine. *Bang, bang, bang-dee-*

37

bang. Fucking crazy, man. Some nights I'd have a girl there. She'd jump out of bed when the sea gales woke up old man tree to begin his mighty beat, and she'd scream the place was under attack. Bare-assed, she'd tumble out the caravan to run back to Whitby, a streak of naked flesh, yelling so loud that it would send all the seagulls spinning up into the air and crying out fit to burst. Man, the times we laughed about that, Clayton and me.

Yeah, an aluminum box in a field. It let in rain. It stank of wet sneakers. It was a mess.

It was home. And that's where we carried our prize.

A shoe box full of gold rings? Stolen cash? Even better, a couple of pounds of pure white coke?

Nah...

"Christ shit on this!" Clayton hooted. "Hey, Nick, whatcha make of it?"

"Jesus, that's never real in a months of Sundays."

"Well, what are those things pointing out the end? They're bone, aren't they?"

"But who'd want to keep a freakin' hand under their freakin' bath?"

Clayton made with the Vincent Price. "It's coming for you, Nick. It wants you."

So, there's that hand lying there on a bed of newspaper in the box. It's a mummified hand; all brown and warty with skin that's dried and shriveled; it looks as if the bones in the hand have been shrink-wrapped. Of course Clayton, the mad bastard that he is, can't resist picking it up and gliding it through the air toward my face while doing the spectral, "It's coming for you, Nick. It wants to feel your balls..."

And I can see the filthy thing is REAL. I see the fingernails with greenie-black grunge stuck beneath them that might be century old boogers; cracks in the skin show bones beneath; I can see the stubby bit of bone that pokes out the wrist where it was chopped from an arm. Remember when Spock used to do that funky salute with his palm flat, fingers stretched out into a kind of V shape? Well, that's how that thing looked, only this had a thumb that looked longer than was natural and it jutted out to a point, hitching a ride to Eternityville.

"Nick...Nick. Look at me. I'm a kid again. I'm sucking my thumb."

"That's gross, Clayton. What if the bastard died of leprosy or cancer or something?"

Now he did a Homer Simpson, glazing his eyes in bliss.

"Hmmm…salty. Like sucking a peanut." He suddenly flashed me one of his crazy leers. "Want a go, Nick?"

And that was Clayton to a T. The first time he really got in deep with the cops was ten years ago when he was fifteen. He broke into a funeral parlor, tipped some old dear out of her coffin, strapped her to the back of a stolen motorbike and blazed through Whitby, sounding the horn, the dead woman's clothes fluttering in the breeze, her head nodding up and down with all the loose-necked frenzy of those novelty dogs you stick in your car. All the time her eyes staring wide like dusty glass balls in her head. "Look at my pussy!" Clayton was yelling. "She isn't wearing any panties!"

The arresting officer puked into his own hat.

«« — »»

We were sober the next morning. Clayton had left the hand on top of the TV. "That's our new ornament," he announced, leering at it with nothing less than sexual pleasure. "We bring it out for the girls when the time is right." He chuckled. "Girls love a finger of fun."

I'd been going through the shoebox. "There's more stuff in here," I said, spreading out papers on the table.

"Cash?"

"No."

"Not interested, then. We got any beer?"

"There's pages that've been ripped from a book."

"Write it down in a letter for me, Nick. I'll read it sometime never."

"No, listen…it tells you about the hand."

"Yeah, as if crap in a book can tell you anything worth knowing."

Clayton doesn't read…can't read. Gets all touchy if someone tells him something about a book. It's as if he thinks all books have stuff written down about him, about what he's really like. You follow? Paranoid is the word, I guess. It gets him punchy. He kicked open the trailer door and stalked off, cursing any bird that flew near him. He'd been gone about an hour when he came back with beer and groceries. He must have snatched them because we hadn't had so much as a penny to scratch our you-know-what for a week. Grunting, he plonked a can in front of me along with a vacuum pack of pastrami. As I ate, I noticed he was watching the hand. Then he looked at the book pages in the shoebox. This went on for a while. Me eating, him pulling on the can of beer, watching. Then at last he said, "OK, then. What does it say about the hand?"

"It's famous."

"The hand? You're pulling my dick."

"No, look for yourself."

"You look for yourself." Touchy again because I showed him the page with all those bamboozling black marks. "There's a photo of the hand in a museum case. Someone must have snatched it then hid it under the bath."

"What is it, then? Egyptian?"

"No, it's local."

"If it's from here it's worth squat, then."

I read it. "In Whitby museum is the grisly relic The Hand Of Glory. The hand came from a gibbeted murderer. After the blood was squeezed from the severed limb it was embalmed in salt and pepper before being dried in the sun."

He opened another can. "Sounds like a streak of piss to me. I mean—why bother?"

"I'm getting to that," I told him. "The Hand Of Glory was used by thieves. When they went housebreaking they'd put this outside the front door of the house with a burning candle wedged between its fingers, then it'd send everyone in the house into a kind of trance. After that, old Johnny Lightfinger strolled into the house and took what he wanted."

"With no one any the wiser."

"Something like that."

He stared at the hand, his big ugly face scowling as he thought so hard the skin from the top of his head to his eyes formed into hard ridges. I thought he'd make his usual scornful remark about the hand, but then he said something surprising. "OK, Nick. Let's try it."

«« — »»

Come to think of it, Clayton is superstitious. Looking back now I realize he never even gets out of bed on a Friday the 13th. Of course he never ever said he was superstitious, only he'd make some excuse about not rising. Not that it was unusual: we didn't have day jobs in the City, did we? Society didn't expect us to fight for the democratic way, did it? Brain surgery would continue without our intervention, right? So we'd settle down for a day's smoking and drinking and a bit of the other if we had female company.

Yeah, so we were losers. Alcohol was the answer to our problems (even hangovers). And there were those purple pills that allowed us to soar with angels.

But then Clayton found the Hand Of Glory. With that, he believed, he could change everything. He could turn our poxy lives into GOLD.

«« —»»

"Why don't we do the Morrelli place?"

He gave me that sneering look of his like I'd just suggested we write a letter to Santa Claus. "Think bigger, Nick."

"Morrelli's the richest man in Whitby. He's out of town. That mansion's sitting up there all alone."

"Duh... Turd brain." He waved The Hand Of Glory under my nose. The brown skin looked like a rotten apple in the moonlight. "What's the point in trying this if the house is empty? Isn't it supposed to put people in a trance?"

"Clayton." My laugh came out on the nervous side. "You don't believe that thing really works, do you?"

"There's only one way to find out, isn't there?"

The time was coming up to around ten as we walked into Whitby. If you've never clapped eyes on the place let me tell you: Whitby is a hunchbacked town. A dark, evil-tempered hunchback at that. With its back to the sea, houses disfigure the hillside like clusters of scabs. Streets are so narrow that all the buildings hang over them with weird frowning faces, and with poxy little windows that look like evil eyes. And those beady little eyes are always watching; they're always hating you and willing the big bad luck bird to come pecking at your door.

In that old monster town there were people about even on a winter's night like this. Most were moving from pub to pub; a few were leaving restaurants as the shutters came down. In houses across the water lights shone where most of the townsfolk eyeballed TV. Clayton couldn't resist a bit of clowning, running the dead fingers through my hair, or putting the hand on girls' shoulders, so they'd look down at it and scream at the sight of mummified flesh. They all thought it was a joke hand. Most laughed. They knew Clayton; they knew what he was like. So did I. An ugly incident in search of an opportunity.

"So," I said, "what big idea have you got for the hand?"

"Just you wait and see. This is gonna blow your mind."

"What's the point in heading up the cliff? There's nothing up here."

"There is." He nodded at a dark column standing above the old church on the cliff-top. "The TV mast."

"What the hell do we want with that?"

"You'll see in a minute...here."

He gave me the hand to hold as he pulled a candle and a glass jar from his pocket. I followed him in the moonlight, with the sound of the sea booming against the bottom of the cliff. I tried not to think about that pound or so of dried skin and bone I held in my hand. And when I felt the fingers twitch inside mine I muttered to myself: "It's only your imagination, it's only your imagination..."

Fifteen minutes later he'd done it. Clayton had climbed the twenty-foot TV mast, lit the candle in the jar (no mean feat with the breeze blowing like that), wedged that and the Hand Of Glory into the front of the transmitter dish, then made me recite the verse with him. I should have felt an idiot chanting that rhyme but instead of feeling ridiculous I felt cold. A great lumbering cold that went to the root of my bones.

"Oh, Hand Of Glory, shed thy light, direct us to our spoil tonight."

Clayton came swinging down the TV mast like an ape, boots clanging the steel ladder, moonlight glinting on his shaved head. "See," he called with a crazy leer on his face. "That didn't hurt, did it?"

"Right," my voice sounded so skeptical it oozed. "What's the point in leaving the hand up the TV mast?"

"Just you wait and see. Now...we've earned ourselves a little treat. Hold out your hand."

Standing in the breeze, the sea whooshing around the rocks below, he tipped half a dozen purple pills into my hand. "As the bishop said to the actress: swallow. We're going to party tonight."

Clayton was in one of his wild 'n dangerous moods. The purple pills were Frankies, some kids called them Frankensteiners. They were made by an alcoholic lab technician who combined uppers, downers, E and some of his own secret ingredients into a mind-bending cocktail for the nark-head connoisseur. Take them and you were launched on a magic roller-coaster ride to hell knows where. As I've said, sometimes you flew with angels. At other times in our aluminum trailer, that leaked, that festered, that smelt of wet sneaker, we conversed with GOD.

I swallowed them.

By the time we walked down the hill into town those Frankies were kicking in. Imagine being rolled easily along on big fat marsh-mallow tires instead of legs; imagine a tropical breeze that warms you through to your gnarly old soul, replaces the cold easterly. You don't feel that headache any more. Those swollen veins in your throat you've got from your dirty rotten drinking stop hurting. You shrug off that burning itch in your dick. And instead of dark wells of shadow in back yards there mushroom these gorgeous mists of indigo and crimson. Lurking houses no longer frown but grin; window eyes now wide open and blazing with JOY. That's how Frankies feel.

We were laughing, waving our arms, excited.

"*Man,*" I sang out. "Why did you put the hand up the TV mast?"

"*MAN!*" he sang back. "Haven't you worked it out for yourself yet? Look!" He pointed along Church Lane as that laugh came bubbling up through his throat again. "Look, Nick. It works. The Hand Of Glory damn well works!"

Jesus...shivers prickled up my spine, my eyes grew wide, as I followed the direction of his pointing finger. I told myself this was a new trick courtesy of the Frankies. But it wasn't. This was really happening. Whitby had fallen asleep. Not only people in their beds, either. Everyone had fallen asleep in their tracks. Men and women lay on the street, or in bars. A man lay upside down on a flight of steps that ran to the beach. A woman dozed amongst fast-food clams spilt from a trashcan. A cold hamburger stuck to her forehead like a huge third eye.

"C'mon, c'mon," Clayton shouted. "You must have worked it out by now?" The sound echoed over a town that was silent as DEATH.

Maybe it was the cold dawn of realization but it rolled back the feel-good warmth of the Frankies. "You put The Hand Of Glory in the TV mast."

The leer went WILD on his face. "You're getting it. And why did I put the hand there?" He walked across the chest of a cop lying on the sidewalk. "...because down here's a dead zone for TV transmissions; that's why they stuck the booster mast up on the cliff. TV signals are scooped up by the aerial then squirted out again down here to all these houses. Only now..." He grinned. "...only now the TV signals go *through* the Hand Of Glory...they AMPLIFY its power...and what you see is what you get. Sleepy town."

He was almost skipping now with a lusty delight. Sometimes he stepped over a man lying there sleeping in the gutter; sometimes he kicked.

"Whoa, Nick! Did you see how his nose just went *POW!*" He hooted. "Christ crap on that...look at all the blood!"

By the harbor it was the same. Dozens of people lay unconscious in the road. Dead, I told myself until I bent down to feel a woman's chest. But there was the heartbeat good and strong. When I held my open palm under her nose I could feel her breath. They weren't dead, only sleeping. The Frankies still worked their magic too. I could see her breath come out as a mist that was pure GOLD.

"Good idea," Clayton shouted.

Finding a pair of women in high-heels and short skirts, he started pulling off their clothes.

"Just opening up a couple of goodie bags." He laughed. "Look at the twin peaks on this. Yooo! Pierced nipples!"

Neither of the women woke or even murmured in their sleep as he went to work on them. The old time phrase for it came to mind. *Sporting the wood.*

Clayton was sporting the wood so hard with one of the sleeping beauties her back slapped the pavement loud enough to echo along those comatose streets for miles around.

Dazed by the sight of all this, I stepped over bodies lying flat out, walked round a car that had run into a store front, the driver lay bleeding (and still sleeping) in his seat. I watched Mick Waterman lying back on a bench with a cigarette smoldering away on his chest. It had burnt a hole as big as a saucer in his best silk shirt. As I turned away his jacket lapel caught fire; a rose colored flame took root there.

Not a whimper from him. Not one.

I turned round. Now I noticed a cat lying unconscious on the ground just a yard away from the sleeping mouse that it had been chasing when the Hand Of Glory blasted out its POWER from the TV mast.

Seagulls littered the quayside. I picked one up. They were warm plump things, heavier than I imagined. I could feel the heartbeat through its feathers. I put it down gently. Then I remembered Mick Waterman with the fire taking hold of his jacket. I went back and rolled him over into a puddle at the side of the road. The flames went out with a long cartoon hisssss...like Tom sinking his burning ass into a bird-bath.

"Give me a hand, Nick. Hey, give me a hand!"

Laughing so hard you'd think his bald head would burst into a million pieces, Clayton sweated as he heaved old Judge Jeffrey over the harbor railing. "Help us out, Nick!"

I kept on walking. It was getting crappy now. An alarm screamed where a house had caught fire (maybe some poor bastard had fallen asleep into their nice log fire). Fish appeared on the water to float there in a shining carpet. Do fish sleep? I asked myself as I walked into a bar. Do they drown if they stop swimming?"

I stepped over a bartender that'd somehow fallen into a sitting position like an obese pixy. There I helped myself to cash from the register.

Clayton walked in over a bouncy rug of fallen bodies (not a murmur, not a sigh from them). He put on a lardy-dah joke voice. "Ah, there you are barkeep, my fine fellow. Your best champagne and your largest cigar."

"Coming right up, sir."

So that's how it went. We drank champagne; we used those sleeping guys and gals as beanbags. Torsos are comfortable, heads are not. We chatted conversationally.

"The cold water never even woke him up." Clayton blew smoke rings at the ceiling. "Judge Jeffrey sank like a stone."

Then the idiot did something stupid. He set fire to a woman's hair. That really does stink vile. We went to the next bar to continue drinking. We also took money from cash registers, purses, wallets. Clayton removed clothes and posed the clientele like models in a hilarious watchem-a-callit...tableaux? Yeah, that's the word. Tableaux. A kind of warped nativity scene with things sticking in here and there. "Won't there be some red faces when this lot wakes up," he told me as he finished off with a few artfully inserted bottlenecks.

A couple of hours later Clayton sighed, "All good things come to an end." We'd just loaded the last bucket full of money into the trunk of a BMW that had caught our eye. Maybe it was time. You couldn't leave those people asleep outside all night, could you?

But when they did wake we'd be long gone. They couldn't pin anything on us.

It didn't take long for Clayton to return to the TV mast, shin up the ladder, blow out the candle and stick the hand wrist first into his pocket with those Spock fingers pointing out.

Then we drove south with the trunk filled to the lid with cash. Lovely liquid untraceable cash. I cranked the CD player until the car shook then we drove with the windows down hollering out into the night air. It felt so good. We were the undisputed Lords of Misrule.

Then we found the truck that'd rolled into a ditch. The driver wasn't dead but I couldn't wake him. We passed more cars. Some had come to a stop with their engines still running, the dozing drivers slumped in their seats. At dawn we reached the city. That was sleeping too. And we knew it was never going to wake.

«« —»»

SHIVERS

Six months have gone. When it's cold we burn banknotes in the hearth. We've as much food and drink as we need—for now anyway. Clayton's messed with those pills too long though. One side of his face is paralyzed. Not that it matters. He's been going insane for weeks now. Not long ago he started screaming, and I figure it's one of those screams that's never going to stop. Me? I'm sitting here writing down what happened to us. There's that mummy hand squatting on the table. Its ugly fingers twitch every now and again; the index finger rises slowly to point—*j'accuse*... I've the loaded revolver here. As soon as I've reached the end of this, my last living testament, then I'm going to suck the barrel until the bullet comes. You follow?

Naturally enough, we speculated after that night in Whitby. We decided that the mast didn't only boost TV transmissions down into the valley, but carried signals back the OTHER way. Spreading the power of that shriveled man-paw along transmitter chains, relay stations and satellite transponders across the world. Leaving us the only ones to be immune. And there's one more thing we figured out. Although we knew how to activate the Hand we didn't know a damn thing about switching it off.

Now I see the results for myself. Men and women sleep out in the streets. They still breathe; but their clothes rot, their hair grows into tangles, while vines snake across their bodies, and moss covers their faces in a soft green rash. For all the world they look like the fallen statues of a dead as bones civilization.

Maybe they will wake up in a thousand years. Maybe they'll never wake. Just like me when I slide the gun muzzle into my mouth, put my thumb on the trigger and begin that final squeeze...

Whisper, When You Drown

Tom Piccirilli

The storm isn't quite loud enough yet to clear all the dead from my head.

Marianna takes me by the wrist and drags me into the living room where they're watching Japornimation and discussing the perimeters of the covenstead. The lady who owns the house is some locally known pagan queen and she's holding court on the stairway with a few kids who think Ozzy invented the pentagram. She says that she and her husband are the foci for earthly power heading in all directions from the house for a mile and a half. She controls the other members of the coven psychically but with beneficence. The kids nod in understanding. The husband pops in another anime tape and him and his beer buddies are talking about *Speed Racer* and the premium that the Japanese put on pubic hair.

The white witch is called Willow, and her man is Mojo. She plays the part pretty well, wearing a white muumuu, hair ringed with plastic daisy petals, tipping two-fifty or so. She's got a real mother nature attitude, and gestures a great deal with her hands, palms up, as if invoking spirits. She talks about energy and the manipulation of the elements, but she never says to what end.

I head back into the kitchen where I've been hiding for the past forty-five minutes, close to the bottle of Jack Daniels, but Marianna tries to draw me from my "self-imposed shell" for purposes unknown. Rain slashes heavily at the windows and I look out the window at the roiling bay. I'm still surprised and impressed as hell that they could afford a house on the water, even this one, which is little more than a shack. A mile up Montauk Highway the homes sell for seven-fifty large, but this far down the lane you can apparently nab one of the old converted fisherman cabins for pocket change.

The swinging kitchen door is kept propped open by a brick brought in from the garden. More goth kids arrive, their mascara and freshly dyed hair running black across their harlequin faces. Willow welcomes everyone with open arms and huge hugs, whether she knows them or not. Perhaps it's meant to reassure or console, but that sort of thing makes me leap out of my skin.

Marianna knows everybody and runs to each new guest with a squeal. One kid in a leather trenchcoat gives her a kiss and then flashes a razor blade between his teeth. She bursts out laughing and I wonder if everybody who's supposed to be on medication has gotten their allotted refills this week. I haven't.

The storm seeks entrance. I know the feeling. The wind doesn't howl now, it mewls, scratching at the shingles, rain tapping like the hands of children. Suddenly the sorrow is on me all at once. It gets like this on occasion, when the blackness swells, tidal and dragging. The three dead girls look bored and I can't blame them. They vanish through the walls but instantly reappear. They say my name and I keep turning, waiting for something more, but there isn't anything else.

I look around the room, hoping to make eye contact with somebody. Willow might be able to send me positive psychic vibes but she's busy giving bear hugs, squashing freaks and stick figures alike. Everyone else is wrapped up in their own conversations or highs, the naked lady-boy cartoons flashing on the tube.

I start to float towards the front door, but I'm stopped cold by a new band of folks coming in. Rain spatters and sprays through the living room like a snipped carotid. More of Mojo's boys, they're all carrying six-packs and tiny knives in their belt buckles. Shoulder to shoulder I brush past a few of them and get the long look, the puzzling frown. Even they know I don't belong.

Marianna thinks I'm oversensitive and gives a sexy sigh. We've lived next door to each other since we were kids, but recently things have changed between us. Some extra tension, maybe a little sexual friction. Or perhaps we've just grown accustomed to one another and seek each other outside the usual circumstances. It's the only reason I can figure as to why she would've brought me here. The dead girls agree.

"What's the matter?" she asks, and I can smell the weed in her voice. She's loose, sort of weaving on her feet, blithe.

"Nothing really, just not my sort of group. I think I should be—"

This dodge annoys her because I've used it so often. I try to think up new excuses and occasionally write them down, but on the spot I can never remember any. "How do you know?" she asks. "You never go to parties. Why don't you just ease up."

"I'm out of my element."

"Oh Christ, not that again. You act like they're trying to hang you. What would you rather be doing?"

"No, see, it's not that, it's just—"

"What, reading? Sitting in some online chatroom?"

"Uhm, well, you—"

"Don't you ever feel ashamed?"

As a matter of fact, I do, but it has nothing to do with what she's accusing me of. Now she's getting me heated. "That's enough."

"Come on."

The rain is as much a draw for her as it is for me. Our bedroom windows at home face each across perfectly hedge-clipped yards. We've stared at each other through panes of glass that pulsed with throbbing water. Sixty feet, and I've watched her undress while on the phone, wrapping the cord around her wrist until it's tight as a garrote. She puts a little skip in her step now and takes my hand, leading me. The girls follow, also skipping. Marianna tows me outside onto the patio, where we watch the thrashing whitecaps of the bay.

She is low-slung in blue, blonde hair darkening as it grows wet, freckles evaporating while droplets swerve across her nose and into the channels of each angle and curve, lovely face topped with shining black eyes. With the moon at its zenith, pale light ignites the glazed dark brick. The street lights are a hazy burn up and down the docks of the pier, the distant lighthouse at the far end of the beach revolving slowly like a geyser of brilliance, waiting for the high night tide, illuminating the thunderous waves.

"Is this better?"

The roar is nice. "Yes," I say.

She's got a strong grip and it means something, in the worsening storm. She shows me her teeth as the rain courses over her lips and funnels from her mouth. My breathing hitches in my chest and I shake my wet curls from the edges of my vision. She keeps leading me, down to the water's wild edge.

"Uh, listen—"

"Come on."

I look back and can see that the roof of the white witch's cabin needs to be fixed badly. The gutters have backed up and are sluicing rain in a mad arch under the dormers. I can imagine the whole house being washed away down the street and into the sea.

SHIVERS

I am pliable but difficult to grasp, as Marianna's hand slips from mine. She grabs hold of my jacket and yanks it from me, and we peel one another as we go. I've got four buttons of her blouse undone, but it sticks to her as she moves, saturated and heavy, and won't come completely free. Her bra opens from the front and I sort of like how it looks there, wet and see-through, with the dark nipples and aureole prodding from beneath, but it suddenly snaps open from the front without either of us touching it. She has larger breasts than I'd thought. I've been looking at her my entire life, so how could something like that get by me?

A rotted rowboat lies upside down on a muddy hill, the rain shifting over its keel. She runs by it, giggling now, pot and expectation shifting her buoyant mood into higher gear. I wish it was catching. Brackish water and brine froth along the canals, seeping from the sumps and flooding the side roads.

"It's the end of the world!" she shouts above the storm. "We'll be consumed by the rain. Let's wallow in the mud!"

Well, I've done a little of that in my time and never thought much of it. She rushes down into the weeds beside the ditch and strips out of her skirt, flings her panties off in one liquid motion. It's so quick that I gasp, beginning to tremble in the cold, wanting her to put them back on and take them off slowly, let me see it happen.

My shirt is gone and my jeans are open as Marianna wheels into the water. It's freezing and she gives a little scream that gets me in a good way, watching as she bobs with her nipples so tight and hard, hair lusciously falling across her face, that I'm growling. I get my pants off, sliding in the mire, and though I've got a mind full of serpents, the lashing rain strikes like a cat'o'nine-tails across my flesh.

This is contrition. This is both too much and not enough. She flails savagely, enjoying herself, but there are jagged hunks of cement around and the guide-poles are old and full of splinters. I stand at the ledge of the jetty and she rises out of the foam and dives into my arms, tiny trails of blood running from dozens of small wounds all over her sleek and glistening body. Slashed by the rocks, with barbs of wood here and there, she tries to force my mouth to her cuts.

Full of salt, Marianna's blonde curls hang in her fiery glare and drape across her breasts, and she takes me down to the bottom of the mauling green world.

The dead girls are waiting. They're silhouetted in silver, back-lit by bright light. I can almost make out the shape of a school bus down there, rolling in the mud, making stops and picking up the kids.

Freddy, the driver, is with us too, smelling like Wild Turkey, and he takes a sip from his flask.

Marianna's eyes keep spinning and I see that she's not just high, she's on something else, who the hell knows what. It adds another reason to why this feels ethereal, as if it's not actually happening between her and me. We swim closely together, kicking our feet hard to stay up as the waves launch against us. Every so often she tires and stops and pulls me under. Her nails scratch at my thighs as she works along my legs, her belly pressing against me. Even underwater she chortles and the sound is everywhere. I wheel and Marianna is right with me, raising her breasts to my mouth, moaning in the wind. I lick her nipples and the sour taste eases into my throat. The stinging rain continues to pelt. Freddy's got an ugly laugh and he lets it out, high-pitched and rapid as a dingo's.

The girls giggle, watching. They never got to live long enough to do this sort of thing, and their resentment boils from them. Marianna goes down for a time, taking me between her teeth, as she floats upwards. There's too much salt as she chokes and spits when we hit the surface. We kiss and our tongues are capped with bits of seaweed.

Boats crash against the docks along the channel, knocking and groaning, sterns rising and battering downwards. Her face is almost lost in the darkness and I edge closer, searching out this girl I know and not being able to find her. She wraps her thighs around me and I press myself into her a half inch.

"Wait!"

"What?"

"Don't you have a condom?"

If she didn't know the answer to that by now—Christ, my clothes are ten yards away up on a muddy hill, and my soaked wallet in the back pocket is empty. "No."

That stops her like a backhand across her mouth. "What? You don't? Why the hell not?"

It's a good question, really, just an exceptionally bad time for it. "I didn't think I'd...uh...get lucky."

"You asshole!"

"Look, we're in the ocean for Christ's sake, shouldn't the salt-water, uhm...isn't it a spermicide?"

"No, I don't think so."

"Well, won't it just wash out of you?"

"I don't know, I'm not taking that chance."

"But—"

"God, I'm tired."

Finally I see Marianna, the girl I've grown up with. We're back to square one, more or less, freezing in the dark night of flooded absurdity. The moment has been doused. She looks up at me and I catch a silver smear of moon in her eyes, and she's yawning. I give her a boost into the weeds.

"I'm bleeding!" she cries, all the way back into herself. Whatever she was on has pretty much worn off. Like that, we're once again staring at each other from a great distance across the pulsing rain. We gather our sopping clothes from the muck, get dressed and head back to the house.

I slosh inside. I'm completely drenched and my jeans squeak against my legs as my sneakers squeal on the hardwood floors. The water running into my eyes takes the edge off the world. Everything has this nice misty glow to it now.

Mojo and his crew are off the Japornimation kick and are now watching tapes of kids' shows from the 70s. *Land of the Lost* is on the screen: Holly sobbing her little pig-tailed ass off, being chased by Grumpy, claymation dinosaurs all over the place, with Will just sort of standing by and watching, overacting *a la* Shatner. Stacked on the television are videos for *Sigmund and the Sea Monsters* and *Thunderbirds Go!* I've got to admit I'm a little curious to see Sigmund again.

I drop onto the couch next to Mojo. He hands me a beer and I shoot it without tasting. Freddy offers me a hit off his flask and I pass. The girls sit on the floor and huddle around the TV.

Willow the white witch is staring at me. At first it's irritating, but after a while, I don't mind. In fact, I find it soothing, even if I don't know why.

Somebody pops in Sigmund and it doesn't take long before I begin snickering. The sea monsters are falling all over Johnny Whitaker and I just can't help myself. Mojo slides a little further away. So does Freddy. I'm laughing so wildly that the others can't help gawking, but that doesn't stop me. This is too good. My God, just look at it, brilliant, hysterical. Sid and Marty Kroft were geniuses, and I can't imagine why the show lasted only twenty-nine episodes. I can hardly breathe through the guffawing, and my face is so tight and frozen that it feels like stone.

They start to scatter. The dead girls peer back at me over their shoulders. Willow wanders over and gets me to my feet and walks me to the stairwell, where she hugs me deeply and I fall into her big body and I don't ever want to leave. We're swaying a little, rocking back and forth, and my tears soak her muumuu.

Eventually we unclench and I take the steps two at a time, with no idea of where I'm going.

I leave puddles behind on the hardwood floor as I waft around the bedrooms, peeking into closets. In the hall I spot a string hanging from the ceiling. I tug on it and another platform of stairs unfolds, leading to the attic. I climb for no reason I can name, and then I pull the steps in behind me.

There's one small fluorescent light burning in the corner of the attic. Mojo and the white queen have a pretty solid stash of hydroponics pot up here. The sprouts are coming up nicely, almost ready to transplant out of the root system tank. There's a fairly sophisticated drip feed going, but the nutrient solution stinks to hell. I back away into the gloom and look around.

"Are you hiding too?" a voice asks from the darkness.

I'm surprised I don't jump. Normally I would've been shocked, but this somehow fits with the rest of the unfolding night.

"I suppose I am," I say.

My eyes are adjusting, and a shard of moonlight slashes in from the attic's single window. She's sitting on a broken rocking horse, one of the old time ones carved from pine.

Shadows from the rain drift against her skin. She says, "You're all wet."

"Ohboy. Yes."

"Will you kill me?"

I look over at the girls and they shake their heads, but for once I'm not listening. They've been with me since I was six and Freddy went off the road. "If you want me to."

Her sable hair falls to perfectly frame her heart-shaped face, those lips a natural red deeper than running blood. She wears a black sleeveless dress cross-laced down her entire back, exposing every muscle, freckle, curve, and scar. I'm suddenly feeling very perky.

It doesn't take long to become haunted.

Her beauty already plagues, entices, even appalls me. She's intangible in this dimness, with the shadows slithering over her, the roof murmuring and grunting in protest beneath the pooling rain.

One thin stream of water has broken through the rafters, dripping down in a near-constant run. She sits beneath it and I go to her. I think it'll feel like the Chinese water torture, the expectation and trauma of each drop driving me out of my head, but it doesn't.

SHIVERS

This presses me further inside, into the scent of the rain, the ebbing of flesh. She's a part of me, working one arm around my shoulders, legs around my waist.

She whispers but I can't quite make out the words. I start to tell her I have no condom, it's a big issue apparently and needs to be addressed now, before I'm all the way in this ocean with her, but she clamps her lips to mine and strangles any concern. She unbuckles my soggy jeans and struggles like a champ to get them down. I pull aside her panties and she's liquid fire against my hand. We kneel before one another and I ease inside her, or she into me.

"Yes," she tells me.

It's hard to breathe. The roof sounds like it's ready to collapse directly over us, the water no longer trickling, but gushing. The storm is inside. Freddy appears to be very scared and his flask is finally empty. He keeps stomping his foot like he's trying to find the brake pedal. I wonder how Sigmund is doing. The girls look terrified, and I keep trying to brush them away with my hands. They don't want to go. They've never wanted to go.

She flows like all my deepest fears swimming up to meet me. Her head bobs as she pours across my skin, squirming like a serpent, like a fish. I'm drowning but I still thirst. That's the way of it. I am in my element now. Rafters croon and wail, about to give way perhaps. Christ, I can still hope. The girls are screaming much louder than they did on the bus. This is absolution, purification. The roof shrieks. The deluge is upon us, yet she continues to whisper and mumble against my tongue as I dive deeper into the consuming wash of our maelstrom.

Hermanos
De El Noche

Bentley Little

"**W**hat the hell are they?" Brock asked.

The tour guide was obviously frightened. His face was pale, his hands shaking. Behind him, in his seat, the bus driver was praying. "Vampires," he said.

Brock tightened his grip on Marnie's hand and stared out the dusty window of the bus. In the darkness of the Mexican desert, the naked men continued to run blindly across the road in front of them. There were twenty or thirty of them, and they ran on and off the pavement and the sand, silently, barefoot, making no sound, not even crying out when their legs collided with bushes or cacti.

One hit the side of the bus with a dull thump.

"What are we going to do?" a woman in the back cried. Her voice was high and panicked, tinged with hysteria.

The tour guide licked his lips. "There's nothing we can do. We cannot fix the tire until morning, until they are gone. We must wait here. And pray."

"They're not vampires!" the old man across the aisle said. "There's no such thing as vampires. That's just stupid." He stood up. "I'll change the damn tire. I'm not afraid of a few dirty wetback homos. Where's the spare? Where's the tools?"

"You're not going anywhere." Brock told him. "You're not leaving the bus. They may not be vampires, but they're crazy. Look at them." He gestured out the window toward where the naked men were running through the desert. "It's dangerous out there."

Marnie squeezed his hand tightly, and he turned to look at her. Her eyes were scared but clear. She nodded her agreement with him.

The tour guide looked at his watch. "It is about six hours to dawn," he said. "Hopefully, they will leave us alone. If we can survive until the sun comes up, we will be safe. I suggest we pray to keep them away."

There was a loud thump as another one hit the side of the bus.

Brock felt Marnie's hand tighten. "Look," she whispered, pointing out the window.

He followed her finger. One of the men nearest the bus was holding in his hand a rodent of some kind. A rat or chipmunk or squirrel. The man twisted off the animal's head, held the body above his mouth and drank the streaming blood. The red liquid dripped down the sides of his dirty face.

Marnie turned away, sickened, but Brock continued to watch as a second man came and picked up the discarded head from the sandy ground. Another man ran forward and began to fight him for it. Brock had never been a superstitious man, but he was not blind or stupid either. He had always believed the evidence of his own eyes, and he believed it now. He believed that the men outside were vampires.

He stared at the naked man sucking the last drops of blood from the rodent's body, his eyes focusing on the dirty skin, the long matted hair. Brock's conception of vampires had been formed entirely by the movies—suave sophisticated seducers, aristocratic men in capes—and he found it hard to reconcile the wild savages outside with his image of the elegant traditional vampire.

The stake and garlic and crucifix and holy water were probably a load of crap too.

On an impulse, he looked up at the bus' large side mirror.

The vampires cast no reflection.

Another vampire hit the opposite side of the bus. And another. And another.

Brock stood to see what was going on, looking over the heads and shoulders of the passengers on the other side of the aisle. Several vampires were throwing themselves against the vehicle, grinning hungrily up at the travelers through the windows. They had obviously discovered that there were people in the bus, and were trying to get inside. The vehicle rocked slightly back and forth.

"Stay inside!" the tour guide warned. "Whatever happens, stay inside!"

More vampires ran up to the bus and began pushing, working in tandem, making a concerted effort to tip the vehicle over. Passengers stood up and began scrambling for their belongings.

"Stay in your seats!" the tour guide pleaded.

"Hell with that!" a man in the back announced. "I'm getting the hell out of here!" He pulled open the bus' emergency exit, and the rear panel opened with a pop.

And then the vampires were upon them.

It happened quickly. Brock saw parts of actions, heard snatches of sounds but so many things were happening that he couldn't really tell what was going on. Naked bodies were swarming through the open exit, and at the same time people were screaming, trying to break windows, trying to escape. As more vampires rushed in, the rocking bus finally tipped all the way over. He held Marnie tightly and tried to shield her face from the shattering glass as both of them fell. His body hit hard metal. The impact jerked his head toward the front of the bus, and he saw the tour guide and driver lying on their sides, feet tangled, still praying. The back of the bus was filled with screams, and when he looked in that direction he saw red blood and yellow teeth, brown skin and multicolored clothes, hair and hands wrestling in a confusing upside-down jumble.

And still the vampires kept coming. An unending stream of naked dirty men crawling down into the overcrowded bus from the broken windows, grinning hugely, showing fangs.

Brock was holding Marnie's hand, and he was suddenly aware that he could not let go of it. He tried to turn, tried to look at her, but his head would not swivel that far to the left. He seemed to be pinned under a crushed seat.

"Marnie!" he cried.

"I'm okay!" Her voice sounded raw, rough, totally unlike her regular speech.

The vampires were feasting now. Blood flowed from crash cuts and incisor incisions, and the filthy men were licking it up, drinking it down. Brock saw one of them rip open a screaming woman's neck. A fountain of blood geysered upward, but the vampire immediately cut it off at the source, placing his open mouth over the spurting wound.

Brock tried to wiggle free. Only eight or ten feet, ten or twelve screaming squirming bodies, separated them from the vanguard of the vampires. Some of the passengers were free and unhurt, but he could see that those who tried to escape were killed immediately, vampires slashing throats with long dirty fingernails, rending flesh with plagued teeth. The remaining members of the tour huddled frozen in place, unable to flee, unable to fight, unable to act.

He felt movement, behind him, and his body stiffened, muscles tensing. "Marnie?" he cried. And then his wife was crawling across the metal floor in front of his face. Her blouse was torn, but other than that she seemed to be unhurt.

"You're trapped under the seat!" she said. She was yelling. "I'm going to try and lift it off of you! See if you can crawl out!"

He could barely hear her over the chaotic jumble of noise about them, but he could read her lips, and he nodded as she sat up and maneuvered into position. The bus was filled with screams, sounds of terror and agony totally unlike the simulations heard in movies or on TV. In films, he thought, when people were menaced by evil or gruesomely tortured, the actors' screams were invariably loud sustained notes, impossibly clear and consistent. But the noises coming from the back of the bus were short, ragged, choked by cries or panicked lack of breath, terrifyingly unpredictable.

A great weight was suddenly lifted from his back, and he knew that Marnie had succeeded in picking up the fallen seat. He used his hands to pull himself forward, out of the way, and sat up, relieved to discover that he had not been seriously injured. His neck and right shoulder hurt, but the pain was really not much worse than a muscle cramp.

He hugged Marnie tightly, quickly, then pushed her away. They had to escape, and they had to act fast. The air was filled with the smell of blood, and he realized with surprise that it did not smell "coppery" as he had read in so many cheap novels but was sickeningly, putridly organic, a cloying almost decaying odor nothing like the clean antiseptic scent of metal. He pushed Marnie silently toward the window above them. The glass was cracked but not shattered. They would have to break the window, pull themselves through it and try to escape. The odds of them successfully doing so were slim to none, but they had no other choice.

Marnie stood.

And the vampires nearby suddenly stopped what they were doing.

The two events happened so obviously one after the other, that even amidst the screaming and fighting and feeding Brock could not fail to notice the causal connection. Marnie broke open the window with someone's bloody boot, cleared the glass, and reached for the frame to pull herself up and out, but vampires were already surrounding her, drawn as if by a beacon. One of the filthy men began bleating in a strange high-pitched voice, and the other took up the cry. The vampires at the rear of the bus dropped their prey and moved forward, toward his wife.

Brock struggled to help her through the opening, but he was roughly pushed aside by one of the vampires, sharp fingernails raking across his face as he was thrown to the floor.

He noticed suddenly that Marnie was the only woman on the bus with blond hair.

One of the vampires, an old man with a wild white mane and

crooked rotting teeth, ripped open Marnie's blouse. She screamed, tried to fight back, but bloody hands held her back. Brock leaped up, crazed. "Leave her alone, goddammit!"

A vampire punched him full in the face.

He thought he had only staggered backward, shaken his head, blinked his eyes, but when he glanced around the bus, he saw that all of the vampires were gone. In the rear of the vehicle, he could see only red blood, bits of clothing and flashes of white bone. Around him, a few other travelers were still alive. Shocked and hurt, but alive. The vampires had left them alone.

And taken Marnie.

He looked out the window and saw the bare backs of several naked men retreating into the desert. "No!" he screamed, but the vampires were already disappearing into the darkness, and the unmoving form which he assumed was Marnie's body was merely a dim white blur which grew smaller and fainter and then was gone.

Brock pulled himself through one of the top windows and out of the overturned bus. His fellow passengers, the ones still alive, were moaning and crying, begging for help, but he ignored their pleas. He had to go after his wife.

He tried to follow the vampires, and thought at first that he was making good time, but the events of the night had taken their toll and he sat down to rest on the sandy ground less than ten minutes after he started, exhausted and possibly in shock. His muscles hurt, his brain felt numb, it was so dark he could see only a foot in front of him. He closed his eyes.

He fell asleep almost instantly.

«« — »»

In the morning he saw that the vampires had been traveling west.

He awoke with the dawn, neck and shoulder throbbing with unfamiliar pain, and found himself in the middle of what seemed to be an endless expanse of desert. He must have walked farther than he'd thought, because although visibility was clear for miles and the land was flat in all directions, he could see no sign of the road or the bus. The trail of the vampires was clear, however, and for that he was grateful. He stood at the bank of a river disturbance in the otherwise untouched sand, staring at the overlapping footprints heading away from the sun.

The sun.

The tour guide had said that they would be safe when the sun rose.

Of course. Vampires were afraid of the daylight. That meant that they couldn't have taken Marnie that far. They had to be within walking distance. If he started now, he might reach them by noon, be able to grab Marnie, stake as many of them as he could and take off.

But where would they go? Mexico City was some fifty miles behind them, the next town was still twenty miles ahead. If they could find their way back to the road.

Maybe the other survivors on the bus would go for help, bring back the authorities.

But maybe the authorities already knew. The tour guide and the bus driver had seemed to know immediately what was happening during the attack. Maybe the authorities and the vampires had reached some type of coexistent understanding.

He couldn't think about that now. He would cross that bridge when he came to.

Brock started walking, following the footprints away from the sunrise. He heard no sound save the soft noise of his shoes in the sand, the sibilant scurrying of lizards under brush, and the staccato ticking of unseen desert bugs. It was hot already, and he took off his shirt, tying it around his waist.

He thought about Marnie.

The two of them had met while juniors in college, ASU, and though he had been involved in several relationships by that time, had been with a lot of different girls, Marnie's life had been much more sheltered and he had been her first real boyfriend. That had been part of her charm, her innocence. It had not hurt that she'd also been extraordinarily bright and interesting. And drop-dead gorgeous.

They hadn't married for another five years, until they were both settled in their careers, until they could afford to buy a house together. A genuine two-story home with a redwood Jacuzzi and an automatic garage door opener. They had always been a pragmatic couple, a modern couple.

And now she had been kidnapped by vampires.

His shoes sunk in the soft desert sand. It was so ludicrous, so off-the-wall unbelievable that even now he had a hard time admitting to himself that this was really happening. Never in his most fantastic imaginings, in his worst-case scenarios, in his direst, most fatalistic projections of the future had anything even remotely similar to this even occurred to him. It was not as if he had been unaware of the downside possibilities. He had always known that he or Marnie or both of them could be involved in an automobile accident, could be shot by a crazed gunman, could even be blown up by a terrorist.

But attacked by vampires while on vacation?

Never.

He continued walking.

The sun grew hotter.

His shadow had shrunk to nothing, indicating that it was near noon, when he came over a slight rise and saw before him a town. At least it looked like a town. There was a metal-sided warehouse, a large water tower, two gas stations, a market, some unidentifiable buildings, and numerous houses, several of them adobe. But there were no streets. It was as if the buildings of a town had been arbitrarily dropped on an empty section of the desert, with no roads leading either to the area or from it. There were no people either, he noticed as he drew closer, and from the drifts of sand piled on the windward side of walls, he would have guessed that the town was abandoned.

But the flood of footprints ended here, individuals branching off from the herd until there was nothing left of the trail he'd been following.

This was the vampires' village.

He walked slowly forward. His heart was hammering. He realized that he had no weapon, and he mentally kicked himself for not thinking ahead enough to at least have taken something from the bus. Someone would have had a knife, a gun, a nail file…something in one of the suitcases.

He had no plan, no idea of what he was going to do, and he stood for a moment outside the first structure he came to: an adobe hut on the outskirts of town. Slowly, carefully, trying to make as little noise as possible, he peeked in through the open door.

He was not sure what he had expected. A coffin, perhaps. A dark cave-like interior where light could not penetrate. Instead, the sight which greeted him was a furnitureless room, ground strewn with straw. A naked man, his chest covered with dried blood, was lying in an indentation in the dirt, directly beneath a shaft of sunlight which streamed through one of the rectangular windows.

Brock stepped forward.

The vampire stirred, turned, sat up.

Brock quickly backed away from the doorway, darting around the corner of the adobe hut. Inside, he heard the vampire moan, stand, walk across the straw, relieve himself.

So that was another Hollywood myth. One which even the tour guide had bought. Vampires were not afraid of sunlight. The rays could not kill them. They simply slept during the day because they were tired.

That made his job even harder. He not only had to find Marnie and figure out some way to escape, he had to do so while avoiding waking vampires.

Why the hell hadn't he brought a weapon?

He waited until the noise within the hut stopped, until the vampire had once again fallen asleep, and then ran quickly to the next house, making sure he was not spotted before darting across the sand. He did not know where Marnie was, or even if she was alive, but he assumed that if she had been taken captive she was probably somewhere near the center of town.

He heard grunting, moaning, and he peeked around the corner of the house to see two of the filthy naked vampires striding across the hot sand toward the warehouse. The duo opened a door, stepped inside, and emerged a few moments later carrying the emaciated body of a small boy. Brock watched them traipse over to one of the adobe homes, holding the squirming boy between them.

After they had gone inside, he turned his attention back to the warehouse. This was obviously where they put the people they cap-tured. It was their refrigerator, their meat locker, the place where they stored food for later.

The idea made him shudder, and he vowed to get Marnie out of there whatever it took.

He waited in place for a few moments, until he was sure that no other vampires were about, and he ran across the open space to the warehouse, opening the door and dashing inside.

The interior of the building was one gigantic room. Ropes and pitchforks and shovels and scythes hung on the pegboard walls in the open section nearest the door. Beyond that, a wire mesh fence rose to the ceiling, penning in the rest of the huge enclosed space. On the other side of the barrier, imprisoned, were scores of jostling bodies, of var-ious ages and nationalities, in various stages of dress and undress, moaning, crying, screaming.

Brock stood unmoving for a moment, overwhelmed by it all, not knowing what to do. There were so many people inside the pen that he could not make out individual faces. He saw only a writhing mass of humanity. "Marnie!" he called, yelling at the top of his lungs. "Marnie!" But his voice was lost amidst the crying of the captives.

He walked forward, up to the edge of the mesh. Fingers pushed through the tiny holes, terrified voices called out to him in Spanish.

"Marnie!" he called again.

Ahead, next to the wall, he saw what looked like a gate in the fence. He sprinted toward it and found that although it was closed, it was not locked. The latch was situated so that it could not be opened from inside but was easily accessible to anyone outside the pen.

With no hesitation, he opened the gate.

And the people streamed out.

It was as if a dam had broken. People were running, crawling, falling, climbing on top of each other, but the overall movement was smoothly fluid as the gigantic pen emptied, the vampires' prisoners running immediately out of the warehouse into the desert daylight.

Brock stood next to the open gate, trying to spot Marnie in the sea of faces flowing past, but though he saw many women, none were blonde or Caucasian.

They were holding her somewhere else.

Outside he heard shouting, surprised cries of pain and terror, and he knew that the vampires had already discovered the escape. He had to get out of the warehouse fast. He stuck his head out of the door and saw a naked filthy man rushing toward him. He quickly ducked around the corner and ran next door to an empty gas station, taking refuge in the open bathroom. He held his breath, waiting for the vampire to burst in on him, but nothing happened.

He counted to ten, then moved outside again. Above the sounds of the fleeing captives and the pursuing vampires, he heard another sound. A sound which chilled him to the bone.

Marnie screaming.

The screams were short, loud, high-pitched, but unmistakably those of his wife. He wanted to scream back, to cry out her name, but he dared not. He glanced furtively around. It was obvious to him now that the prisoners he had freed had not a chance in hell of escaping. Dozens of naked vampires were bounding after them, laughing, playing, taking them down.

Marnie continued to scream. She was close, somewhere nearby, and he ran away from the vampires in the direction of her voice, toward the center of town. He passed a house, past what had once been a market, not checking to see if he was unobserved, simply running. The screams seemed to be coming from a sandstone building which looked as though it had been some sort of government office, and he ran unthinkingly through the open doors.

The screams were definitely coming from here. He rushed past a pile of broken overturned desks, down a hallway, and into the first room he saw.

—where Marnie was naked, spread-eagled on a stained mattress on the floor, her hands and feet tied with twine to metal stakes embedded in the concrete, a filthy rhinestone tiara hanging crookedly off her head. She was screaming, crying, trying to jerk free, her red face streaked with tears and blood, her body covered with welts and bruises. A short vampire, semen dripping from his still tumescent penis, was moving off of her, away from her.

Eight other vampires stood waiting in line across the room.

"No!" Brock screamed.

He was grabbed from behind, but he lashed out. "She's my wife, goddamn it!" His elbow connected with flesh, and the vampire was knocked to the floor. He had half-expected to hit a body hard as steel, but the vampire's flesh was surprisingly pliant, human. The vampire stood, and Brock kicked him squarely in the crotch. The grimy creature doubled over.

"You very brave."

He whirled to see another vampire standing less than a foot away from him. Unlike the others, this one was clean and wearing clothes, an expensive white suit. Brock was surprised by the vampire's softly accented voice, even more surprised by his appearance, but that did not stop him from taking action. He swung at the vampire's face. The vampire caught his fist before it connected, squeezing until bones popped.

"Do not do that again."

"She's my wife!" Brock screamed.

"She's our wife. She's our new queen."

Brock looked toward the mattress. He could not see Marnie's head or body for the filthy vampire pumping away on top of her, but he could hear her screams.

"Our old queen is dead."

"Leave her alone! Let her go!"

The vampire chuckled. "You are feisty one," he said. "Very resourceful. I like you. That is why I not kill you yet."

"Let her go." Brock could feel the tears stinging his eyes, escaping against his will.

"She is ours."

"Why?"

"Our village is lonely. We want children. It is natural desire, yes?"

Brock's head was spinning. He was standing here with a broken hand, talking with a vampire about *natural* desires while other vampires were lining up to gang rape his wife.

Marnie screamed as the dirty vampire pulled out of her.

"Let her go, damn you!"

"Can you not understand why we want children?"

"You can turn whoever you want into goddamn vampires! What the hell do you need with children?"

"It is not the same," the vampire said quietly. "Adopted children are never the same as your own."

Brock kicked out. He must have caught the vampire by surprise because his foot connected with a shin, but the vampire's grip never lessened.

"Yes," the vampire said in that same low voice, and Brock could see his sharpened teeth. "You are right. We can make whoever we want into one of us."

He bent down and bit.

Brock felt the slashing sting of pain, felt the blood being sucked from his neck, vacuumed out. "Marnie!" he cried. He tried to call out again, but he was too weak, too dizzy.

His legs gave out as the vampire released him, and he crumpled to the floor. His vision blurred and darkened and then disappeared, taking with it all sound.

«« — »»

Images.

A dark room. Sand. A cave. The sweet herbal smell of blood. Blood. Faces. Male. Female. The vampire: "He is strong and resourceful. He will be asset to the community." A woman, hissing: "No." Marnie. Where was Marnie? Naked, crying, screaming. The line grew longer. Long men. Waiting. Pleading people. Slashed throats, gushing. Blood. Warm blood. Warm delicious blood. Warm wonderful blood.

«« — »»

His vision gradually became clearer, surrealistic shapes hardening into focus, becoming the concrete outlines of a room. A dark room with adobe walls. Outside it was night, and the stars shone with an extraordinarily brilliant clarity.

For a second he was not sure where he was, what had happened. Then he remembered. He sat up quickly and was surprised to find that he was naked. His skin was filthy, covered with dirt and dried blood. He could feel burrs in his hair, thick stickiness on his teeth.

Two vampires walked into the room, carrying between them a trembling Mexican girl who could not have been more than six or seven. One of the vampires held the girl on the ground while the other brushed long black hair from the child's neck, gesturing for Brock to take her.

Instinctively, with no hesitation, feeling only the hunger in his gut, he bit into the soft warm brown neck and felt the hot deliciousness of the blood spurting into his mouth as the small body thrashed on the dirt floor.

He drank.

After, he walked unhampered and unattended across the sand to the government building. The night air felt cool and refreshing on his skin. He passed through the front office to the back room, pushing his way past the line of waiting men. The place had changed. It was now adorned with gauche trappings of dimestore royalty—garish paintings, gaudy candlesticks, a tacky throne.

Marnie was lying on a raised mattress covered with a red velvet bedsheet. She saw him but did not recognize him. Brock doubted at this point whether she could recognize anyone. Her face was blank, her eyes vacant, showing more white than iris. There was an unfamiliar cast to her features, madness in the set of muscles beneath the skin. No sound came from her open drooling mouth.

She appeared to be several months pregnant.

How long had he been out?

The next vampire in line moved forward, bowed ceremoniously, climbed on top of her.

Brock watched as his wife, slack-jawed, lay unmoving on the mattress, small muscles in her feet twitching involuntarily as she was violated by the vampire. He remembered the first time they had made love, frightened yet desperately passionate in the back seat of a cramped Pinto. He remembered how she had looked in her wedding gown. He remembered the trips they had taken, the places they had gone, the people they had met. He remembered that she liked raspberry yogurt. He remembered all of this and he saw her now and he wanted to care, but he did not.

He could not.

She whispered something as the vampire crawled off her. It sounded like his name.

"Brock."

He looked at her, felt nothing.

A strong hand grasped the back of his neck, and he turned to see the white-suited vampire standing behind him. The other vampire nodded, smiled, motioned toward Marnie, toward the line.

Brock returned the nod.

And moved back to the end of the line to wait his turn.

Walking with the Ghosts of Pier 13

Brian Freeman

O n these hot summer days at the beginning of the New World, we're all walking with the dead.

That thought—so simple, yet so complex—seized Jeremy's mind as his sandals smacked down hard on the splintered boardwalk. It *was* a hot summer day. Sweltering, in fact. The sun was bright and scorching, and the blinding light reflected off the odd copper-colored sand like a field of broken glass. The wooden sidewalk that marked the boundary between the beach and the town was old and weathered and covered with litter that migrated in tiny cyclones of wind. The boards creaked under Jeremy's weight.

There weren't many people around—just a dirty bum here, a dirtier teenager there, along with a few elderly couples who obviously had nowhere else they could go. Most of the shops were closed, their heavy hurricane doors bolted shut. Normally the boardwalk and the beach and the small town of Penny Beach would be packed with people this time of year—couples on holiday, families with kids, retirees who spent most of their time at Pat's House of Bingo at the north end of the boardwalk, and beautiful singles who mixed and mingled on the sand before heading to the Bermuda Bar and Grill—but not today. Not now.

In the distance, Pier #13 floated on top of its thick, wooden supports. The long, wide summer microcosm stretched out over the beach, and then on over the changing tides and the fingertips of the Atlantic ocean. Jeremy could see the wooden roller coaster at the end of the pier, and although the ride was racing along the track, there were no people in the bright red seats. The black, padded safety bars only restrained the air.

SHIVERS

Jeremy deeply inhaled the salty sea breeze as he watched the waves breaking on the beach. The water was blue and beautiful. The sky was clear, nearly perfect. Today could be Webster's definition of a summer day, if there were people here to experience the perfection. In one corner of his mind, Jeremy could hear the drone of the small airplanes pulling advertising banners across the sky. There were no planes today, but he still heard them, and the crowd, and the shopkeepers selling their wares, and everything else that had made the beach his summer home as a child, when his family had lived in New York City and spent the summer relaxing here, without a care in the world. Everything real from those memories was gone, but their ghosts remained.

"One please," Jeremy said when he reached the ticket booth at the entrance to Pier #13. The booth was old and narrow and weather beaten, like everything else. A painted sign hanging from its roof stated the various rates for the amusement park. Inside the booth was a kid about Jeremy's age. He wore a red uniform that hadn't been washed in a few days, and he looked tired and bored, and maybe a little scared, too.

"One ticket, or one All-Day pass?" the kid asked. His face was acne scarred, his skin tanned. A small fan blew humid air around the booth and a beat-up radio sat next to the window. From the radio came the voice of a solemn reporter reading something off the news wire. Something dreadful and horrifying, Jeremy suspected. The kid added: "We don't got many rides running. Most everyone quit."

"Why are you still hanging on?" Jeremy asked.

The kid shrugged. There was a bead of sweat forming on the end of his pimpled nose, near the metal stud protruding from a self-piercing that looked infected. Bubbling puss filled the wound. "Don't got anywhere else to go."

"Yeah, ain't that the truth. Just one ticket, please."

«« — »»

Jeremy roamed the pier, past the empty game booths and the hulking rides that remained motionless and quiet. The amusement park was like some ghost town in the middle of the Nevada desert, only with the sound of the ocean forever in the background. When Jeremy finally found another human being, he couldn't help but want to communicate. He needed to talk. He needed the human contact.

"Nice day, isn't it?" Jeremy said to an older woman in the same type of red uniform as the ticket kid. She sat on a tall chair by the Swing-Go-Round, running the oversized swings every three minutes on schedule, although she had no riders. She sat directly in the hot sun even though there was a bent umbrella laying on the boards nearby.

"Is that you, Ralph?" she called, her voice raw and aching, her eyes searching wildly, as if she was blind and didn't know it yet. "Goddamn you, Ralph! Why'd you bring the kids to the park today! Why? Goddamn you, Ralph!"

Backing away slowly, Jeremy continued to explore the park without saying another word.

«« — »»

Soon he found a middle-aged man who was selling funnel cakes. Jeremy bought one. He felt bad for the man dressed in his neatly pressed red uniform. The man probably had a family to support, if he was still working in this lifeless place.

"I loved these as a kid," Jeremy said as his food was prepared. He smiled. The man didn't reply, and Jeremy could see the worry in his eyes. He probably did have a family, and he was thinking about them, wondering if they'd be alive when he got home... if he'd make it home alive.

Jeremy thanked the man, paid for the funnel cake, and dropped it into a blue trash barrel the moment he was out of sight of the booth. A flock of seagulls descended in a pack and began tearing the food apart. Their cries were pitiful and dreadful, all at the same time. Jeremy walked away. He certainly had loved funnel cakes as a kid, but now the sugar tasted sour to him. A lot of things had soured.

«« — »»

When he reached the wooden roller coaster—the ride was called the Screamin' Demon—Jeremy stood silently and watched it run. Thirteen empty cars, chasing each other in circles, always starting at the same place and ending right where they had begun their journey. The mid-day sunlight cooked them, baked their paint. The peak of the first hill was at the very end of the pier, hanging out over the ocean. It was the most beautiful view in the world. Jeremy knew that for a fact. He and his brother Jason had ridden the ride a million times when they were kids. They had loved the roller coaster.

The sign over the entrance for the Screamin' Demon was blackened and scarred. The railed walkway that wound back and forth to the loading area for the ride was twisted and burned. A hole in the wooden planks was covered with heavy plywood. Yet the Screamin' Demon was still open for business.

The red cars (the sides of which had bright yellow flames and grinning skulls painted onto them) roared by, the grinding metal on metal louder than normal, like the ride was about to rip apart. It only took Jeremy a moment to realize why the sounds were so intense. There was no one around to make any other noise: no shrieking riders, no talking parents, no teenage park employees pushing metal carts filled with ice and bottles of Coke. Without the people, there was just the cars on the track and the ocean down below. The waves, breaking, again and again, always and forever, from the beginning of time until the end. Repetitive, hypnotic. Beautiful.

"You want to ride?" the teenage girl who was running the Screamin' Demon asked. She sat on a tall, three legged stool under a tattered yellow umbrella. She sounded hesitant and lonely at the same time. She probably felt the need for human contact, too, Jeremy guessed. She was pretty in a simple, girl-at-the-beach kind of way with her long blonde hair tied up in a pony tail, her blue eyes, her tanned skin. She somehow managed to make the drab red uniform look good. She added, "Just two tickets."

"Oh, I only have one. When I was a kid, it only cost one."

"That's fine," the girl replied. "I really don't care. I'm not coming back tomorrow."

"Quitting like everyone else?"

"My paycheck is probably gonna bounce. Why bother?"

"I haven't been on this pier in a long time."

"Since you were a kid, right?"

"Yeah, my brother and I loved this place."

"Well, I hate it. My boyfriend and I are running away tonight."

"Where you going?"

"Anywhere but this shitty town."

"That's what Jason and I said."

"You queer?"

"No, Jason was my brother."

"Where's he now?"

"Dead."

"Oh."

"He was here last month, waiting in line."

"Oh. I'm sorry."

"Yeah," Jeremy said, handing the girl his only ticket. She ripped it in half as he moved to take his seat. "I didn't really think the park would even be open, let alone with the coaster running."

"You heard the President, didn't you?"

"Go on living, right?"

"Like nothing has changed," the girl added. "Like there's nothing to fear."

"You scared?" Jeremy asked.

"Out of my mind."

«« —»»

At the top of the first hill, the roller coaster paused for just a second, allowing Jeremy to take in the full view. The blue, sparkling waves of the Atlantic had conquered the world from below his feet to the horizon a thousand miles in the distance where the ocean met the beautiful, clear sky. The dazzling sunlight formed an elongated diamond of fire on the dancing water. Jeremy's skin tingled in the heat even though the ocean wind was whipping past him as he sat at the highest point on the pier. He could hear the squawk of seagulls, the crashing of the waves against the supports under the pier. He deeply inhaled the salty sea air again, bringing back a million memories of summers long gone, bringing back a million ghosts who still lived here, and only here, and only in the summer.

"I miss you, bro," Jeremy whispered, and then his stomach rushed into his throat as the roller coaster roared down the hill, the tracks and cars screaming like terrified school children in a horrible, hot place like Hell. He laughed like a kid. He laughed to release the pain. He laughed because he had to laugh or his heart would explode in anger and sadness.

When the ride was over, he was crying, and the laughter had been lost to the waves.

«« —»»

"You okay?" the girl in charge of the Screamin' Demon asked. "Oh man, you didn't break your teeth on the safety bar or something, did you?"

"No, I'm all right," Jeremy said, removing his seat belt, pushing the safety bar up so he could exit. "I just..." He didn't finish the thought.

SHIVERS

"You're scared, too, aren't you?"

"Yeah, a little."

"We're probably safe here, you know? I mean, they blew up rides in Hershey Park the week after they hit us, they shot up all those elementary schools in Baltimore last week, they destroyed some malls in North Carolina on Monday, and they hit Disney in Florida two days ago, so they're kind of moving away from us. So we might be safe here."

"What did they do at Disney?"

"Man, don't you watch TV?"

"Lately I've been... lost."

"Well, yeah, a bunch of them landed in Disney in a small plane and started shooting everyone and everything with these big machine guns. Park security was useless. They got shredded all to hell. CNN showed it live, too, from a local traffic helicopter. Probably three hundred people dead, lots of kids. The bastards were dressed in black masks and long, heavy jackets and when they were finally cornered by the Army, they blew themselves up. Took another fifty people with them."

"Makes what happened here last month look like small potatoes, doesn't it?" Jeremy asked, studying the scarred sign, the twisted metal, and the plywood covering the hole in the pier. This was where Jason had died. This was where Jason had spent his last moment alive. What had he been thinking right before the bomb went off? Had he been watching the ride following the tracks? The beautiful girls in their bikinis? The seagulls swooping down for pieces of pretzels on the boards? What had been going through his mind? Only he knew, of course, but his ghost lingered.

Jeremy thought about what it must have been like to be standing in line, enjoying the day even though you were packed in with hundreds of other sweaty summer revelers, waiting for your turn when... Well, what happened next? It wouldn't be like the movies where you know what's coming thanks to the music.

No, not at all like that.

There would be no warning. One second you'd be alive and unaware, the next second there would be a roar of concentrated thunder.

If you were really close to the bomb, the force would just shred your body instantly. You wouldn't hear or feel anything. One second you'd be alive and smiling (or laughing or shading your eyes from the sun or wiping your brow or memorizing the curves of the hot chick

72

running the ride), and the next second you'd be gone into the thick darkness that was the realm of the dead. You'd never have to worry about how your death was going to affect your family. You'd never have to think about the things you were going to miss or the things you would never get to do or see.

If you were a few yards away from the blast, you might hear the thunder before the explosion ripped the life from your body, but there wouldn't be time for you to truly understand what was happening. A loud sound and then darkness. No pain, no thoughts.

But if you were a dozen yards away, the odds were good you might be one of the unlucky ones who was wounded severely enough to slowly bleed to death. You might hang on for minutes or hours, knowing you were doomed once the confusion settled within your mind. You'd be frightened and angry and you'd spend your last moments facing down every regret you ever had while wondering how the people you loved would take the news of your death. There would be a lot of pain, and not all of it would be from the shrapnel that tore your flesh apart, that severed your limbs or blinded you. Then, slowly, darkness and death.

When the girl didn't reply, Jeremy rephrased his comment and said again, "What happened last month really was small potatoes, wasn't it, at least to the people who weren't here?"

The girl asked, "Small potatoes? Well, do you see all the reporters and cops?"

"What?" Jeremy replied, glancing back at the virtually abandoned amusement park behind him.

"Exactly. They're gone. We're old news."

"Did you know anyone who died?"

"A couple of employees. One of my best friends. He was killed instantly, I think." A tear had trickled past her nose and bulged out onto her lip. Jeremy stared at her for a moment, at the tear, at her blue eyes, and he wondered if her eyes were even more blue than the sea. The beautiful, haunted sea. "At least I want to believe that. Probably isn't true. I miss him."

"We're all walking with the dead, I think," Jeremy said and walked away. The girl called after him, but he didn't look back.

«« —— »»

"Was it worth the trip?" the kid in the ticket booth asked as Jeremy left Pier #13 and stepped back onto the boardwalk.

"Huh?"

"Coming to see what they did."

"Yeah, I guess so. My bro is dead, you know. Died here."

"I'm sorry." The kid with the pierced nose sounded sincere enough. "Don't worry, the Army will get the fuckers."

"Anything new on the news?" Jeremy asked, pointing at the busted radio sitting in the booth. The fan continued to blow warm air around, back and forth, again and again.

"Not really, just that the Prez is pretty sure this has something to do with the Middle East. Some new group of extremists with a crazy name."

"How do they know it isn't homegrown?"

"Americans? Doing this shit to ourselves? Are you crazy?"

"You never know."

"Someone would have to be really fucked in the head to strap bombs to their chest and kill innocent people."

"Or really angry."

"Yeah. But what about? What could make some dudes do this shit?"

"Maybe they don't think they'll be heard any other way. You never know what angry young men will do."

Before the kid could respond, the radio crackled. He adjusted the tuning and turned up the volume. An earnest reporter stated: "The FBI alerted police in the major cities about possible threats to theaters either today or tomorrow. The threat is said to be credible, although the FBI gave no other details..."

"This shit is never going to end, is it?" the kid asked, turning the radio off with a disgusted flick of his hand.

"Not for a long time." Jeremy turned away. His face was covered in sweat. The sun was cooking him, burning him up, and it felt good. The heat felt perfect.

"Hey, where you going now?"

Jeremy looked back over his shoulder. "I was thinking of heading to New York City. I used to live there, with my brother and our parents. It's been a long time since I've been back."

"Well, stay away from Broadway, man. You heard the news."

Jeremy began walking, the boardwalk creaking under his feet, the hot sun beating down on him harder and harder, a cyclone of wind-blown trash floating past him in slow motion. He didn't reply. Instead he thought of Jason and the wooden roller coaster and the ocean and the summers of years past. He thought about anger, and what angry young men can do when they feel there is no other course of action to achieve their goals, when they need a means to an end.

He thought about Jason at Pier #13.

He thought about the explosion and the deaths and the things to come.

He thought about the last thing Jason had said to him the day he died: "On these hot summer days at the beginning of the New World, we're all walking with the dead. Love you, bro. Miss you."

And Jeremy thought about all the people who might be attending a Broadway play or musical on any given night. He tried not to think of their families, of the family and friends they loved and might have already lost. He tried not to think about all the people who were still going to die in the months to come.

Instead he remembered the people *he* had loved and lost. He remembered the ghosts that haunted him, the ghosts that he loved, the ghosts that guided him. Some of them still lived on Pier #13, some only lived in his heart, but he could feel them everywhere he went.

He vowed to never forget his brother, no matter what happened.

Jeremy thought about anger and angry young men with a cause, and he walked with the ghosts, and he prepared himself for one last trip to New York.

265 and Heaven

Douglas Clegg

1

What do we all live for? the bird asks.
This.
A glimpse of heaven.

2

The town at night seemed all crumbling brick and leaky gutters, alleyways washed clean by the summer rain, the stink of underground swamp, and grease from burger joints in the air. He was always on shift at night, and so it was the town he grew to know: the rain, the steam, the smells, the red brown of bricks piled up to make buildings, the hazy white of streetlamps. The same haunted faces downtown at night—the lonely crowd, the happy crowd, the people who went from diner to movie to home without walking more than a few feet, the kids in their souped-up cars, the old men walking with canes, the brief flare of life in the all-night drug stores.

All of it he saw, and it was for him the world.

But then one night, he saw something else.

It began as a routine call about an old drunk out at the trash cans. Paul was six-months new to the uniform, having only seen a couple of drug busts of the non-violent variety and one DUI. It was that kind of town—one murder in the past six years, and one cop killed in the line of duty since 1957. He and his little sister had lived there five years, and picked it because it was fairly quiet and calm, a good hospital, good visiting nurses' association, and no one to remember them from nine years before. He had been a security guard back in St. Chapelle right after college, but it had been his dream to be a cop, and now he was, and it was good, most nights. Most nights, he and his partner just trolled the streets for small-time hookers and signs of domestic violence. Sometimes they arrived too late at a jumper out on the Pawtuxet Bridge. Sometimes, they watched the jump.

Paul couldn't shake the vision in his head of the kid who had jumped two weeks ago. Damn lemmings, some of these kids were. Just wanting to get out of town so bad they couldn't wait for the bus.

"Some guy's over in front of the Swan Street apartments knocking over cans and covered with blood," the smooth voice of the dispatcher said.

"Christ," Paul muttered. "Swan Street. Why does everything seem to happen over there?" He glanced at his watch. Nearly midnight.

His partner, Beth, sighed and shook her head when the call came from dispatch. "I bet I know this guy," she said, "Jesus, I bet it's this old clown." She turned left at Wilcox, and took two quick rights until they were on Canal Road. The night fairly steamed with humidity, and the sky threatened more rain. Paul wiped the back of his neck, feeling the slickness.

"He used to be with the circus, a real carny-type." As she spoke, Beth managed to reach across the dash, grab a cigarette from the pack, thrust it between her lips and punch in the lighter while still keeping her eye on the road. "He spends half the year God knows where and then comes back here in the summer. We had to ship him out twice last year."

"What a night," Paul said, barely hiding the disgust in his voice. The flat-topped brick buildings, dim blue windows, dark alleys of downtown bled by as he looked out the window. The streets were dead.

When Beth pulled the patrol car to the curb, Paul saw him. A fringe of gray hair around a shiny bald scalp, the checkered shirttail flapping, the saggy brown pants halfway down his butt. The guy stood beneath the streetlamp, his hands over his crotch. "He jerking off or what?" Beth asked, snorting.

"Poor old bastard," Paul said. "Can we get him to the station?"

"Easy," she said, "you just tell him we're taking him for some free drinks." As she opened her door, she shouted, "Hey! Fazzo! It's your friend!"

The old man turned, letting go of his crotch. He hadn't been masturbating; but a dark stain grew where he'd touched. He cried out, "Friends? My friends!" He opened his arms as if to embrace the very darkness beyond the streetlamp.

Paul got out, too, and jogged over to him. "Buddy, what you up to tonight?"

Looking at his uniform, the guy said, "I don't got nothing against cops. Believe you me. Cops are gold in my book."

Paul turned to Beth, whispering, "His breath. Jesus."

She gave him a look like he was being less than professional. He was new enough to the job to not want to get that kind of look.

The guy said, "I just been having a drink."

"Or two," Beth said. "Look, Fazzo..."

"Fazzo the Fabulous," the guy said, and did a mock-spin. "The greatest magician in the tri-state area."

"We got to take you to another bar."

"You buying?" he asked her.

"Yeah sure. You got a place up here?" Beth nodded towards the flophouse apartments beyond the streetlamp.

Fazzo nodded. "Renting it for thirty-five years. Number 265."

Paul shined his flashlight all over Fazzo. "I don't see any blood on him."

"It's the piss," Beth whispered, "someone reported it as blood. It happens sometimes. Poor old guy."

Beth escorted Fazzo to the car. She turned and nodded towards Paul; he took the signal. He went over to the back staircase. The door was open. He walked inside—the carpeting was damp and stank of mildew. A junkie sat six steps up, skinny to the bone, leaning against the peeling wallpaper, muttering some junkie incantation. Paul stepped around him. The hallway above was narrow, its paint all but stripped off by time. The smell of curry—someone was cooking, and it permeated the hall. When he got to 265, he knocked. The door was already ajar, and his fist opened it on the first knock.

There was a light somewhere to the back of the apartment. Paul called out to see if anyone was there. He gagged when he inhaled the fetid air.

All he could see were shadows and shapes, as if the old guy's furniture had been swathed in dropcloths. He felt along the wall for the light switch. When he found it, he turned on the light. It was a twenty-five watt bulb which fizzled to life from the center of the living room ceiling. Its light barely illuminated the ceiling itself. The chairs and couch in the room were covered with old newspapers, some of them damp from urine. The old man hadn't even bothered to make it to the bathroom anymore. There was human excrement behind the couch. Empty whiskey bottles along the floor in front of the television set.

Paul didn't notice the strong stink once he'd stayed in the apartment for a few minutes.

Beth arrived at that point. "I got him cuffed, not that he needs it. He fell asleep as soon as I sat him down in the car. Jesus!" She covered her mouth and nose. "I thought he'd been living on the street." Her eyes widened as she took in the other sights.

"Look at this," Paul pointed to the windowsill, shining his flashlight across it.

It was black with dead flies, two or three layers thick.

He continued on to the kitchen. "Should I open the fridge, you think?"

"Sure," Beth said. "Looks like Fazzo the Fabulous is going to end up in state hospital for awhile. What the hell?" She picked something up off a shelf and held it up. "Paul, look at this."

In her hands, what looked like a wig with long, thin hair. "You think Fazzo steps out on Saturday night in pearls and pumps?"

Paul shook his head, and turned back to the refrigerator. He opened the door, slowly. A blue light within it came on. The refrigerator was stacked three trays high with old meat—clotted steaks, green hamburger, what looked like a roast with a fine coating of mold on it. "Shit," he said, noticing the flies that were dead and stuck against the wet film that glazed the shinier cuts of meat. "This guy's lost it. He's not just a drunk. He needs serious help."

Beth walked into the bathroom, and started laughing.

"What's up?" he asked, moving around the boxes in the kitchen. Paul glanced to the open door.

The bathroom light was bright.

"It's clean in here. It's so clean you can eat off it. It must be the one room he never goes in." Beth leaned through the open doorway and gestured for Paul to come around the corner. "This is amazing."

Paul almost tripped over a long-dead plant as he made it over to where she stood.

The bathroom mirror was sparkling, as was the toilet, the pink tiles. Blue and pink guest soap were laid out in fake seashells on either side of the brass spigots of the faucet.

Written in lipstick on the mirror: a phone number.

For a second, he thought he saw something small and green skitter across the shiny tiles and dive behind the shower curtain. A lizard?

Paul went to pull the shower curtain aside, and that's when he found the woman's torso.

Paul washed his face six times that night, back at the sheriff's office. He wished he hadn't found it, he wished it had been Beth, or some other cop, someone who could take that kind of thing. It was the sort of image he had only seen in forensics textbooks, never in living color, never that muddy rainbow effect, never all the snake-like turns and twists…he had to put it out of his mind. He did not want to think about what was left of the woman in the tub.

He had not seen her face, and he was glad. She wasn't entirely human to him without a face.

Her name was Shirley. Fazzo the Fabulous told him. "Shirley Chastain. She was from the Clearwater District. She ran a dry cleaners with her mother. I thought she was a nice sort of girl right up until I cut her. I dug deep in her. She had a gut like a wet velvet curtain, thick, but smooth, smooth, smooth. She had a funny laugh. A tinkly bell kind of laugh." He had sobered up and was sitting in county jail. Paul stood outside his cell with the county coroner, who took notes as Fazzo spoke. "She had excellent taste in shoes, but no real sense of style. Her skin was like sponge cake."

"You eat her skin?" the coroner asked.

Fazzo laughed. "Hell, no. I'm not some damn Jeffrey Dahmer wannabe. I mean it *felt* like sponge cake. The way sponge cake used to be, like foam, like perfect foam when you pull it apart." He kneaded the air with his fingers. "I'm not a freakin' cannibal."

Paul asked, "You were a clown or something? Back in your circus days, I mean?"

"No, sir. I wasn't anything like that. I was the world's greatest magician. Even Harry Blackstone told me, when I was a kid, he said, 'Fazzo, you're gonna be the biggest, you got what it takes.' Didn't mean shit, but my oh my it sure did feel good to hear it from him."

"I guess you must've been something," Paul said.

Fazzo glanced from the coroner to Paul. "Why you here, kid? You busted me. What are you gawking for?"

"I don't know," Paul said. "You kind of remind me of my dad I guess." It was a joke; Paul glanced at the coroner, and then back at Fazzo. Last time Paul saw his dad, his dad's face was split open from the impact of the crash.

"Shit," the old guy dismissed this with a wave. "I know all about your old man, kid. It's like tattoos on your body. Everybody's story is on their body. Dad and Mom in car wreck, but you were driving. Little sister, too, thrown out of the car. I see it all, kid. You got a secret don't you? That's right, I can see it plain as day. You shouldnta never gone in 265, cause you're the type it wants. You're here because you got caught."

"*I* got caught?"

"You went in 265 and you got caught. I pass it to you, kid. You get the door-prize."

"You're some sick puppy," Paul said, turning away.

Fazzo shouted after him, "Don't ever go back there, kid. You can always get caught and get away. Just like a fish on the hook. Just don't fight it. That always reels'em in!" Paul glanced back at Fazzo. The old man's eyes became slivers. "It's magic, kid. Real magic. Not the kind on stage or the kind in storybooks, but the real kind. It costs life sometimes to make magic. You're already caught, though. Don't go back there. Next time, it's you." Then Fazzo closed his eyes, and began humming to himself as if to block out some other noise.

It sickened Paul further, thinking what a waste of a life. What a waste of a damned life, not just the dead woman, but this old clown. Paul said, "Why'd you do it?"

Fazzo stopped his humming. He pointed his finger at Paul and said, "I was like you, kid. I didn't believe in anything. That's why it gets you. You believe in something, it can't get you. You don't believe, and it knows you got an empty space in your heart just waiting to be filled. You believe in heaven, kid?"

Paul remained silent.

"It's gonna get you, then, kid. You got to believe in heaven if you want to get out of 265."

Then, Fazzo told his story. Paul would've left, but Fazzo had a way of talking that hooked you. Paul leaned against the wall, thinking he'd take off any minute, but he listened.

4

I was famous, kid, sure, back before you were born, and I toured with the Seven Stars of Atlantis Circus, doing some sideshow shit like sword-swallowing and fire-eating before I got the brilliant idea to start bringing up pretty girls to saw in half or make disappear. This was way back when, kid, and there wasn't a lot of entertainment in towns with names like Wolf Creek or Cedar Bend or Silk Hope. The Seven Stars was the best they got, and I turned my act into a showcase. I was hot, kid. I blew in like a nor'easter and blew up like a firecracker. Imagine these hands—these hands—as I directed the greatest magic show in the tri-state area, the illusions, kid, the tricks of the trade, the boxes with trapdoors that opened below the stage, the nights of shooting stars as I exploded one girl-filled cage after another—they turned into white doves flying out across the stunned faces of children and middle-aged women and old men who had lost their dreams but found them inside the tent. Found them in my magic show! It was colossal, stupendous, magnificent! I gave them a night of fucking heaven, kid. We turned a dog into a great woolly mammoth, we turned a horse into a unicorn, we turned a heron into a boy and then into a lizard, all within twenty minutes, and then when it was all done, the boy became a rabbit and I handed it to some thrilled little girl in the audience to take home for a pet or for supper. Once, traveling during a rainy spring, the whole troupe got caught in mud, and I used my knowledge of traps and springs to get us all out of there—and was rewarded with becoming the Master of Ceremonies. It was practically religious, kid, and I was the high priest!

But the problem was, at least for me, that I believed in none of it. I could not swallow my own lies. The magic was a fake. I knew where the animals were hid away to be sprung up, and the little boy, bounced down into a pile of sawdust while a snowy egret took his place, or an iguana popped up wearing a shirt just like the one the boy had on. The boy could take it, he was good. Best assistant I ever had. The woman, too, she was great—saw her in half and she screamed like she was giving birth right on the table—not a beauty except in the legs. She had legs that didn't stop at the ass but went right on up to her chin.

When she got hit by the bus in Memphis, everything changed for me, and I didn't want to do the act again. Joey wanted to keep going, but I told him we were finished. I loved that kid. So, we quit the act, and I went to do a little entertaining in clubs, mostly strip joints. Tell a couple jokes, do a few tricks with feather fans—voila! Naked girls appear from behind my cape! It was not the grandeur of the carnival, but it paid the rent, and Joey had a roof over his head and we both had food in our mouths.

One month I was a little late on the rent, and we got thrown out. That's when I came here, and we got the little place on Swan Street. Well, we didn't get it, it got us.

But it got you, too, didn't it, kid? It wasn't just you walking in to 265, it was that you been preparing your whole life for 265. That other cop, she lives in another world already, 265 couldn't grab her. But it could grab you, and it did, huh.

I knew as soon as I saw you under the streetlamp.

I recognized you from before.

You remember before?

Hey, you want to know why I killed that woman? You really want to know?

Watch both my hands when I tell you. Remember, I'm a born prestidigitator.

Here's why: sometimes, you get caught in the doorway.

Sometimes, when the door comes down, someone doesn't get all the way out.

You want to find the other half of her body?

It's in 265.

Only no one's gonna find it but you, kid.

You're a member of the club.

5

Paul was off-shift at 2, and went to grab a beer at the Salty Dog minutes before it closed. Jacko and Ronny got there ahead of him and bought the first round.

"Shit," Paul said, "it was like he sawed her in two."

"He saw her in two? What's that mean?" Jacko asked. He was already drunk.

"No, he sawed her in two. He was a magician. A real loser," Paul shook his head, shivering. "You should've seen it."

Jacko turned to Ronny, winking. "He saw her sawed and we should've seen it."

"Cut it out. It was...unimaginable."

Ronny tipped his glass. "Here's to you, Paulie boy. You got your first glimpse of the real world. It ain't pretty."

Jacko guzzled his beer, coughing when he came up for air. "Yeah, I remember my first torso. Man, it was hacked bad."

"I thought nothing like that happened around here," Paul said. "I thought this was a quiet town."

Jacko laughed, slapping him on the back. "It doesn't happen much, kid. But it always happens once. You got to see hell just to know how good the rest of this bullshit is."

Paul took a sip of beer. It tasted sour. He set the mug down. "He called it heaven." But was that really what Fazzo the Fabulous had said? Heaven? Or had he said you had to believe in heaven for 265 to not touch you?

Jacko said, "Christ, forget about it, Paulie. Hey, how's that little Marie?"

Paul inhaled the smoke of the bar, like he needed something more inside him than the thought of 265. "She's okay."

6

When he got home to their little place on Grove, with the front porch light on, he saw her silhouette in the front window. He unlocked the front door, noticing that the stone step had gotten scummy from damp and moss. The early morning was strung with humid mist, the kind that got under skin, the kind that permeated apartments and houses and alleys. Humid like an emotion. Inside, only the bathroom light was on. He walked in, glancing at her, sitting in the living room.

"Marie," he said.

"I couldn't get the t.v. to work." Her voice was humid.

"Sorry, kid," he said, trying not to show exhaustion. "I'll get it fixed tomorrow. You should be asleep."

"I should be," she said.

"Well, try and get some," he whispered. He went into the darkened living room, careful not to trip over the books she always left on the rug, or the Coke bottles, or the newspapers open to the comics pages. As he knelt beside her, he touched the top of her head. "How was Mrs. Jackson?"

"Oh, she was something," Marie said, and Paul was always amazed at her acerbic way of saying things. But it was nearly three a.m. on a Friday. No school tomorrow. Nothing for Marie but a vast day of nothing to do.

"How's the pain?"

She didn't answer.

Paul kissed his little sister on the forehead. "Well I need to go to bed. You should too."

Marie pulled away, turning her chair back towards the window. "I hate what you did to me," she whispered.

She said this more than he cared to remember.

"I hate it, too," he said. Trying not to remember why she could say it in the first place. "You keep your oxygen on all day?"

She may have nodded, he couldn't tell in the dim light.

"I hate what I did to myself," she whispered, but he wasn't sure. She may have said, "I hate what I do to myself." Or, "I hate what I want to do to myself." It was late. He'd had a couple of beers. She had whispered.

The three possibilities of what she had said played like a broken record through his mind every now and then, and in the next few days—staying up late, staring at the ceiling, hearing the hum of the machine that helped keep his beautiful twenty-year-old sister alive, he was sure she'd said the last thing.

I hate what I want to do to myself.

7

Clean-up crew had been through, photographers had been through, the apartment was cordoned off, but not picked over much—with a full confession from Fazzo there wasn't much need of serious evidence. Paul stood in the doorway, nodding to one of the detectives in a silent hello.

He glanced around the apartment—it was trashed. Just a crazy old drunk's shit-hole.

The bathroom light seeped like pink liquid from under the door.

He didn't go in.

He didn't want to.

He wanted to not think about the torso or the magician or even the lizard he'd seen scuttle into the bathtub.

But it was all he thought about for the next six months.

8

On his nights off, he'd sit in the living room with Marie and watch television. Marie loved television, and besides her reading, it was the only thing that got her out of herself. "I saw a great movie last night," she told him.

He glanced at her. The small thin plastic tubing of the oxygen like a Fu-Manchu mustache hanging from beneath her nostrils, hooked up to the R2D2 Machine. The braces on her arms that connected to the metal brace that had become her spine and ribs. The wheelchair with its electric buzzes whenever she moved across the floor.

Still, she looked like Marie under all the metal and wire and tubing. Pretty. Blond hair cut short. Her eyes bright, occasionally. Sometimes, he thought, she was happy.

"Yeah?" he asked.

"Yeah. It was amazing. A man and woman so in love, but they were divided by time and space. But he wanted her so badly. He sacrificed his life for her. But they had this one…moment. I cried and cried."

"You should be watching happy movies," Paul said, somewhat cheerfully.

"Happy or sad doesn't matter," Marie said. "That's where you mix things up too much. Happy and sad are symptoms. It's the thing about movies and books. It's that glimpse of heaven. No one loves anyone like they do in movies and books. No one hurts as wonderfully. I saw a movie about a woman in a car wreck just like ours, and she couldn't move from the neck down. Her family spurned her. A friend had to take care of her. She thought of killing herself. Then, the house caught on fire. She had to crawl out of the house. A little boy helped her. The little boy couldn't talk, and they became friends. I cried and cried."

"I don't like things that make you sad," he said. He meant it.

"This," Marie nodded to the machines and the walls. "This makes me sad. The stories get me out of this. They get me into heaven. Even if it's only for a few minutes, it's enough. You want to know why people cry at movies even when the movie is happy? I've thought about this a lot. It's because life is never that good. They know that when the screen goes dark, they have to go back to the life off-screen where nothing is as good. People who have cancer in movies have moments of heaven. People who have cancer in real life just have cancer. People in car wrecks in movies and stories get heaven. In real life…"

She didn't finish the thought.

"So you feel like you're in heaven when you read a story?"

She nodded. "Or see a good movie. Not the whole movie, just a few minutes. But a few minutes of heaven is better than no heaven at all. You know what I dream of at night?"

"No machines?" he said, hoping she would not be depressed by this comment.

She shook her head. "No. I dream that everything is exactly like it is, only it's absolutely wonderful. Then, I wake up."

They were silent for a moment. The movie on television continued.

Then, she said, "I know why people kill themselves. It isn't because they hate anyone. It isn't because they want to escape. It's because they think there's no heaven. Why go on if there's no heaven to get to?"

9

Paul went to see Fazzo the Fabulous on Death Row. Fazzo had gained some weight in prison, and looked healthier.

"I have to know something," he said.

"Yeah, kid?" Fazzo looked at him carefully. "You want to know all about 265, don't you? You been there since I got arrested?"

Paul nodded. Then, as if this were a revelation, he said, "You're sober."

"I have to be in here. No choice. The twelve-step program of incarceration...Let me tell you, 265 is a living breathing thing. It's not getting rented out any time soon, either. It waits for the one it marked. You're it, kid. It's waiting for you, and you know it. And there's no use resisting its charms."

"Why did you kill that woman?"

"The forty million dollar question, kid. The forty million dollar question."

"Forget it then."

"Okay, you look like a decent kid. I'll tell you. She was a sweet girl, but she wanted too much heaven. She and me both. Life's job is not to give you too much heaven. But she got a taste for it, just like I did. You get addicted to it. So," Fazzo gestured with his hands in a sawing motion. "She got in but the door came down. I mean, I know I cut into her, using my hands. I know that. Only I wasn't trying to cut into her. I liked her. She was sweet. I was trying to keep it from slamming down so hard on her. They thought I was insane at first, and were going to put me in one of those hospitals. But all the doctors pretty much confirmed that my marbles were around. Only all that boozing I did made me sound nuts." Fazzo leaned over. "You got someone you love, kid?"

Paul shrugged. "I got my little sister. She's it."

"No other family?"

"I got cousins out of state. Why?"

"Okay, now it's clear why 265 chose you, kid. You're like me, practically no strings, right? But one beloved in your life. Me, I had Joey."

Paul grimaced.

"Hey!" Fazzo flared up. "It wasn't like that! Joey was a kid whose family threw him out with the garbage. I gave him shelter, and that was it. Wasn't nothing funny about it. Sick thing to think." Then, after a minute he calmed. "I gave Joey what was in 265 and everything was good for awhile. Joey, he had some problems."

"Like—"

Fazzo shrugged. "We all got problems. Joey, he had leukemia. He was gonna die." Then it was as if a light blinked on in the old man's eyes. "You know about Joey, don't you? It touched you in there, and it let you know about him. Am I right? When it touches you, it lets you know about who's there and who's not, and maybe about who's coming soon. You know about Joey?"

Paul shook his head.

Fazzo seemed disappointed. "Sometimes I think it was all an illusion, like my bag of tricks. In here, all these bricks and bars and grays—sometimes I forget what it was like to go through the door."

"What happened to Joey?"

"He's still there. I put him there."

"You killed him?"

"Holy shit, kid, you think I'd kill a little boy I loved as if he were my own son? I told you, I put him there, through 265. He's okay there. They treat him decent."

"He's not in the apartment," Paul said, as if trying to grasp something.

"You want me to spell it out for you, kid? 265 is the door to Heaven. You don't have to believe me, and it ain't the Heaven from Jesus Loves Me Yes I Know. It's a better Heaven than that. It's the Heaven to beat all Heavens." Fazzo spat at the glass that separated them. "You come here with questions like a damn reporter and you don't want answers. You want answers you go into that place. You won't like what you find, but it's too late for you. 265 is yours, kid. Go get it. And whoever it is you love, if it's that sister of yours, make sure she gets in it. Make sure she gets Heaven. Maybe that's what it's all about. Maybe for someone to get Heaven, someone else has to get Hell."

"Like that woman?"

Fazzo did not say a word. He closed his eyes and began humming.

Startled, he opened his eyes again and said, "Kid! You got to get home now!"

"What?"

"NOW!" Fazzo shouted and smashed his fist against the glass. The guard standing in the corner behind him rushed up to him, grabbing him by the wrists. "Kid, it's your sister it wants, not you. You got caught, but it's your sister it wants. And there's only one way to get into heaven! Only one way, kid! Go get her now!"

10

Paul didn't rush home—he didn't like giving Fazzo the benefit of the doubt. He'd be on shift in another hour, and usually he spent this time by catching a burger and a Coke before going into the station. But he drove the murky streets as the sun lowered behind the stacks of castle-like apartment buildings on Third Street. The wind brushed the sky overhead with oncoming clouds, and it looked as if it would rain in a few minutes. Trash lay in heaps around the alleys, and he saw the faces of the walking wounded along the stretch of boulevards that were Sunday afternoon empty. He passed the apartments on Swan Street, doing his best not to glance up to the window on the second floor—265, its three small windows boarded up. No one would live there, not after a woman's torso was found in the bathtub. Even squatters would stay away.

He dropped by his apartment, leaving the car to idle. He just wanted to see if she was watching her movies or reading.

He didn't believe the old man.

Fazzo the Fucked Up.

In the living room, her books, the television on.

Soft music playing in the bathroom.

Paul knocked on the door. "Marie?"

After four knocks, he opened it. His heart beat fast, and seemed to be, not in his chest, but on the surface of his skin—

The machines were off, and she lay in the tub of pink water. On her back, her face beneath the water's surface like a picture he'd seen once, when they'd both been children, of a mermaid in a lake.

Scratched crudely on the tile with the edge of the scissors she'd used to cut herself free from the flesh, the words:

I don't believe in heaven.

11

It was only years later, when he saw the item in the papers about Fazzo the Fabulous finally getting the chair, after years of living on Death Row, that he thought about 265 again. He heard, too, that the apartments on Swan Street were being torn down within a week of Fazzo's execution.

In his forties, Paul had led what he would've called a quiet life. He'd been on the force for fifteen years, and the town had not erupted in anything more than the occasional domestic battle or crack house fire. He kept Marie's machines in his apartment, and often watched television in the living room feeling as if he were less alone.

But one evening, he went down there, down to Swan Street, down to the rows of slums and squats where the city had turned off even the streetlamps.

Standing in front of the old apartments, he glanced at the windows of 265. The boards had come out, and the windows were empty sockets in the face of brick.

He carefully walked up the half-burnt staircase, around the rubble of bricks and pulpy cardboard, stepping over the fallen boards with the nails sticking straight up.

The apartment no longer had a door. When he went inside, the place had been stripped of all appliances.

The stink of urine and feces permeated the apartment, and he saw the residue of countless squatters who had spent nights within the walls of 265.

Graffiti covered half the wall by the bathroom—spraypainted cuss words, kids' names, lovers' names...

Scrawled in blue across the doorway to the bathroom, the words: THE SEVEN STARS.

The bathroom had been less worked-over. The shower curtain had been torn down, as had the medicine cabinet. But the toilet, cracked and brown, still remained, as did the bathtub and shower nozzle.

Paul closed his eyes, remembering the woman's bloody torso in the tub.

Remembering Marie in the pink water.

When he opened his eyes, he said, "All right. You have me. You took Marie. What is it you want?"

He sat on the edge of the tub, waiting for something. He laughed to himself, thinking of how stupid this was, how he was old enough to know better...how Fazzo the Fabulous had butchered some woman up here, and that was all. How Marie had killed herself at their home, and that was all.

There was no heaven.

He laughed for awhile, to himself. Reached in his pocket and drew out a pack of cigarettes. Lit one up, and inhaled. The night came as he sat there, and with it darkness.

Sometime, just after midnight, he heard the humming of the flies, and the drip-drop of rusty water as it splashed into the tub.

In a moment, he saw the light come up, from the edge of the forest, near the great tree, and two iguanas scuttled across the moss-covered rocks. It came in flashes at first, as if the skin of the world were being stripped away layer by layer, until the white bone of life came through, and then the green of a deep wood. The boy was there, and Paul recognized him without ever having seen his picture.

"You've finally come to join us, then," the boy said. "Marie told me all about you."

"Marie? Is she here?" Paul's tongue dried in his mouth, knowing that this was pure hallucination, but wanting it to be true.

The boy—and it was Joey, Fazzo's friend—nodded, holding his hand out.

The world had turned liquid around him, and for a moment he felt he was refocusing a camera in his mind, as the world solidified again. The great white birds stood like sentries off at some distance. A deer in the wood glanced up at the new intruder. Through them, as if they were translucent, he saw something else—like a veil through which he could see another person, or a thin curtain, someone watching him from the other side of the gossamer fabric. Lightning flashed across the green sky. A face emerged in the forest—the trees and the fern and the birds and the lizards all seemed part of it. A face that was neither kind or cruel.

And then, he saw her, running towards him so fast it took his breath away. She was still twenty, but she had none of the deformities of body, and the machines no longer purred beside her. "Paul! You've come! I knew you would!"

She grabbed his hand, squeezing it. "I've waited forever for you, you should've come earlier."

Joey nodded. "See? I told you he'd come eventually."

Paul grabbed his sister in his arms, pressing as close to her as he could. Tears burst from his eyes, and he felt the warmth of her skin, the smell of her hair, the smell of her—the fragrance of his beautiful, vibrant sister. He no longer cared what illusion had produced this, he did not ever want to let go of her.

But she pulled back, finally. "Paul, you're crying. Don't." She reached up and touched the edge of his cheek.

"I thought I'd never see you again, I thought—" he said, but covered his face to stop the tears.

"Yes, you did," Marie said. "You believed in 265 all along. They told me you did. They knew you did."

"Who are they?" he asked.

Marie glanced at Joey. "I can't tell you."

"No names," Joey whispered a warning.

The rain splintered through the forest cover like slivers of glass, all around them, and the puddles that formed were small mirror shards reflecting the sky.

Marie grasped Paul's hand.

He could not get over her warmth. "How...how did you get here?"

She put a finger to her lips. "Shh. Isn't it enough that we're here now, together?"

Paul nodded his head.

"It won't last long," Marie said, curiously looking up at the glassy rain as it poured around them.

"The rain?" he asked, feeling that this was better than any heaven he could imagine. This was the Heaven of all heavens.

"No, you being here. Each time is only a glimpse. Like striking a match, it only burns for a short while."

"I don't understand," Paul said.

Marie looked up at him, and all he felt was joy. He had never remembered feeling so alive, so much a part of the world, so warm with love. Again, his eyes blurred with tears.

"It's only a glimpse," she whispered. "Each time. When Fazzo was executed, he was the sacrifice. But they need another one. This time, they want the sacrifice to be here, on the threshold. It works longer that way. Just one. Each time, for you to be here."

Then, her mood changed, as she smiled like a child on his birthday. "Oh, but Paul, it's so wonderful to see you. Next time you come I'll show you the rivers of gold, and the way the trees whisper the secret of immortality. The birds can guide us across the fire mountains. And I have friends here, too, I want you to meet."

"I don't understand," Paul whispered, but the rain began coming down harder, and a glass wall of rain turned shiny and then melted, as he felt her hand grab for him through the glass—

He was sitting in the darkness of the bathroom at 265, a young woman's hand in his, cut off at the wrist because the door had come down too hard, too soon.

12

For Paul, the hardest one was the first one. He found her down in Brickton, near the factories. She was not pretty, and looked to him to be at the end of her days from drugs and too many men and too many pimps beating her up. She had burn marks on her arms, and when she got into his car, he thought: I won't be doing anything too awful. Not too awful. It'll be like putting an animal out of its misery.

"You a cop?" she asked.

He shook his head. "No way. I'm just a very desperate guy."

He told her he knew this place, an old apartment, not real pretty, but it was private and it got him off. When they reached Swan Street, she laughed. "I been in these apartments before. Christ, they look better now than I remember them."

He nodded. "Will you be impressed if I tell you I own them?"

"Really? Wow. You must be loaded."

Paul shrugged. "They went for cheap. The city was going to tear them down, but I got that blocked, bought them up and fixed them up a bit."

"They look empty."

"Just started getting them ready for tenants," he said. They went upstairs, the green lights of the hallway like haloes around her red hair. Inside the apartment, he offered her a drink.

"All right," she said.

"Need to use the bathroom?" he asked, opening the freezer door to pull out the ice tray.

"If you don't mind," she said.

"Go ahead. Take a shower if you feel like it."

"Well, you're buying," the woman said.

When he heard the bathroom door close, he went and took the key from the dresser. Standing in front of the bathroom door, he waited until he heard the shower turn on.

He checked his watch.

It was two minutes to midnight.

From the shower, she shouted, "Honey? You mind bringing my drink in and scrubbing my back?"

He opened the bathroom door. Steam poured from under the shower curtain. When he was inside the bathroom, he turned and locked the door. He put the key in his breast pocket.

"That you?" she asked.

"Yeah," he said. "I'll join you in just a few seconds."

He crouched down. Beneath the sink, a large wooden box. Opening it, he lifted the cloth within. He grabbed the hand-ax and then closed the box.

He set the small ax on top of the sink. He unbuttoned his shirt, and took it off. He hung it on the hook by the door. Then, he stepped out of his shoes. Undid his belt, and let his trousers fall to the floor.

"Baby?" she asked.

"In a minute," he said. "We'll have some fun."

Pulling off his socks, and then his briefs. Grabbing the hand-ax. Looking at himself naked in the mirror, ax in fist.

For a second, the glass flashed like lightning, and he saw her face there.

A glimpse.

Then, he pulled back the shower curtain and began opening the door to Heaven.

The Sailor Home from the Sea

John Pelan

A pub in midsummer can be a funny place, you go in expecting to see no one yet wind up running into just about anyone. So it was on a hot August day when I dropped round The Smoking Leg to return a stack of CDs that my friend Ian had lent to me.

The Smoking Leg is usually fairly quiet in the afternoons, good for a cup of coffee or tea and a chat with Ian, and every so often he'll share one of his odd experiences that ends up making its way into a book or magazine by way of my computer. This afternoon proved to be a bit different...

Ian was picking up a chair, which was next to one of the small and flimsy tables that appeared smashed beyond any hope of repair. Only two customers were in the bar, old Curly who sat quietly in the corner mumbling to either himself or his glass of white port, and Arne something-or-other. Arne was a semi-regular that I'd never had occasion to chat with, seemed a nice enough guy but we'd just never had any reason to exchange more than the standard nod that one gives to a familiar face. Arne sat at the bar holding a towel full of ice to his eye, apparently I'd just missed some sort of row. I quickly moved to help Ian straighten up the tossed-about furniture and asked him what the hell had happened; (The Smoking Leg just isn't the sort of place where fights break out, at least not in the afternoon).

"Shit, one of Arne's old buddies came in to buy a pack of smokes, he saw Arne and they started talking. Next thing you know they're trading punches and knocking furniture about." He glanced at Arne disapprovingly and went on. "They'd both be banned from here, but I saw that the other guy started it and Arne's never given anyone any trouble before."

I looked at Arne; he'd be sporting an impressively swollen eye for a few days, but other than that seemed to be in fine shape. "Ian why don't we all have a drink on me," and (I nodded to Arne), "maybe you can tell us what all the fuss was about?"

Arne nodded and asked Ian for a large, (very large) schnapps and I settled for a cup of coffee that had obviously been brewed some hours earlier, it was as dark and bitter as a story by Ambrose Bierce, but ultimately as satisfactory. Ian poured himself a cup of the thick brew as well and sat down on the other side of Arne.

"Well, suppose you tell us what the hell that was about..."

Arne shrugged and took a gulp of his drink. "He offered me a job and I wouldn't take it, then he called me a coward..."

"What sort of job? There's got to be a bit more to it than that."

"He wanted me to go fishing again, as mate on his boat. I told him I'd never leave dry land again for any amount of money and he called me a coward. I'm asking you, is a man a coward because he wants to stay alive?"

Ian frowned at the man's comments. "Go to sea, again...I thought you worked in construction?"

"Yeah, I do now. But I'm a Sigurdson, my father was a fisherman as was his father, my uncles, cousins, and my grandfather and his kinsmen before them. Back in Norway our family's been going to sea as long as anyone can remember. I'm the first of our family to walk away from it and stay on the shore. It pisses me off to be called a coward by a man that's never seen the things I've seen or been in the situation that I'm in now. I'd ship out with him in a heartbeat if I could, but it would bring doom on me and perhaps everyone on the boat; I'm no coward, but I can't risk that sort of thing happening."

He paused and glanced around the bar as if half-expecting to see someone else listening in.

"Either of you been out fishing before? Out on the open ocean?" We both shook our heads in the negative.

"Then let me tell you what happened to me and why I can't go back to it. I'm no coward today, though perhaps I was a coward once before when I didn't stop a horrible thing from happening, though I've thought about it a lot and I really don't think that there's much of anything I could have done at the time...

"You've never been out on the Bering where it's deathly quiet except for the sound of the wind, not even any gulls wheeling overhead like you see in more temperate waters, just the frigid wind and the sounds of the cables pulling the crab pots up. Hoisting up some three-hundred pounds of clacking, fidgeting crab out of the water and stacking the damn cages three to four high on a slippery deck is enough to make most men wish they'd never signed on. The sea is as dark as pitch and there's a cold that gets into you no matter how well you're bundled up. And the quiet, the quiet is nice for a while and then the silence starts to eat at you until you wish you could swim for shore. The sea's a terrible place, but the money's good and it's what I grew up expecting to do. I'd be doing it still except for what happened...

"Of all the things to fish for, crab are the best and the worst of it. Like I said, the money's not bad at all and you can make a go of it with a small boat on account of the price they fetch. But they're not like catching fish in a net or on a hook, you have to lower mesh cages to catch 'em and the damn things weigh a ton when you pull 'em up. Many's the ship that's capsized under the weight of its own crab pots when they're full up. The worst of it is that you have to keep the damn things alive until you can get them to the processor, you look at those crabs trapped in the wire pots and peer into their eyes and I think that maybe you're looking right into a bit of hell. That if there's a devil maybe his eyes look something like that; crabs are strange and evil creatures, they stare at you with those beady eyes and the briny drool running from their mouths as they wave those claws around and wish they could get hold of you. Imagine what those fiends can do to a man in the water, legs as long as your arm and pincers that can shear through flesh and bone as though it were putty; I've caught a million of 'em, but I'd never eat one; damn things have always given me the creeps.

"*Bering Belle* was the name of the ship that I worked several seasons on, right out of Seattle and skippered by a childhood friend, Eric Ronning. Ronning's family has been in the fishing business as long as mine, but they were wise enough to buy a license rather than working for someone else. The *Belle* wasn't a huge vessel, just a sturdy thirty-footer, big enough for a crew of eight with private quarters for the skipper and more than adequate enough to take the pounding of the Bering Sea without tipping over when fully loaded. The seasons were a lot longer then, you could be out till you caught your fill, into port and the processors and then back out again. Three months at sea wasn't unusual; not like now with the two-week seasons and limits they've got.

"You could keep a good crew together then too, no need to recruit every time you wanted to take the boat out, guys found a good captain and a fair share and stayed on. This was before the big companies took to buying up all the licenses. I worked for Eric Ronning, we'd gone to high school together and spent our summers working for his father on their boat. When the old man retired and Eric became a skipper it was only natural that I'd wind up as first mate. We had a Japanese engineer name of Takemura, what he didn't know about engines isn't worth the telling, the rest of the seven-man crew was comprised of our friends from school that had grown up with fisherman's blood in their veins.

"I think back now that if only Eric hadn't been stuck in such a miserable marriage and if only we had taken shorter trips, things might not have turned out as badly. Most men with families are glad to get home and pretend to have a normal family life if just for a couple of months, not Eric; he'd married way too young and all he saw was blonde hair and big breasts. All his wife Kirsten had seen was a fisherman's income and more credit cards than she knew what to do with. Hell, they were in separate bedrooms before they'd been married a year.

"Eric didn't much care, although I suppose that's about when he began to hate women in general and the ones close to him in particular... Sort of made for a recipe for disaster when he wound up meeting Tanya at a Dutch Harbor tavern one night.

"Living in a small fishing village in Alaska can be hell if you're an attractive young woman with her mind set on having the finer things in life. Tanya was of Eskimo and Russian ancestry with the blackest hair and eyes that I've ever seen and a figure that would've shamed most girls in a beauty pageant. She and Eric hit it right off, they both liked to drink and they were both out to see what each could get out of the other; a perfect combination for a one-night stand, but this one lasted, lasted all of one season and into the next.

"I'd have never figured it, like I said Eric had nothing but contempt for women and Tanya seemed to have little use for Eric other than getting her pleasure and having her bar tab paid for. Their usual routine was to drink until they started arguing, then she'd slap him and he'd knock her about a bit and the next thing you know they'd be climbing all over each other like rabbits in heat. Funny relationship, but none of my damn business; or at least so I thought...

"The second year after our skipper had started his affair was when things started to turn to shit. The fishing was still good and the money better but something had gone sour. Ronning had never permitted drinking at sea, but now he'd taken to carrying a flask with him wherever he went. No one dared say anything about it, after all he was the skipper and if you'd ever seen him in a bar fight then you'd know that he wasn't anyone to provoke. Besides which, it wasn't like it was affecting anything other than his moods, moods that were getting progressively bleaker the longer we were at sea.

"The routine changed only by Eric shunting off more of his duties to me while at sea and his temper getting worse than ever. Fortunately, we wound up with a sizable catch in record time and were able to put in with several weeks left to spare. We spent the time in Dutch Harbor relaxing, that is if drinking round the clock with the occasional fist-fight can be said to be 'relaxing'. Eric spent a good deal of time with Tanya as might be expected, and they picked up right where they'd left off, fighting and screwing like mink.

"She spent near as much time on the ship as she did at her own place, the two of them keeping us up with their fighting and cursing. Of course she'd always make sure that we got a good look at her long legs or a glimpse of breast, as she'd walk out in the morning wearing one of Eric's shirts. The sort of thing drove Eric mad with jealousy, but what could he say to her? She played him like a well-tuned guitar, toying with him and goading him into rages and then laughing at him when he hit her. We used to joke that one of them would kill the other before too much longer... Doesn't seem quite so funny in retrospect... She kept at him about marrying her and Eric kept dodging the issue by running up his credit card, ordering her all sorts of clothes and jewelry from the finest stores in Seattle.

"Wasn't long before she started staying on board full time, she'd look at us all as though we should be bowing and scraping for a chance to near her and then they'd head into his cabin with a bottle or two. It was the same every night, quiet while they sat and drank and then the row would start, she'd be screaming at him calling him every name in the book and then there'd be crashing and banging as he slapped her around. Then we'd hear his bed thumping against the wall as they spent their passion. A deal like that can't go on forever, not when both parties really have contempt for each other and the self-loathing that comes from being trapped and being afraid to do anything about it.

"The explosion came at the Salty Dog when Eric made the mistake of knocking her around in full view of the town cops. Eric knew better than to fight, even as drunk as he was, you don't jeopardize your relationship with the town by fighting with cops; plus, that's a real good way to wind up getting shot and dropped off a pier. She taunted him unmercifully as he was being led away, said she'd find someone else that could satisfy her if she had to try every man in the bar...

"We went back to the boat knowing he'd be turned loose in the morning and that that would be the end of it. I don't think any of us had really paid attention to Tanya's raving and ranting. After all, it was just an angry woman's drunk talk, or so we thought. When she came onto the boat no one was more surprised than me. Maybe this was an act of cowardice, maybe not being able to say "no" made us all guilty, but like I said she was beautiful and we'd been at sea for a long time. I was on the deck with Morey (one of our old buddies from high school) when she came up the pier and strode onto the *Bering Belle* as though she owned it.

"She'd been home to change clothes, she was wearing a long leather coat (no doubt ordered from the lower forty-eight with Eric's credit card), and as I soon saw, that was all she was wearing. She undid the belt and opened up the coat to give us both a look... I just about lost it right there, her breasts were large and perfectly formed with the nipples stiffened in the arctic wind. Even with the chill, I could feel the heat radiating from her and I knew why Eric had endured her temper these last two years. This was a woman you'd do anything for, even knowing that you might lose your soul in the process. She looked us both over as if choosing dinner off a menu.

" 'Arne, you're next, let's go below.' That was all she said to any of us other than 'you're next'. I've never been with a woman like that before or since, part angel and part fiend; I've still got scars from her nails and teeth. It was a night to remember, we all took turns and she chewed us up and spit us out in the morning when she left. Ronning was back a couple of hours later and went straight to his cabin. A good thing as I don't think any of us could have faced him. It's a terrible thing that we all did, but what came later was much, much worse.

"It's sad, if only we'd have been able to leave then it would have been all right, but two days can be an eternity. Two days was just enough time for Tanya to demand that Eric marry her, two days was enough time for them both to get drunk again and for everything to go straight to hell.

"We spent the evening at the 'Dog trying to get lucky but just getting drunk, Hansen being the youngest, had stayed on the ship with the promise that we'd bring back some beer for him and that Tak and I would relieve him on watch. Tanya and Eric were unusually quiet the whole evening and all the way back to the boat; Eric's mood seemed a bit less black than usual and even Tanya wasn't playing the bitch-goddess for a change. I looked forward to a peaceful watch of drinking beer with Tak and then a sound sleep; but it wasn't to be...

"No sooner had we sent Hansen below with a six-pack then Tanya brought up marriage to Eric; usually he'd dodge the question and change the subject, but this time he flat out told her 'no'. And he wasn't very subtle about it either.

" 'Marry you? Hell you're a good lay and fun to drink with, but I'm already stuck with one bitch; why would I want another?'

"For a moment I thought she was going to attack him, and even though Eric towered over her I wouldn't have bet against her, but what she did was much worse than scratching his eyes out...

" 'You stupid bastard, you're lucky I spend any time with you at all. You're not a man; you've never satisfied me, your whole crew is better than you are, I've tried 'em all on and there's not a one of 'em that isn't more of a man than you are!'

"Eric recoiled as if he'd been punched. 'What do you mean, bitch?'

" I let them all have me, the night you were in jail, I came here so I could have some fun. They're not your friends, there's not a one of 'em that couldn't wait to stick it in me as soon as you were out of the way...'

"We were stunned, stunned by her words and the look of hate that Ronning gave us, he grabbed her arm and headed belowdecks, she didn't struggle, she'd pissed him off and humiliated him in front of his crew and that's exactly what she'd wanted. It wasn't any surprise to hear the screaming and carrying on that came from his cabin. Tak and I assumed our place at watch as the rest of the crew turned in.

"It was a few hours later when I heard the skipper's footsteps...I heard his slow, measured steps before I could see him clearly in the dark. Eric walked slowly as if he were either very drunk or as if carrying a heavy load; placing one foot in front of the other slowly and carefully. I turned and squinted into the night to see that it was the latter, that he was carrying something...

"'Arne, what am I supposed to do now?' Ronning's voice reminded me of a time in the sixth grade when he'd broken his arm playing football. There was the same note of pain and confusion in it. Then I saw what he was holding, and I stifled an urge to vomit.

"He'd beat her terribly, in the silence I could hear the gentle spatters as droplets of blood hit the deck. He must've hit her with a bottle, the side of her head was caved in and one of those beautiful dark eyes lolled onto her cheek. I didn't have to ask if she was dead or not.

" 'You have to help me Arne, this is partly your fault...'

"Maybe this is where I was a coward, maybe I should have run off into the night and returned with the police, but maybe the guilt of betraying my friend was too strong, maybe I thought by helping him I could atone for my actions. I don't know what I thought, but one thing was certain, Tanya was dead and Eric was alive; there's nothing to be done for the dead, but sometimes you can help the living.

"I was almost unaware of Tak coming up behind me, I heard his soft voice as his logical engineer's mind analyzed the situation and came to the only conclusion possible.

" 'Skipper, you have to get rid of the body. There is no other way. Fasten her to one of the pots and put her in the water. The crabs will take care of the rest.'

"I started, here was the gentle man who raised bonsai and wrote constant letters to his family calmly talking about feeding a woman's body to the crabs, a woman that he'd had sex with just hours before... I guess you never know about the way some people's minds work, but Tak was right. There was nothing to be done but to get rid of the body. Tanya had lived by herself, by the time anyone thought about her as being missing we'd be on our way home and the crabs would have reduced that beautiful body to bones that would lie under the dark sea forever.

"Somehow we managed it, lashing her with baling wire to one of the crab pots, Tak loaded some extra weight into the cage just to be on the safe side and over the side she went. The dislocated eye staring unseeingly at us as she sank from sight beneath the frigid waters."

Arne paused here, signaling for another glass of schnapps. I could see why he was so reluctant to return to the sea, the memories of that night would torture anyone but a sociopath.

"We made it home okay, the rest of the crew never knew anything about it and if they ever talked about screwing the skipper's girlfriend, they never did so in my hearing. I made good money on the trip and made a down-payment on a house, I guess even then I was thinking that I might not be going fishing much anymore. Eric came home to find divorce papers and his credit cards at their max. He was too shaken by the events in Alaska to even think about contesting anything. His wife walked away with half his income, the house, car, and dog. Eric spent most of the time in Ballard Avenue taverns drinking by himself and managing to avoid being tossed in jail more by luck than by design. We were all glad to get back to sea, and, I think, had come around to thinking of Tanya's death as more of an unfortunate accident than a willful murder...

"You know, I've heard some people say that they think love is forever, well if that's true, then what about hate? Can the venom and bile that drives one to hate someone else be chilled by death? Somehow I think that if love can last forever, perhaps hate can last even longer...

"Almost a year to the day Eric and I stood on the deck watching the borealis dance and shimmer. It's a strange time, mid-summer out on the Bering, the lights from the borealis and the stars illuminate the horizon, but from where you're standing on the reeling deck of a crab boat it's as black as pitch ten feet in front of you.

"The thump was so soft, that I thought nothing of it, a piece of driftwood perhaps, a float from another vessel. It was when I heard the clank and rattle of baling wire that I looked and saw what was coming over the rail...

"The jet-black hair hadn't changed, even with all that time in the sea, most of the flesh was gone, the beautiful breasts that I'd squeezed and caressed mere months earlier were ragged tears of skin flapping softly as the thing moved towards us. But the face was by far the worst part, the horribly shredded cheeks and brow, that and the gaping hole near her temple that was festooned with barnacles and limpets. The eye that had dangled on her cheek was long since removed by an ocean scavenger. I could tell right off it was Tanya, and so could Eric. He didn't even make a move to defend himself as the thing went for him with long blackened nails strengthened and sharpened by months in the brine. Maybe I was a coward then, or maybe I just knew that ultimately death was what Eric wanted. Like I said, he made no move to defend himself as the thing ripped at his face and dragged him over the side.

"My entry in the log was stated simply, our skipper had been lost at sea, an apparent accident with the possibility of alcohol being involved. Eric's reputation as a big drinker had preceded him and there was no inquest. People are lost at sea all the time, if I'd said what really occurred I'd have been shut up in an asylum. Old man Ronning sold the *Bering Belle*; license, gear and all to one of the big seafood companies. I spent the next year trying to make up my mind whether or not to sign on with another crew.

"Even with the constant nightmares, waking up seeing her ruined face and grasping hands looming over me, I still thought about going back out. There's something about the fisherman's life that gets into the blood even with a greenhorn that's on their first trip and with me, fishing was bred in the bone. I'd almost made up my mind to go back when I ran into Tak.

"He was working for one of the big trawlers, keeping their huge turbines purring along, a good position with a great salary. We hooked up at a bar here in town and spent some hours talking about the old days and trying unsuccessfully to keep the conversation from drifting to talk of Eric Ronning and his disappearance at sea. I think that Tak always knew that there had to be more to the story than what I'd let on, but if he thought me a liar he never said anything to indicate it.

"Tak seemed to be doing well, except for his marriage, which had ended with his wife quietly packing up kids, clothes, and furniture and returning to Japan. We sat with a pitcher of Red Hook between us as the jukebox played songs that had been old when I was in school. I couldn't help forcing a smile as Johnny Horton sang about the riches waiting when one went 'North to Alaska'… One pitcher led to another and we found ourselves chatting until nearly closing time. What we didn't talk about hung over the table like a morning fog, just as thick and omnipresent…

"The two of us talked of boats and beer and bad marriages and tried to forget about the image that had burned into our souls nearly a year ago.

"A picture of that beautiful long black hair draped over the horrid wound in the side of Tanya's face as we'd lowered her into the sea. I couldn't bring myself to tell Tak what had happened to Eric. Some things are too terrible to talk about no matter what the circumstances. More cowardice? I don't know, I had no reason to think that any of us were in danger, a hateful hand had reached from beyond the grave to avenge a murder, but we hadn't really *done* anything…

"Tak's ship was to stay in port for a few days while they loaded up supplies, there was an offer of a job tendered, not as demanding as my previous position, but a salaried position with a share of the catch… I thought long and hard about it and had almost made up my mind to say 'yes', when Tak disappeared. We'd closed Pete's Place down and headed our separate ways, me to my little house in Ballard and Tak back to the ship. He never made it back. No body was ever found; questions were asked but no one had even a hint of a motive.

"I know what happened to him, and I suspect I know where. I think it has to do with the stars and the seasons being right, that and the fact that she can't leave the water; or at least I don't think that she can. I'm pretty sure that Tak made it as far as the pier and then something came up out of the sea and took him, something of bone and baling wire and black barnacles all held together by hate.

"That something's waiting for *me* out there somewhere, somewhere out in the sea. Y'see, I'm not a coward like that guy accused me of being, I've damn good reason to stay away from the sea…

"She's as vindictive in death as she was in life, she's after me now and *I didn't even do anything to her*...neither did Tak and now he's gone. I look at the calendar that marks the dates of Eric's death and Tak's disappearance and I wonder when my time will come. I asked a woman that told fortunes if there was any significance to those dates and she said something about water signs, the unquiet dead, and atonement... Sounded like either a bunch of bullshit or like maybe she really saw something in the cards that she couldn't bring herself to talk about. I take a little bit of comfort in being pretty sure that she can't come up on the dry land, but lots of nights I lie awake and think about the night that she said "Arne, you're next..."

Ian and I glanced at each other and I pulled a ten-dollar bill out of my wallet to cover our drinks. I finished my coffee and bought the former fisherman another drink; (he looked like he could use it). I headed home, making sure to take the long route through the city, well away from the waterfront...

This Is The End; My Only Friend, The End

David B. Silva

Russell McDaniel found his wife, Phyllis, sitting at the kitchen table, her face buried behind the morning newspaper, a cigarette burning in the ashtray to her right... He pulled out a chair and sat at the table across from her, his head still pounding from last night's New Year's Eve party at the Henderson's... A low-pitched buzzing sound had brought him awake this morning... It was still with him, vibrating persistently just beneath the surface like a bad case of tinnitus.

"How long have you been up?"

She glanced over the top of the paper, her eyes clearer than he would have imagined after all the drinking she had done... "Well, look what the dog dragged in... You look like living hell."

"I feel like living hell." He tried to swallow back the dry, cottony taste in his mouth, then rested his head in the crook of his arms on the table top and closed his eyes.

That sound...that low-pitched sound...thank God today was a holiday.

Phyllis laughed at something in the paper.

"What's so funny?"

"I just realized...the new millennium...it's finally arrived... And what do you know? The world's still in one piece."

"Uh-huh."

"All the naysayers...with their Y2K, and their apocalypse, and their Book of Revelations and the end of the world and all of mankind...they were wrong... I love it!" She laughed again, then folded the newspaper in half and set it aside... "You really do look like hell."

"Do you hear that sound?"

"What?... The refrigerator?"

"No... It's like a low-pitched buzzing sound... Like an electric razor."

Phyllis listened, then shook her head. "It's the hangover."

"Maybe."

She stood, took one last drag off the cigarette before smashing it out in the ashtray, then started out of the kitchen... "I'm going to take a shower... Don't forget...we're supposed to meet Jimmy and Marge at the Cinema 10 at one."

Russell nodded... He placed his head in the crook of his arms again, closed his eyes, then let his thoughts wander... This year's resolution: no more drinking... Well, no more over-drinking... He tried to move the pain further to the back, hearing Phyllis laugh again, then silently agreeing with her: it was nice to finally put an end to all the millennium naysaying.

He heard her laugh again.

Then he heard something else: a familiar, yet disturbing squeal just above the electric-razor buzz that seemed to be charging the air around him... This was faraway, he thought... Not something in his head, but something real.

Russell raised up and glanced around... It had sounded, he realized now, like one of his wife's sharp, little yelps that escaped whenever he was driving and she was afraid an upcoming car might pull out in front of them. Phyllis would yelp, then brace herself against the dashboard for an impact which invariably never occurred.

He stood up from the table.

Best to go make sure nothing was wrong.

Passing through the living room, something caught his eye... Russell stopped, then backpedaled... Through the picture window, he could see out across the street to the Duncan's front yard... There were dark, angry clouds overhead, and the Duncan's had their sprinklers running... Weird enough... Only the water...the water was black... How odd... It had already collected into a huge dark pool on their lawn, the run-off rolling across the sidewalk and down the gutter like a thick, viscous oil slick.

Russell stared at it a moment, thinking how dark it looked, how it almost seemed to be consuming whatever it touched... Then he heard another sound, this time from the bathroom, and he continued down the hall to check on his wife.

He found Phyllis in the shower, the faucet spitting and hissing.

"Are you all right in there?"

"Help me!"

He opened the shower door, then fell back... Pouring out of the showerhead...that same black water had covered most of his wife's body, neck to waist... She looked at him, her eyes wide... Water had splashed across her chin and her lower jaw... They were gone now, replaced by an infinite, black nothingness, as if they had never existed at all... Rivulets of nothingness trickled down her legs, leaving behind an incomprehensible, anatomical jigsaw puzzle of flesh, cartilage and bone.

Then Russell noticed the huge, black hole that had opened in the back of the shower stall, and in the floor beneath her feet... Nothingness...gobbling up everything it came in contact with.

More of Phyllis disappeared into the abyss.

Then outside, somewhere overhead, a loud clap of thunder shook the house, and Russell heard the first few heavy drops of nothingness strike the roof.

White-Out

Peter Crowther and Simon Conway

WE HAVE NEVER HEARD THE DEVIL'S SIDE OF THE CASE
BECAUSE GOD WRITES ALL THE BOOKS.
—*Samuel Butler*

O TELL HER, BRIEF IS LIFE BUT LOVE IS LONG
—*Alfred, Lord Tennyson,* from *The Princess IV*

"Tell me again what happened," Jack Medley said. "But more slowly."

Victoria Matheson walked across the room, carefully avoiding the flower-bedecked bars printed on the bright orange carpet, and leaned against the window. The glass felt cool on her face and she could feel the winter trying to break through into the false warmth of the centrally-heated office.

Far below her, on the choppy water of the East River, a solitary boat wound its way towards Brooklyn, trying to beat the coming storm. She had never seen a boat on the East River before, not in her eight years in New York City. Not one boat.

She had seen other things, of course.

She had seen a bum with a gangrenous leg, swollen to twice its size, begging for change in the dimly lit catacombs of the 14th street subway station and rewarding all who contributed with a piece of home-spun advice. "Watch out for those pots and pans," he had told her in a rasping voice dulled by a steady diet of surgical spirit and food-scraps. "They'll getcha ev'ry time," he added with a conspiratorial wink of a rheumy eye. And all for one shiny quarter.

She had seen a seemingly well-dressed man (until you noticed the sneakers, the Band Aid across the bridge of his spectacles and the tattooed serpent on his left cheek) carrying the stiff body of a cat into Saks Fifth Avenue, the carcass held by the tale like a hold-all.

And she had seen a man in mirrored sunglasses—sitting cross-legged alongside a dog dressed in a full suit, shirt and vest, smoking a pipe—reading animatedly from a book of Walt Whitman's poetry while passers-by studiously failed to acknowledge his existence.

She had even seen a drive-by shooting, her first, on her way to LaGuardia. The victim looked to be around 14 years old. In the ensuing traffic snarl-up she had told the police she hadn't seen anything.

But she had never seen a boat on the East River. But then, you waited long enough, maybe you could see anything and everything in this city. After all, she had seen her husband come into her room for three consecutive nights, smiling at her, smiling as he pulled back the sheets and crawled in beside her, his body cold and clammy, and then—

"Victoria?"

The images of Robert faded with Jack Medley's voice, dear Jack…long-standing friend, confidante and one-time lover. Now all that remained was the boat, straining for the shoreline. It was like an omen, that boat. But was it a good omen?

"You okay, Victoria?"

She felt rather than heard the good doctor's feet approaching from behind and she spun around, gasping, one hand going to her neck and the other…the other *covering* herself. Covering where Robert had been.

Jack Medley stopped where he was. "Hey," he laughed, hands held with their palms towards her, "it's only me, okay? Loosen up."

"I'm sorry. I really am sorry, Jack, but I don't honestly think I'm in the mood to go through it all again right now." She pointed to his desk and the open file lying on its polished surface. "It's all there. It would be just the same if I went through it all again. Sure a word or two might be different, but the basic facts would be the same. I am not imagining this."

He looked around for something to lean on, something neutral, so she wouldn't feel threatened. He moved a pile of books from the back of the sofa and dropped them on the floor. Shuffling onto the vacated space, he clasped his hands on his lap and said, "Why don't you just humor me, Victoria. We've known each other for a long time and—"

"Eight years."

Jack Medley nodded. "Eight years. That's a long time."

She shrugged. "It's eight years is what it is. What's your point here?"

"Well, my point is, doesn't that time qualify me to ask you to tell me it all again? Right from the beginning? Maybe there's some—"

"Uh uh. No more. I'm not in the mood for any more right now, okay?"

He shrugged. *Sure it was okay, but if you don't want to try to resolve this problem why come to me for help,* his expression said. *Shit or get off the pot already, for crissakes.*

She turned back to face the window and her reflection set against the late afternoon gloom. "I don't want to go home."

"Okay, that's fine. But you don't go home, where will you go?"

Now it was her turn to shrug. "Somewhere he won't find me."

The sigh came out against his wishes—and against his better judgment.

Without turning, she said, "See, I told you you wouldn't believe me."

"I believe *you* believe, Victoria." He stood up and rubbed a spot on his backside that was going into pins and needles. "But, you know—" he laughed gently "—these things just don't *happen.*"

"You examined me, Jack, you saw the marks…and the *bruises,* you—"

"I saw evidence of sexual activity, Victoria, sure." He rubbed his hands together like he was cold. "That doesn't mean diddly and you know it."

What he meant was she was a healthy, good-looking woman who had, he knew, an active sex life. He was too polite to come right out and say it but Jack Medley thought she had gotten the marks from one of her overly attentive lovers *and* she was losing her mind—the latter part of which was beginning to sound like a reasonable prognosis to her, too.

"Well, let's see what the test results show."

She was getting pissed and she didn't want to get pissed with Jack. Not Jack. She looked back out of the window and saw that the boat had reached the Brooklyn shoreline. She thought she could see figures moving around, getting down onto the dock and carrying things. She tried to imagine their conversation…tried to picture their expressions: normal people going about their business, going home to normal houses and normal relationships.

I told you, Robert had said, *I told you I wouldn't let you go.*

She gave an involuntary shudder as she recalled his voice, a deep and hollow rumbling, like the sound of the late night trains on the Sixth Avenue subway, rattling the shelves in their first apartment in a dingy three-floor walk-up on 44th Street. That voice had been a different one than the one he had had while he was still alive.

Behind her, Jack Medley cleared his throat.

She looked up and watched a helicopter wing its way up from...from where? And where was it going?

"Victoria, you have to let me recommend somebody for—"

"I'm not losing my mind, Jack. And I am not going home." She turned around, smiled once and walked across to the sofa. "I'll sleep here tonight," she said, patting the cushions affectionately.

"Wha—"

"I'll be fine."

He shook his head. "But, you can't just—"

"Why can't I? Why can't I stay here, Jack?"

He shrugged and ran his hands through his hair. "Jesus Christ, Victoria, I—"

"There's no reason is there? No reason that you can't just leave me here for the night." She sat down on the sofa and swung her legs up onto the cushions. "A sheet or blanket or something would be good."

"And what about tomorrow? And the next night? You've got to face this, Victoria."

"I'll worry about tomorrow tomorrow. You'll have the test results then and you'll know," she shouted. "You'll know I'm not losing it."

He walked back to his desk and hit the intercom button. A shrill voice answered.

"Sally, could you find me some blankets? Mrs. Matheson will be sleeping here tonight." The voice started to say something and Jack Medley picked up the receiver. "I think there are some along the hall. And could you turn down the sofa in the waiting area please." A pause. "Yes, that's right. Could you call them and say I can't make it tonight. We'll re-schedule."

Victoria watched him replace the handset. "You don't need to do this, Jack," she said. "I'll be fine by myself."

For a second he thought about making some crack of hitting on her but then thought better of it, one dim section of his head—the part connected directly to his groin—thinking maybe that was a possibility...maybe that was what all this was about. But then, there *were* the bruises...

Instead, he shrugged. "I'm sure you will. But if it is...you know, if it isn't Robert but something else..."

"You mean if it's just my imagination."

"Well, let's say maybe it's something that you're doing that you don't realize you're doing and, if it *is*, then just changing your bedroom—albeit across the city—won't necessarily stop you doing it."

"You think…you think I'm doing this to myself, don't you? You think I'm dreaming I'm awake and Robert's ghost—who I can *feel*, by the way—he's raping me while I'm busy *masturbating*…is *that* what you think?" She stared. "Is *it*, Jack?"

"I think you're very scared and in this present state the mind can play some pretty amazing tricks. Okay? That's what I think. Nothing more." He held up his hands palms-forward to show he was telling the truth. "Okay?" he asked again.

She nodded and smiled. "Okay, point taken." He smiled back. Victoria clasped her hands together and looked down at them intently. "Well, I have to say I'm glad you are staying," she said, softly, like she meant it.

"You are?"

She looked up and, for the first time, Jack Medley saw genuine fear etched into her face, tugging at her eyes and pulling down the corners of her mouth. "Yes," she said. "I'm glad because I don't see why a ghost—if it *is* a ghost—I don't see why it wouldn't know where to find me."

The doctor felt a sudden chill down his back.

She wrapped her arms around her chest and stared past him across at the darkness outside the window. He followed her stare and saw that it had started to snow, hard.

"I think he'll come to me here," she said with a confidence that sounded absolute.

««—»»

"Another hour and I think we might've starved," Jack Medley said as he dumped the last of the food containers in the trash. The whole place smelled of egg foo young and he moved across to the window in a vain attempt to reach at least the impression of fresh air.

Outside, the world was white.

"There's not a thing moving down there," he said, "not a single thing. We must have had a foot of snow in the past couple of hours." He turned around and saw that Victoria was not paying him any attention. He looked back out of the window and saw his reflection looking back at him.

"How about we watch a little TV?" He clapped his hands and dropped the blind with a loud rattle. "How about that?"

Victoria looked up at him as though she had just woken up. "Huh?"

"TV. I said, do you want to watch TV?" He picked up the remote and surfed the channels until he hit the local news.

"Sure," Victoria said lazily from the couch. "Whatever."

"The forecast calls for more accumulation over the next 24 hours and Mayor Sarah Veggas has told non-essential city workers to stay home tomorrow," the newsreader said chirpily.

"Public transportation is already at a standstill and it seems the only way to get about is on skis!" The accompanying picture showed two men walking along Wall Street—evidenced by a quick cutaway shot to the street sign—wearing full skiing outfits. They smiled dutifully at the camera.

The picture suddenly cut back to the studio to show the female anchor grinning and shaking her head in amazement. *"You going home that way, Bill?"*

Bill shook his own head and smiled too.

Not to feel left out, Jack shook his head. This was one hell of a funny show.

"Well, Andrea," Bill confided, *"I don't think so. Maybe the two of us are just stuck here."* He gave a small laugh and turned to face the camera.

"Meanwhile," Bill droned on, *"a police spokesman tells us that crime has virtually come to a halt in New York City...as Adam Flanagan over at the 7th Precinct reports."* He looked down at his monitor, smiled, and said, *"Adam?"*

Jack Medley hit the off switch on the remote before Adam could make any cheap cracks. He couldn't take any more merriment.

"Did you hear that?"

Victoria didn't answer.

"Hey, if nothing's moving, maybe Robert won't be able to get here," he said and immediately regretted the cheap crack. Maybe Victoria couldn't take any more merriment either. He looked down at her and was pleased to see her grimace and throw a cushion across at him. Okay, it was a half-hearted throw...but it was a throw. He was about to respond when the phone behind him rang out. "Saved by the bell," he said and was pleased to see that Victoria returned the smile.

"Jack Medley," he said.

"Hi, Doc, it's Mike," a gruff voice announced. "Mike Eiseley, the janitor?"

"Hey, Mike, what's up?"

"Well, it's this way, Doc. The heating system is crapping out on me down here—snow's blocked up the outlet vents or something."

"Sounds bad."

"It's gonna get worse, Doc, believe me."

Jack waited for something else but Mike said nothing. "Something I can do, is there?" he ventured.

"Oh, hell no, Doc," the janitor said. "I'm just calling around to find out who's still here so's I can turn off all the unoccupied suites. You staying?"

"Looks that way, Mike. That a problem to you?"

"Hell, no. I wanted to find out who was still in. I'm gonna turn off all the unoccupied suites—like I said—and that way I'll minimize the pressure on the whole goddamn thing. No problem you staying, though. No problem at all."

"That's good," Jack said.

"Once I've done that I'm heading off myself. Before things get too much worse. You been watching the news reports?"

Jack made a *gabb-gabb* mouth with his hand to Victoria who sniggered. "Yes," Jack said, trying to keep his own amusement out of his voice. "Just turned it off."

"Yeah, don't blame you. It looks like hell out there."

"Except hell's warmer," Jack said.

"'Except hell's warmer'...hey, I like that," Mike said. "That's a good one." He chuckled to himself and, for the first time, in the background, Jack could hear the sound of the boilers and fans down in the basement.

"Oh, Mike, just one other thing," Jack said in an attempt to bring the conversation to a close.

"Shoot, Doc."

"Who else is here, here in the building, overnight?"

"You kidding me? There's only you, Doc. Everyone else must've got out while the going was still possible. Me, I only live two blocks across First. Should make it sometime tonight."

"Fine," Jack said, smiling across at Victoria. But it didn't *feel* fine. It didn't feel fine at all. "You take care on the way home, okay?"

"You got it. Be seeing you, Doc." The line went dead. Jack held onto the handset for a few more seconds and then dropped it back onto the cradle. When he looked across at Victoria, she looked away. But in that split second, when their eyes met and said the things that only eyes could say to each other, she had picked up Jack's concern. And, as she turned, Jack had picked up hers.

I'm scared, it had said.

««——»»

"You want me to leave the light on?" Jack asked once he had ensured that Victoria was comfortable on the sofa.

"No," she said, nodding to the windows. "It's light enough out there."

It was true. Despite the fact that it was now a little after 11 PM, the world outside the wall-length window seemed bright and somehow almost inviting. The snow was still falling—maybe heavier than ever—and the entire wall seemed alive with movement, hypnotic in its slowness. Calming, even…or so Jack hoped.

Victoria turned to him and gave him a tired smile. "Anyway," she said, "I tried leaving the lights on at home." She didn't need to say any more.

"Well, I'm right outside the door if you need me."

She nodded thanks and shuffled herself further into the makeshift bed.

"You need the bathroom, it's right over in the corner." He pointed to the door behind his desk. "The bathroom leads out into the corridor but I've locked and barred the door."

"Thanks. I'll be fine."

"Okay. G'night."

"Night," Victoria agreed.

As Jack pulled the door closed behind him, Victoria added, "And thanks."

"No problem," he said, and he closed the door.

««——»»

Jack stripped down to his shorts before crawling into the warmth of his sofa-bed. He propped up a couple of pillows and settled down to read Victoria's file. *Patient is clearly distressed,* it began.

Genuinely scared of something which she seems to have manifested into nocturnal visits from her dead husband. She believes these visits to be some kind of punishment—patient has recently commenced a new relationship which she feels is contrary to the wishes of her late husband, Robert Matheson. Patient becomes agitated when asked about the visits and when asked about her husband. However, responses to non-Robert-related questions are normal. Healthwise, she seems okay. ECG and blood pressure normal.

Mild bruising to inner thighs and breasts; possible scratch on left side of abdomen could be self inflicted. Next to this, the doctor had written, *What other answer could there be?*

He put the book down and leaned back. What other answer indeed. Either Victoria Matheson was responsible for the scratch herself or someone else had done it and she was blaming her two-years-dead husband. Why would she do that? To protect the real culprit?

Jack frowned. Protect him from what? And, anyway, if she had not brought the scratch and bruises to someone's attention nobody would ever have known about them. He settled himself, tented his hands on top of the file and, just for a second, suspended belief. Say Robert *had* done it. The hypothesis was difficult but he made it stick. So far, so good. But, if he *had* done it, *why* had he done it? He picked up the file and continued to read.

Significant bruising to the vaginal walls consistent with aggressive intercourse. But no evidence of sperm or of prophylactic lubricants. Of course, it was also consistent with *excited* intercourse. And as for the lack of sperm or evidence of sheath contact…well, as his father used to say, *That plus a quarter will buy you a donut.*

He shook his head, got out of bed and tip-toed across to the water cooler by the window, suddenly realizing that he was hungry again. That was the problem with Chinese food: soon as you finished it, you wanted to eat something else. He poured a cup of water and looked down at the street. All he could see was his own reflection.

He walked over to the wall and killed the lights before wandering back to the window again. Hell, it was something to do.

Everywhere outside was white and deserted, the snow still falling hard and drifting up against the buildings. Only the river, glistening blackly as it rolled by, was untouched by the whiteness. It was a silent world…silent as the grave. He shuddered as he took a drink, wishing it were something a little stronger than water, but the bourbon was in his office…now Victoria Matheson's bedroom.

I told you I wouldn't let you go. That was what Robert had allegedly said to Victoria. If he had said that, *why* had he said it? And why had he waited almost *two years* to say it? He crumpled the cup and tossed it into the trash can. Punishment? Maybe Robert didn't like the idea of his widow making it with another guy. Made sense in a *Twilight Zone* kind of way. But, again, it all came back to why now? Why wait so long?

Victoria had been going with the new guy for…how long was it? A little over a year? Something like that. Jack had even met him. He had gone for a meal with one of his two ex-wives to discuss alimony and she had wanted to go to the Russian Tea Room on 57th. It figured.

Then, a little after 11 o'clock, while Jack and Eleanor were finally getting down to business across a table littered with the remains of chicken Kiev, blinis and borscht, in walked Victoria and her new man. They had been to a concert across the street at Carnegie.

Jack leaned on the windowsill and stared into the whiteness. What the hell was his name? He remembered it reminding him of an old time private eye's name—Sam? No, not Sam for crissakes. Maybe he should speak to the guy. Now that was an idea. But what was his name? Brick? Rock? Tad? What *was* the—Philip! That was it. His name was Philip, as in Marlowe. Hell, he had even looked like an old-time private eye.

He would give him a call. It was decided. But how would he do that? Victoria would never agree to him talking to Philip. *Hey, Phil, Victoria tells me she's being screwed by her dead ex-husband...do you feel this puts any pressure on your relationship?* Uh uh.

Jack turned from the window and looked straight at Victoria Matheson's purse. It was hanging from the coat stand with her trenchcoat. He bit his lip and checked his watch. Not yet midnight. It was late, sure, but he would still accept a call. Wouldn't he? But would Victoria carry an address book in her purse? The $64,000 Question!

He walked across and turned the lights back on, then lifted the purse from the stand.

He opened the purse. And he saw the book.

This was going too easy. He almost felt better when he pulled the book out of the bag and saw it was a diary. Then he flicked through and saw the address list at the back. And there it was: Philip Ellik, 255 Riverside Drive. Complete with telephone number.

Jack looked around the room guiltily and checked the door into his office.

Okay, next thing was to get the details written down and get the book back into the bag and the bag back onto the stand.

He found a message pad and pencil and scribbled the number. But before he put the book back he decided to check the diary section for the last few days. They were blank. He went back one week and saw that the last entry was on the Tuesday. *Going to tell Philip about Robert!*, it said, in Victoria's finely scripted hand, two small incomplete circles above the 'i's in Philip and one more beneath the exclamation mark. He had no idea what she was going to tell Philip but at least it showed that all roads led to him. All one of them.

He put the book into the bag and the bag back onto the stand.

Another check around. All quiet.

He sat down in Sally's chair and dialed the number. It rang, once...twice...three times. There was a click and a voice message kicked in. *Hi, this is Philip. I'm not in or can't get to the—* "Don't believe a word of it," a man's voice suddenly interrupted. "I'm here and I've got the phone."

"Philip Ellik?"

"Yes, this is he," the voice said. "Who's that?"

"Have I disturbed you Mr. Ellik?"

"No, not at all. We were just watching the news. New York is currently being buried beneath 16 inches of snow...and still rising. Who *is* that?"

Jack was frowning. *We?* "You don't know me, Mr. Ellik...although we met once. In the Russian Tea Room? You were with Victoria. Victoria Matheson?"

The smile had gone from Philip Ellik's voice when he spoke again. "Oh, right," he said. "I think I do remember now. Were you a friend of Victoria's? A doctor...something like that?"

"I still am," Jack said, "on both counts. A friend of Victoria's and a doctor."

There was a grunt, then, "And how can I help you, mister...?"

"Medley, Doctor Jack Medley. As to how you can help me, well...this is just a little difficult."

"Try me."

"Okay. It's actually about Victoria that I called, Mr. Ellik. She's having—"

"Look, can I stop you right there, Doctor. I really don't want anything to do with Victoria Matheson at all. She and—"

A woman's voice asked something from Ellik's end of the line and Ellik must have turned and spoken to her. He had covered the mouthpiece but Jack could still hear the conversation. The woman was telling Ellik to hang up. Ellik came back on.

"Look, I really have nothing to say to you, Doctor Smedley."

"Medley."

"Whatever. Victoria and I broke up a little over one month ago now and that's as much as I want to say."

Jack was stymied. "Okay, fine...that's fine...but I just wanted—"

"Did you understand me, doctor? I have nothing to say."

Jack bit his lip and waited. He *did* have something to say, though. Philip Ellik was holding onto the receiver over there on Riverside Drive desperately needing to say something to somebody. To anybody. That was why he hadn't just hung up the telephone. Jack waited.

"You know she's not right, don't you?"

"I'm sorry, how's that, Mr. Ellik. Not right? How is she not right?"

Ellik laughed. It was a hard mean short laugh, a guffaw. It was the laugh of a hurt man, someone whose dreams had been dashed. "She's out of her fucking *tree* is how I mean—if you'll pardon my French."

Jack reached for the message pad and the pencil. "She's come to see me because she's having…" Jack searched for the right words. "She's having problems at home which I feel could be related to the breakdown of her relationship with you." He cringed and waited.

"Well, that may be," Ellik said. "I'm afraid I couldn't comment on that."

"I wonder…I wonder if you could just explain how you did break up, Mr. Ellik."

"Hasn't she *told* you?"

"Well, she's a little distressed and she's not actually making a whole—"

"What *has* she told you?"

Jack paused. Too long.

"Did you…did you think that she and I were still…no! Surely not."

"Mr. Ellik, if I could—"

"You *did*, didn't you. Get her to tell—" There was more background conversation from Ellik's end and his voice grew momentarily distant—like he had turned around to say something to somebody. "I don't give a shit what the law says," he snapped. This time he had not covered the mouthpiece. He came back and said, "Get her to tell you about Robert. Get her to tell you that."

The phone went dead.

Jack waited, listening to the static. It sounded like the souls of the damned whispering…like they were trying to tell him something.

«« — »»

While Jack was talking to Philip Ellik, Victoria was looking out of the window of Jack's office. She was watching the snowflakes tumble down out of the sky, spiraling, twisting and turning…trying to fix her eyes on any one flake and go with it all the way to the ground. She would get about halfway down and lose it, and then she would have to lift her head up again and concentrate on another flake. That one. No, that one.

Meanwhile, New York City settled itself under this unexpected white blanket.

Victoria grew tired of the snowflake game and looked across the East River. It was dark and, although lights flickered on the distant shore, it wasn't much to look at. She walked across to the main side window, stared down First Avenue and, despite herself and everything that had happened, she smiled.

It was truly a beautiful and wondrous place...a city of excesses. Hell, in New York City you didn't just *see* ghosts...Nah! You got *screwed* by them! Hell, it would almost be funny if it weren't so damned terrifying.

Victoria wanted to be angry but, particularly these past few days, she just couldn't get herself worked up enough.

Instead, she got under her blankets dressed only in her T-shirt and panties, rolled onto her left side facing the back of the sofa bed and tried to sleep. But sleep would not come. She could feel the office behind her, feel its dark places and all its nooks and crannies, feel its space. And beyond the office, behind the thin glass window, she could feel the city, feel it breathing. She could feel the shadows that moved amidst the whiteness...shadows that people could not normally see. She held her breath and listened.

Was that a noise?

She listened harder, suddenly aware of the sound of her own heart, a strange, internal sound that was at once both reassuring and threatening. But above the sound of that deep, resonant *thrump-mp, thrump-mp*...there *was* something else. The gentle movement of clothing? The soft intake of breath?

Keeping her eyes tightly closed, Victoria forced herself to turn onto her other side to face the office. Her hands formed fists and she brought them up to protect her breasts while her knees came up to complete the fetal position.

She listened some more to the sound of her heart—

thrump-mp, thrump-mp...

and then opened her eyes. The office was empty.

She breathed a sigh of relief and settled onto the sofa-bed, relaxing her hands and her knees. She felt the tension slip away.

Maybe Robert *wouldn't* be able to find her here.

Maybe she *was* going to be able to sleep.

She felt her eyelids growing heavier, starting to close. The darkness became absolute.

And then it happened.

At first the change was all but imperceptible, the slightest, vaguest sense of things being— She searched for the right word, the right expression that would sum it all up neatly, a concise box-description all tied with a happy-looking pink bow the way her mom used to tie her birthday presents. Then she found it: altered. It felt as though things were being altered all around her.

Steadfastly refusing to open her eyes, she said, "Robert?"

It was a gentle word, bearing no malice, no impatience, no bad vibes at all. Just a word...a question.

The alterings continued, maybe even speeded up. As though, maybe, the need for stealth was gone.

She opened her eyes and looked across the office. Robert was sitting in the middle of the room in Jack's swivel chair, jerking it side to side. He was naked, his legs wide apart, and he was erect.

Without opening his mouth—which was smiling—he said *Hi, Babe*, the words echoing hollowly in Victoria's head. *Told you I wouldn't let you go.*

She tried to scream...but couldn't.

She tried to move...but couldn't.

She wanted to cry...but the tears just would not come.

The only thing she was able to do was to force out one word. "Why?" She almost whispered it.

Robert looked suddenly hurt. He frowned, made a sad mouth and pointed down at his lap. *I brought you a present*, he said, his mouth still not moving, the words forming slowly and coldly in Victoria's head.

"But why?" she said again. "Don't you just want to...to talk?"

Now he smiled and shook his head. *Wrong verb,* the words in her head said.

With that, Robert got up and walked towards her while Victoria watched in dumb fascination. The thing at her husband's groin seemed to move with a life of its own and, in spite of her terror, she found herself transfixed by it. *Is that what it used to look like?* she wondered.

He was upon her before she could come up with an answer.

Victoria felt his clammy cold body move on top of her, his hands moving down her thighs and forcing them apart. She suddenly worried about getting an ice-burn—

down there!

—like she'd got that time she'd lifted the popsicles out of the freezer after it had had some kind of power surge. Then, pulling the crotch of her panties to one side, he was inside her.

It was like no feeling she had ever known.

As he moved on top of her Victoria just lay there, staring into those cold, dark eyes—

not Robert's eyes, surely to God...

and she felt his rhythm strengthening. It was like all the other times: something was being removed rather than added. She felt parts of herself being vacuumed up and spirited away. *Spirited away!* She could almost laugh if only it didn't hurt so. And it did hurt...more even than the other times.

What was he doing that made it hurt so?

He's taking something from you, warned a faraway voice in her head. *He's taking your soul.*

Victoria bucked and gave, bucked and gave, wincing with every thrust.

He bent forward and licked her neck and that single act, thankfully, brought forth the scream that would not come earlier. And as she screamed she felt something inside her dwindling away, wilting like a flower.

Somebody was thumping on the door.

Robert grunted. *Yesss!* She heard his triumphant voice deep in her brain.

She wanted to shout some more, wanted to reach for the wilting thing inside her...to grab a hold of it like she had tried to grab a hold of the brass ring on the merry-go-round of her youth. But the thing she grabbed for now was even more elusive than that ring. It slipped and slid, twisting and turning inside her, fading to infinitesimal smallness.

Then it was gone.

The thumping was still there, more insistent now, and somebody was shouting something...but she couldn't quite make out what it was.

She felt Robert pull away from her but she would not open her eyes. By keeping them tightly closed she felt more able to look inside herself...more able to find what it was that Robert had destroyed.

Suddenly there was a crashing sound and the room was bathed in light.

"Victoria," Jack Medley shouted. "Jesus Christ...you locked the door."

She opened her eyes and Robert was nowhere to be seen. "Locked the door?" she said, turning to face Jack. "I didn't lock the door."

The two of them looked around at the door, which Jack had smashed open with such force that it had crashed into the glass-doored bookcase against the back wall.

Jack shook his head. There *was* no lock on his office door, just a handle. Then why had he been unable to open it?

Victoria was sobbing.

Jack turned around and looked down at her.

She was sitting on the sofa with her knees up around her chin and her arms folded around her legs, rocking back and forth.

"Victoria? What's the matter?"

She kept rocking as she looked at him, her bottom lip shaking.

"Victoria, talk to me."

"He was here, Jack," she said. "He was here and he did it again."

"Robert?"

Victoria nodded. "And...and this time he took something from me."

"He took something from you? What? What did he take?"

"I think...I think he's taken my soul," she said. "Does that sound...does that sound silly?" And then the tears came.

Jack kept on staring at her. This was the crucial moment in their conversations. At this moment he could tell her not to be so stupid, that there was no such thing as ghosts—

And so how did the unlockable door get locked?

—and that the door got jammed and that every UFO sighting is reflected car-lights or a particularly bright Venus. He could tell her all that and risk losing her forever. Or he could ask her why she thought that her dead husband would want to steal her soul.

"Why do you—Victoria...Victoria...look at me."

She looked up at him, the tears streaking her cheeks.

Jack sat down beside her and put his hand gently on her shoulder. "Why do you think Robert wanted your soul?"

"I think...I think maybe it wasn't Robert."

"See." Just for a moment, Jack felt that he was making real progress. Now, if he could just get her to admit that it was her guilt all along...guilt at her having found this new man and this new relationsh—

"It was somebody else," she added.

"Somebody else?" *Who? The Tooth Fairy? Santa Claus? The Bogeyman?* "Who was it, Victoria?"

She looked up into his face, drew in a shuddering breath and frowned. "Who is it takes souls, Jack?"

"What? Are you kidding with me now? The Devil?" He tried hard not to laugh but could not prevent an impatient snort from escaping. "You're telling me the Devil came in here and stole your soul?" *Back off, hombre, back off*, an inner voice said.

"Okay, okay." He rubbed his face with his hands. "Okay, but why would the Devil want to do that?"

The answer was both immediate and succinct. "To punish me."

Jack felt a slight ache in the pit of his stomach. Something was coming. He could sense it. Something was coming and it was not good.

"And why would he want to punish you, Victoria?"

She told him.

«« —»»

Alone in his office—the police having taken Victoria away—Jack went over the story one more time. It was a straightforward tale, nothing new, nothing unusual. But then all such tales were really only variations on a well-tried theme.

She had met Philip Ellik around 18 to 20 months ago, long before Robert's tragic accident. It had been a fraught time in their marriage.

Robert had been spending more and more time at his office and Victoria had been spending more and more time either at her own work—which was not as demanding as Robert's—or at home alone. She was an attractive and intelligent woman—she still was, Jack noted as he called up her image, staring out of the window at the snow-covered streets below as they had both been waiting for the police. She had needed attention and she had needed inspiration. But, at the time, Robert provided neither.

The close confines of a working environment brought Ellik and Victoria closer together. Ellik was single and, according to Victoria, had clearly been attracted to her. She had flirted with him, harmlessly at first but then the flirtation had grown more serious...at least as far as Victoria was concerned.

This had taken almost a year.

She had shamelessly made a play for him on more than one occasion but Ellik, as refreshingly traditional in such things as he was interesting and entertaining, had skillfully avoided intimate situations. Perhaps that had been one of his great attractions. Perhaps if he and Victoria had succumbed to a brief but passionate affair, the tragedy that was to follow might have been avoided. But they had not succumbed.

Alone every night, thinking of Philip Ellik, Victoria had reached a decision.

Ellik would never want to come between two people. He was simply just like that. He did not want to cause upset. So Victoria could never ask for a divorce. And anyway, hadn't Robert always told her he wouldn't let her go?

No, the solution—if there were to be one—had to be something that was both more definite and seemingly nothing to do with Philip Ellik.

The fire in Robert's office building that had claimed five lives had not been an accident. Victoria had gone to the building on the night that the design team was putting the finishing touches to an important campaign and she had doused the first floor hallways with gasoline.

Robert's office complex had its own restrooms and its own cooking equipment and microwave. There was no reason for any of them to leave the office once they were in there except to go home. And Victoria knew that they would not be going home until maybe three or four in the morning.

It had been a little after 1:30 when she had finished. The street had been completely deserted.

Then she had calmly walked back inside and tossed a match. By the time the fire had reached the door to their office, on the fourth floor, the rest of the building was an inferno. There had been no way for them to get out.

Two of the men—Victoria had known them all—had got out onto the ledge in an attempt to escape the flames. They had fallen.

Robert and his assistant and one other man had stayed inside. Nobody knew why they too had not gone out onto the ledge, though there had been no means of escape there. But Robert himself had no head for heights.

It was an old building and it went down like a pack of cards before the fire department could get anywhere near. Victoria, who had started worrying immediately about gasoline traces, thought that was probably a good thing. The cause of the fire had been attributed to faulty wiring. There had been no reason to think otherwise.

Victoria had been distraught. *Oscar-nominee distraught*, Jack now realized.

Jack could remember it all clearly and he now remembered—hating himself for it—spending time with her to try to help her come to terms with her loss.

But Victoria had received other consolations that Jack had known nothing about.

Philip Ellik had been almost as devastated as Victoria. He looked after her, went to the funeral with her—Jack had had to fly to London and simply could not get out of it—and, while she stayed at home apparently grieving, he would visit her. All innocent—at least as far as Ellik was concerned—at first, and then, quite naturally, the relationship developed.

How Victoria could have managed to shoulder such a burden—the taking of five lives!—Jack Medley could not understand. He did not *want* to understand.

But the knowledge she carried around with her had clearly been taking its toll.

Inevitably, more than one year after Robert's death, Philip Ellik had proposed.

It had been everything that Victoria had wanted, everything she had fought—and killed!—for. But even that was not enough. Ellik's traditional stance on these things had caused him to make a confession. He had had one other close relationship, albeit some years earlier, that had almost resulted in marriage. Ellik had wanted Victoria to know this, and to know that that other woman had never meant one fraction of what she now meant to him.

Victoria was touched by the confession and loved him all the more.

But she now realized that she should confess her own background.

It took her some weeks to reach a decision to tell Ellik about what she had done to Robert. Jack Medley could only guess at the nights she had spent alone in her apartment fighting over her decision. But, she had rationalized, Philip had told her that nothing in her past mattered. He had told her—when she had hinted at something she wanted to share with him—that he was not interested. This made her all the more determined.

Then, one night, she had told him.

The incredulous Philip Ellik had been devastated. Victoria had not understood why he would act that way: hadn't he told her that nothing mattered? Hadn't he told her that he loved her no matter what she had done before?

Ellik had left that night.

The next night, Victoria's dead husband had paid his first visit.

The whole thing had, of course, been guilt but Victoria had rationalized it one step further: all this time, Robert had been on 'the other side' believing that his death had been an accident. But now, now that she had openly confessed her crime, Robert had heard. And he wanted his revenge. Worse still, Victoria had told Jack, maybe *something else* now knew what she had done.

When she had reached the end of her story, Jack had said nothing. What was there to say? He had told Victoria that he had to call the police and she had nodded.

"At least he won't be coming back," he had told her. "Robert or whoever you think it really was."

She had nodded without turning around. "There's no need," she had said. "He has what he came for."

The reception door buzzer interrupted his thoughts.

He went to the door and peered through the spy-hole. Police again, this time different officers. Jack opened the door, a twinge of anxiety starting in his stomach.

"Doctor..." The taller officer glanced down at his notepad. "...Medley?"

"Yes?" Jack shifted his glance between them, first one and then the other one, a smaller man with a face that bore the traces of bad acne.

The first officer frowned and looked at his partner. "You called? About a half-hour ago? You have a—"

"She's gone," Jack said, blurting it out.

The tall officer looked up from his notepad. "Gone?"

"I mean," Jack said, "you're too late."

"Look, er, Doctor Medley..." The other man had stepped forward. "We got a call about, oh, about 30 minutes ago now saying you had a possible murder suspect here and that we should collect her. We got here as fast as we could, okay?" He stopped and shook his head. "It's like *Doctor Zhivago* out there, you know what I'm saying? People are actually skiing in Times Square for crissakes. We got here as fast as we could, so, you know, if—"

"No, you don't understand. She's actually gone. The other policemen...*they* took her."

The officer frowned. "Other policemen? How long ago?"

Jack shrugged. "Ten, fifteen minutes. I remember thinking you'd—*they'd*—got here fast...the weather and all." He pictured the two men who had called at his door—just like these two—both in uniform, both in caps, both wearing badges. He could see their names—or at least one of them—in his mind's eye.

"One of them—thin, good-looking guy—his name was Madrid." Jack shrugged his shoulders. "I remember thinking, you know, Madrid? Sunny?"

The two policemen looked blankly at him.

"You know...Madrid? It's in Spain...hot..." He pointed back into the office at the window. "With the snow, it just seemed kind of funny."

The tall officer's face hardened. "Look, if she's in here Doctor—"

"She isn't here. I told you."

The cop's eyes burned into Jack's. "And the other guy?"

"The other guy was..." What was he? He was just a cop. Jack

smiled a weak and apologetic smile. "I don't know. He was a cop...just a cop."

"You get his name maybe?"

Jack closed his eyes and called up the image again. He could see both of the men's shields and, yes, he could make out some part of a name...Hen-something. "Hen-something?" he said, opening his eyes. He shrugged again. "Henderson? Could it be Henderson?"

The tall cop looked at his partner and some kind of recognition seemed to pass between them. He turned back to face Jack. "Hennessey?"

Jack nodded. "Yes, Hennessey. I think it might have been Hennessey." He ran his hands through his hair and realized he was very tired. "But...you know, I can't be absolutely sure."

The small cop—Jack saw that his name was Garbezie—flicked the guard off his holster. "You mind if we come and take a look around, Doctor Medley?"

Jack stood back and waved them inside. Officer Garbezie drew his gun and slid along the wall into the reception office. The other one—Manners, his shield said—stayed with Jack.

A minute later Officer Garbezie re-appeared from Jack's office and holstered his gun. "I don't know what's going on here, Doctor Medley, but I'll just put it down to cabin fever, okay? Let's go, Jimmy."

"But...wait a minute...you can't just—" Jack had suddenly noticed the little patches of water outside his door, down on the floor by the men's feet. He looked up and saw that their tunics were wet. The snow was still falling outside and their tunics were wet. But the tunics of the first two men had been completely dry. Perfectly pressed, spot-lessly clean and completely dry. And it had not stopped snowing for about twelve hours.

"So who were those guys?" he said.

Officer Garbezie smiled without warmth or humor. "Officers Madrid and Hennessey were killed in active service about two years ago. I don't know what game you're playing here, Doctor Medley, but we're tired and—"

"Game? I'm not playing any game here...I—"

"You called in to say you had a suspect here for collection," Garbezie continued. "When we arrived you unlocked the door. The suspect is not here. If she ever *was* here, then you must have let her out and re-locked the door." He shrugged. "Then there's the little matter of the dead cops." He shook his head and *tut-tutted*. "You've been lis-tening in on police wavebands Doctor Medley."

Jack frowned. "Listening in on—"

"Oh, you didn't hear about the investigation?" Officer Garbezie slapped his forehead theatrically. "Oh, you didn't happen to hear that on your radio. Tsk tsk. Well, it just so turns out that those officers have been dishonorably discharged...posthumously. Never happened before—least not in our precinct."

"Turns out they were taking lookaway-money for a dealing syndicate operating out of Jersey," Manners added.

Garbezie shook his head. "Lot of dead kids. Not popular...you know what I'm saying? When they were killed, they were heroes but now..." He shrugged. "Now they're just dead meat—*tainted* dead meat."

The other officer reached out a hand and patted Jack's shoulder. "Seems to me like you been spending too much time with the wrong kind of people, Doc." He smiled a smile that was entirely without warmth and adjusted his cap. "Maybe you ought to try get out more."

The men turned around and started off along the corridor.

"But, if they were somebody else—imposters maybe—where *are* they now?"

Without turning, Officer Manners shouted over his shoulder. "The snow was banked up against your entrance Doctor Medley, about 12-15 inches. Smooth and untouched. Nobody has either left or arrived here for hours."

Jack waited until the men had turned the corner at the end of the corridor and then he listened to the sound of the fire-escape door slamming behind them. Suddenly it seemed very quiet. He turned back to face the empty office.

Outside, the wind had increased and the snow was billowing against the glass in thick flurries. Even from where he was standing he could hear its plaintive moan...the softly insistent sound of torment.

"WE MAY NOT PAY SATAN REVERENCE, FOR THAT WOULD BE INDISCREET, BUT WE CAN AT LEAST RESPECT HIS TALENTS."
—*Mark Twain*

The Holding Cell

Jack Ketchum

O nly one of them looked or acted crazy.

Only one of them even looked dangerous.

Two out of six, he thought.

It could be worse.

The door slid shut behind him, clanging into place.

"Cell," muttered the crazy guy, head swaying side to side, his long matted hair swaying too. That was how he knew the guy was crazy—saying "cell" like that and swaying back and forth. "You're in it now."

Well, he knew that too.

The walls of the holding cell were cinderblock, painted white. Before that they had been red. The underpaint showed through like veins in a bloodshot eye.

"You're in it now."

He walked past them and sat on a wooden bench in back, one of only four benches for the seven of them, aware of their eyes on him, on his new silk shirt and two-tone Paul Stuart shoes. *How come they didn't take the laces? he thought, along with his belt and tie and blazer.*

You could hang yourself with a pair of laces, right?

Not that he was about to hang himself over a DUI. Even if it was his first. Still, he considered it a strange omission.

Somebody else could hang you.

The others were all wearing jeans and running shoes in various states of repair. Teeshirts. A black kid in a tie-dye muscle-shirt. Even the little thin guy in back with glasses—jeans, a teeshirt and running shoes. Variations on a theme. What had he expected? Imagination? Everybody but the tall, sandy-haired guy sitting in front, across from the enormous sleeping fat kid. The sandy-haired guy was wearing prison orange and a red ID bracelet on his wrist. He looked like a hospital attendant, only nastier.

He did have the Reeboks, though.

He was aware of class distinctions.

The cell smelled of pine disinfectant, human shit and more faintly, urine. A metal-frame toilet sat in the middle of the room—aside from the benches its only item of furniture. Apparently it had been recently used. He hoped he wouldn't need to.

He sat back against the wall, closed his eyes and tried to sleep. The walls were moist, damp, almost sticky. But he knew that sleep was the best thing now. Sleep would see him through.

It was going to be a long night.

His arresting officer, J. Johansson of the SPD, badge number 42789, had explained to him that under Florida State Law DUI carried a minimum of eight hours dry-out before you could even make bail.

It was now, he guessed, about three in the morning. That was only an estimate. They'd taken his watch and he'd seen no clocks around anywhere. Already his sense of time was tenuous. Probably they had planned it that way. But assuming it was three that meant it would be eleven, minimum, before he could get out of there, even if everything was all right with Ann, if she'd found her way home all right and was working on bail.

And that was not wholly certain.

She was new in town for one thing. Brand new job in a brand new State. Didn't even know all the streets yet. And the layout of the town didn't help. From what he could see it was a fucking maze—old bumpy roads intersecting into new stretches of highway, half of them one-way, the other half unmarked. Swamp to the left and swamp to the right.

He bet these roads *ate* out-of-towners.

He wondered where she was. Or if she even *knew* where she was.

It wasn't her fault. He couldn't even blame her for getting them lost and then telling him to turn when it was really too late to turn, so that he had to slam on the brakes and veer from the left lane into the right, which was what had got him noticed by the cruiser in the first place. She was new. He was just a visitor. It was a case of the blind leading the blind, both of them drinking—moderately, he'd thought, and then only wine—at her office Christmas party.

He'd blown a hefty .165 on the intoxilyzer.

He guessed that, moderately or not, seven to eight hours was a lot of drinking.

Jesus. I hope you made it, Annie…

Because there was also the fact that she'd given the cops one hell of a hard time. It wasn't too difficult to imagine her sitting in county jail herself—women's division. He remembered her leaning out the driver's side window, halfway out the window, looking like she was about to climb out the rest of the way and punch somebody as they told him to recite the alphabet and close his eyes and touch his nose and walk the line heel to toe, heel to toe, frisked him and cuffed him and stuffed him into the squad car. He remembered her screaming, what the *hell* are you *doing* to him? crazy about her for her relentless Irish temper even as he was scared for her when Johansson said to *get back in the car! Right! Now!* hand on his revolver and command-voice up full throttle, no doubt fully aware that he would not be the first or last cop to be blown away by some irate lady on the occasion of her husband's arrest.

He was worried about her. She was angry. She was easily as high as he was. And as of a few minutes ago, she was not home.

At the station they'd booked him, printed him, taken mug shots, relieved him of his cigarettes and valuables, frisked him a second time, read him his Miranda, had him sign six or seven forms he was much too wired and basically disoriented to even bother reading, questioned him, and then allowed him his phone call.

He left a message on her answering machine. *Help!* probably sounding a lot more cheerful than he felt because by then the headache had kicked in in a big way and he was cold without his blazer, shivering with nerves and the cold damp of the station house, and he had just been booked for committing a crime for the very first time in his forty-five year-old life.

He felt no guilt about it. He had somehow contrived to feel guilt about almost nothing these days.

He could try to phone again later, they said.

Great.

It was something, he guessed, to look forward to.

He gazed around the holding cell. He did not like the look of the crazy guy, who was unfortunately sharing his bench, sprawled across it lying on his back and leaving him only a narrow spot against the wall, staring up wide-eyed at the ceiling, eyes glazed, pupils darting like flies trapped under milky glass. He did not like the way the lips moved soundlessly.

"Whatcha in for?"

It was the guy sitting across from him.

The guy looked middle-aged, maybe fifty-five—and harmless

enough. His jeans and Nikes were new and clean and he did not seem to need to glare or mutter.

"DUI."

The guy shook his head knowingly. "Me too," he said. "You want to hear the worst fucking thing though? It was my goddamn *wife* who turned me in. You believe that? I go out for a six-pack, she calls the cops and tells them I'm fucking drunk out there and driving without a license. Tells them right where I'm headed. Do you *believe* that shit?"

He had the attention of everybody in the cell, all except the fat kid up front sleeping off his drunk. Even the crazy guy had turned in his direction. Everybody smiling. Amused.

The guy himself was not amused.

"I get out of here, I'm gonna cut her *tits* off!"

"First time?" It was the sandy-haired guy wearing prison orange. Getting up and walking over, laughing. Then squatting, digging in his shoe and pulling out a cigarette from one side and a book of matches from the other.

He took a glance toward the narrow cell window, cupped the smoke and lit it.

"Nah."

"Guess you should of cut 'em off last time then."

"You're right. I should've. Jesus! I been dying for one of these! What you in for?"

He took a deep drag and passed it to the guy. He spoke with a deep southern accent. "Skipped bail on a second-offense armed robbery. Guess I'll be around awhile. Fuck it."

They smoked in silence, waving the cigarette like kids in a high school boy's room to make it less conspicuous.

The crazy guy got up, walked over and held out his hand. The hand was black with matted filth. "Mind?"

"Fuck it." The con in prison orange handed him the butt. "Finish the damn thing."

The crazy guy took two deep drags. Then the cigarette disappeared into his clenched fist, ember and all. He lay down again. The fist went up to his mouth. He commenced chewing.

They're all crazy, he thought.

It occurred to him, not for the first time, that he could have been in bed with Ann by now. Every fine, smooth, fragrant inch of her.

Just sleep, he thought. *Get some sleep. In a while try to make your call again. Meantime, try to pass the night. Sleep. Get yourself lost. Get the hell out of here…*

And miraculously, he did sleep.

Maybe it was the alcohol working or the late hour or the nerves exhausting him or all of these together but he slept, head pressed back against the sticky cinderblock wall.

He slept fitfully. Waking often.

There were snatches of conversation.

"Jesus! What time is it? You'd think they'd give you a fucking *clock* at least!"

"...ran a warrant for beating up on her."

"...second offense. Let's see. I think it's a $500 minimum and ninety days. I'm not sure though..."

"Did you *taste* that stuff? What the hell was that stuff?"

"Peanut butter."

"*Peanut* butter? The fuck it was peanut butter!"

From time to time the door would slide open and a guard would call one of them outside. They'd be gone a while and then come back holding a single sheet of paper. He was not even curious as to what was written on the paper. He assumed he'd find out, eventually.

Instead, he was wholly engulfed by a single urgent need—to escape the whole damn thing. The only escape available to him was sleep. The crazy guy was snoring. So was the kid with the enormous belly. He envied them the thoroughness of their immersion.

Finally, he heard his name.

He got up and saw that they'd all been sleeping, the sound of his name and the sliding metal door blinking everyone suddenly awake.

The sullen black kid in the tie-dye muscle-shirt was gone. It didn't even occur to him to wonder where or why. The rules here, the everyday reality of the place, were unknown to him.

In the hall a guard handed him two sheets of computer paper mounted on a clipboard and told him to sign the top copy. The other one was his. NOTICE TO APPEAR FOR ARRAIGNMENT the papers said. They noted the charge, the date, his docket number, and the amount of his bond. The bond was all that interested him — $369.00. He felt relieved. It was not going to be a problem. Ann would have that much on hand.

If he could reach her.

"Can I try that call again now?" he asked.

"What call?"

"I couldn't get through before. They said I could try a little later."

SHIVERS

The guard looked at him without expression and nodded. He unlocked and opened the holding cell door.

"I'll let you know."

The door slammed shut. He walked back inside. The holding cell was silent. They sprawled across the benches. The belly of the fat kid looked like it was melting all around him under the dirty white teeshirt. The crazy guy was still snoring. Despite the missing black kid there was no more room for him now than before.

He decided to try the cell floor. At least he could lie down.

He curled himself up into a fetal ball, one arm raised to pillow his head. And in moments he was asleep again. A strange half-sleep in which he was partly aware of his surroundings and even of himself thinking, of his mind working, and partly not.

He thought he had never slept like this before in his entire life.

It was as though he was allowing himself to disappear. Hoping to disappear off the face of the earth.

You are very depressed, he thought.

It didn't take a degree in psych to figure what this was. It was total avoidance, total *immersion* in avoidance—some waking part of him considered this even as he was dozing. He felt thin inside as a piece of paper, weightless, waiting to be lifted out of here. By contrast, his head felt thick and heavy with sleep, as though he'd been drugged. He didn't sense any contradiction there. It seemed only right in this place somehow. The only thing, sensibly, to be and to do.

The next thing he was aware of was that somebody was moaning. He shut it out.

The sticky concrete floor seemed to soften, to allow him to sink deeper. He slid into blank empty space and shut it out. Shut it all out.

Then he heard the sliding door again, and his name.

The door must have been opened at least once before that—the little guy with glasses was gone now too, his bench looking oddly desolate and sad. He hadn't heard anything but that didn't surprise him. Probably it was mostly the sound of his own name and not the door opening that had roused him even now. His hangover was raging. Wine, he thought. You ought to have known better. His head pounded. He was trembling.

He dragged himself outside.

It may have been a different officer, maybe not. In his condition they were all looking pretty much the same.

"This way," he said.

They turned a corner. He dialed at the telephone on the grey concrete wall.

She picked up immediately.

"Ann?"

"My god, Richard! Are you all right?"

"I'm freezing, I'm exhausted, my head is killing me. But yeah, I'm all right."

"Listen. I've been out of my *mind* here. They won't tell me *anything*. I've been calling and calling and...all they keep saying is you're not on the computer yet. It's like you're not even *there*, Richard!"

He smiled. "Oh, I'm here. Believe me."

"Have they set your bail yet?"

"Yes. Three hundred sixty-nine dollars. Can you manage it?"

"Of course I can manage it. I'll get down to the bank right now."

"Don't hurry. I'm not getting out of here for a while. According to Johansson they keep you eight hours minimum from the time of arrest—or booking. I'm not sure which. What time's it now?"

"Almost seven."

"Jesus. Four more hours."

"Oh god, Richard. I'm so sorry!"

"Hey, it's not your fault. It was just bad luck, that's all."

"If I hadn't told you to turn..."

"I know. And if I didn't have some squad car behind me. And if we hadn't been drinking all night. And if I hadn't come down here in the first place. Forget that. You can drive yourself crazy."

"Do you regret it?"

"What?"

"Coming down here."

"No. I *regret* being arrested."

"You swear?"

"I swear. Not for a minute."

He could hear her thinking about that. And the truth was he really did have no regrets in her regard. After so many months of separation he'd been surprised to get the invitation in the first place. And even more surprised at how glad he was to see her.

Before she left him there'd been nothing but fighting, for a long while. Probably, the marriage had made them both too...passionate for their own good about one another's faults and neglected the virtues. He didn't know about her, but he now found himself less frenzied. A year apart had taken care of that. It made for easier sledding. If he missed the sheer intensity sometimes—and he did—he didn't miss the drunken anguish that, all too often, went along with it.

He felt softer now, more flexive.

He hoped that in her own way so did she.

"All right," she said. "I'll try to get a couple hours sleep and set the clock for eight-thirty. By nine-thirty I'll be at the bank and down there by ten with the money. Just in case you can get out early. I just wish they'd get you on the goddamn computer. You've been there four hours! How long does it take?"

"I guess they figure they've got time."

The guard was tapping him on the shoulder, motioning him back inside.

"Gotta go," he said.

"Richard? Is it horrible?"

"Bearable. I'm trying to sleep as much as possible."

"Good. I miss you. I'm sorry. I'll see you soon, all right?"

"Okay."

He hung up. Wondering, strangely, if he'd ever actually see her again.

Get a grip, he thought.

Good god.

Inside the holding cell the fat kid was still snoring, looking bigger and softer than ever, his breasts spread out across the sides of his flabby biceps. The con in prison orange was asleep directly across from him. But the crazy guy was wide awake.

"*Cell*," he said. "*You're in it now.*"

Right. That again.

The eyes darted warily. The man closed them and lay back down. Seconds later he was snoring too. All three of them were snoring. It would have been funny if it hadn't been so disgusting. Like the toilet sitting there in the middle of the room was disgusting.

The guy whose wife had turned him in was gone.

Richard was glad for the empty bench.

He lay down. The bench smelled of alcohol and aftershave. The scent of the guy who'd been lying there.

As though part of him had bled right into it.

«« —— »»

It came without warning.

One minute he was trying to get comfortable, trying to relax against the pounding in his skull—and suddenly he was asleep again.

It was like entering a black empty room without doors or windows, a room that swayed and shifted like the surface of a pond under a breeze, as though he were riding that surface, a place where neither day nor night nor time of any recognizable sort even existed—or if it did exist, could possibly matter—just silent, constant, nearly unnoticed movement, some slow-moving drift that seemed to well up out of the vague internal shiftings of the earth like magma. He had a sense of indifference, not only his own indifference but something in the nature of things which absorbed without judging, without sense of right or wrong, strong or weak, clean or dirty or even yes or no. It was as though the world were a stewpot—on simmer. And he was a scrap of meat.

Breaking down.

The holding cell, he thought.

Holding. Cell.

The words sounded odd in his head.

And then he was the fat kid—no, he was the fat of the fat kid and he was melting, scalding human gravy running all along the bench and over the floor, pooling at the wall, an obscene sticky mess running off over muscle and bone, a surprising lot of muscle for a kid so fat—but who was he to criticize. He was the juice. He was the problem.

He woke. The door clanged shut.

The fat kid—the *real* fat kid—was gone.

The con in prison orange sat up on the bench across from him, waking, rubbing his eyes.

Then staring at him.

"You ever been in a holding cell before?" he said.

Richard's mouth felt dry. "Unh-unh."

"Shit. I'd ask *him* but he's fucking bonkers." He nodded toward the crazy guy, still sleeping. "Thing is, something ain't right here."

"What?"

"Asshole. If I knew that, I wouldn't be talking to you, would I."

Richard decided not to comment.

"Ought to be more of us, for one thing. Usually you get people parading in all night. Second thing, I never been in this *particular* cell before and I thought I seen every damn one of 'em in the whole damn county. Third thing is, where the fuck's everybody got to?"

Richard shook his head.

"You make your phone call?"

"Yeah. A while before. You were sleeping."

"I been sleeping like the fucking dead. You gettin' bond?"

"Bond?"

"A bail-bondsman. You getting a *bail-bondsman.*"

"My wife...my ex-wife. She's—"

He laughed. Surprisingly it was not an unpleasant laugh. "You got an ex-wife'll make your bail? Very nice."

He smiled. "That's if they can find me on the damn computer."

"Computer?"

"As of around seven I wasn't on it."

"Bullshit! You're on the fucking computer the minute you step *into* this place. *Before* that. In the fucking car you're on the computer. That's bullshit!"

"That's...that's what they told her."

"It's a fuckup. It's some fuckup then."

He shook his head again, ran his hand through his thinning sandy hair.

"This fucking place..."

"*Cell*," said the crazy guy. "*You're in it.*"

There was an edge to his voice this time, something sort of excited, and they looked at him. He was sleeping, talking in his sleep.

"You're in it," he said. He was tossing on the bench, legs wobbling every which way like they were made of rubber.

"Asshole," said the con. He lay back down again.

Richard's head felt worse than ever—soft, eggshell-thin. He pressed it gently back against the wall.

I swear to god, he thought, *I'll never drink again.*

Not wine at least.

He closed his eyes for a moment.

And it was as though he could see through the eyelids, a thin pale red-veined film over everything, over the con on his bench and the crazy guy on the other, over the gleaming metal toilet in the center of the room and the door with the single small window behind it—as though he were the blood-shot walls of the cell itself. Watching. He could even see himself sitting there with his legs spread wide, shirt and trousers wrinkled, his head pressed to the damp wall.

He presumed he was sleeping again, his access to sleep just that sudden.

It shocked him, that access. Frightened him.

Nobody should sleep like this, he thought.

Nobody.

What was it the con had said?

I been sleeping like the fucking dead.

What kind of sleep was this anyway?

And what kind of dream where he could watch them, both the con and the crazy guy, start to struggle weakly—could see *himself* start to struggle—against the shifting tides that were the room—faces, bodies going soft, growing indistinct and somehow particulate, breaking down, blending *into* the room, *part* of the room, looking like something he'd once seen alive through a microscope, some amoebic protoplasmic bacterial *something*, even the toilet losing its precise form now, dark inside the gelatinous mass, its flowing nucleus.

A shitter. The nucleus of a cell.

He almost laughed.

Instead he screamed soundlessly and tried to wake.

The con was on his feet—or on his knees—his feet and calves sinking suddenly into the shimmering floor, absorbed instantly to the knee. For a moment the flesh of his face resolved into an expression of fear and astonishment, then slipped away as the con himself slipped away somewhere in front of what moments ago had been his bench.

The crazy guy was already gone.

An atomic swarm like thousands of tiny dots on an empty tv screen, drifting.

He felt a helpless panic.

He looked down. The silk shirt, the beltless pants, the socks. All sinking into him. His flesh blood and bone sliding gently back into the wall, into the bench, the bench sliding down into the quivering shifting floor...

He fought his assimilation for quite some time.

The Paul Stuart shoes were the last to go—laces and all. He was actually glad to see them.

Inside the holding cell, almost everyone was wearing Reeboks. Thousands of them.

He guessed it didn't hurt to be different.

The Wager

Thomas F. Monteleone

For an instant, Gordon Kingsley had forgotten where he was. Had he drifted off to sleep? Impossible! After what he'd just experienced...no, it was plainly impossible.

And yet he'd felt himself blink, felt his entire body spasm, as though he'd been abruptly awakened, as though from a trance.

The darkness held him like a fist, and although he had not reached out to touch the walls of the coffin, he knew the prison of its wood loomed terribly close. He wished he had his watch with its luminous dial, just to check the time. But that would be against the rules.

The bastards, he thought with amusement. They're all probably jowl-deep in their *Wall Street Journals* by now, but Gordon knew at least one of them would be monitoring the simple control panel Huntington had designed for this particular little adventure.

That was one of the conditions—someone would always be monitoring both of them in case there was either (a) an emergency, or (b) capitulation.

Gordon Kingsley cleared his throat, wondering if the sound was loud enough to arouse whoever might be listening. No, that's right; they couldn't hear him unless he flicked on the mike. He thought about turning on the light, but that would enact one of the other conditions— for every minute you kept your light on, one was subtracted from your total time.

No, he thought. For now, I'll just lie here in the dark and think about why I'm here...

Murder is always murder. So is theft.

Gambling, however, is one of those fascinatingly odd pastimes that wears the clothes of its practitioner. If you're tuxedoed to the nines

145

at Barclay's Casino in Soho, playing roulette and baccarat all night, you're the jaunty gentleman. But if you're throwing dice behind the YMCA or getting toasted at Aqueduct's two-dollar window, you're the biggest scumbag in Manhattan. There is something elegant about betting with bankers and industrialists, but altogether tatty when you do it with steamfitters and housepainters. Gambling carries both its own social stigmata and imprimatur. It's not what you do; it whom you do it with.

And so it was with the members of The Colonial Club—the oldest men's club in New York, dating back to the earliest days of New York's inclusion into the original thirteen colonies. Gambling among its brethren was as natural as hand-rolled cigars or imported sherry. To hear a wager being offered or taken in the Club's drawing room was as acceptable as a market price being quoted. Topics ranged from the most mundane of sporting events to personal boasts of prowess to the outcomes of political and financial futures. Amounts ranged from paltry dinner tabs to portfolio items. In all, the Colonial Club found gambling to be a delightful pastime.

But sometimes, a wager could take on a new level of meaning, of competition, and perhaps an even sinister nature.

This kind of bet was rare, and usually only witnessed between men who were sworn adversaries. There are certain types of men who require a personal nemesis to give them the energy needed to live life most fully. Men such as these are resolutely bored with the usual challenges in life; they have met these impediments and have vanquished them. In other words, they have made their fortunes, raised their children, divested themselves of sour marriages, traveled the world, and proved their manhood in all the other customary ways.

To truly enjoy their jaded lives, men such as these need a personal demon, someone to hate, someone they can best at all costs, someone whose misfortune will make them feel good.

The Colonial Club stabled men such as these—J. Gordon Kingsley and Henry Pearce Huntington being the most notorious.

Gordon had taken an instant disliking to Huntington the moment he'd met him. The Huntington family had only come into their wealth during the Thirties. Before that, they'd been a loose circle of laborers and railroad louts. The worst part of this history was that Huntington continually blared out his nouveau riche status, as though he were proud of the fact that his grandfather swung from the back of a caboose. He may as well have declared that his ancestors swung from trees. Gordon was certain that if he searched through the Huntington genealogical record, he would find more than one Irishman in the woodpile, and that would more than account for the lack of Henry Pearce's manners and general sense of decorum.

At fifty-five, Henry Pearce Huntington was in remarkably good shape, boasting at the amount of exercise in which he indulged. Despite his suspected mongrel status, Huntington sported the finely-chiseled features of true nobility. This too irritated Gordon Kingsley, who had allowed himself to grow soft and weak as time and gravity stepped up their assaults. Indeed, everything about Huntington grossly annoyed Gordon Kingsley. Gordon found himself actually studying the man, watching his every move and hanging on his every word, searching for ever more reasons to loathe this poseur to true American aristocracy.

And so, Gordon Kingsley never let an opportunity pass wherein he might embarrass, chide, or challenge Henry Huntington. Not that the former had any trouble carrying on his end of the unspoken agreement; it seemed that Huntington found Kingsley's neo-Tory arrogance and his corpulent presence an equally hated target. If these men had lived in the age of dueling, they would have both carried more slugs than an uzi's magazine. Neither man could hurl enough insults at the other. They were the Ford and Chevy of their social set; the oil and water; the ying and the yang.

Tensions between them became the norm at the Colonial Club, and their tête-à-têtes became legendary sources of interest and amusement. A wager between the two men invariably meant bravado, guile, and a certain amount of spectacle.

The latest engagement, however, had no equal.

Huntington had been sitting in the lounge sipping, contemplating the onion in the depths of his martini, when Gordon had entered the room. Feeling flushed from the victory of their last showdown—a marathon poker game in which one or the other would clean out his opponent's $100,000 table stakes, Gordon had let loose on Huntington.

"So, Henry Pearce, how's it feel to be a hundred thousand lighter these days?"

Huntington forced a smile to his lips, enacted a shrug dripping with ennui. "A straight flush beats a full house every time, Gordon. I can live with that."

"What's that supposed to mean?"

"Only that any baboon can draw cards to his hairy belly," said Huntington, warming to the call to combat.

"I'm not sure I follow you, old man," said Gordon.

Huntington smiled. "Really? Well, follow this: don't start bragging about luck. Your winning hand had nothing to do with your skills or abilities—unless you've got a talent for leger de main?"

"Are you accusing me of cheating?" Gordon Kingsley's voice ascended the octave range.

One could almost hear the collective attention of everyone in the lounge shift to the molten core of their conversation.

"How declasse," said Huntington. "Of course not, enemy mine. What I mean is this: a reliance on luck cheapens the contest, don't you think?"

"Cheapens!?"

"Just so. However, I've been considering a wager that depends upon nothing but the sheer, tensile strength of our wills, Kingsley."

"How's that?"

"Have you ever read Poe's 'Premature Burial'?"

"It's been a long time—at Andover, but yes, of course. Why?"

"Ever think about what it must have been like for any of those poor bastards who woke up in their coffins, sunk six feet in black dirt?"

"What's the game, Huntington?"

"Ever think about what it would be like if you woke up in your coffin?"

Gordon paused, hesitant to say something, anything he might later regret. He didn't like the gist of their conversation. Something lurked beneath its polished surface. Something dark and slippery. Something dangerous. What the hell was his nemesis getting at?

"Earth to Kingsley...are you there, Gordy?"

"Yes," he said softly. "Yes, I've thought about it. Haven't we all?"

"I would think so," said Huntington. He sipped his martini with a measured precision, then stared at his adversary.

This made Gordon uncomfortable but he forced himself to look directly into Huntington's eyes. Something was going on behind them, dark and slick as Timkin bearings, and he had to fathom it out. He could not let his sworn enemy think he might be getting the best of him.

"Is that it, then?" asked Gordon. "I mean, come on now, Henry—what's the point of all this? All this talk of the dead and their coffins...?"

Huntington smiled. "Hold on! No one said anything about the dead..."

"No, I suppose you didn't. But what of it? What's the game, Huntington?"

Henry Pearce Huntington, that living monument to the nouveau riche, grinned like a Cheshire. "Simply this: do you think you could (1) stand to be buried in a coffin wide awake, and (2) stay down there longer than me?"

The silence that punctuated his question hung heavy in their midst. The eavesdroppers seemed to hold their breath as one. Could he be serious? Had he gone too far this time? What kind of a mind could even conceive of such a proposition?

Gordon scratched his nose, cleared his throat. A quick glance about the room confirmed the stolid gazes of his fellow Colonials— each one trying to seem less interested than the next, but attentive as hungry dogs nonetheless.

"What kind of a question is that?" he said, his words seeming to actually boom throughout the room.

"Just what it sounds like," said Huntington. "I've offered you the terms of a wager, Gordy. Are you man enough?"

"You're insane," said Gordon.

"Most likely. But I've got another hundred thousand that says I can stay down longer than you."

"What?!"

A soft murmur colored the room.

"If we both stay down for 30 days, we call it a draw." Huntington smiled. "What do you say?"

Again, the weighty silence enclosed as the room itself seemed to take anxious pause. They were all listening, all waiting to see what kind of a man he was. Kingsley had agreed to the sky-diving and the bungy-jumping and even the William Tell re-enactment, but this latest escapade, this one danced upon the wall of true madness. Gordon had always believed he was a touch claustrophobic, and just the thought of being in that kind of tight space made him shudder.

"Well, what's your answer, old sport? Have I finally called your game, or what?"

"Can I assume that you've already worked out all the details? And that you've put together a set of conditions?"

Huntington grinned. "After all this time, all the wagering we've done, how could you even ask such a question? But yes, I thought I might call them ground rules, eh?" He laughed at his small pun.

Gordon nodded, swallowed hard. "All right then...let's hear them."

"Does this mean you're on?"

Gordon hesitated only for an instant. "I'm game. One hundred thousand."

Someone coughed; the tension in the room spidered and cracked like an old windshield. Exclamations of shock and encouragement, salted with the odd deprecation, filled in the empty spaces between his thoughts. What the hell had he just agreed to? What came next?

Huntington smiled broadly, bringing together his hands in a steeple. "All right, Gordy. Here's the way I envisioned it. If something offends you terribly or strikes you as unworkable, just raise your hand and stop me. We can talk about it, okay?"

"Go on..."

Huntington hunched closer across the bar, warming to the subject. His eyes grew brighter, the voltage of his imagination having been stepped up a few notches. "Okay, here's the way I see it. Two coffins, buried side by side, you in one, me the other. I have a game preserve in Hansford, Connecticut. Plenty of land, we can do what we want there without any interference or prying of the locals. Anyway, we outfit them with some special equipment and supply lines."

Gordon raised a hand, feeling foolish for acting so obediently. "What kind of special equipment?"

"I think we'd want an intercom, and maybe a lamp of some sort. Then there's air, food, water, getting rid of waste. A system of buried tubes and cables should do it just fine."

Gordon shuddered again. The thought of being down there long enough to want to eat, to have to take a piss...who could last that long?

"And you solved these problems?"

Huntington nodded. "I'd say so. Studies confirm we could live on nutrient-enriched liquids for months if necessary. And we don't have to worry past thirty days, right? A catheter and a simple pump will take care of liquid waste, and there wouldn't be any solids—a good nutritionist could see to that."

Again the image of actually being in the coffin slammed into his thoughts like a left jab to his jaw. It was madness! No one could go through with it, he thought. And perhaps that was the rub—this was an elaborate joke on Huntington's part. An attempt to show him up, make Gordon look silly.

"What's the matter, Kingsley? Having second thoughts? I know what you're thinking, and I had a hard time getting used to the idea myself. All that dark earth on top of you, all around you, and that little tight, dark space for a home. The Brits have a name for coffins, you know—narrow houses! I'd say they're right, eh?" Huntington laughed, tossing back his head dramatically like the villain in a bad Thirties film. Gordon watched him, thinking he looked more than a little mad.

"No light, no sound. Just the hammerfall of your own pulse in your ears, and of course the faint burrowing of the worms, trying to get through to you!"

Again a murmur suffused the lounge. The Club members were getting their money's worth this day.

"Yes, I've thought about it," said Gordon, running his fingers through his pale, thinning hair. "and as bad as it sounds, I know I can outlast a loudmouthed showman like you."

"Well, we're going to see about that," said Huntington. "Any last questions?"

"Only one," said Gordon. "When do we start?"

«« —»»

...and so went the preamble to what now transpired.

Gordon stared upward in the darkness, noticing for the first time how he was already losing sense of spatial orientation. Were it not for the insistence of gravity, he wouldn't know which end was up. It made him think of a study he'd read somewhere—the Smithsonian or some other pop-science magazine—about subjects who underwent sensory deprivation tests. Seems that when you put someone in a special chamber that canceled all sense of smell, taste, hearing, feeling, or seeing, you were pretty well sure of pushing them off the edge of rational thought and experience. What usually happened, the researchers discovered, was that when a person cannot receive any sensory input from outside himself, he will create his own. Subjects reported seeing strange creatures, hearing bizarre music, etc.

Would that eventually happen to him?

And what of Huntington? If he went mad, how would he know Gordon had bested him?

Stop thinking about it. Just lay here and take it like a man. Right. Easy to say. Gordon had kept reminding himself that the best way to handle the situation was to try not think to about where you really were. Yes, of course, but that would be—

"I say, old sport, are you there?"

The voice was canned, electronically flavored, but achingly familiar. It poured from a speaker near Gordon's head. What was going on now?

"Kingsley, are you there? Don't tell me you've had your overdue coronary and we can just leave you down here?"

"Fuck you, Henry."

"Ah…! There you are! Good to hear your usual self."

"Would you mind telling me what the hell's going on?!" Gordon tried to sound most outraged, but honest to tell, he welcomed the human contact, even from a fool like Huntington.

Laughter filtered into the narrow house. "Did I forget to tell you we'd be connected by the intercom system too?" Huntington paused for effect. "Yes, Gordy, just a little extra bonus I thought up at the last minute. And, it's on its own channel, so anybody on the monitoring equipment can't hear us. Just you and me, buddy."

"You never cease to amaze me with your boldness, Henry."

"Thank you."

"I mean, why? What's this for? To irritate me? To amuse yourself? Isn't it a violation of your own rules?"

"Of course not! No contact with the surface, remember? We're both down here. Nothing said or agreed that we can't talk amongst ourselves…"

"Henry, I've known you too long. What gives?" There was a bad smell to things already. Gordon felt himself tensing up, he fought the urge to push upward on the solid lid just inches from his face. At any moment everything could just collapse in on him.

Soft laughter.

Then silence.

Henry Pearce Huntington was obviously going to play psych-warrior. Well, fuck him. Gordon could play too. Don't give him the satisfaction of a reply.

Seconds ticked past him like gnats crawling on his arm.

Finally the speaker crackled: "You know, Gordy, I'd bet it's never occurred to you that you've been had…"

Don't answer him. Ignore the nonsense he was suggesting.

"I mean, how do you know, really know that I'm down there with you, old sport? Sure you saw me get sealed in, just like you. But did you see my coffin get lowered into the ground and the dirt piled on…?"

How could that be? Impossible. The Colonials…there were witnesses…

"And don't think I'm not beyond paying off a member or two…or that there aren't larcenists in our little Club that are down on their heels enough to take a bribe or a little blood money…"

"Don't be ridiculous!" The words escaped him like air from a ruptured bellows. He hadn't wanted to sound so out of control.

Again soft laughter. "Is it, old sport? Well, you'd better hope so…"

Gordon waited for more, but there was only a deadly silence. The closeness of his prison suddenly gripped him, even in the absolute darkness. He thought about the PVC airshaft ever flushing the chamber with fresh oxygen, suddenly realizing what a totally fragile connection to the surface that tube represented. How easily it could be interrupted or sealed off with something as silly as a sock or as intentional as a cupped palm.

Huntington wasn't that crazy. Murder could not be explained away...

"We're an influential lot, we Colonials. A police inspector would be told to listen closely to whatever we said, Gordy. We—"

"Shut up, you moron!" Gordon stiffened, pushed against the sides of the enclosure. It was like the bastard was reading his mind, anticipating his every thought...

"Yes, Inspector, it was an unfortunate accident. We were engaged in a...a contest, if you will. Sort of an initiation into a secret order of the Colonials. Oh yessir, you know about such things. Yes, that's correct, they have them at places like Yale and Harvard, sir. And yessir, I do believe our current President is a member of a such a secret club. Well, at any rate, it was a terrible accident when the air compressor failed like it did...yessir, it was very tragic, and yes, we at the Colonial Club would certainly appreciate the lack of publicity concerning Mr. Kingsley's unfortunate demise..."

"I said shut up, Henry! You're just trying to shake me up." said Gordon, summoning up what strength remained to him. "What happened? You get down here and realize you're not going to be able to take it?"

A chuckle fell from the little speakers, clattered all about Gordon's head.

"You underestimate me, old sport. That's why you lose so many of these little wagers."

"What do you mean?" Gordon fought to keep the panic from his voice.

"Don't you know that if I'd really intended to outlast you, I'd have trained for the event long before wising you to the game! Why, I'd have been sleeping in a casket, with the lid up, then down, then spending a few hours every evening in my little narrow house— building up my endurance, acclimating myself to the environment."

Gordon was stunned by the concept. Of course! That's exactly what Huntington would do!

Without thinking, Gordon had put his hand to his mouth. It was an odd uncharacteristic gesture, made more awkward by the cramped area in which he could move his arm. He reached down to the toggle switch on his left and clicked on a soft halogen lamp.

Almost instantly, he wished he hadn't.

The light only served to emphasize the horrible closeness of where he was. The satin lining of the casket, with its sickly pearlescent shine made his stomach lurch.

Is this what it's going to be like?

Forever...?

He could see his stockinged feet seemingly so far away. What had it been like to actually bend and touch them?

So close.

Nowhere to move.

Nowhere to go.

Just stay right where you were. Just like this. Forever.

Thumbing the toggle switch, the darkness engulfed him and he welcomed it. The lamp, he realized now, had been another velvet trap set by Huntington. There was no comfort in its hard illumination, only a special kind of horror.

"Earth to Kingsley...come in..." the speaker crackled, followed by the softest hint of Huntington's sardonic laughter. "I know you're down there..."

The bastard! Gordon had no idea what to do. much less say. If what Huntington said was true, then no one knew they could converse like this. If his opponent was trying to psych him out and Gordon panicked, pushing the alarm button on the right side of the casket, then he would not only be scammed, but he would lose the wager.

But how could he even think about something so mundane? The primitive forebrain of his consciousness was screaming at him to preserve the life essence, to get out of this hellish prison at any cost. Fuck the wager! And fuck Huntington!

Surely he could prove that there had been tampering, collusion, or whatever you'd want to call.

"Earth to Kingsley..." His nemesis paused as if savoring the phrase. "You know that's quite a pun isn't it, under the, shall we say, 'gritty' circumstances..."

"Dammit, Huntington," he said softly, trying to retain control. "This is a shabby stunt. Trying to trick me into quitting the game. You must be desperate."

"You mean you still really believe I'm down there with you? Do you actually think I'd be stupid enough to let myself be interred in a bloody fucking coffin!"

More laughter. This time a brutal cascade full of mocking disdain.

"Especially when you consider where you are…"

"Why, Huntington? Why all this? Because you're such a sore loser, you had to cheat your money back? By conning me into quitting? Because if you think—"

The remainder of his sentence stuck in his throat. Silence held their conversation in a timeless void. Licking his lips, he forced himself to speak.

"…Huntington, what did you just say…? If I consider what where…?"

"You really are a piece of work, Gordon." Then more of that idiotic chuckling.

"Get to the point, man! What're you talking about?"

"Just two interesting points of fact. One—that you didn't inquire as to why I selected the particular location for this wager, and two—that you're interred in land once owned by your family. Bought and sold several times before I purchased it, of course."

"I'm afraid I don't follow you…" Gordon's mind galloped ahead of his words, of Huntington's reply. There was something ominous, something sinister in the man's tone. Even in the tight space, Gordon felt the leathery pouch of his scrotum tighten, contract.

"Your family is from Connecticut, Kingsley. Originally from the town of Hansford, which is the name of my game preserve. Strange that you didn't comment or make any connection… I half-expected you might."

What in God's name was Huntington getting at? "Hansford," said Gordon. "Should that name mean something to me?"

"Come on, Gordy, didn't your father ever tell you about the Hansford Sanitarium?"

"Other than the fact that Grandfather had built it, or that we owned it…no, why?"

Huntington clucked his tongue, sighed. "Did you ever remember hearing or reading about the Great Influenza Epidemic of 1918?"

"Huntington, cut to the chase, would you!? You can damn well bet I don't know what you're talking about!"

"It was a terrible thing. More than thirty percent of the population of the cities on the East Coast died in a 12 month period. A half million dead. People were dying so fast, nobody knew what to do with them.

"Nobody except your Granddad, that is…"

There was an absence, a distinct void, as Huntington's voice trailed off. Gordon felt himself almost lurch forward in the oppressive darkness. He knew he didn't want to hear what Grandfather might have done. And yet, he must. When he spoke, he sounded hoarse, weak, even puny.

"What did he do…?"

Huntington cleared his throat. "Well it seems your grandfather had a small army of Irish laborers working in his quarry near Wallingford. When the influenza ripped through their ranks like cavalry, the poor micks swelled the Hansford Sanitarium to bursting. When they started dying like blowflies, your grandfather didn't want to be bothered with the details and the expense of getting them all back to their Manhattan tenement families…"

"What're you talking about? What did he do?" Gordon shifted uneasily on the soft padding of the casket.

"A most ingenious solution, really. He had all those dumb Irishmen's bodies thrown into lorries and hauled off to a big quicklime pit he'd dug just beyond the trees on the Sanitarium grounds."

"Huntington, you're a lying bastard!"

There came a soft chuckle. "No, old sport, I'm afraid you're the one who's lying—right in the middle of that nasty old quicklime pit…"

Like a blade, something twisted in the core of his being. He could not keep a silly, melodramatic gasp from escaping him.

"Oh, I know it's been a while now, Gordy, but I'd say you're not very far from a big pile of those poor micks' bones.

The confines of the casket were suddenly smaller, the air staler. His entire world reduced to a six-foot wooden hull embarked upon a journey into madness. His skin felt dry, itchy. Places he couldn't reach had started tingling with histaminic urgency. Although clutched in darkness, Gordon's eyes remained tightly shut. He didn't want to think about what lay beyond the thin wood of his cell.

Just get out. Just open your mouth and start screaming and push the button and get yourself out of this fucking pit.

…No, wait, stay calm.

"As a matter of fact, being a betting man, I'd wager there's more than one angry Irish ghost twisted up in the dirt and the bones that're wrapped around you like a fist."

Stay calm. Talk it out. Get a grip.

"Is this what it's all about, Henry? All this business about the Irishmen— Let's see if I can figure this out. Let me tell you what happened: my grandfather threw yours in the quicklime, right? I always thought that crap about railroads was just crap. Your grandfather was nothing but a common laborer, and his son made his money bootlegging with Joe Kennedy's bunch!"

"Ah, Gordy, you make me proud, me boy! You're smarter than I ever gave you credit for. But did you ever imagine that all the years and all the wagering has been nothing but a setup?"

"What's that? What're you talking about?"

"Revenge, old sport. Someone said it's served best when served cold, and I have to agree with that."

"You're a madman! A fucking loony!"

Huntington chuckled. It was a lilting, almost musical sound. "But not as crazy as you're going to be before you ever get out of there. By the time they get to your fat ass, you won't even know it."

"I'm sounding the alarm," said Gordon, summoning up the most authoritative voice he could find. Fumbling for the switch at his right hip, he massaged the button, but didn't push it.

"Kiss your money good-bye, Gordy..."

Caressing the button, his fingers tapped it lightly, but not enough to actually depress it.

This was exactly what Huntington had wanted all along, had been manipulating everything to get things to this point. The slick son-of-a-bitch thought he was going to con him out of the money, but Gordon Kingsley would show—

The sound was so subtle, so soft, he almost missed it...

"So, where's the alarm, Kingsley? I'm sitting here waiting for you."

"Shut up, you blathering idiot! Shut-up-shut-up-shut-up!"

Huntington chuckled softly, but Gordon was listening to another sound—the barely audible sound of something scrabbling through the dirt, pawing, scraping, clawing...

He was suddenly aware of grinding his teeth together. The muscles in his jaws felt like piano wire, stretched to its limits. He tried to open his mouth, but couldn't. Something was wrong here. Something not right, and—

A new sound.

Not a scrape as much as a *tick!* along the side of the casket.

Along the outside.

Holding his breath, Gordon listened. The sound repeated itself. A rhythmic, series of tappings, as though something were signaling him in Morse code.

He had no idea how long he listened to the sound.

SHIVERS

In the darkness, it was everything. There was nothing but the tapping on the wood. Time lost its sense, its measure. Gordon lay in the thrall of the sound and nothing else. Inanely, the notion that knocking on wood brought good luck passed through him, the shock of conscious thought released him from the hypnogogia.

He pressed his hand against the left wall of the casket, felt the vibration of the impact. Something was out there.

But that was ridiculous.

Impossible.

Out there.

As he struggled to rein in his panic, he realized the tapping had ceased.

But only for an instant.

To be replaced by a scraping sound. A deliberate gouging of the wood as if by some sharp tool, like an engraver's awl, or maybe even a…

…fingernail, or a

…finger-bone.

He must have cried out, but had no memory of doing so. His mind full of white noise static, a radio burst of pure terror. A muffled voice spoke to him that could have been Huntington, but he was beyond the comprehension that accompanies hearing. The measured pace of the gouging and scraping had increased, faster and faster until it sounded like the machine-like digging of a dog for his bone. Kingsley, in fact, had begin his own gouging and scraping, having torn away the satin ceiling of his narrow house, and his own fingernails as he clawed at the wood just inches from his face. Maple has a sturdy grain and he'd made little progress, but he was beyond notice.

The thing that so furiously worked the wood at his left shoulder had fared far better.

When Gordon toggled his lamp and sounded the alarm, the last thing he saw was the splintered wood collapsing in…towards him.

«« — »»

"Oh yes, Inspector, most tragic," said Henry Pearce Huntington. "How could any of us have known old Kingsley's ticker was bad."

He stood in the four-car garage of his Greenwich, Connecticut estate. In addition to the police lieutenant, there were two uniforms and the county Medical Examiner, who was inspecting a body in a casket. The casket rested on a large table, trailing several tendrils of electric wire and plastic tubing.

The Inspector shook his head gravely. "Of course not, Mr. Huntington. I mean, who could know?"

Huntington nodded gravely. "And of course, I'm sure you're in agreement that there should be no publicity. Some of our most respected institutions have secret societies and initiation rites…"

The Inspector grinned. "Hey, what're you kiddin'? I heard the President was in one of these secret clubs when he was at Yale!"

"That is correct, sir," said Huntington, as he followed the Lieutenant to the side of the casket.

The Medical Examiner looked up, away from the slack jawed, sunken eyed corpse of Gordon Kingsley. His hair a dead-white, Einsteinian nimbus.

"Something scared the shit outta this guy," said the M. E.

One of the uniforms chuckled. "Guy must've been a flake," he said. "I mean, if he'd been buried in the ground, hey that would be one thing…but this guy, I mean, he was just layin' here in his buddy's garage."

Always Traveling, Never Arriving

Robert Morrish

Sweating profusely from the hot lights and the lingering late-night heat, Ken watched as the man reached up and grasped his nose, tugging rudely on it until it yanked free with a fleshy popping sound. Ken never took his eyes from the man, studying his every move as if prepping for a final exam.

"The essence of true horror," Ken finally said, "is the clown at midnight—at least that's what Robert Bloch said."

"Robert who?" said the man, still holding his nose.

"Robert Bloch. He was a writer. A great writer."

Bored, uncomprehending eyes gazed back at Ken.

"Never mind, it's not important."

The man dropped his ruddy red clown nose on the makeshift dressing table and continued working in silence, dabbing adhesive from his cheeks and his real nose.

"The nose is always important," tried Ken. "In *Killer Klowns From Outer Space,* the only way to kill the klowns is to shoot them in the nose."

The clown ceased the deconstruction of his face, twisting in his seat to look at his visitor, who sat awkwardly, long legs accordioned, knees almost reaching his chin, on a steamer trunk in the corner. "What the fuck are you talkin' about?"

Ken shrugged, felt fresh beads of sweat pop up on his forehead. "Nothing. Just trying to make conversation."

"Yeah? Well go make it somewhere else. Shouldn't you be takin' down tents, or somethin'?"

"Right, probably should be," mumbled Ken as he rose. "Sorry to bug you."

"Sorry," he tried again as he ducked out the RV's door, but the clown had already turned back to the mirror, a pint of amber liquid now tipped to his lips.

Ken was shaking his head as he swam out into the swamp air of a July Alabama night. *Maybe I should've told him how a clown was the personification of pure evil in Stephen King's* It. *Maybe he could've related to that concept.*

A quarter-moon shimmered low in the sky as he picked his way through the dark alleys formed between the maze of RVs and trailers, heading for the midway, where tear-down was well underway.

Every step of the way, he was carefully observed, like a microbe wiggling beneath the lens of a microscope.

Unaware of the surveillance, Ken stepped out of the shadows, pulling a pair of work gloves from his back pocket and venturing into the brightly-lit heart of the carnival.

《《——》》

Something less than three hours later, Ken was sweating even more profusely, although the night had cooled considerably by then. He could feel his heart pummeling his chest wall, although he couldn't say if it was from exertion or emotion. Darby Jo Conley's skin stuck to him like, well, like a second skin. It peeled away like old scotch tape as he rolled off her and onto his back. He looked over at her in the darkness, as if to reassure himself that she was still there.

"I hope we weren't too loud," she said, panting slightly herself.

"We? Who's this 'we'? I was quiet as a church mouse. You're the one who was making enough noise to wake the dead."

She threw a half-hearted punch into his stomach, giggled into his chest. "You bring out the animal in me."

Laughing, Ken reached down to the floor beside the bed, then stopped. "Shit."

"What?"

"I keep forgetting that I quit smoking. Old habits, you know."

Darby Jo brushed brown hair—hers, this time—back out of her face. Her hair was almost exactly the same color as Ken's, and virtually the same length, reaching almost to her shoulder blades, but where his was iron-straight, hers was a never-ending mess of twists and turns.

"How long has it been now?"

"Almost four months. I knew I had to quit before I joined the carnival; all the hours on the road, the dead time, strange places, strange beds—" He winked at her, the movement nearly lost in his long, narrow face, tinged by darkness and a well-past-five-o'clock shadow. "Hard to believe it's been that long."

"Since you quit smoking or since you joined up?"

"Both." He laid a forearm across his forehead, as if he were trying to block out a memory. "But in some ways, you'd think I just got here yesterday..."

Darby Jo scooted closer, placed a hand on his chest. "What do you mean?"

"Just the usual complaint." He sighed. "People around here—with the notable exception of you—act like I've got the plague or something. I tried talking to Ray after the show and he basically told me to fuck off. I don't know what they have against me..."

"It's not you. It's just how they are. They close ranks until you prove that you're genuine, that you're...part of the family. Believe me, it took them a long time to open up to me, too. I think maybe I had to prove to them that I was going to stick it out; that I wasn't going to be a first-of-May fly-by-night who split after a few stops."

Ken laughed. "Even though that's exactly what you intended to do."

"Well, yeah. It was a nice fantasy, but by the time we got to the west coast, I'd come to my senses. But you've heard that story..."

Ken nodded. Darby Jo had told him how she'd quit her job in Greensboro and joined the carnival, planning to stay only until they passed through Southern California, at which point she'd journey to Hollywood and land a job as a make-up artist. Somewhere along the way, in the endless miles between Gibsonville and Glendora, she'd realized the dream was more likely a delusion. And she'd grown to enjoy carnival life—the constant parade of new places and faces, and eventually the carnie folks themselves, once they'd warmed to her. And she was able to ply her trade as a make-up artist, helping prep the clowns and some of the least-abnormal freaks, although the majority of her work was in the various gaming booths, where her infectious smile and busty figure were a perpetual lure for the rubes.

Ken smiled as he remembered their first conversation. He'd been eyeing Darby Jo for days before he'd finally learned enough about her to provide a stake for an opening gambit. Her aptitude for teasing had quickly proven to be an excellent match for his fresh-faced gullibility. The exchange was still fresh in his mind.

Having learned of her affinity for make-up work, Ken had taken the first opportunity to compliment her on her handiwork...

"Oh come on, you're just saying that," she'd replied modestly.

"No, really. What you do with the clowns and some of the folks in the freak tent...like the AmphibiMan—that's amazing work."

"I don't do the AmphiMan's make-up."

"You don't? Who does?"

"If anyone does, it's him—but I'm not sure it's make-up. I've never seen him out of it. I don't think anyone has."

"Really...? Wait a minute, you're pulling my leg, aren't you?"

"No! What makes you think he isn't real?"

The conversation had gone on like that, Darby Jo continuing to tease and test, Ken gradually gaining the confidence to offer humor in return, grins increasingly tugging at the corners of both their mouths.

"What are you smiling about?"

"Just remembering our first conversation, when you were feeding me tall tales about the AmphibiMan."

"Tall tales? You mean to tell me that you still don't believe he's legit?"

"Don't even start with me," chuckled Ken. "I know my freaks."

"Oh, really?"

"Well, maybe I should say that I know freaks in, umm, popular culture."

"Popular culture? Meaning...?"

"Fiction, films, art..."

"Oh, really! Do tell..."

Ken gave her a wry look. He'd been avoiding this conversation since he'd started seeing her, but perhaps this was as good a time as any. "Okay, but just remember you asked for it... Freaks have always been popular subjects in the arts. The grand-daddy of them all is probably a story called "Spurs" by Tod Robbins. He shows the *real* monsters to be the so-called "normal" people in the carnival. The story later got made into a film called *Freaks* by Tod Browning, in 1932." Ken's words picked up speed, his enthusiasm a locomotive headed downhill.

"When they made the movie, they brought in real circus freaks to play some of the roles. Problem was, the showbiz people weren't too happy to rub shoulders with the freaks. In fact they were, and I quote, 'shocked and nauseated' to have to eat next to them in the MGM commissary. And the film itself didn't fare too well, either. First, they had to cut more than half an hour just to get it past the censors, and then after it was released, it got a lot of bad press and got withdrawn from circulation. And it was banned in Britain for nearly forty years."

"I guess that's not surprising," Darby Jo said, half to herself.

"Audiences want to see beautiful people on movie screens." Her expression of calculated skepticism was melting into something unidentifiable.

"True…but people seem to have a morbid fascination with freaks. After all, 'Spurs' and *Freaks* are just the tip of the freak iceberg. There have been at least three anthologies devoted to freaks, the most recent being F. Paul Wilson's *Freak Show*, as well as novels like Jeffrey Sackett's *The Demon* and Katherine Dunn's *Geek Love* and lots more short stories, like Nancy Collins's "The Two-Headed Man," and Robert Bloch's "Freakshow" and Ramsey Campbell's "The Next Sideshow" and…" He paused and snickered. "OK, OK—I can see your eyes are starting to glaze over. I'll stop now."

"It's not that. It's just…I thought you were kidding when you said… My gosh, Ken, how do you *know* all this stuff?"

He just stared at her for a few seconds, then looked down wordlessly at his hands, as if searching for an answer there.

"Ken? What? Is something wrong?"

He laid back, turning his gaze at the ceiling. She waited.

Finally, he said, "There's something I need to tell you."

"Oh-oh," Darby Jo murmured, with obvious worry.

"What? I haven't even told you anything yet. How can you sound so dejected?"

"Those words—'There's something I have to tell you'—and that tone of voice, and the way you won't look at me…? There's never anything good that comes after that."

"No, no." Ken forced a smile. "It's nothing all that bad. At least I don't think so. I haven't lied to you, I…just haven't told you every last little thing."

Darby Jo's expression didn't change but she sat up, pulling the sheet up almost to her chin. "OK, I'm braced. Go for it."

He finally met her gaze, mentally crossed his fingers that this would go well, and began. "Well, I didn't exactly get sick of academia like I said; didn't decide that I needed a total change in my life—that's not why I joined the carnival. I'm here because I'm writing a thesis on the carnival, and this summer is part of my research."

Darby Jo's mouth opened slightly, but otherwise she showed no reaction. Lacking alternatives, Ken plunged ahead.

"Specifically, my thesis is on carnival folklore and mythology, including its expression through popular culture. The freak-oriented material I was talking about is just one aspect of that. I…I didn't tell anyone because I was afraid they wouldn't agree to hire me in the first place, and even if they did, nobody would want to talk to me. 'Course, people have wound up not talking to me, regardless… But, anyway…I haven't told you, in particular, up 'til now because… I guess because I was afraid at first that you'd shut me out, and then the longer things went, the more involved we got, the worse it seemed that I hadn't told you already.

"But it's been driving me crazy not telling you," he added. "I couldn't stand to keep it from you any longer. I don't want to keep anything from you." Ken reached over, held her hand. She didn't pull away, and that was good. He watched her, waited.

"Well," she said finally, "I don't know what I expected you to say, but that sure wasn't it."

Ken had to fight the urge to jump in and further his explanation. Something told him that it was best to be patient, keep quiet, and let her mull it over.

Darby Jo shook her head. "In a way, I guess you're right—what you've been keeping to yourself isn't all that bad. But just the fact that you *have* kept it to yourself…I have to admit that hurts."

"I know, I know—and I'm sorry," said Ken. "I really am. If I could do it over, I would've told you a long time ago. I probably would've told everyone, and just taken my chances."

Darby Jo was quiet for a while. "So tell me more," she said finally. "Make me understand why this is so important to you."

That he could do. Ken propped himself up on one elbow to make his case, eyes alight.

"Like I said, freaks are just a small part of it. The folklore of the carnival as a whole is a powerful, pervasive thing. There's a huge amount of fiction that's been written about carnivals, and a lot of films. A lot of that material has been horror- and fantasy-oriented, and that's the focus of my thesis—examining the stories, and the themes expressed there, tracing them back to their origins in folklore.

"There's so much I could tell you. Just the books… For starters, there's Ray Bradbury's classic *Something Wicked This Way Comes,* and Charles Finney's *The Circus of Dr. Lao,* and Tom Reamy's *Blind Voices,* and Tom Monteleone's *The Magnificent Gallery.* Not to mention Al Sarrantonio's *Totentanz,* and Dean Koontz's *Twilight Eyes* and *The Funhouse,* and A.R. Morlan's *Dark Journey* and Theodore Sturgeon's *The Dreaming Jewels.*" He took a quick breath and continued, "Plus books by James Blaylock and William Gresham and others, and a ton of short stories, and…"

"Wow," interjected Darby Jo. "You know your stuff. But…it's not *just* a thesis to you though, is it? I can tell."

"No," he admitted. "I've been fascinated—some who know me might say *obsessed*—with carnivals and circuses ever since I was a little kid. Every year, a small carnival came to my hometown and set up in a field about a quarter-mile down the road from my parents' house. They'd be there three days, and I'd be at the carnival for every bit of that time, spending all the money I'd saved, soaking up the atmosphere, and generally driving the carnies crazy following them around and asking questions. I don't know why I thought it was so interesting, even back then. All I know is that I've always found something about carnivals to be captivating. My course of study is just one outgrowth of that, I guess."

Ken hesitated; there was more to it than that, but this didn't feel like the right time to dig his hole any deeper. He tossed back the covers suddenly, rising and stepping carefully across the small, darkened interior of the trailer. Opening a cupboard, he pulled out a file box, which seemed full to bursting, with paper and folders threatening to explode out at various angles. He sat back on the bed, one leg tucked beneath him, and switched on a small lamp.

"These are some of my files," he said. "Notes and drafts and Xeroxes and film stills and artwork—all sorts of stuff. I couldn't bring much of it with me, but I needed to have some of it."

Ken started to page through the collection, then thought better of it and just pulled out a stack and put it on Darby Jo's lap. She hesitated, then reached down and picked through it, settling on a group of film stills. Flipping through them, she recited the caption titles with a pronounced, melodramatic inflection: "*Berserk*; *Carnival of Blood*; *Circus of Horrors*; *ClownHouse*; *The Clown Murders*; *Psycho Circus*... Geeze, Ken, this stuff is almost enough to make me quit the carnival."

Ken smiled. "Yeah, it can be pretty gruesome at times." He eyed Darby Jo as she continued to flip through the stills, trying to gauge how his revelation was going. Not *too* badly, or so it seemed. If he was reading her right, it seemed she might just forgive him for his dishonesty. She seemed clearly intrigued by his story, and that might just be a smile threatening to have its way with her lips, but her posture was still standoffish, arms folding across her chest now as she put down the stack.

She looked up at him with a furrowed brow. "Some of these have 'circus' in the title. Are you lumping carnivals and circuses together in your thesis?"

"Good question. And the answer is no, not really. Although circuses and carnivals share a lot of the same elements and imagery and there're plenty of circus-oriented stories, too—like Alan Ryan's *Dead White* and Angela Carter's *Nights at the Circus* and Stephen King's "The Night of the Tiger"—my thesis is concerned primarily with carnivals *per se.* I do some comparing and contrasting, but the focus is on carnivals. "

"There's one other thing I don't understand," said Darby Jo. "If your thesis is about fiction and movies and folklore, why do you need to spend time traveling with an actual carnival?"

"Because the carnival itself is so central to what I'm writing. I didn't want to be writing about it from a distance, making points based on book references and old hearsay. I felt like I needed to really *experience* it all, first-hand—"

Ken stopped suddenly and peered out the RV's small, louvered window.

"What is it? What's wrong?"

"Nothing. I just thought I heard something."

"What?"

"It sounded like someone was laughing right outside the window."

«« — »»

Three weeks later, Alabama had been replaced by Missouri, the sweat-sticky weather supplanted by even hotter temperatures, and the locals' Southern drawls were beginning to give way to a nasal Midwestern twang.

Ken absently wiped sweat from his brow, a gesture that had almost become automatic over the course of the summer, as he ambled down the midway, enjoying some rare free time and mingling with the sizable early evening crowd.

The people came in at one end, traversed the midway, and eventually exited; ingested and disgorged—minus some cash—by the carnival. Bone-tired and feeling strangely detached from the hubbub around him, Ken watched the families and couples drift by, spores carried by an unseen wind.

In many ways, the last few weeks had likewise glided effortlessly by, an unending stream of brief stands in new towns, the tear-downs almost stepping on the heels of the setups. But when it came to Darby Jo, Ken would have to say that events had occurred at a glacial pace. After that night in the trailer, after Ken's 'confession,' she'd asked for some time to herself, to think things over. Ken had tried to give her the space she asked for, but every time he saw her, every time she averted her eyes and avoided his path, it tore at his heart. He'd never expected to become so attached to this girl, but it had happened, and now he was in deep, straining to grasp hold of their relationship again before it could be snatched away by a whirlpool of regret and disappointment.

But honoring her request and keeping his distance had ultimately turned out to be the right thing to do. A little over a week ago, Darby Jo had finally approached him and said she was willing to try to mend her trust; in the last few days, their relationship had become physical again, quickly moving beyond hesitant first kisses. There were still occasional awkward moments and far-away stares, but for the most part, it seemed she had been able to put the episode behind her. Her forgiveness had finally dismissed the gnawing feeling that had been worming its way into his gut, the dull ache that was threatening to put down roots in his head.

Of course, what remained unspoken was how his revelation—and more importantly his planned departure, looming only a few weeks ahead—affected any longer-term aspirations that either of them might have. They had studiously avoided the topic so far.

He didn't know if he would be able to just walk away from her when the time came. But he at least had a few more weeks before he had to face any such decision. In the meantime, he would savor his time with her. He kept himself busy when they were apart, clearing lots, pitching tents, selling tickets, generally losing himself in the odd variety of tasks that constituted his job, and squeezing in a few stray hours on his thesis when he could.

He walked on, watching the people who in turn eyed the attractions—the house of mirrors; the whirl-a-gig and ferris wheel and other rides; the haunted house; the freak show; the fortune teller; the gaming booths—each serving to attract certain patrons and repel others. It was fascinating, or perhaps just folly, to play psychiatrist and try to guess what it was that led individuals towards certain tents, and away from others.

Still idly scanning the crowd, Ken suddenly spied Mr. Morgan, the carnival boss, lingering in front of the freak tent, listening to the barker and watching the crowd's reaction to the pitch. He was always "Mister Morgan," never just "the boss" or "the manager" or any other term; and certainly never called by his first name. In fact, Ken wasn't even sure what his first name was. As Ken drew closer, the man suddenly turned toward him.

"Young Mr. Rivers." The greeting was pure Morgan; he affected the ways of earlier times in conversation and comportment. A big man, towering tall and massive across the chest and shoulders, with just a hint of padding from the years, he was made even more noticeable by the frilly tuxedo shirts he sported, covered by paisley vests; the piped pants tucked into shiny mid-calf boots; and a pattern of speech that seemed better suited for a much earlier decade.

"Mister Morgan," acknowledged Ken with a nod. "How're you?"

"Fine, just fine, thank you. And I imagine you're doing much better of late, eh?"

Momentarily confused, Ken could only stare back without speaking. It almost seemed as if he was referring to Ken's reconciliation with Darby Jo. But there was no way... They'd been careful to keep their relationship hidden, right from the beginning, not wanting to draw unwanted attention.

"Well, yes, I guess so. But why..."

Before Ken could finish his question, angry shouts erupted a bit further down the midway, on the far side of a knot of teenagers. Morgan wheeled and charged around the group, moving with a grace that belied his brawn. Somewhat reluctantly, Ken followed a few steps behind. He was hardly of the demeanor or physique to play the role of bouncer, but it was one of the many hats he occasionally had to don. Thankfully, there'd always been several other carnies around to lend a hand whenever such a need arose.

Once he maneuvered past the gawking teenagers, Ken saw Calvin, one of the game booth operators, facing off with two obviously drunk townies, one of whom was wielding a glinting object of some sort. Without hesitating, Morgan waded into the fray, grabbing the wrist of the man with the weapon and then swinging his other arm up underneath the man's elbow, driving it in a direction it was never meant to take, the movement ending with a sickening crack. The man's knife fell to the ground. A cry of pain had barely escaped his lips when Morgan spun him around and smashed his head into one of the wooden posts framing the booth.

The swift violence of the scene took Ken's breath away. And obviously that of the other drunk as well, for he held up his hands in surrender and began pleading for some mercy for his broken, bloodied friend. Calvin and two others swept in, herding the two towards the exit, none too gently, while Ken stood by feeling useless.

Morgan wiped his hands together with a dusting-off motion, a satisfied expression on his face. He turned to Ken and said, "Sometimes you have to inflict a little pain, to keep the carnival healthy. You'll learn that, when it's your time." He smiled grimly and walked away.

«« —»»

The carnival had at last managed to evade, at least briefly, the heat wave that had doggedly trailed them for much of the summer. They'd finally found a welcome patch of coolness in central Oregon, but with it came the forced realization of just how quickly the weeks had passed. Labor Day weekend was upon them, and soon, in less than two weeks, Ken was supposed to end his summer of first-hand research and return to every-day life of academia. Each day closer left him a little more unsure of what he would do.

The cool weather had also ushered in a crowd of rainclouds. Off-and-on sprinkles for the first couple days, but then last night a full-fledged rainstorm had descended on the carnival caravan as they headed from the last town to the next, connecting two dots on the map.

The caravan stretched out for what seemed like miles along a desolate two-lane highway, its length expanding at times, contracting at others, undulating around curves like a sinuous snake. Near the tail, Ken drove alone, clinging tenaciously to the faint tail-lights in front of him, struggling at times to keep the bulky RV from hydroplaning. His solitary status was often a blessing of privacy but had seemed a curse during the storm, when a shotgun navigator would have been welcome. He rode alone because he owned the RV, a fact that had helped convince Mr. Morgan to hire him in the first place, since Ken's presence wouldn't further cramp the quarters of the other carnies. Ken had expected the RV would be a major point in his favor; it was, in fact, why he'd arranged to purchase the aging, well-worn vehicle shortly before inquiring about a job.

The rain had lashed the caravan mercilessly during the last hour of their trek, forcing Ken and the other drivers to squint through spattered windshields while searching for unfamiliar landmarks and strange-sounding street names. The rain had fled with morning's arrival, but it had left their staging area—the open space just beyond the outfield fence of a ball-field —a bog of ankle-sucking mud dotted with deceptively deep puddles. Ken was out early with the other roustabouts, marking off spaces for the booths and tents and throwing down loads of sawdust along the paths and the wide track destined to become the midway. As he worked, Ken sang quietly to himself:

171

*"With a cannon blast, lightning flash, moving fast,
through the tent, Mars-bent,
    He's gonna miss his fall. Oh God, save the human cannonball..."*

"Wild Billy's Circus Story" was one of his favorite songs, and as usual it was in heavy rotation in his head. Finishing with the sawdust, Ken armed himself with tent stakes and a mallet. He and the song continued on, in auto-repeat mode...

*"And the ferris wheel turns and turns like it ain't ever
gonna stop,
    And the circus boss leans over and whispers into the little
boy's ear, 'hey son, you wanna try the big top?'
    All aboard, Nebraska's our next stop."*

«« —— »»

Three hours on, with blisters threatening to form around the calluses he'd already built up in weeks past, the tents and booths were mostly up and some of the men were heading over to help finish the amusement ride set-up. Ken got the OK from the crew boss to take a break. On his way to the mess tent for a cup of coffee, he went looking for Darby Jo. They'd grown more lax about being seen together, but still avoided any public displays of affection, hoping people would figure them to be good friends. Judging by the frank appraisals they received as they walked into the tent, those hopes were probably unfounded.

Finally seated with a tongue-numbing mug of coffee in front of him, Ken looked across the folding table at Darby Jo and said, "You look as tired as I feel."

"Gee, thanks. Aren't you a master of flattery?"

"Sorry...but you know I didn't mean it that way. I'm just so tired I can't think straight. Leaving as late as we did, and then with the rain slowing us down... I don't think I got to sleep until about four. And then I had to be up at seven."

"It was a long night," agreed Darby Jo. "I didn't think those police were ever going to let us leave Prineville."

"No kidding. Apparently cops in rural Oregon haven't heard of that whole 'innocent until proven guilty' thing."

Darby Jo sipped at her coffee. The tent brightened briefly as the sun threatened to emerge from behind a canopy of clouds. "Well, the carnival is automatically a likely suspect if somebody disappears while we're in town. Blame the outsiders, the wandering gypsies. What do you call it—xenophobia?"

"That's it. If you try to imagine yourself in their shoes, I guess the attitude isn't surprising. Not that that makes me feel any better right now." He closed his eyes for a second, opening them only reluctantly.

"You know…" started Darby Jo.

"What?"

"This isn't exactly the first time that this has happened."

"Not the first time we've been hassled by cops?"

"That, too. But I was thinking this isn't the first time someone's disappeared while we're passing through their town. Since I've been here, this is at least the fourth or fifth time—that I've heard about—that local police have come out to ask about someone who's missing. It seems like it happens a lot." She circled a finger around the rim of her mug. "You don't think anyone from the carnival could've had anything to do with the disappearances, do you?"

Ken shook his head. "People disappear all the time. The statistics on it are amazing. And you said it yourself—when anything happens, we're the usual suspects." Ken took a long swallow, mulled a thought. "And, let's face it, we've had, what, three kids join on this summer, all of them looking for a way out of whatever crappy little town they were in. It's no wonder carnivals are the first to be blamed."

Darby Jo sighed. "You're probably right.

"Is that what's going to happen to you?" she said suddenly. "Are you just going to disappear one night?"

Ken regarded her. "I guess you're asking what happens to us when I'm supposed to leave."

Darby Jo looked down, unable to meet his eyes.

"Don't think that it hasn't been on my mind a lot. More every day. I know we've been avoiding talking about it… The truth is, I don't know if I can leave you. I don't know if I can leave the carnival."

She looked up and gazed into his eyes. After a moment, Ken suddenly realized how quiet the mess tent had become. Every one of the half-dozen other people in the tent were staring at them.

«« —»»

If pressed on the matter, Jerry Guynes would have to admit that he'd had one too many. Okay, maybe two or three. Four at the most.

Absolute tops, five—but only if you started counting the shots and beers he and Mickey had put away before leaving home. Jerry had long ago learned that nothing or no one of any great value ever came to Baker, and he should have known better than to bother with this Podunk, half-ass, two-bit excuse for a carnival. Rip-off games, sad-sack freaks, and rickety rides that couldn't thrill a three-year old. The only things that saved the whole experience were the flask under Jerry's shirt and the fact that the Jaycees had a beer tent out front. And Mickey didn't care all that much for Jack Daniels, so that meant most of the flask was Jerry's. Speaking of Mickey, Jerry hoped the sonuvabitch wound up catching herpes from that Marlow bitch that he'd abandoned Jerry for. Here they were, supposed to be best friends, and yet there he went, chasin' after the first piece of tail waggin' in front of him.

Disgusted with his fickle friend, with the boring carnival, with the state of his life, and with his almost-empty and slightly-warm beer, Jerry did something about the latter, since that was the only item from the list that he had any control over. He pitched what was left of the beer into the nearest booth, drawing a yell from a big-titted booth babe.

"Sorry," he grinned, hoping she could tell that he wasn't, "I was aiming for that trashcan in the corner."

"That's not a trashcan, you idiot. That's a prize bin," she said, shaking wetness from her arm.

"You call that shit prizes? Those stuffed animals are god-damned Goodwill rejects."

At that, the woman turned and said something to someone in the shadows at the back of her booth. Jerry thought that might be a good signal for him to get the hell out of Dodge. He started to make a brisk beeline in the general direction of the exit, or at least he tried to. In truth, he was doing a fair bit of staggering, and not moving very damned fast at all. He could see word being relayed from booth to booth and carnie to carnie as he passed, some of them pointing and yelling at him. The exit was still quite a ways off and this wasn't working out quite like he'd planned. Evasive action was called for. Jerry veered toward the opposite side of the midway and cut between two tents, flailing his way under a rope with a "no admittance" sign and stumbling into the shadows.

His eyes were just beginning to adjust to the darkness when hands grabbed him from behind and he felt a lightning flare of pain on the back of his head…

<<«——»>>

It was starting to drizzle again as the two carnies dragged the inert form between them, up a short flight of steps and into a dimly-lit, well-appointed trailer. They lugged him across the interior, his feet scuffling over a thick, embroidered rug, and then dumped him unceremoniously at the foot of an ornate, high-backed chair, the size of which was equaled only by the man seated there.

The prone man groaned and forced his way up to his hands and knees. After a moment, he opened his eyes and saw a pair of polished boots just inches from his face. A voice boomed from above, knifing through his haze of pain.

"Feeling a little worse now, are we, young Mr. Rivers?" Morgan accented his question with a mocking laugh.

Ken forced himself to look up, even though the movement seemed to jam a crown of thorns down over his head, and sent dots scurrying across his vision. He could feel blood running down his neck.

"What…happened?"

"Why, we found you out, Mr. Rivers. Caught you red-handed, I'd say."

"Caught me? I didn't…"

"Save it. We've seen your handiwork. Most unfortunate—a perfectly good patron of the carnival, murdered for no good reason. He may have been a little drunk, and a tad annoying, but that was no reason to kill the poor man."

Ken tried to gather his thoughts. It seemed Morgan was right: there was no point in denial. It was time to speak directly. Everything had been leading up to this moment.

"There was a reason," he managed. "I did it for the carnival… You know why."

"For the carnival, you say? I'd certainly like to hear how you think that was an act committed for the carnival. Whatever would make you think such a thing?"

Ken could still hear the ridicule in Morgan's voice; he was no doubt enjoying making Ken squirm. But if Morgan needed proof of Ken's knowledge; of the depth of his dedication, then he'd give him just that.

"When I was ten years old, your carnival came to my town. My best friend was a kid named Jeffery. He got it in his head to sneak into the carnival after hours, spy on the carnies, maybe find something worth stealing. He convinced me to go along. But when the time came,

I got scared and stayed home. I figured he'd chicken out, too. But I don't think he did. I don't know for sure, though, since no one ever saw him again after that night.

"I was the only one who knew what he'd been planning, and I was too scared to say anything, or maybe too embarrassed, since I'd been afraid to go with him. I kept thinking that maybe if I'd gone along, he'd still be OK.

"I heard that the police questioned you, but they had nothing to link the carnival to Jeffery's disappearance. But I knew what had happened. You took him." Ken paused, pushed himself up, hands on one knee, struggled to his feet. Morgan's men took a step forward, but saw that Ken posed no threat. He could barely stand.

"For a long time," he continued, "I was scared of carnivals, maybe even hated them. But I needed to understand. I needed to know why you took my friend. So I started reading, researching. At some point, it became my whole life.

"I learned things about carnivals that the world had forgotten centuries ago; roots leading back to legends of supernatural nomads and caravans, in Zoroastrian and Egyptian mythology—"

Morgan sneered, shook his head.

"Until finally, I did understand. I wasn't scared any more. And I wanted to help keep the carnival alive. The tradition is too old, too important—"

Morgan suddenly stood up, looming over Ken, his head nearly brushing the ceiling, a scowl draped upon his face.

"Let me see if I have this straight—you thought you could just go out and murder someone, and their death would, what...*feed* the carnival?" The carnival boss looked down at Ken incredulously. "Are you insane?"

Ken took a step backwards, shocked by the intensity of Morgan's denial. He couldn't have been wrong. There was no way—

Morgan shook his head sadly. "There's a lot more to the ceremony than that; a lot more," he said. "Tie him up, boys. Good and tight. Let's show him how it's done."

That Extra Mile

David Niall Wilson
and Brian A. Hopkins

T he road ahead shimmered in the heat, warping Scott's vision with myopic waves and shifting perceptions. He brushed sweat from the corner of his eye. Four miles already. Two more to go. A mile further than he'd ever gone, and on this scorcher of a day no less.

Three months earlier, if anyone had told Scott Danning he'd be four miles into a six mile run and smiling about it, he'd have laughed in their face. What had started as a dare from his athletic wife Jean had become a fast addiction. He'd never been very athletic, might have even been considered a wuss by many. They might like him—he was an extremely affable fellow—but they'd never pick him first for their ball team.

Now he religiously did four miles a day at lunch time, often skipping his meal entirely. He couldn't remember a time when he'd ever felt better. His waist had begun to trim down and overall he'd dropped fifteen pounds.

Christ, he thought as he rounded the final curve and began the last long stretch of road leading to his health club, *I'm actually starting to enjoy this.*

His legs were moving rhythmically, beyond the need for conscious control. His mind was wandering. He wondered briefly if he might be pushing himself too far too fast, but the thought slipped away. With the exception of a slight tingling sensation at the back of his neck and a few fleeting moments of imbalance, he felt fine.

Endorphins, he acknowledged with a grin. He'd learned about the natural, exertion-produced drug from the half dozen or so jogging and running books he'd bought since launching his new fitness program. The beginning of a run still hurt, but it was more than worth it for the exhilaration he felt once that "high" had been reached.

The fifth mile was behind him now. He could feel the pavement, hot beneath his feet. His concentration centered less and less on the road in front of him, seeming to jump perspective every few strides.

There was a car pulled off to the side of the road up ahead, an old Dodge Charger, and two figures stood in the ditch beside it. There was something odd about the two, but he was having a hard time concentrating on them. Something...one of them was on his knees. *Her* knees. She was blonde, young, attractive. The other was a burly, long-haired man in dark glasses and an expensive three-piece suit.

The images shifted in and out of focus as he neared the car. The lightness in his head was making his knees rubbery. Neither the man or the woman looked up as he approached, even when he managed a hoarse, "Hey!" The man had his hand raised above his head, and something in it glittered brightly in the sun.

Lurching awkwardly, Scott fell. The car was there, then it wasn't. As he reached out to steady himself against it, he pitched headlong, narrowly missing the side of the pavement with his shoulder and scraping his knees painfully.

"What the hell?" he exclaimed, pushing himself to a sitting position. He was in the ditch beside the road, directly to one side of where the car had been parked and almost on top of where the man and woman had been only moments before, and yet he was alone. There were no people. There was no car. There were, in fact, not even marks in the gravel to indicate it had *ever* been there.

Shaking his head, which brought on a sharp pain and a wave of nausea, he rose unsteadily to his feet. Closing his eyes tightly, he used his shirt tail to wipe the sweat from his face. When he opened his eyes, nothing had changed, but the pounding of his heart had begun to settle. After giving his scraped knees a final, apologetic wiping off, he turned toward the club once more.

The half mile that remained seemed more intimidating than the entire run had when he'd begun, but he managed it at a slow, labored pace. His mind was fuzzy—out of focus—and he kept reviewing the run like a strobed slide show, trying to sort out what might have happened.

The only explanation that made sense was that he had just overdone it. The day was hot, he'd gone a mile further than he'd ever attempted before, and it had just proven too much for him. He was still trying to convince himself of this when he rounded the corner of the parking lot and headed on into the club.

He waved absently at Carol, the receptionist, and headed straight for the locker room. His knees were beginning to ache, and he wanted very much to just sit down on the bench in front of his locker and catch his breath, but sitting would be the worst thing to do after a run. A hot shower was the answer. He stumbled into the locker room, peeled off his sweat-soaked clothes and stepped into the shower.

As the steaming water washed over him and down the drain, it carried some of his weariness with it. His mind began to clear. By the time he'd finished and was toweling himself off, he was chuckling over the incident, and by the time he'd reached his car for the short drive back to work, he'd forgotten it almost entirely.

«« ── »»

"I'm telling you, Jean," he said around a mouthful of lasagna, "it was the strangest thing I've ever experienced. The damn car was there, and then it just wasn't. I fell right through the thing."

"It sounds like you were working too hard," she said, concern wrinkling the corners of her eyes. "It was pretty hot out there today, Scott. I want you healthy, sure, and you're starting to look really great, but I want you alive too."

"But you should have seen that woman's face, hon. She was terrified. And that guy had a knife; I'm sure of it. I saw him pull it back like he was going to cut her throat or something."

"Well, it's a good thing they disappeared before he had a chance," Jean smiled at him with good-humor. "I still think you're just working too hard."

"Maybe. I know I'll be sticking at four miles for a while, that much is certain."

And that was that. He didn't bring the subject up again, and there were no recurring "mirages" during his daily run. It would no doubt have slipped his mind completely, had it not been for their puppy, Yap.

Yap was a half-Chow, half-Labrador puppy that had wormed his way into their lives about a month earlier. He was a good dog, all in all, but he was not completely housebroken. In fact, his training had barely reached the point where he was leaving his nightly surprises on a sheet of newspaper just inside the door. Every night, Scott spread a new set of papers out in the hope that, come morning, he'd find that the pup had wised up.

It was the Saturday following his odd encounter on the roadside, in the middle of the afternoon—he was placing the newspaper early because the previous evening he'd forgotten—when he stumbled across an article that changed everything. It was on the front page of the paper, a page he didn't pay enough attention to, favoring instead the sports page and the comics.

The photo was of a car—*the* car—and it was parked right where he'd seen it, alongside that road. Replacing the front page with another section of the paper, Scott took the article back into the front room and sat down to read it.

VIOLENT MURDER LEAVES LOCAL POLICE BAFFLED, read the title. He read it quickly, his heart pounding faster and faster. A young woman, Eleanor Chandler, had been brutally murdered and left in the ditch beside the road. Cause of death: multiple stab wounds. The killer had escaped cleanly. The police were still searching, said the article, but had made no progress. Scott let the paper fall to his lap and stared at the wall.

"What is it?" Jean asked, looking up from her book. "You look as though you've seen a ghost."

He stared at her dumbly. Without a word, he rose and brought her the newspaper, then stood beside her chair while she skimmed the article.

"I read this when it first came out," she said finally, looking up. "It's strange, but why does it bother you so?"

"That's the car I saw," he said slowly, "the other day while I was running. It's parked right where I saw it, and the man had a knife."

"Well," Jean said, brow furrowed in concentration, "is there any chance you read this, or saw the picture and then heard some friends discussing it? I mean, it is on the front page."

He thought hard. Of course it was possible, but it just didn't seem right. "I don't know," he said at last. "It didn't seem like I was seeing the car for the second time when I saw it on the road—not like it did when I saw this photo. And the two people I saw—they aren't in the photo."

Actually, the woman's face was smiling up from the newspaper. A small photo of her was included alongside the larger one of the crime scene. The man was what was missing.

"Honey," he said, a thought tickling at the back of his mind, "you read the paper every day. This was a week ago—have they caught this guy yet?"

Jean frowned. "I don't think so. I saw a little piece on it again last night. They had a couple of suspects, but nothing concrete. Why?"

"Don't you see," he answered earnestly, sitting down on the arm of her chair, "I saw this guy. He wasn't in the newspaper photo. I saw him do this. I saw her face." Still, he thought, the time frames were all screwy. The article said the coroner estimated the woman's time of death at between nine and eleven p.m. Thursday night. Scott's mysterious vision had occurred on his Friday run.

Jean wrapped her arms around him, concern in her voice, and said, "You know that's crazy."

"Yeah, I know," he replied, untangling himself, "but I'm going to have to prove that to myself. I think I'll go down to the club for a run."

"Now?" she said, voice bordering on exasperation. "Why?"

"I'm going to go that extra mile, maybe two," he said. "I'm going to run until I'm so tired that my eyes swim from it. Maybe I just hallucinated, or maybe it has something to do with those damned endorphins you told me about. Whatever, I need to get this out of my system."

"Don't forget you agreed to go to that party with me tonight."

He had forgotten. Jean's friends were all health food nuts and there was some sort of "new age" feast scheduled for that evening. He knew it was important to her that they *both* show up. "I didn't forget," he lied. "I can be back in plenty of time to go eat health food. Besides, just think of the appetite I'll have worked up."

"It's not health food, Scott. I told you that."

"Uh, yeah, right."

"It's brain food, silly," she laughed. "You could probably use some. It's natural things like ephedra and caffeine, plus smart drugs like piracetam, vasopressin, and the like."

"Can't wait." He gave her a quick kiss. "I'll be back soon, okay?"

She got up from the chair. "No. I'm coming with you. If you're going to pass out along a road somewhere, I'm going to be there to haul you back. Besides, I could use a good run."

«« — »»

The sun was still high in the sky when they reached the club. The heat rose from the pavement like shimmers of steam above a boiling pot of water, and it wasn't long before Scott was completely drenched in sweat.

Jean trotted easily at his side, only the faintest traces of moisture near the nape of her neck and on her upper lip giving evidence of any undue exertion. He knew she would be running much faster if it weren't for him.

He ignored her, concentrating on keeping his own pace slightly above what he was used to. The blood was pounding through his veins, and his head was feeling lighter. He could sense the extra effort draining his reserves, but he could also feel his body responding—the exhilaration of the wind in his face and the smooth rippling of his leg muscles as he stretched them out heading into the final mile.

Endorphins, he recited from memory, having reviewed the subject in one of his books just before leaving the house, *are similar in chemical structure to the analgesic morphine.* In 1973, morphine was found to act on specific opiate receptors in the brain, spinal chord, and nerve endings. This discovery led to the identification of small protein molecules produced in the body that also act at opiate receptors. These morphine-like proteins were named endorphins—short for endogenous morphines. Endorphins are produced mainly in the pituitary and related regions of the hypothalamus. Endorphins act through the opiate receptors by modulating nerve impulses across the synapses.

Vaguely, as if from far away, he could hear Jean's voice. At first she just seemed to be talking, babbling, then the sound grew more insistent. He blocked her out, concentrating on the road ahead. He could feel the heat through the rubber soles of his shoes. His fatigue was gone, erased by a sudden flow of energy—his "second wind."

Suddenly it was there. It was exactly as he remembered it, the car, the man and the woman in the ditch. It was like watching a tape he'd shoved into his VCR. He concentrated as he neared the two, moving slightly to the side of the road. He couldn't quite make out the man's face. He kept straining to get a look, a glimpse.

He could sense Jean moving up next to him, and he pushed himself a little harder, pulling away and moving further down the hillside into the ditch. He couldn't hear her, though he had the vague notion that she was screaming at him. He moved in a dreamy haze, carefully concentrating on keeping his balance as he ran over the uneven ground.

The man's hand began its plunge, and Scott had a clear view of the fear in the woman's eyes. She didn't beseech Scott's help—she didn't even seem to be aware that he was rushing down on them at reckless speed. She was not blonde…?

He saw the knife, a curved blade, like the ones used by carpet layers. He saw clearly in that instant the image of a green dragon on the man's forearm. It twined nearly all the way around his wrist and back up toward his elbow, fangs gaping.

And then he was on them. He cried out, reaching up to stop the plunging blade, staggering and pitching headlong. His last view was that of the blade, plummeting toward his chest, and of green eyes, glittering with malice as they stared through and beyond him. Then it was dark—dark and silent.

«« —»»

The cool brush of damp cloth across his forehead brought him back to bright light and searing pain. He heard the murmur of voices, Jean's and one other, and he tried to push himself upright, regretting the rashness of this movement almost instantly.

"Wha…" he stammered, his voice dry and sluggish. "What happened? Jean?"

"I'm right here," she replied, her voice tight with concern. "You're going to be fine. Good sized lump on your head, but otherwise you're intact. Just what the hell did you think you were doing out there, anyway?"

"What do you mean?" he asked. He remembered the run, the car, and the woman's eyes in a sudden rush. Nausea nearly brought his breakfast back for a return engagement.

He opened his eyes carefully, squinting into the bright light of the health club's lobby and his wife's face. She was still covered in a light sheen of sweat, her hair slightly mussed and her eyes wide with emotion. *Beautiful*, he thought.

"You went running down into that ditch all of a sudden," she said, "screaming like a banshee and raising your arm over your head like some sort of damned super hero. You were really moving, too. Lucky you didn't smack your head on a rock or something when you fell."

Somehow he pulled his thoughts together quickly enough not to say anything just then. He managed a sheepish smile, raising a hand to gingerly probe the growing knot on his head. Carol was standing behind Jean with a bored sneer on her face that showed clearly how much respect she had for a man who'd been carried in by his wife.

"Let's just get home," he said quickly, swinging his feet off the bench where they'd laid him.

"Home and straight to bed," Jean agreed. "You need to sleep this one off."

"But your party—"

"Forget the party," she interrupted. "I really don't want to go anyway."

"You're a piss poor liar, Jean."

"No, really, I—"

"You've been talking about this damn shindig for the last two weeks, hon. Soon as I get a shower—" he touched his forehead again, grinning "—and maybe a Band-Aid, we're going to that party."

"But—"

"No buts. We're going. Case closed."

««—»»

Percy Simms was a complete bore. What's more, he was an educated bore—Harvard Med and all—which made it twice as annoying to be around the old fart because not only did he rattle on and on about meaningless drivel, his drivel was of the sort that made you realize how ignorant you were. Scott tolerated the retired physician because he'd been Jean's family doctor going way back to her diaper and teething years, but the man's parties were guaranteed sleepers.

Scott took another sip of the drink Percy had handed him and made a face. "Tastes like Tang. Sour Tang." He had to speak up to be heard over the crowd. As a result, Jean heard what he'd intended only for the doctor.

She punched him on the arm. "It's called a think drink, Scott."

"Vitamins, fructose, choline, phenylalanine, ephedra, and caffeine," Percy explained, taking a long pull from his own glass.

"Needs some vodka," muttered Scott.

"You've slaughtered quite enough brain cells already," Jean scolded.

"This drink," explained Percy, "is intended to heighten your mental faculties—"

"What little you have," Jean slipped in playfully.

"—not anesthetize them."

"Okay, okay. I know what fructose and caffeine are, of course, but what about the others? Jean mentioned ephedra this afternoon."

"Ephedra's an herb. Phenylaline and choline are amino acids. Like caffeine, they're stimulants."

"But not the kind you get from a can of soda pop, eh?"

Percy smiled. "We're not into anything illegal yet, Scott. Everything in that drink can be bought at a health food store. Think drinks improve memory, concentration, alertness, problem solving abilities...they even delay the cognitive effects of aging."

"And a mind is a terrible thing to waste," Scott joked, but he was thinking about his present problem. Twice now, he had watched a woman being murdered. And twice he'd been incapable of stopping it. He'd bet his last dollar that tomorrow's newspaper would confirm what he had seen that afternoon. The problem, as he saw it, was two-fold—two *barriers* actually. He needed to overcome the barriers of place and time. Somehow he needed to "break through" so that he could save the next victim. And somehow he needed to do it retroactively since it appeared that he was witnessing the events *after* they happened. The think drink was certainly in order. He'd need a "cognitive boost" if he was going to solve this one.

"Percy's into nootropics," Jean explained.

Scott blinked. "New who?"

"Nootropics," Percy answered, "pharmaceuticals for cognitive enhancement."

Scott did a quick count in his head: five words, 15 syllables. That had to be a record, even for Percy.

"Let me show you."

And the next thing Scott knew, Percy had his arm and was weaving him through the other guests, touring him about the room and pointing out party tables which might normally have sported marguerites, daiquiris, finger sandwiches and crunchy treats, but were now covered with blenders, fruit and vegetable drinks, and colorful bowls of drugs. Jean was left behind to mingle with the other health food nuts.

"Here you've got your tyrosine, lecithin, ginseng, and Ginkgo biloba. Over here your Hydergine, vasopressin, Lucidril, choline, and Deaner. There, piracetam."

Looking at the sea of pills and powders, punch bowls and glasses, Scott had a sudden intuition. "I don't understand," he lied. "What are they all for?"

Percy smiled patiently. "Well, take the piracetam for example. As you know, the left and right sides of the brain act like two computers linked by a data bus." (Jean had obviously explained to Percy that Scott worked with computers.) "This link is called the corpus callosum. Piracetam tablets speed up the data transfer rate of the corpus callosum. Smart pharmaceuticals like piracetam are prescribed in Europe, Japan, and China for victims of stroke and memory impairment."

"No shit? What about these?"

"This is a homemade phenylaline-choline derivative—"

"Homemade?"

"As Jean said, I've taken an interest in nootropics, even going so far as developing some of my own. This is a simple one."

"How does it work?"

"The brain's supply of neurotransmitters, particularly dopamine, serotonin, acetylcholine, and norepinephrine—" He broke into a grin suddenly, and for the first time Scott thought that the old guy might be more than a bothersome bore. "Don't worry, Scott, there won't be a test afterwards."

Scott laughed. "It's a good thing."

"Anyway, these neurotransmitters can be restored with their precursors, amino acids such as these. Phenylaline and choline, for example, combine in the brain to produce norepinephrine and acetylcholine. Amino acids also eliminate age-accelerating agents known as free radicals."

"And you've been making your own versions of these drugs?"

Percy was on a roll now. "These and more. Let me tell you, Scott, the real frontier of nootropics is NGFs, nerve growth factors. NGFs not only regenerate old neurons, they actually stimulate the growth of *new* ones!"

"Incredible." And he meant it. As boggled as he was by the barrage of multi-syllable words, he could imagine what NGFs would mean to alzheimer's and stoke victims. *Good God*, he thought, *NGFs might be capable of eradicating senility!* But at the same time he was thinking about something else entirely. He was wondering what effect such cognitive enhancers would have on a brain already high on endorphins.

"The problem pharmacologists are wrestling with is getting these agents into the brain. You see, NGFs are incapable of crossing the blood-brain barrier. Several approaches have been tried with various success: attaching the NGF to a blood-brain permeable molecule and injecting it into the bloodstream, using neural transplants from fetal brain cells, and injecting genetically engineered cells that produce NGFs directly into the brain. But—" and here Percy's eyes positively glowed "—I think I've developed the first over-the-counter, workable solution, an NGF you take as easily as aspirin."

Scott smiled. "Please, show me."

«« — »»

Six thirty, Sunday morning. The rising sun was broiling off Saturday night's dew, cloaking ponds and low lying ground in a mantle of translucent gauze. The day promised to be another scorcher. The thermometer had already topped eighty.

Scott hit the streets, the right front pocket of his sweats bulging with pills he'd stolen from Percy Simms. His stride was measured and certain. He was planning a long run this morning.

He'd left his wife a note:

Jean,

Didn't want to wake you. I've gone for an early run.

I don't quite know how to explain this, so I'll just write it as simply as possible. I know that what I saw while running that day was real. Somehow (hell, not SOMEHOW, it's the endorphins high, I'm sure of it) during my run I stepped outside the "here and now" as we know it. I know that sounds crazy, but I've no other way to explain it. I didn't tell you, but it happened again yesterday when you and I went running, just before I fell and blacked out.

I saw him kill another woman.

ANOTHER woman, Jean. If there was any doubt, I had only to see this morning's newspaper. Check the paper yourself after you read this. Front page. Same M.O. Same vicinity. She drove the same kind of car as the last victim. She was murdered late Friday night. The police have acknowledged that it's a serial killer.

I know I can find him. And when I find him, maybe I can stop him. I also know if I don't try, and he kills again, I'll feel partly to blame.

The endorphins got me close to him, but not close enough. I need to step across that line, step completely into his timespace. What I need is some sort of booster. I borrowed (sorry, honey, I STOLE) some pills from Percy, hoping that they'll give me a boost.

Please don't worry.

Scott

«« — »»

The pills had virtually no taste, but they left him with a greasy feeling in his mouth. He chewed rather than swallowed the pills , reasoning that they would take effect faster that way. His knees and head were still throbbing from his previous falls, but these were only mild irritants. His legs were pumping in a steady, road-eating rhythm, and he was surprised to find that he felt pretty good.

The first two miles took him past his health club. When he reached the corner where he would normally turn back, he took the opposite turn, heading toward the park. There was a long, looping trail that wound through the trees there, and Jean had told him it was about five miles long. That, along with the two from the club and the two back, would be well past his tested limits.

He didn't notice any effect from the pills, nor did he look for any; he just concentrated on passing each level of fatigue, pushing himself that little bit further to kick his metabolism into a higher gear. By the time he reached the park, the sun was well up in the sky, and his skin was coated with a bright sheen of sweat. He grinned, realizing that he wasn't even tired yet.

By the time he'd looped around the park and made it back to the edge of the road, his body was totally on automatic pilot. His thoughts were disjointed, wandering, and his sight was slightly fuzzy from the combination of fatigue and the sweat collecting in the corners of his eyes. He wiped them clear on the sleeve of his t-shirt and pushed onward. Two miles to go, less than that to the roadside where he'd twice witnessed a murder.

He wasn't even certain what he planned to do. At the very least, he was going to make it down far enough into that ditch so he could positively identify the killer. If Percy's "drugs" came through, maybe he could do more. The fact that this made no sense did not sway him.

The pavement disappeared beneath him, entire blocks slipping by without any conscious notice of them, minutes flashing into the past without being acknowledged in the present. The last stretch loomed ahead, shimmering and wavering as the heat rose to confound his eyes. Sweat, now pouring down his face, burned his eyes unmercifully. He squinted, blinked, fought to keep them clear. Everything might depend on how well he could see, how closely he could describe the killer.

It was there! The same Charger, the same man—and the same brunette woman he'd seen on yesterday's run. This had to mean that the killer hadn't struck again since Friday night and Scott was still focused on that murder. No matter. All that really mattered now was to maintain his "high" and get there before it was too late. His legs were moving like pistons, eating the ground hungrily, and he could feel a new energy, a new level of stamina flowing through his bloodstream.

Offering a silent prayer to Percy, his chemicals, and the great god Endorphin, Scott plunged down the last few hundred feet, trying to be more careful than the last time, trying not to kill himself in the process. He moved into the ditch, watching for ruts and stones. He would do no good at all if he slipped and went tumbling again.

Twenty yards ahead of him, the killer raised his knife.

"I'm here!" Scott screamed. "I see you, you son of a bitch!" And he did see him. Carefully, he memorized every line of the killer's face, made mental notes on his size and weight, the tattoo running up the length of his arm, the dirty brown of his hair, the ice blue of his eyes as he looked up at the mad jogger bearing down on him and his victim.

"Shit," the killer muttered, his eyes fully focused on Scott.

The killer could see him! Scott came to a skidding halt, going down as he slipped on the loose gravel. The killer could see him! Scott looked to the victim, hoping to confirm in her eyes that he was indeed occupying the same space and time, but she was scampering through the ditch, taking advantage of her assailant's momentary distraction to scramble away from the bright little blade.

"Bad time to drop in, buddy," the killer hissed and he lunged toward where Scott sat on his rump.

My time, Scott thought desperately, as if this was something he could control, *take me back to my time!* Nothing happened. The killer took a mad swing with the knife and Scott felt a sting and the warm rush of blood down his forearm. He kicked out clumsily, somehow managing to trip his assailant, and scrambling backward like a crab, he maneuvered out of reach as the killer took another swipe at him from the ground. Then he was up and on his feet and running. Scott heard the killer struggling to his feet behind him, and he risked one quick glance back over his shoulder to confirm that the maniac was indeed chasing him.

When he reached the street he spotted a man walking his dog. Scott screamed for help, but the man appeared to be deaf. When Scott tried to get his attention by grabbing his arm, he passed right through, as if he were a ghost. Only the dog seemed aware of his presence, barking and straining at its leash. Its master merely cursed and pulled harder on the leash, continuing down the road.

The killer swung wide to block Scott's flight down the street, passing right by the dog and owner as if they weren't there.

Because they aren't there, Scott thought as he stumbled back the way he had come, back into the ditch. He was, once again, seeing into another timeline, perhaps his own, the one he'd left to get here. Scott's arm was dripping thick red blood and it had begun to throb painfully. He clamped his left hand over the gash to stem the flow of blood, desperately looking left and right for an avenue of escape. The far side of the ditch was hemmed by a chain-link fence topped with barbed wire. Further down the road, the ditch ended at a culvert that was much too small even for Scott's slight frame. He was trapped.

He cast about for something to use as a weapon. There was nothing. The killer's original victim had scrambled up the bank to her car. As Scott looked on, she started the engine and sped off, spewing gravel and dust. Scott had a brief second in which he contemplated this unexpected expression of gratitude, then the knifeman was upon him again.

Scott feinted toward the fence-side of the ditch and dodged to the other as the killer reacted. The slope was steep. Several steps into it, Scott realized his reserves were running out. The long run and his wound were taking their toll. He could hear the killer panting behind him, thought at one point he even heard the hiss of the knife slicing air at his back. Near the top of the bank, his feet slipped in gravel and he went down on his belly for a second. In that instant he was certain the next new sensation for him would be that wickedly curved little blade slicing through his spinal cord, but on hands and knees he kept moving, kicking up nearly as much gravel as the Charger.

He ran head first into her legs, almost bowling her over. Looking dumbly at the ground before him, he suddenly recognized Jean's running shoes as she turned around to look down on him. He didn't stop, but continued to scrabble forward, trying to drag her with him, screaming at her to run even before he looked up at her face. She didn't budge.

"Scott, what's wrong? My God, you're bleeding!"

Trying to calm his nerves, he glanced quickly over his shoulder. There was no one behind him. He looked twice in both directions up and down the ditch. No one.

Jean knelt beside him. "Let me see your arm. I think we'd better get someone to call 9-1-1."

"No, I'm fine," he stammered.

"The hell you are! Look at that gash."

The cut was real. Fresh blood ran in rivulets down his arm, dripping from the tips of his fingers. It *had* happened. "I must have gotten cut on something when I fell," he lied. He hated lying to her, but there was no way she was going to believe this.

"Stay here," she ordered. "I'm going to run up to the club and get help."

"No," he told her, using her arm to pull himself to his feet. "I'm going with you. I can walk."

Jean looked doubtful, but at his insistence she let him lean on her arm and accompany her to the club. "When I saw your note, I came looking for you," Jean explained as they walked. He could tell she was talking just to hear her own voice. He'd definitely scared her. He felt bad for having done it, but thought that what he had accomplished more than justified her discomfort. He knew what the killer looked like. *Exactly* what he looked like.

"I'm really worried about you, Scott," Jean continued. "All this nonsense about Dodge Chargers and murdered women—"

"I'm not crazy," he told her. "You looked at the paper, didn't you?"

She looked more concerned than ever. "Scott, there was nothing in this morning's paper about a murder. I checked the front page, the back page, the whole damn paper."

Nothing? But he had seen the article...? And then it hit him. He had changed it. He had stepped back in the past and stopped it from happening. Of course there was nothing in the paper when Jean checked. Because of his interference, it had never happened.

"I want you to see a doctor, Scott."

"Sure," he said, not really listening. He had altered history. Scott Danning, time traveler. Scott Danning, protector of the weak and helpless. He liked the sound of that. The pain in his arm suddenly seemed less. "A few stitches and I'll be as good as new," he told Jean.

"I'm not talking about a doctor for your arm, Scott!"

"Sure, hon, anything you say." If he had done it once, he could do it again. The killer was still out there. Scott could give the police his description, but they'd never believe how he had gotten it. And there remained the first woman he'd seen murdered. Could he go back and save the blonde as well? But once both women were restored, there would actually be no crime for the police to investigate, no charges to be brought against the maniac with the knife. The man would be free to kill again—or for the first time (all over again). The time complications of the whole mess were mind-boggling.

It was a paradox to which he saw only one solution. He, Scott Danning, would have to take care of this. Save the first woman. Kill the maniac with the knife. His pocket still bulged with Percy Simm's nootropic pills. With some careful planning, he could do both those things—perhaps even at the same time. Couldn't he?

"Scott, are you listening to me?"

"Sure, hon. I'm listening."

"Maybe you should quit jogging."

He smiled and kissed her on the cheek. "Not a chance."

Bleed With Me:
A Brackard's Point Story
Geoff Cooper

Respect to Ulcer, and the Ft. Myers crew.

"**C**ome on, Mark. It ain't the end of the world, you know?"
He looked at me, eyes ablaze with emotion I had never experienced. It was pain, true, but more. Much more—hatred, self-pity, injustice, self-loathing, and rage so powerful it bordered on passion. My friend was crazy, driven so by his ghosts. He had been for months. Every time he started to recover, he would slide back down again. It did not take much to set him off. A word taken the wrong way or an allusion to a situation similar to his own would undo him all over again. The guy was a wreck.

I felt bad for him, but was powerless to help. I had not gone through his trials. My life had not blown up in my face, left me shattered. My sense of self had not been pulverized. I could just be his friend, be there for him, sift through the fragments and pick up pieces not lost. Sometimes, though, he made it damned difficult for me to help.

"Listen to me," I said. "One day? This will all be behind you, and you'll be happy again. I swear, you will." I felt as hollow saying it as a campaigning politician promising no new taxes and a thousand points of light.

(*"Read my lips..."*)

Mark shoved back the stool, set his beer on the counter, and said, "You know? I've had about enough of your Pollyanna bullshit, Ron." He nodded over to Valerie, gestured toward his beer mug.

Val caught his nod, gave him the "Give me a minute" finger, finished washing some glasses. Mark looked back at me, eyes alight with madness and pain. "You want to know something?"

(Not really.) "What?"

He wiped his mouth with the back of his hand. "Everything sucks."

"Oh, dude, don't even—"

"No, fuck you. Listen. Everything sucks, *all the time.* Just that sometimes you're too frigging stupid to realize it. That's how it *is,* man. That's how it's cut."

"Mark," I shook my head. "It's not always like that. Not *always.*"

"Whatever," he muttered, scanned the other side of the bar for Valerie and our beers.

"Mark, man, I know everything pretty much sucks right now, but dude, whether you like it or not? You're going to eventually move on."

"Not unless I die tomorrow."

He did not even turn to look at me when he said it.

From anyone else, I would have looked deeper into that statement. Mark would never. No way. I knew he *considered* it constantly. What happened over the next few weeks was his form of self-annihilation: he systematically killed the man he used to be. Through symbolic death, Mark sought rebirth. He found it.

«« — »»

The tattoo was the first I saw of it. Mark pulled up his jeans, took off his sneaker and sock to expose it all. The tattoo had a rose that stemmed from his Achilles' tendon, up the back of his calf. The bloom was in a woman's mouth. She bit down with a smirk both sexy and sadistic. Thorns pierced her lips, petals stuck out from between her teeth. Blood dripped, marred her chin.

I did not need to question the symbolism.

Valerie leaned over the counter to check out the new tat. "You're crazy, Mark," she shook her head. "You know that, right?"

"Yeah," he laughed. "Ain't it cool? Now how's about a beer?"

"You too, Ronnie?"

"Sure," I said. "Why not?"

I was closer to the tattoo—I could see more of the detail: the grain of the stem's bark, the veins in the leaves, the cruelty of the thorns. I could see the familiar creases of the tattoo's lips (lips that once promised me pleasures—a secret I kept from him still). It was *her*, from the nose down. I remember being silently glad Mark did not use her whole face. I might have worried more, then.

He gauged me for a reaction. I became aware of him, inspected the

GEOFF COOPER

art further, but saw nothing more. I had plenty of time to see it in its entirety. He was obviously waiting for a response, so I said the first thing that came to mind: "Jesus, that must've hurt like a bitch."

Stupid, I know. Stupid and obvious. Someone rattling needles on your tendons cannot feel good.

Mark grinned. "It didn't hurt enough."

Something in that smile disturbed me. I turned away, looked to the bar for Valerie and our beers.

"It was a certain type of unpleasantness," he continued. "I could have taken more."

"I don't get it. Why would you *want* it to hurt?"

"It's like life, man. It's supposed to."

Unwilling to argue, I shrugged.

"And, unlike *some* things I could mention—that bitch, for example—a tattoo is forever."

Cynical bastard. I wanted to smack the shit out of him.

"This," he motioned to his leg, "is, though. *This* I keep with me. To remind me of the things that *do* last. Like pain. Like hate. Spite. Revenge." He pulled his pant leg back down, put on his sock and sneaker.

"So, you got a permanent image of her mouth for spite and revenge? Dude, you're fucked up."

"No! Goddamnit! You're not fucking listening to me!"

I did not mean to, but I jerked back in my stool. If I were someone else, I think he would have taken a swing at me. He still might have if Valerie had not arrived with our beers.

"Calm down, you two," she said. "You're giving the old men coronaries." She gestured toward the other side of the bar, where two of the regulars hunched over their ashtrays and muttered to themselves about us both.

"Ain't my fault Ron's thickheaded," Mark said.

"Talk about the pot and the kettle..."

"Oh, Jesus H. Christ in a chicken basket," Val said. She grabbed a bottle of Dewars' White Label from under the bar, and three shot glasses. "Now," she said as she poured. "Friends? All of us?"

Mark looked sheepish, and slowly raised the glass. "Yeah. Sorry dude."

"It's cool."

"Great," Val said. We clinked glasses and fired the shots down.

"Thanks," I told her after I recovered my breath. 86.8 proof has a nasty habit of burning a bit when taken raw.

195

SHIVERS

"Don't sweat it," Val said, and gave my hand a squeeze.

"Why don't you two just bang and get it over with?" Mark asked.

I'm not sure who told him to fuck off first—Val or me. He was always trying to get us together, moreso since his relationship went sour. I wondered if Mark believed he could have a relationship by proxy if he was to ensure Valerie and I hooked up. Val thought he wanted to live vicariously through us. I didn't like the sound of that, because that would mean that Mark secretly—or not so secretly— wanted to sleep with her. That thought brought on the jealousy bug.

Okay, fine, I wanted her. Happy? But…we were friends. I didn't want to fuck up our friendship. Besides, cool as Val was, the girl had a couple of issues. She told me about them, sort of. Not nice things to think about. Sometimes, when I looked at her, I could see the emotional scars in her eyes. They were like ghosts, dim little reminders of past trauma.

She often said the same thing about me. Whatever.

"Oh, come off of it, you two. You know you want to—"

"Dude, drop it."

"Oh, come on."

"Mark," Val's voice was a warning. She gave him a look, then collected the glasses and went to tend to her other customers. It was a few beers later before she returned for more than an alcohol delivery.

By then, both Mark and I had a good buzz on. We talked about the Yankees, and how nice it was of them to let Arizona have the pennant that time. We talked about the Bank of New York being robbed last week. We talked about a lot of non-subjects. Time-passers.

Once Valerie came back, we started having an actual conversation. Mark was precariously close to drunkenness at that point, so, at first, we both blew him off when he asked us: "You guys want to know how to deal with pain?"

I looked at Valerie, she at me.

(Here he goes again.)

We both said, "sure," or something similar. There was no stopping Mark now. If we declined the offer of his wisdom, he would have went on regardless. Mark did not notice, but both of us sighed, and leaned a little heavier on the bar. He also did not notice Valerie's arm and mine were touching (which is how we both knew he was smashed).

"The way you deal with pain, I mean, *real* pain, emotional pain?" He paused, sipped his beer. "Is to make it physical. I swear, when they were doing those straight lines on my Achilles' Tendon there, I bit my tongue till I bled, I wanted to scream so bad. But now? I'm *glad* I suffered through it. I made it through, and now, I'm better for it. I've got something very cool. Very special. I mean, it's all *from* the pain."

"Kind of like catharsis," Valerie said.

I said nothing because it made sense, and I did not want to admit that Mark's sense and mine were in alignment because I knew Mark was as fucked up as a football bat about his situation, and if he made sense to me, then, perhaps I was still fucked up. I liked to believe I was, as they say, *over it*. Yet, when I heard his theory, I had to admit— if only to myself—that it was, indeed, sensible. Damn him.

"Exactly!" Mark sipped his beer, set it down on the bar, then gestured with both hands as he clarified. "You take the deep pain—the shit in your soul, and put it in the flesh, where it heals faster. Once it heals, you have something tangible to remember *why* you suffered. You've got something that comes from *yourself*. You take *control* of the situation that way. Not someone else. *You.* You take control, to begin to heal. It becomes manageable."

"So, what you're saying is, whenever someone hurts you, get a tattoo?" I asked.

"Well… no." His brow darkened but his eyes and smile gleamed bright with something sinister. "It doesn't *have* to be a tattoo."

He slowly unbuttoned his shirt. Pulled it open.

Chrome flashed at us—reflecting the smoky bar lights. Metal studs with pointed ends shot through each one of his nipples. From his armpit to his waist, all the way down the ladder of his ribs, were a series of metal hoops, gradually growing larger as they descended.

Valerie gasped. I could only stare. It was everything I could do to keep my mouth from falling open.

"Jesus H. Christ in a chicken basket."

The piercings were out of character, but nothing I had not seen before. I just never expected to see them on *him*.

They did not bother me as much as the scars.

Shiny, grainy tissue crisscrossed his stomach: long, deliberate trenches carved into his skin. Above them were pinwheels, as if he poked something through his flesh and twisted until it ripped away. Mark's pectorals looked clawed, gouges torn outward from center. As if talons had dug into him. As if he tried to tear out his own heart.

"This," he said coldly as he held his shirt wide, "is what it looks like on the inside."

Empathetic hate surged within me. I closed my eyes. I turned to my beer, and swallowed deep so I would not speak. The beer had no taste. It could not wash away the bitterness on my tongue.

I thought about what he went through. Would I be that strong? Would I have survived? I could not positively answer yes. I did not know.

My thoughts grew heavier and my head dropped into my left palm as I leaned against the bar for support. I stared at the bottom of my beer mug, slowly shook my head.

It was wrong, all so very wrong. Mark made sense. The tattoo and the piercings and the scars—the transference of pain—made sense to me. So help me, it made *perfect* sense. It was so simple.

"Ronnie?" Valerie's concerned voice, her small hand gentle on the back of my head. "You all right?"

I lied: "Fine."

I saw ghosts of pain in her. They identified with Mark's statements. With his shiny scars. She must have seen it in me, too.

Everyone has a haunting regret that causes sleepless nights decades after the fact, causes moments of remorse when we permit remembrance. Everyone has a ghost. Mine were not as bad as some, worse than others. It was only pain. *My* pain. My albatrosses to carry. At times, their weight hung my head.

I did not go to the funeral, but have visited his grave in Gethsemane Cemetery. Last time I was there, I could not bring myself to even mutter an apology to his stone. I merely stood, stared, read the dates that were far too close together. Where the flowers were supposed to go, I placed a kickball and hoped that was enough. Hoped the dead forgave easier than the living. At least, easier than we forgave our own transgressions.

Hers was worse. I knew part of it—more than I ever wanted to, because I did not like picturing such things happening to a young girl—any girl—anyone—much less someone with whom I was friends: someone I cared about.

It had to do with her mother's boyfriend, a bottle of Jack Daniel's, four short bungee cords, and a four-poster bed. Any questions?

"Val, I need another drink," I said.

"You're not even done with that one."

"I need something stronger."

She went to the shelves.

"Dude?" I began. I was deeper than intrigued. I wanted to learn. *How... why...* Questions I didn't know how to ask. I understood only the answers: only half of the equation. Unacceptable. I needed more.

"Fuck," he answered—and waved any discussion away. "I'm done. I ain't talking about it no more. Not tonight. Val—give me one of those, wouldya?"

I have no idea what Valerie poured into that glass. I drained it immediately.

"So much for sipping whiskey," she muttered.

Mark chuckled.

I laughed as well, but the heat in my throat strangled the sound. "I'll sip the whole damned bottle right about now."

It sounded like a good idea.

«« — »»

Valerie stayed in my apartment that night. She was still there in the morning. I smelled her on my pillow when I woke up.

No. Not woke up. "Waking up" is what one did after sleep. I did not *sleep*. I *passed out*. Therefore, the correct wording would be "when I *came to*."

Physically, I felt the standard consequences of drinking to excess: bright light sensitivity, nausea, a headache and trembling that measured in the upper echelons of the Richter scale. The dirty sock fairy visited while I was unconscious, left each of my teeth encased in a small, well-worn woolen sock. Or so it felt. The back of my head had a monstrous lump. My hair lay matted against my head in a line of caked blood, but I did not remember hitting it on anything. A few bits and pieces, but little more. It was all very foggy. I decided I was better off kept in the dark. I did not want to know.

If Billy Joel was to give me one hint, honey I sure did put on a show. Yes, yes, I had to be a Big Shot, didn't I?

Valerie tried to be quiet as she rustled in the kitchen. I heard the coffee pot hiss and burp.

Coffee, I thought. *Thank God.*

I knew I loved that girl for a reason. I stumbled into the kitchen.

"How do you feel?" she swung a mug into my hand and poured.

"Like stir fried dog shit," I said. I meant it. The coffee was good: caffeine to offset the alcohol. What goes down must come up, and I had a long lonely climb to complete coherence. I needed all the help I could get. I rubbed my head. From inside my skull, Billy Joel still sang, a smartass *Ha-Ha! I'm-Not-Hungover* smirk in his voice: *"Go on and cry in your coffee; don't come bitching to me..."*

Fuck you, Piano Man—go ahead with your own life and leave me alone.

"You look it." Val turned her back toward me, vigorously washed her hands in the sink.

"Thanks."

Valerie asked me to hand her a dish towel.

"They're all dirty," I said. "All I got's paper." I reached for the roll.

"Uh…all right. I guess."

"You guess? You want to dry your hands or not?"

"Umm…"

I looked into the sink. Blood stained the white porcelain. Red on white screamed in my vision, such blatant contrast.

My system was already precarious, thanks to the hangover. Seeing the blood threw me completely out of synch. My lungs operated out of rhythm, refused to relinquish their grasp of the last breath. A glacier inched from the back of my neck to my spine, from my spine to my gut, as a burning lump of heat lodged in my throat. It tasted like beer foam and bile, and was difficult to swallow back down.

Blood dripped on the sink surface. Each droplet an entity, unique in shape and size. The only common factor was their content. They slid together and formed puddles, large enough to have ripples. Depth.

So entranced was I by the droplets of blood themselves, I did not think to look for a source, obvious as it was. Val's left hand. A deep cut between her thumb and forefinger—the web of her flesh gashed to the meat, if not the bone. Blood ran between her fingers, slipped under her rings, dripped off the curled knuckles.

"What did you do?" I asked.

"Nothing. I'm fine. I was just…" her explanation died on her lips.

I knew. I knew what she was doing. Mark's theory.

"What's wrong, Val?"

She said nothing as she took the towel from me and wrapped her hand. Her lips crunched in thought as she watched the stain spread.

I watched her. Held her. She was preparing not to answer, but rather to make a confession. Though my stomach felt toxic and my head pounded from the agony of being upright, I stood there, watched her think it through—how to word it for me. How much to omit.

I set the coffee cup down to hug her. Painful answers always come easier when spoken to the chest of someone you trust.

She did not speak. Not right away. She sobbed for a while, and I stood there, head pounding, guts churning on stale beer foam and whiskey, my mouth full of paste. Her tears and her blood soaked into my shirt.

"We should call Mark," she said after what seemed an eon. "See if he's all right."

I made to move for the phone. "I'll give him a—"

"But not yet," she squeezed me tight. "Please?"

Her voice. So small. Muffled. Needing.

I held her, felt her soft cheek against my chest. I looked down, saw the wetness on my shirt. Her tears. Her blood.

I held her, placed my head against hers. I held her, smelled stale cigarettes in her hair. I gently touched the puckered gash between her thumb and first finger, and wondered what pain she needed to purge. If it were me. If I was at fault. If I should even ask.

I held her tight. Held her until I felt a burning in my chest. Until I felt a scar form on my heart.

"You want to talk about it?"

"No."

"You sure?"

"Yeah, I'm sure, but..."

"But what?"

"Ronnie?"

"What?"

"Will you..." She abandoned speech, nuzzled against my chest again, hiding her eyes from me.

I breathed. Once. Twice. She wasn't going to continue. I prompted: "Will I what, Val?" and held the third.

Her left hand found mine. Fingers intertwined. She looked at me with age-old hurt in her eyes, ghosts of bungee cords and rape, and saw the broken body of my childhood friend at the base of Hook Mountain.

Our ghosts recognized each other for what they were. They saw— thus, they knew: instant acceptance. Our pain did not like being lonesome. Our ghosts did not like being cold. Lonely.

Such distance, reaching across years to the woman that was already in my arms. Feeling her reach to me. Reaching from the deep well of memories we tried to forget, but in so trying, remembered far too often. Such distance traveled—from our childhoods to that moment.

By the time I exhaled, we had lived a lifetime together: we'd suffered. Agonized. Been betrayed by those we trusted, and abandoned by those we needed. Loved those that died and killed those we loved with hurtful words and good intentions. We'd both been wronged, and exacted revenge on ourselves—(*yes, we'll show them*)—we did so out of anger, out of rage, out of spite, out of pain: all the things that lasted.

We lived in that half-breath's lifespan. Lived together, and fell in love.

Hurt to hurt, scar to scar, ghost to ghost, we embraced.

She gurgled in her throat—a moan she tried to swallow down. Then, she spoke, answering the question I posed twenty seconds before. A lifetime ago.

"Bleed with me."

We kissed deeply.

Our lips did not break contact when the razor bit. When the pain flashed forked tongues of lightning across our eyes, when we stained the floor and table, we did not break. The exorcism weakened our legs, and we collapsed to the floor. The kitchen tile was cool, soothing against our flesh, raw from the gleaming razor's caress.

We remained locked, our lips slick with each other. We murmured promises into each other's mouth: of love, of truth, of eternity. Of shelter from pain, of warmth for our ghosts. Of acceptance and understanding (nothing that lasted).

We will never scab, for our lives are open wounds. We will never scar if we forever bleed.

The Green Face

Al Sarrantonio

L anois, who listened to the green face in the window, sharpened his knives and wept.

"I will not do what you want this time!"

There was no answer, but when he looked through the window, the Green Face was there, hanging suspended like a perfectly sculpted marble bust, smiling, lit bright green from within, framed by night.

And he did as he was told.

«« —»»

She was a loose girl, given to loose blouses and a top that showed her erect nipples. Men came to her, but tonight, a languid slow night, she was drawn to the streets by the humidity and summer itself. Heat coated her but radiated from her body, her long legs, her still-tight tummy, her triangle of hair. A pool of perspiration dripped between her heavy breasts, and her full mouth was open and moist. She pushed back her short hair, which clung damply to her skull.

She wanted a man inside her, but didn't know why.

«« —»»

Lanois stumbled into the night from his home. The gate creaked mournfully on its hinges. There was a fog around the streetlamps, and the shops were closing, winking out like eyes, closing against the mist.

Lanois was a petite man, but handsome. He kept his beard trimmed tightly against his sharp chin, and his eyes were intelligent and moist behind his spectacles. He worked figures at his job, and looked like such a man. He was reserved and women took this for character.

He pushed himself down the street, toward the closing town. A deep bell somewhere announced ten o'clock. The grocer, also a small man, nodded to him knowingly, pocketing his key and hurrying away into the swallowing fog.

Lanois pushed onward, and encountered the girl.

"Ah! The accountant!" she said, smiling, stopping him as he sought to move away from her with a strangling cry in his throat. "What's the matter—won't you buy a girl a drink?"

He looked at her, and nodded, his voice still a croak. "All right," he said.

She took him to the expensive place, because she knew he had money. "You have a nice house," she said, and smiled again. Her lips were wet.

"Yes," he said, trying not to look at her, but listening to the loud chatter in the cafe. He felt oily, as if the night were adhering to him.

"Take me home with you," she said, pressing against him and pushing her drink away.

He trembled, and said, "All right."

Outside, the night had thickened. The fog pressed toward the ground, a green vapor. She led him, holding his arm because he seemed either drunk or unwilling.

"Here it is!" she said, pushing open the moaning gate.

Inside, she slammed the door and pushed him away. Her eyes looked full of tears, but her warmth reached him. She undid her top and let it fall to the floor, as an almost ripe odor assailed him from her breasts.

"Take me here," she said, pulling him down toward her as she lowered and stepped out of her blouse, kicking her shoes expertly off in the same motion.

Lanois, mewling, drew his knives crosswise from his pockets as he fell toward her, and, with both of the blades, crying out deeply, cut his own throat.

«« — »»

A deep winter day. Snow had fallen in abundance, and there was a cold smell in the air that topped the redolence of the radiators. Lanois moved from his bed, scratching himself and yawning. His feet missed their slippers, and he returned groggily to his bedside, slipping the footwear on where they lay by the bed's foot. He put his robe on over his gown and yawned again.

Saturday?

No. But a holiday!

He retrieved his rolled paper from outside the front door, thankful for the robe but still shivering. The day was suffused with light, the white snow only more blinding than the now-sapphire sky. The air smelled cold and clear in the aftermath of the storm.

He retreated to his kitchen and brewed coffee, the rich hot smell soon filling the room.

Opening the paper, he scanned the columns, noting the day's international events, another African war, the troubles in the colonies. Idly, he looked for news of his own death, and, finding none, was relieved.

Of course it was a dream, he thought.

The girl's murder was on page two.

Gasping, reading closely, he learned that she had been beheaded; that her head had been found in the gathering snow at the edge of the town park, the body nearby in an obscene position.

"The force of the beheading was gargantuan," the pathologist was quoted as saying. "I doubt one man could have done this."

Lanois's coffee turned cold, and he laid the paper down.

«« —— »»

Dressed in his working clothes, Lanois entered the prefect's office and was met by the prefect himself.

"Lanois!" the man said, smiling. "What brings you out on a holiday in such weather!" He advanced, holding out his hand.

Lanois did not take it. "The murder," he said. "I have something to report."

"Oh?"

Lanois pushed ahead, toward the prefect's office. "Please," he said.

His brow furrowed, the prefect followed.

«« —— »»

"But this is preposterous!" the prefect said, after Lanois had told his story. "In the first place, in your dream, you were with her in the summertime, not the dead of winter. And you said yourself, you cut your own throat."

"Nevertheless. And this has happened before, other murders…" The prefect traded his scowl for a smile. "Lanois, go home! You've been working too hard! Today is a holiday, and I suggest you use it as such. And I expect to see you at our weekly card game tomorrow evening!"

"Perhaps…" Lanois said.

The prefect's hand was on his shoulder, and Lanois looked up into the man's wide, kind face. "You had a dream," the prefect said, his hand squeezing Lanois's shoulder. "You didn't kill anyone. Anyhow, you are not capable of such an act. If you were, I would catch you!" The prefect laughed. "Now go home, and rest yourself. At the most, you had a strange dream. Leave it at that."

Lanois nodded briskly, and rose.

"Perhaps," he said.

"Good! And remember—you will lose money to me tommorow night!"

Lanois managed a slight smile. "I'm sure I will," he said.

«« — »»

A week later Lanois packed for a trip. The snow had melted as if by magic, leaving the February streets clean and clear. Spring could almost be tasted, though not yet arrived. Trees in Lanois's yard, pear and peach, had begun to show faint buds, and the air was unaccustomly mild and sweet.

The clock in the hall struck eight, and Lanois looked up from his valise, knowing he would be late if he didn't hurry.

He snapped the valise closed and his eye was drawn to the window.

The Green Face was hovering there.

In an instant, it was gone. As Lanois's heart skipped a beat, the window was once again clear, half-raised, letting in the oddly warm air.

Lanois stared at it, waiting for a reoccurrence, and then quickly crossed the room to shut and lock it.

Outside, in his backyard, a bluejay sat on the branch of the nearest fruit tree and cocked its head at him.

Lanois finished packing, pressing two knives into his open suitcase before closing it, and left.

«‹—»»

The trip was as uneventful as all trips were. The weather turned toward winter again, a cold front driving cold air and flurries into the northern city he was visiting, and leaving the sill of his hotel window covered in snow dust. Lanois pulled the shade and sought to nap until the night's meeting.

He closed his eyes, and almost immediately opened them as a knock came upon the door.

"Valet, sir!" a voice called.

Lanois rose, and, sighing, opened the door to reveal a young man with his bagged suit, pressed and ready.

The young man entered, and Lanois took the suit, realizing that his wallet had been moved to the dresser.

"Come in, please, and wait a moment," he said.

The young man, not more than seventeen and smiling, obeyed and entered the room, stopping a discreet distance inside the door.

Lanois retreated to the dresser, opened the top drawer and withdrew the two knives from where they lay atop his folded underclothes.

"Close the door, please," he said.

The young man obeyed.

Lanois was instantly upon him, driving him against the door.

He registered the terror in the young man's eyes.

Lanois raised the two knives and crossed them, driving deep, into his own neck.

«‹—»»

The next morning, in his hotel room, Lanois read of the murder of the valet, whose bisected body had been found in the hotel's laundry chute.

This he read before he opened the window.

Bright sunshine assaulted him, and the day was already warm, heading toward the heat of spring. The trees in the hotel's courtyard were in full bloom, filled with robins, and squirrels chased one another from bole to bole.

The green face was there, a stringless balloon, three dimensional, perfectly formed.

His face.

"It doesn't matter if you're dreaming, does it?" the face said. It even had the fussy straight part of his hair, in bright green. "It doesn't matter if you dream of winter or spring, or if robins chirp or squirrels play. If you see me, you will then dream, and they will die." The face smiled. "Is this not so?"

"Yes," Lanois said, "it is so. You have proved it. The murders are real, and you have caused them to happen."

"Don't you want to know where I come from, Lanois? If I am a creature of your own mind, or a monster from the deep of cold space or roasting hell itself, come to feast on you?"

"It doesn't matter. You exist. I'm sure now."

The face laughed again. "Quite so. Next you will dream of the Prefect's wife, who you admire greatly. She is a handsome woman. They will find her legs cut off, and her tongue and hands."

Lanois turned his back on the face.

"Don't you approve?" the green face laughed. It moved in closer to the open window, hovering above the sill, tilting slightly to stare at him in amusement.

"Of course I do," Lanois said, turning back with both of the knives, crossed with immense tension at the blades, in his hands.

He lunged at the green face, and thrust both of the sharp weapons deep into his own throat.

His green throat.

Tender Tigers

Nancy A. Collins

The Ogre does what ogres can,
Deeds quite impossible for Man,
But one prize is beyond his reach,
The ogre cannot master Speech:
About a subjugated plain
Among it's desperate and slain
The Ogre stalks with hands on hips,
While drivel gushes from his lips.
—*The Ogre*, W.H. Auden

«« — »»

Y ou don't hear much about ogres nowadays. There are tons of books and movies and other media tie-ins about fairies and elves out there. That's because they're supposed to be cutesy-poo make-believe shit, even though I know better.

The same goes for the proliferation of vampires in pop culture, except in that case they've been reinvented as the ultimate misunderstood bad boy. It's hard to believe that humans can take reanimated corpses who feed on the blood of the living and turn them into romantic icons, but there you go.

It doesn't work for ogres, though. They're too scary for the modern nursery, and they certainly don't cut it as sex symbols. Not unless your idea of a romantic evening is a close cuddle on the couch with Leatherface.

In a world that can produce the likes of Jeffrey Dahmer and the Trenchcoat Mafia, stories of cannibal monsters who look enough like humans that they can marry into normal families without anyone noticing the difference cuts a little too close to the bone. So ogres have been downgraded from superstition to folklore, along with all the other long-legged beasties and things that used to go bump in the night. Which suits them just fine. It's much easier to get about your work when nobody believes you exist.

As Pretenders go, ogres are something of an embarrassment. They lack the vampires' mesmeric powers and the were-races' ability to shapeshift, nor do they possess the *strega* and the *sidhe*'s inborn talent for sorcery. What they do have in their favor is that they are very, very strong and the females of the species are, for the most part, indistinguishable from humans. The males can only pass while still young. Once they start developing bull-ogre attributes, there's no being mistaken for "normal" in human society, at least not without considerable camouflage.

If the stories are true, the ogres once battled with and preyed upon the Neanderthals, over whom they had significant advantages in the survival of the fittest department. In their way, they were kings of Shit Mountain back then.

Then Homo Sapiens made the scene.

Although they might have been considerably smaller and physically weaker than the ogres, Cro Magnon had the nasty habit of using tools. Especially sharp ones that could be used from a distance. Things soon got out of hand, as far the ogres were concerned.

Still, with their immense strength, hardy physique and smallish brains, ogres have found a place for themselves in Pretender society by providing muscle to those who require it. They make loyal servants and tireless watchdogs. And, in their own odd way, they are dedicated parents. As commendable as that might sound, you have to bear in mind that they raise their young by stalking human families, hollowing them out, and living inside them. Not literally, mind you. But close enough.

I've had more than a few run-ins with ogres over the years, but mostly because they were in the service of a vampire noble or doing scut-work for human crime bosses or foreign military regimes. But every now and again I come across the odd free-range ogre...

«« — »»

Its not that unusual to see unsupervised youngsters on the city street going to and from the laundromat with bundles of clothes. What caught my eye was how young this particular child was; she couldn't have been any older than seven years old. She was far too small to be manhandling a wire-shopping cart full of clothes and laundry supplies so late at night. She could barely see over the top of the cart, which she pushed with both hands.

As she doggedly maneuvered the overloaded cart up the street, I scanned a half-block before and behind her, trying to spot any adult who might be accompanying her. There was none to be found. This made my antennae go up. Unattended children are the favorite prey of virtually every breed of Pretender, not to mention run-of-the-mill human monsters.

As a precaution, I opened my sight even farther, scanning the pedestrians and other passers-by in the area. While there were plenty of seedy types loitering on the surrounding doorsteps, none of them were werewolves or vampires.

As the child rounded the corner and headed up a side street, I decided to follow her. I kept to the shadows, trailing a safe distance behind but not so near that I would be noticed, yet close enough to act should a smiling stranger emerge from a doorway or lean out of a passing car.

Suddenly, without any warning, one of the wheels on the over-loaded laundry cart gave way, jack-knifing its contents onto the pavement. The girl gave a horrified gasp and clapped her hands to her mouth, a look of fear on her face more in keeping with someone who has foreseen their imminent death, rather than a child who has had a small accident.

That's when I decided to surrender the shadows in favor of stepping forward.

"Hey, kid, you need some help?"

She spun to face me, panic in her bright blue eyes. Then, upon seeing I was a stranger, the fear was replaced by relief.

"Fiona's gonna be mad," she said simply, and then stooped to gather up the clothes.

"Is that so?" I replied as I righted the cart. "Is Fiona your mom?"

"No," she said, with an emphatic shake of her head. "My mommy's dead."

"Then who is this Fiona then?" I asked, taking an armload of laundry, still warm from the dryer, and dropping it back into the cart.

"She's my daddy's wife."

I lifted an eyebrow and tried to smile as openly as I could without showing my teeth. "My name's Sonja. What's yours?"

"Tiffany."

"That's a pretty name."

Tiffany shrugged shoulders as fragile as those of a baby bird. "My daddy says I'm named after a lamp."

"They're very beautiful lamps."

A look of curiosity crossed her pale features, transforming her weary features into those of a child again. "Really? Have you seen one?"

I found her excitement contagious, and I couldn't keep myself from chuckling. "Not only have I seen one, I actually *own* one."

"Wow! Could I see it sometime?" Tiffany asked, her eyes sparkling like her namesake's.

"Nothing's impossible."

"Tiffany!"

The voice was as shrill as a dentist's drill and just as pleasant to experience. I looked up in time to see a woman with a towering bouffant, heavy thighs, and ample bosom, dressed in skin-tight zebra-print leggings and an appliquéd kitty-cat sweatshirt, rapidly bearing down on us. Tiffany's face drained of all color and animation, returning to its previous gray slackness.

"Fiona," she said dully, in way of explanation.

As Tiffany's stepmother drew closer, I caught a scent not unlike that of the lion house at the zoo. It was clear that my presence had not gone unnoticed as well. The ogress froze in her tracks, her piggish eyes narrowing at the sight of me. She tossed her head and made a snorting noise, like a wild boar that's caught wind of a mountain lion.

In such close quarters, it was easy for me to spot the flaws in the ogress' "disguise", as her fingernails were unnaturally long and curled inward, with elaborate tribal totems etched into them. She was one of the crested species, as opposed to the tuskers, and the bouffant served as camouflage for her peaked skull. Her skin was coarsely grained, like the leather of a well-oiled catcher's mitt, and she gave off a raw, animal stink redolent of the big cats. Her teeth were small and sharp, and there were far too many of them, which accounted for her clipped manner of speaking.

"Tiffany," Fiona said, lowering her voice so it no longer sounded like a table saw cutting through sheet metal. "What's been keeping you, child?"

Tiffany glanced in my direction before answering. "The wheel on the cart came off again, and this lady was helping me fix it."

"I'll take over from here, if you don't mind," Fiona said

brusquely. She took a step forward, extending her hand towards Tiffany. "Come along, dear. Your dinner's getting cold."

Tiffany frowned, clearly baffled by Fiona's behavior. Clearly the presence of strangers had never been enough to keep her stepmother's wrath at bay before. She looked at me again, her brow furrowed.

"No problem," I said, keeping my voice as even as I could. "I'll be more than happy to help push the cart the rest of the way."

Fiona's eyes clicked back and forth, trapped. She was unprepared to face a predator of my stature, yet we both knew she could not relinquish the child.

"Hey, Mama! S'up?"

The ogre who came to Fiona's side was young, probably no more than nine or ten years old, but he was already the size of a fifteen year-old boy, with a jutting jaw, beetling brow, splayed nostrils and jagged teeth. His shoulders were wide and heavily muscled, with long arms and oversized hands. His legs were bandy and his feet wide, although his build was hidden, for the most part, by ultra-baggy hip-hop pants and matching shirt. A multi-colored knit stocking cap was pulled low over his thick brow. He was odd looking, but still capable of passing for human in public. Judging from the size of his feet and the width of his shoulders, he would be at least seven feet tall, possibly more, by the time he reached his full growth.

"No, Garth," Fiona said, patting her offspring's shoulder. "There's no trouble. *Now.*"

"Come along home, Tiffany, dear," Fiona said, displaying a fearsome set of shark-like teeth. She knew I would not risk a confrontation with two ogres. I had no choice but to relinquish my grip on the cart. "We mustn't keep your daddy waiting."

There was nothing I could do but stand and watch as Fiona and her hulking son escorted Tiffany towards an apartment building on the corner. For appearances sake, Fiona was actually pushing the heavily laden cart instead of Tiffany.

I knew the ogres would be watching me to see what I would do next, so I turned and headed back up the street without looking back. Once I rounded the corner, I broke into a run towards the street that ran behind Tiffany's building. I entered the cramped lobby of the tenement that stood back-to-back with the apartment building the ogres had entered and pushed all the intercom buttons until I was rewarded with a buzz. I ignored the dingy elevator, taking the crooked stairs three at a time. I made the roof in less than ninety seconds.

A quick glance told me Tiffany's building had a courtyard that served as a holding bay for the tenants' garbage, which put at least thirty feet between her rooftop and the one I was on. I moved to the far end of the roof and made for the opposite ledge at a dead run. One moment I was bound by gravity, the next I was flying through the air, my nostrils filled with the pungent reek of rotting garbage rising from five stories down.

I hit the rooftop, rolling with the fall like a paratrooper, and came up on my feet. I quickly brushed myself off and trotted to the fire escape at the rear of the building. I eased myself onto the metal stairs, careful to avoid the potted plants and hibachis illegally stowed on the landings by various tenants. I had learned a long time ago how not to be seen, but not being heard was another question. I had to be careful not to alert not only my prey, but their neighbors as well.

It didn't take me long to figure out which apartment was Tiffany's. The reek of cooped-up ogre radiating from their third story window was strong enough to cut through the stench from the rotting garbage below me. Careful to remain in shadow, I peeked in through the window.

My first impression was that the room was full of jellyfish. Then I realized what I thought were tendrils drifting from the ceiling were actually scores of yellowed, insect-encrusted flypaper strips. The room looked to be the kitchen and living room, as well as the bathroom, judging from the tub located next to the decrepit stove.

Tiffany's father sat at the filthy Formica dinette table near the window. He was dressed in a dirty polo shirt and a pair of stained khaki pants. With his sallow complexion, bleary eyes and unshaven jaw he looked like a junkie. He was strung out, all right. But not on smack or crack, or even that old standby, demon rum. No, the drug he was on was far more insidious than any that could be snorted, smoked, guzzled or run up.

As I peered in the window, the front door of the apartment opened and Fiona and Garth entered, followed by Tiffany, who was once again pushing the heavy cart. The moment the door was closed behind them, Fiona's mouth pulled into a snarl that would have backed down a mandrill.

"Stupid, horrid little bitch! How many times have I told you *talk to no one!*"

She cuffed the girl's ear so hard she fell to the floor. Tiffany's father flinched as his daughter was struck, but did not open his mouth or try to stand up.

"Yeah," Garth said, grinning like a jack o-lantern, drool dripping from his lower lip. "You're stupid! Stupid! *Stupid!*"

Fiona whirled and slapped Garth in mid-taunt. The young ogre rubbed his jutting jaw, an uncomprehending look on his face.

"What'd I do, Ma?"

"You're no better than she is! You don't even realize how much danger we were in out there!"

Garth furrowed his brow and stuck his lower lip out. "I could have handled it…"

"She was *enkidu*, you witless fool! She would have torn you apart like fresh bread!"

Garth blinked a couple of times as he attempted to process the information he'd been given. He pulled the stocking hat off his head, revealing a bald, leathery pate stretched across a peaked skull.

"That was a *vampire?*" he said after a long pause.

Fiona did not bother to answer, but merely shook her head in disgust. Her gaze fell on Tiffany, who was still huddled on the floor, struggling to control her tears.

"Stop your whimpering, you little wretch!" She grabbed Tiffany's arm, roughly yanking the child onto her feet. "You still have chores to do before you're fed!"

"Let go! You're hurting me!" Tiffany cried as Fiona's bird-like talons bit into the flesh of her upper arm.

Tiffany's father's eyes flashed and his body jerked as if he'd been given a jolt of electricity. "Let her go, damn you!"

Fiona let the child's arm drop and turned to face Tiffany's father. *"My-my-my!"* she sneered. "Looks like you need another fix, sweetie! I can't have you growing a backbone on me *now*, can I?"

Tiffany's father twitched and a look of anticipation mixed with sick fear crossed his wasted features. She was threatening him with what he both dreaded and lived for. He licked his lips with a dry tongue.

"Please," he whispered hoarsely. I couldn't tell if he was begging for mercy or pleading for more.

Fiona pulled her sweatshirt off, baring her upper torso. Her breasts were large and heavy, the nipples the size of a man's thumb and the aureole were the color of a bruise. Tiffany's father's twitch became a full-blown tremor, vibrating his chair like a tuning fork, as he stared at Fiona with lust and horror. Garth smirked as his dame removed her leggings and chuckled in anticipation. Tiffany lowered her head and hurried from the room, her cheeks burning bright red.

The ogress stood nude before her human husband, her taloned hands planted on her hips, legs splayed to better display her sex. Her lips pulled into a twisted smile as she studied her victim's face.

"Oh, yeah. You're jonesing bad, aren't you?"

She grabbed Tiffany's father by the throat, lifting him from his seat as if he weighed no more than his daughter. His eyes bugged slightly from the pressure on his carotid, and although his mouth worked like a goldfish's, he did not put up a struggle. Fiona tossed him onto his back, where he laid, the only signs of life the movement of his eyes and the erection tenting his pants.

The ogress straddled Tiffany's father, unzipped his fly and, after a few seconds of rummaging, freed his hard penis. She laughed and glanced over at her son, who grinned and nodded his head, sharing an unspoken joke between them. Then, without further preliminaries, Fiona lowered herself onto Tiffany's father and began pumping her hips.

I was reminded of a farmer milking a cow instead of the sex act. This was something she had to do to keep control of her household situation, nothing more, nothing less. Tiffany's father's eyelids trembled like those of a junkie on the needle and his jaw dropped open.

Since the scattering of their tribes and the rise of the human empires, ogres have managed to continue by making sexual slaves of human males and using them as camouflage while raising their young. The mucous membranes of an ogress's vagina are impregnated with chemicals that act like a cross between Spanish Fly, Viagra and crack, liberally mixed with DMSO. The moment a human male sticks his dick in an ogress, he's in for the fuck of his life, no two ways about it.

Ogresses seek out widowed or divorced human males and utilize their desperation for sexual relations to gain control of them. The human males they pick are usually passive types to begin with, and once the ogresses work their erotic arts, they are in complete and utter thrall. In time, the human decoys lose interest in bathing, eating, drinking…everything but the one thing they must have.

I grew bored watching the ogress rape her decoy and decided to see where Tiffany had gone. I eased myself over the fire escape railing and crawled headfirst around the corner, clinging to the brick face like a lizard on a garden wall.

I found Tiffany in a cramped bedroom, peering into a white crib with a large picture of a yellow duck carrying a red umbrella emblazoned on the headboard. The floor of the room was littered with empty beer bottles and upended buckets of take-out barbecue ribs, the gnawed bones scattered about the floor like jackstraws. A plastic pail behind the door overflowed with dirty diapers.

"Look who's awake from his nap! Can you give Cissy a smile, Cully? That's a good boy!" Tiffany smiled down at the occupant and gave the Winnie-the-Pooh mobile hanging over the crib a spin. "What? You want me to play peekaboo?" She picked up a stained blanket draped over the foot of the crib and held it in front of her face. "Where's Cully? Where'd Cully go?" Whatever was in the crib gurgled in delight. "Peekaboo! There he is!" She said with mock surprise as she dropped the blanket away from her face. It was the first time I saw anything resembling a little girl shining in her eyes.

The bedroom door crashed open with such force it was knocked off its hinges. Fiona filled the threshold. She was still nude, her monstrosity exposed for all to see. Her toenails were long and curved, like the claws of an iguana, and her carefully maintained bouffant had unraveled, revealing her pointed skull. Still, as ogresses go, she was quite the looker.

"You know you're not supposed to play with the baby!" Fiona shrieked as she advanced on Tiffany. *"You're a bad girl!"* Fiona rasped. "You know what happens to *bad girls*, don't you?"

Tiffany mutely shook her head. She was too frightened to even cry.

"They get eaten up by monsters!" the ogress said, licking her lips with a pointed tongue.

As Fiona grabbed Tiffany's upper arm, the child finally found the breath to scream. It was a high, thin cry, like that of a kitten being tossed down a well. Fiona snarled and backhanded the girl, sending her flying across the room, where she slid, unconscious, between the bed and the wall.

That was my cue.

The ogress spun around as I entered the apartment in a shower of glass. Her lips drew back in a jagged grimace. "I told you to keep your distance, vampire! The morsel's mine!"

There was no point in trying to tell her I was not interested in Tiffany as food. She wouldn't believe me even if I tried. So I bared my fangs and growled deep in my chest. Before I could move on Fiona, I was slammed into the wall hard enough to shake the plaster loose.

"I've got her, Ma! I've got her!" Garth crowed.

Fiona's piggy eyes bulged in consternation. *"Garth! Get away from her!"*

"You should really listen to your mother," I said, as I grabbed his head and jerked it in a direction it was not designed to go. There was a loud snapping sound, like that of a bundle of dry kindling being broken in half, and the young ogre fell to the floor.

I was lucky Garth was a preadolescent. Had he been a year or two older, there would have been no way I could have broken his neck so easily.

Fiona stared at the body of her son for a long moment, then looked directly into my face. Her lips pulled back, exposing rows of needle-sharp teeth, and then charged, her talons at the read, for she was fighting not only for her life, but the life of her remaining offspring.

The ogress' fingernails were hard as thorn and sharp as knives, slicing through my leather jacket like it was tissue paper. I felt something warm and sticky spread across my belly, signaling she had drawn first blood. If I didn't want to find myself tripping over my own guts, I would do well to keep some distance between us.

I tried to reach into her mind, but Fiona had been around long enough to know what a probe felt like. She furrowed her brow and snapped her teeth in rage, saliva flying from her lips. It would take too much time to wrest control of her motor center. Better to get this over with as quickly as possible, before the neighbors finally decided to call the cops.

I flexed my right arm, freeing the switchblade from its sheath inside the jacket's sleeve, and it fell butt-first into my cupped palm. I ran my thumb across the dragon wrapped about the hardwood handle, pressing the ruby chip that served as its eye, and was rewarded by its silver blade springing forth, quick as a serpent's tongue. The ogresses' piggy little eyes narrowed in confusion as she spied the weapon. Vampires don't need to fill their hands in combat.

I feinted with the knife, making as if I was going to stab her in the belly. The ogress moved to block the blow, just as I knew she would. At the very last moment, I drove the blade into her left eye. Unfortunately, doing so meant I was within striking distance of her talons. I felt a sharp pain, and then saw the end of my nose fly across the room in a spray of blood, but I did not dare let go of the switch-blade as I *twisted* it in the socket.

The ogress shrieked like a wounded panther and pushed me away. She staggered drunkenly towards the crib, the switchblade still jutting from her eye socket, blood pouring from her nose and ears. Ogres were not fatally allergic to silver like vampires and werewolves, but a knife in the brain is a bad thing, no matter what species you are.

Fiona's legs buckled on her third step and she grabbed the crib to keep from falling, smearing gore across the headboard. She gargled something in the language of her kind, doubtless a curse on my head, and collapsed, face-first, onto the floor, the switchblade punching its way through the back of her skull like an ice pick going through a ripe cantaloupe.

I nudged her in the ribs with my boot, and then flipped her over in order to retrieve my blade, wiping it clean on my jacket sleeve. As I stood up, I touched the tip of my nose or, rather, where the tip of my nose *used* to be and came away sticky with the thick, blackish-red ichor that passes for my blood. It would take a day's rest to reconstruct the damage, nothing more. I'd have to spend the rest of the night walking around looking like Michael Jackson, but it was far preferable to trying to get across town while holding my intestines in place with a borrowed dinner plate.

Now that Fiona and Garth were taken care of, the last thing on my "to do" list for the night was to dispose of the whelp. I leaned over the crib, knife at ready, but all I found was a tangle of bedclothes and a teddy bear with chewed-off ears.

"Don't hurt my brother."

Tiffany was standing in the farthest corner of the room, clutching a squirming bundle to her thin chest. I have to admit I was surprised to see the girl was still alive. Although there was a bruise spreading its dark bloom across her cheek, and her lower lip was swollen to twice its normal size, she seemed otherwise unharmed.

Realizing what I must look like, I tried my best to get the whelp away from her without frightening her. "Tiffany…honey. Give me the baby."

Tiffany tightened her grip on the whelp and drew away, even though she knew she had no hope of escaping. "I won't let you hurt Cully."

"Tiffany…He's *not* your brother. Fiona tricked your father into thinking Cully was his so he would help feed and care for it. Once it got old enough to walk and talk, Fiona was going to *feed* you to it. It's an ogre…a *monster*…just like Fiona and Garth."

Tiffany shook her head, tears building in her eyes. "But he's just a *baby!* See—?" She flipped back the blanket, exposing the whelp's face.

To my surprise, it was actually cute, although in the same way baby rhinos and gorillas are "cute". It looked human enough to fool the casual observer, although the width of its jaw and the shape of its skull and brow were somewhat odd. The fact it already had a full set of teeth was something of a giveaway, too.

"You love your cissy, don't you, Cully?" Tiffany cooed. The whelp smiled broadly and reached out with a pudgy hand capped with tiny, pointed fingernails, and squeezed Tiffany's nose, giggling with babyish glee.

"See? He *loves* me!" she said, holding Cully out for my inspection. The ogre whelp bared its milk fangs and hissed like a startled kitten, clawing the air in my direction.

"Yes. I see." I replied, stepping forward.

"*No!*" Tiffany wailed, pulling her precious bundle tight to her chest. "Who *says* he has to be like them?"

"He's an *ogre*, Tiffany. That's just how ogres *are*."

"But what if I teach him to be a *good* monster?"

Jesus, the kid was really busting my chops.

"Tiffany," I sighed. "That's impossible."

"Why?" she asked, her voice trembling on the verge of tears. "Just because he *is* a monster doesn't mean he has to *be* a monster! *You're* a good monster, aren't you?"

I opened my mouth, but could not find anything to say.

"I *knew* you weren't going to hurt me," Tiffany said. "Fiona thought you wanted to eat me. But *I* knew you were different. I don't know why, but I just *did*."

I cocked my head and dropped my vision into the occult spectrum. There was a faint glimmer of intuition about the child's head—not enough to qualify as a sixth sense, but enough to be of use in tight situations. I wondered if she had been born with it, or whether her ordeal with Fiona and her demonic brood had forced its development.

I turned and left the bedroom, stepping over the cooling bodies of Fiona and Garth, and entered the combination living room and kitchen. Tiffany's father was curled up in the middle of the floor in a fetal position, muttering to himself under his breath as he rocked back and forth. He quickly lifted his head upon hearing my footsteps.

"*Fiona—?*" he whispered hoarsely.

I grabbed Tiffany's father by the back of his neck and carried him into the bedroom like a kitten. Upon seeing the body of his wife splayed in a slowly expanding pool of her own blood, his entire body began to shake.

"*Thank God*," he sobbed. "*Thank God, thank God...*" He staggered as I let go of him. I didn't know how much longer Tiffany's father had, but at least he possessed enough sanity to rejoice over his captor's demise.

"Do you have family elsewhere?"

Tiffany's father nodded weakly. "Back in Kentucky."

I reached into the breast pocket of my jacket and removed a thick fold of hundred dollar bills I keep there for emergencies. "Take this. Pack what you can in two suitcases and simply go. Don't worry about the cops. There's no way in hell the authorities are going to pursue this, believe me. Besides, homicide only applies to human beings. Take Tiffany and the baby and walk away like this never happened."

Tiffany's father shot a fearful look at Cully, who promptly bared his little milk fangs and growled. He swallowed loudly, and then looked back at me.

"Are you sure?"

I glanced at the snarling ogre whelp, then at Tiffany's tear-stained face.

"Family is family. Whatever else Cully might be, he's still your son, " I lied.

Having said that, I turned my back on Tiffany, her father and Cully and walked out of the apartment and their lives. I had done what I could; now it was up to them. I have not seen or heard from them since. Nor do I expect to.

Every now and again, though, I wonder whether I made a mistake not destroying the ogre whelp when I had the chance. But then I remember how it smiled and cooed in Tiffany's arms, and how brightly the love in her eyes had shone for the monstrous infant she claimed as kin, and my doubts are set aside.

There is a character from one of the old Oz books called The Hungry Tiger. Like his companion, The Cowardly Lion, he was a most uncommon talking beast. Although The Hungry Tiger longed to eat fat babies, even drooled when he thought about it, his tender heart would not allow him to do such a horrid thing.

There is no telling what role nature plays over nurture in human families, much less those of ogres. If it turns out I made the wrong decision, Tiffany and her father shall no doubt pay with their lives, if they have not done so already. But if it turns out I made the right decision...well, the world could stand a few more tender tigers.

Spin Cycle

David G. Barnett

o ahead. Drive home, you bastard. Show the bitch.
The wind cold on the flesh as the hilltop sinks into black. The moon doesn't shine here. Darkness enters every pore, seeps through to the marrow.

The bottle slips from his hand. The grass catches it and the earth gulps greedily at its flowing contents. The night wraps itself around him and squeezes 'til he pukes. Sickening stench fills his nostrils. The bottle is back in his hand. Empty, cool, hard.

Right up side her fat, fucking face.

The bottle feels good. Thirst hungrily for its warm comfort. Nothing. The night welcomes the empty bottle and swallows it whole. There is no more. A quick thought of licking the wet ground. Pathetic.

The truck?

Frantic searching—nothing. Angry fists pound cool metal. A frenzy of motion. Long, black, greasy hair thrashes in the night. Flannel whips and slaps dirty bluejeans. Steel-tipped work boots dent the door above three-year-old rust. Decayed, metal flakes drop to the ground—mashed in by stomping feet.

Projecting the anger does no good.

Gotta take it out on her. Boot right in the ass.

A loud slam. The hilltop explodes in a halogen flame. Silence disappears as eight cylinders scream into the night. The road is shown no mercy and a dust cloud, obscuring two red, demon eyes growing smaller in the distance, is left to settle slowly.

Here I come baby.

Cold tears dry on a warm cheek.

SHIVERS

She stood there while the cops told him to take a drive. Not much else they could do. Dog ain't no good. Licks his balls and looks the other way. Three beers and momma's already out. She gonna be pissed in the morning when she ain't got no beer and no money for more. Her old man ain't gonna give her no money if'n she wasn't there tonight to suck him dry. She gonna bitch at me.

The rifle. Full, cool, hard.

Show him what I got. Show him real good. One step and...

A rumble from the chair. Oughta give her one right in the head. Put her outta her misery. Bitch stinks. Still, momma gave him a good wallop. Black eye for sure. Serves the fuck right. Expecting me to cook him dinner after doing welfare all day.

Long, and hard. A sense of arousal as hands caress black steel. Tongue moistens lips. A desire down below. Pathetic.

«« —»»

Hard at the thought of cracking her in the mouth. Hands grip the wheel tighter.

Cops said take a drive...calm down. Fuck 'em! First her, then her goddamn momma.

A quick glance in the mirror. Eye swollen like a ripe plum.

She gonna get it. Get it good.

Foot pressed to the floor. Road rutted from last nights rain. Shocks reaching limits. Steering wheel slipping from grip. Tires losing hold.

Faster. Faster. Faster.

Gonna slap the shit outta her. Then fuck what's left.

Road coming too fast. *Crack.* Drive shaft drops. *Clang—Clang— Clang.* Hot metal ping-pongs under the carriage. Shard enters front tire. *Blown.* The roll comes quickly. Fraction of a second. A tree stops the motion. *Instant.* Some bark lost, spackled over with flesh, painted in blood.

No explosion. Not a movie...real life.

No death at first. Only excruciating pain. Then shock. Then dark silence.

Real life.

Real death.

DAVID G. BARNETT

«« — »»

Two years after and the grieving is long past, interrupted after only two weeks. Uncertain sadness, outweighed by the need for beer and grass. Plenty of men with change for both. Whored out for a good meal. Hundreds of men and not one wants her for keeps, only for a quick suck, fuck and slap on the ass.

«« — »»

She got a new man, one that wants her for more than just her hole. Bigger, stronger, meaner than the last. But she needs him.

Suck him hard when he wants. Food when he wants. Cold beer when he wants. Punching bag when he wants. But she needs him.

«« — »»

Trailer bitch, but sucks a mean one. Hole's too loose for his liking, but got another whore for that shit. Only that one's got a kid. Can't handle no fuckin' kids. This one gets pregnant. Bam! One in the gut and it's floatin' in the water. Take care of that shit.

Get her goddamn momma off the couch and back to her old man. Needs a good ass-kickin'. Bitch stinks.

Dog don't like him none. Trip to the woods. *Bang!* Bullet to the head. Take care of that shit.

Get home, get some food. No suck tonight. Gotta save the load for the tight whore. Give me any shit about goin' out—*Bam!* Fist to the head. Take care of that shit.

«« — »»

Welfare ran out a few months ago. Made her get a job. Strippin' out at Lou's. She don't like to work. Got the job because she could suck, not because she could strip. Little room in the back. Twenty-five-buck-suck; she sees ten of it. Make's a cool two-hundred sometimes, maybe more, all in one night. It's a skill.

Moved up to whiskey.

«« — »»

Bitch is rakin' it in. New tires for the truck. New dog. Sittin' pretty.

225

SHIVERS

«« —»»

Whiskey's making her lazy. Gettin' flabby. Strippin' ain't no good. Only laughs and jeers. They only want to see her pick up change. Squat down, no hands. Freak. Twenty-five-buck-suck only now.
    Good money, but it's all gone. New tires, *shit.* Killed the dog. Says it ran away—*bullshit.* Time to tell him to get. There's always another one. He's gonna be pissed.

«« —»»

Wants to beat her, beat her til she drops. Can't do it. She's his bread and butter. Can't damage the goods.
    Manhandled out the door and shoved into the shed for a few days. That'll show her. Teach her not to fuck around anymore.
    Ragged screams in the night. No one for miles, but the sound gets to him. A flick of the latch and a small dark shape is tossed into the blackness of the shed. The screams stop.
    That 'coon'll shut her fat face up.

«« —»»

The cops told him to take a drive. Nothing else they could do. Shouldn't have come back. Should've just left her.

«« —»»

Bang! Bullet in the head. She warned him. No uncertain sadness this time.

«« —»»

Self-defense. She showed them the 'coon bites. No prosecution. Told her story on a dozen talk shows. Lots of sympathy. Lots of money. Better trailer.
    Moved up to scotch.
    Momma still likes her beer. Still stinks.

«‹—»»

No more money. The trailer ain't lastin' much longer. Body's turned to shit. No more strippin'.

Needs a man.

Outside, gravel crunches under heavy tires.

«‹—»»

Met at the door by polyester stretched taut and the smell of Salisbury steak TV dinners. Good meal, good suck, and a good night sleep. Dirt scrapes off on the welcome mat. He looks down, dirty old boots. Gotta get this bitch to work.

Throwing Caution to the Wind: Crypts, Cartes, Crimes, and Camaraderie

Kelly Laymon

Author's Note: This article tells the tale of what is now known as the Horrorfind Weekend, which you may be attending right now. Two years ago, over Labor Day weekend, Brian Keene (one of the head honchos of this here event) demonstrated his ability to summon authors and fans from every corner of the country for what amounted to a keg party. We called it Keene Con. Seriously, folks showed up from Seattle, Los Angeles, the Bronx, Chicago, Buffalo, San Diego, and many locals from Maryland and Virginia. There was one person in attendance from Ireland. So, here's how it all started! And every word is true, that's the scary part. Have fun and enjoy!

«« — »»

M y weekend fell into place when the Rastafarian mozied aboard the airplane holding only a pair of rollerblades, a Bible, and a hackey sack. I spent my entire flight from Los Angeles to St. Louis watching out of the corner of my eye as he bobbed and shook his fists above his head in praise while reading the Bible.

That was the sign. I was going to Keene Con and there was no turning back.

When I arrived in St. Louis, I decided to give Brian Keene a call. I wasn't sure how I was getting from the airport to the party once I landed in Baltimore. Brian informed me that *he* was shitfaced, that Ed Lee and my father were *really* shitfaced, and that the least shitfaced person at the party would be driving out to pick Geoff Cooper and I up in a car at the airport.

Oddly enough, this was no cause for concern for me. I was afraid that *everyone* was going to be shitfaced and that Brian would send Irish horror writer Eoghain O'Keeffe to pick Geoff and I up on a bicycle.

The flight from St. Louis to Baltimore was uneventful. I *was* riddled with anticipation though. I knew that once I got off that plane, a weekend of insanity would officially begin.

I stepped out of the jetway and walked down the concourse. Down a distance, I could see four of my friends dressed in black, and one man I didn't know clad in safari attire. (I was dressed for a luau, so we were quite the motley crew.) As I approached, the five men dropped to their knees with raised arms and bowed repeatedly in praise.

I walked up to them, laughing my ass off, and they stood up.

Geoff Cooper ran up to me first. He hugged me, picked me up, then started to walk away with me lifted six inches off the ground. I was still holding my duffel bag in one hand and rolling my suitcase by its handle with my other. As Geoff walked and carried me in his arms, Brian Keene snatched the duffel bag from one of my hands, but I continued to roll the suitcase behind Geoff and I for a good fifty feet until Mike Oliveri caught up with us and grabbed it from me. After Geoff put me down, it was Brian's turn. Brian picked me up and turned me sideways. I was parallel with the ground for a good minute or two.

My feet stayed on the ground when I hugged Eoghain and Mike. I was then introduced to Mark Lancaster. I had never met him before, but was familiar with him through his postings on the *Masters of Terror* message boards.

We were ready to roll.

We hadn't even been together five minutes before crimes were committed, the least of which was being drunk and disorderly conduct.

Brian frolicked through the airport with my multi-colored Punky Brewster style duffel bag over his shoulder, saying in his best gay voice, "Do you like my purse? I think it's colorful. It's lovely, really. My name is Bruce."

Sobering up for a moment, Brian pointed out to me, "You realize, right, that you were the only woman on that plane who had five men bowing to her?"

No one remembered where the van was parked. After wandering through the empty airport for some time, Brian dropped the luggage and decided to stand on his head. Far too drunk to complete the stunt, he rolled around on the airport carpet on his back with his ass in the air.

"I'm *way* too drunk to do this. Ask me again when I'm sober," he assured us.

As we crossed a bridge from the airport to the parking garage, we stumbled across a *Caution: Wet Floor* sign. Upon seeing the sign, Geoff said to me, "Oh, I *so* want that."

But Geoff kept walking.

Since I was taking up the rear, I shouted back to him, "You really want it?"

He nodded his head enthusiastically.

Brian and Mike had taken my bags, so my hands were free. I snatched up the sign and walked away. When Geoff looked back and saw that I had made the catch, he quickly shoved his lit cigarette into his mouth to free his hands, stopped rolling his suitcase, and unzipped it. After I caught up with Geoff, I handed him the sign and he stuffed it into his suitcase.

As we nonchalantly walked away from the scene of the crime, Geoff said to me, "By the end of this weekend, I'm gonna find a fuckin' use for this ganked sign."

We found the van and moved the luggage off the rented Smarte Carte and into the trunk. Geoff then decided that he also wanted the Smarte Carte. He raised the luggage cart over his head and crammed it into the trunk saying, "We're takin' this fucker too."

Eoghain was reluctant and argued, "No, Geoff! No! We can't take this too! We already took a safety sign! We can't take the trolley as well! Take the trolley out of the boot, Geoff!"

But Geoff, after much effort, managed to close the trunk door and we were off...until someone remembered about the guard post at the parking garage exit.

Brian removed the Smarte Carte from the trunk and hopped into its place.

Mark took the wheel, while Mike, Eoghain, Geoff and I sat in the two rows of back seats and Brian curled up in the trunk.

"No one wants shotgun?" Mark asked the group.

We were in our own worlds. Brian was in the trunk and that was fine by us. The doors were closed and we were off...really this time.

Keene Con? Huh?

Maybe this would be a good time to quickly explain just what was going on. Why had Geoff, Eoghain, Mike, and I traveled to Baltimore from Seattle, Ireland, Chicago, and Los Angeles for Labor Day weekend? A friend threw a party, it was just that simple. Brian Keene (*More Than Infinity*) wanted to spend some time with his horror writing buddies in between organized conventions, and we all answered the call.

During the course of this endless drive from the Baltimore airport to a town called Cockeysville, yes Cockeysville, many things happened…

Geoff Cooper (*Bad News, A Darker Dawning I & II*) found a blanket under his seat, lifted it up to show us, and yelled, "See this fucker here? It's a blanket! We coulda used this to cover the cart. We didn't need to leave that fucker! And I *would* have gotten the luggage cart past the guard. Trust me on that."

In between requests that Mark replay King Missile's "Detachable Penis," Eoghain O'Keeffe assured me that my act of petty larceny was all for the best and said, "If I was a sign, I'd rather be at Keene Con. Personally, I think it will be happier at Brian's."

Sitting in the trunk, Brian nervously notified us of people who were tailgating, saying, "Mark? Whatever you do, don't stop right now…or now."

More than halfway home, Brian looked around the inside of the van and screamed, "Holy shit! We lost someone!"

We were all confused and assured him that no one was missing.

Brian was convinced we had left someone at the airport and reasoned, "But the front seat next to Mark is empty and there are supposed to be six of us. Mark, Mike, Eoghain, Geoff, and Kelly. That's only five! *See*?!?! I told you we lost someone. There are only five of us here!"

The four of us in the back seats quickly turned around to face Brian, pointed at him, and shouted, "Six! You're six!"

Brian still didn't buy it and argued, "What did we do with Judi? Or Lee? Did we put Vince somewhere? Are they *really* all back at the house? I could have sworn there was one more here. To come and pick up Kelly and Geoff, right? They didn't come with us? There was another."

Mike assured him that they were all back at the house with Dick and Ann Laymon.

After Brian considered this flood of information for a moment, he asked, "Shit…then why am I sitting in the trunk then?"

Not wanting to waste the front seat, Brian climbed over the two rows of seats holding Mike, Eoghain, Geoff and I and squeezed himself through the gap between the driver's seat and the passengers. He turned himself forward as he fell on his elbow and yelled an expletive, then he sat down.

Before we arrived at Brian's house, Geoff needed some smokes. We found a Rite-Aid after we got off the freeway, and Brian and Geoff went in. Since I had to get out of the van to let Geoff exit, I stood at the sliding van door while they were in the store. While I was standing there, Mike and Eoghain cheerfully told me about the "endless hilarity" that ensued earlier in the evening as my shitfaced father struggled to remain seated in a rocking wicker chair. I responded, "Are you sure he's shitfaced? He's capable of that sober."

After a while, the remaining four of us wondered what was taking them so long. We even started to contemplate what we were going to do if Brian and Geoff came bustin' outta the store running, yelling "Go! Go! Go! Drive! Drive! Drive!"

Eventually I went in. They were at the counter paying for their goods. I told them what we had been discussing. Brian laughed and said, "Kelly, go back out to the van and say, 'Oh my god. I don't believe it. Oh my god.' Act really worried, like we're doin' something horrible in here."

I walked back out to the van shaking my head in disgust. I jumped back into the van and said, "I don't know what they're doin'. Oh god. I don't know. What a mess."

Inside the Rite-Aid, Brian and Geoff hatched a plan that made the clerk lady say, "Oh, I get it. You two are a coupla clowns, huh?"

Sure enough, a minute or so later, Brian and Geoff came bustin' outta the Rite-Aid at full speed. Their arms were flailing and they were running as fast as they could. They also had a large black security guard hot on their trail. Everyone in the van laughed. After the scene died down, Mike Oliveri (*Deadliest of the Species, 4x4*) said, "Man, I woulda believed it until I looked back at the security guard and saw that big ole grin on Shaft."

Then we arrived at the party.

Sure enough, people *were* shitfaced. My father's tongue was hanging out of his mouth, his voice was squeaky, and one eye was drooped shut, but he was hell bent on taking blurry, lopsided pictures of everyone. It was time to go back to the Econo Lodge. Ed Lee (*The Bighead, City Infernal*) was also staying at that motel, so he rode back with us.

The next morning, Saturday, when my parents and I met up with Ed, we compared notes on the three different rooms we had occupied. We quickly discovered that a leaky sink and tub that wouldn't drain were features of every room. "Hey," Ed said, "I mistook this place for The Four Seasons."

When we returned to Brian's, I immediately whipped out an Easy Mac meal I had brought with me from home and ate lunch. I saw a giant plastic twelve-inch deep blue bowl in the sink filled with dingy and clumpy water. The edges of the bowl were crusted with brown chunks. Everyone *told* me it was from the chili, but I had my doubts. (By the way, the bowl stayed there until Monday morning.) I decided that I would be the control of the convention. I wouldn't eat *any* of the food served, and then if everyone died but me, we'd know that Brian made a bad batch of "chili."

I found a topless Brian Keene barbecuing in the yard. A picnic table was covered with assorted goodies, from potato chips and cookies to brownies and salads.

Then it started to rain. Geoff, who had been standing out in the yard with me and some others, ran into the house and came back with the *Caution: Wet Floor* sign. He proudly propped it up on the porch and looked around at the rest of us with a nasty grin.

Not concerned enough, and too intrigued to take it in, I watched the potato and pasta salads drown in the rain. By evening, they had worked their way into the kitchen and were mingling with the fresh dinner food. No one was the wiser.

Despite the rain, Brian kept barbecuing. The hamburgers and hot dogs cooked in a puddle on the tin foil of the tiny barbecue. Some of the food was moved into the house, and a few of us stood outside with Brian as he cooked in the rain.

Inside, my father and Ed Lee signed books for some fans attending the event, while a soaked Gerard Houarner and Linda Addison arrived by car. A car with about five inches of water in it.

Later on in the day, Brian handed out door prizes. The door prizes consisted of freebies sent by publishers who wished to attend the event and books Brian had doubles of. For example, I got his old paperback copy of Peter Straub's *Ghost Story* because he had recently acquired the hardbound.

Brian also held a trivia game for goodies brought by Keene Con attendees. In my suitcase I had packed a few copies of the Headline paperback edition of *Come Out Tonight*. Gerard Houarner came with copies of *Dead Cat Bounce*, while Linda Addison had her novel, *Animated Objects*, up for grabs. Dan Harm's *The Necromonicon Files* was also given out. Vince Harper, of Bereshith and Shadowlands Publishing, brought proofs of his soon-to-be-published Tom Piccirilli novel, *The Night Class*.

Brian had a special gift ready for eleven-year-old horror fan and writer Sarah Keddrell, whose short story, "Batteries Not Included," was printed in the sixteenth issue of *Jobs in Hell*. Brian gave her a three volume set of the complete works of H.P. Lovecraft.

I stuck my head into the guest room to take a peek at the interview

Holly Newstein (*Out of the Light*) was conducting with Brian and some of the other attendees for *Hellnotes*. I saw Geoff, with a lit cigarette in one hand and a cup of coffee in the other, hopping up and down wildly, shouting, "The fucking fucker is fucking fucked," at Holly. She took it well.

During the course of Friday, Saturday, Sunday, and Monday, we spent much time talking with friends both near and far. Telephone calls were made to and received by Mikey Huyck, Regina Mitchell, and Tom Piccirilli, all of whom could not make it to the bash.

In the evening, a viewing was held of Clifton Holmes's film adaptation of my father's novel, *In the Dark*. Although I've seen the movie at least once and I always rewatch the Mayr Heights massacre, Ed Lee's humorous and often naughty commentary made this second viewing all the more enjoyable.

One not-so-risque highlight: After a male character told the female lead, "You're dressed like a hooker with a gun in your hand," Ed Lee announced, "Sounds like my kind of woman."

Luckily, the young Sarah didn't stick around for the entire screening of the ultra-naughty *In the Dark*, with even worse commentary by Ed Lee, but earlier in the evening she *did* manage to earn herself the nickname "Nutcracker." According to Sarah, "I didn't mean to injure Geoff! I was just swinging my arms back and forth, Geoff walked in behind me and *wham*! I hit him. I started to laugh and cry at the same time because I was so embarrassed. I ran out of the kitchen and out into Brian's back yard. I came back into the house, and my mom was smiling at me when I peeked into the kitchen. I went back in and apologized to Geoff."

An amused Geoff remembered, "My *God* that fuckin' hurt."

After the movie was over, Feo Amante and Julie Morales finally arrived. Feo drove from San Diego to Buffalo to pick Julie up before heading down to Maryland. Long after Feo should have left on this trek we were still noticing updates on his website.

The first thing Julie wanted upon her arrival was a mixed drink. Brian stepped up to make her a juice and vodka. When he was done, he added some clear booze from a bottle with a label printed in Russian. Julie and I looked at each other with concern.

"What's that you're adding?" she asked.

"It's okay Julie, I think Vince brought it," Brian told her.

Julie took a sip or two and said, "Man, this is *strong*!"

When Julie finally woke up, she did so with one doozie of a hangover.

When we drove Ed Lee back to the motel with us, we said our good-byes. Ed Lee was going home Sunday morning. Ed, who loves a party, especially a good party with good booze " had a friggin' blast. Even the hangovers were great!"

On Sunday morning, we were preparing to go to Brian's for the day when my father went to the ice machine and never came back to my mother and I. We figured he must have run into Ed Lee. (Or, as Ed described it, he was "eaten up by the great Lee dragon.") When I went off in search of my father and never came back to my mother, it became a given. My mother finally came along in search of my father and I and joined the party. We spent about another half hour talking with Ed Lee before his cab came.

When we arrived at Brian's we were informed that a field trip was planned. We were all going to troop down to Edgar Allan Poe's grave.

Earlier in the week I had been telling Geoff about an experience my parents and I had at the Edgar Allen Poe house in which we were almost taken down my some crackhouse thugs. Before the group left, Geoff pulled me aside and said, "Kel, if you want it, I've got my Taurus."

I hadn't been drinking, but, caught off guard, I said, "Oh, well I think we've got plenty of cars."

Geoff wrinkled his face and said, "Like you have your Sig, I have my Taurus."

"Oh!" I exclaimed. "I think we'll be okay. We're in a big group and we're only going to the grave, not the house that's in the center of gangland. Thanks."

As it turned out, it's a good thing none of us were packin' heat that day. Once our caravan of six cars parked a few blocks from the grave, we got into even more trouble.

The Edgar Allen Poe grave was closed.

Brian walked around to the brick wall on the side of the graveyard, ran at the wall, jumped, and climbed it. Brian sat on top of the wall with a skinned knee and smiled for a few minutes before Feo joined him. They sat and contemplated what to do, then Brian jumped down and the crowd on that side of the wall disappeared. Everyone went around to the front of the graveyard except Feo and I. Feo was on the wall and I was on the ground.

"What should I do?" Feo yelled down to me. "Everyone left!"

"You really want to put your business cards on the tomb, right? Go for it. You can only do this shit once. Do it!" I persuaded him.

Next thing I knew, Feo was gone. He was down on the ground inside the graveyard with his stack of business cards out and ready.

I quickly ran around to the front of the graveyard to join the rest of the group and watch the scene transpire through the black metal bars of the gate. Sure enough, Feo was walking right up to the grave.

A window cleaner perched on scaffolding outside the church at the graveyard yelled, "Hey, what're you doin'? This place is closed."

Feo, quick on his feet in both mind and body, said, "I'm just a great admirer of his work. I'm paying my respects," as he placed two FeoAmante.com business cards on each side of Poe's grave.

Then Feo booked over the spiky black metal rod gate.

We failed to take into account the fact that Feo had the exact same advertisement, logo, and contact information from the business card plastered across the back of his car in a giant decal.

"They got the car too?!?!" we planned on saying to the police officers.

We spent the rest of the day at the Inner Harbor, shopping, eating lunch, and cringing as Judi Rohrig stood in the middle of a busy Baltimore street to take a group photo.

Sunday evening was the night of the beer penis. As Tom Piccirilli jokingly said upon hearing bits of this story, "Beer penis? You know, there are times when I'm sorta glad I didn't make the party."

Julie, Eoghain, Brian and I were all in the guest room talking and joking. Brian turned away, and when he turned back around to face us he had his beer bottle jammed in the zipper of his jeans. He posed for Julie's camera. Within seconds, Eoghain was on his knees in front of Brian. A picture was to be taken of this scene. As Brian walked toward Eoghain with the beer penis ready to go, the open and full bottle spilled onto Eoghain's slacks as he knelt there.

"Ooops! I was a little early there," Brian said apologetically.

"That's okay," Eoghain comforted him. "It happens."

Later that night, Julie and I logged into the Horronet chat room to see what was going on. There weren't going to be many people in there since most of our crew was under one roof. The only person we ran into was Regina Mitchell. Brian joined in and we all talked with Gina for a few minutes until the readings began.

We were treated to selections of fiction from Mike, Geoff, Brian, and Feo. They all shared unpublished projects they had recently completed. We also experienced our first exposure to the fiction of Eoghain O'Keeffe. We had a blast.

Even later that same night, Eoghain logged onto Horrornet and ran into Scary Redneck Weston Ochse. I knew this was bad news. During the week prior to Keene Con, Weston had used some choice words with Mike Oliveri and I when we were getting all giggly about the impending event.

"Fuck y'all, okay," he told Mike and I.

When Eoghain encountered him Sunday night, he told Eoghain to "Fuck off!"

I don't blame Weston. We did have a great time with our friends. I'd be envious of us too.

All day Monday, we picked up the pieces of Keene Con. Geoff Cooper left for the airport at the crack of dawn. Later on, Mike and Melissa Oliveri embarked on their drive back to the Chicago area. My parents went out to lunch with Eoghain, Julie, Feo, and Dan, and from lunch, Julie, Feo, and Dan left for Buffalo. Brian and I stayed behind and vacuumed in a futile attempt to dry up a giant wet puddle in the hallway carpet near the bathroom. Where was that sign again?

My parents dropped me off at the airport on Tuesday morning, and my weekend ended in much the same way it began; with an annoying person at the airport. I rode on a jitney from Baltimore to New York City. They called it an airplane, but I called it a bus with wings. I had never been on a plane with propellers before, and the plane never got more than fifty feet off the ground. Before take off, in prayer, I recited lines from "Chantilly Lace" and "Peggy Sue."

Once I landed in New York, I had to ride a bus from the patch of grass near JFK on which the pilot landed the jitney to the actual airport. I offered up my seat to an elderly woman. She did not thank me, but replied in a snotty voice, "Age before beauty, right dearie?"

I asked myself, " What would Geoff Cooper do?"

I don't think she had ever had a Jets hat stuffed there before...

Portrait of a Sociopath

Edward Lee

T he beach. The crashing waves.
The beautiful bodies...
There's something idyllic about the beach, isn't there? Where the sea meets the land and all that?

That's where I live now. That's where I'll *always* live.

Because here, at the beach, all I gotta do is look out my window to see heaven. Oh, yeah. I can see them lying there on their blankets, their suntanned flesh shellacked with oil, their sex beckoning me.

All the beautiful bodies...

My feast.

«« —»»

I killed the folks when I was seventeen. Dad wanted me to go to college—you know, Harvard, Princeton, some blueblood school like that—but I didn't wanna. So one night I took his Webley out of the closet and blew his head off while he was working in the den. That Webley—Christ!—it was loud. Mom, of course, she never heard the shot. She was upstairs in bed—in the middle of the afternoon, for Christ's sake—tranked out on valium. I decided I had to make a good show out of her; I carved her up right there in bed—Sheffield makes the best carving knives, take my word for it. I figured doing it up real sick was the best way. Who'd ever suspect a seventeen-year-old kid of slicing his mom up like Thanksgiving turkey and throwing her guts around the room?

Took six weeks for the will to get out of probate. Dad was worth millions, plus there was the trust fund I got to take when I turned eighteen.

So what did I do? Not two months after dear old mom and dad were in the ground?

I moved to the beach...

«« — »»

No, I'm not crazy, which is probably what you think. I guess I'm what they call a clinical sociopath. Don't take drugs. Was never slapped around as a kid. Never got sodomized by an uncle or a babysitter, and I swear I was never locked in a closet.

So why did I kill my parents?

Same reason I killed over twenty more since then.

For the hell of it, that's why.

«« — »»

I planned it out pretty smart so I wouldn't take the rap. We lived in this big stuck-up ritzy house in Potomac, and there was this guy who'd come by every week or so and clean the pool. This guy had a real scumbag look to him, and the kid who worked with him told me he also had an arrest record for peeping in windows about ten years ago. So the night I punched mom and dad's ticket, I went to this guy's apartment and put the Webley and the carving knife under the front seat of his truck.

Asshole. Somebody should've told him to lock his doors.

He went up for life without parole.

«« — »»

Yeah, sure. Money. That's as good a reason to kill people as any, isn't it? Next thing I know, I'm rich, I can do anything I want.

So I bought a house on the beach, nothing too showy, just a decent place sitting up on this sandy hill overlooking the water. Close enough to walk right out to the waves, but no neighbors, you know?

No one to hear the pretty screams.

«« — »»

A murderer, a sexual sociopath—you'd think they'd have a *look,* you know what I mean? But not me. I look just like anyone else— better, actually. I keep in shape. I run ten miles a day, that's right, *ten miles.* It's great to run up and down the beach, checking out all those hot bodies. Plus I eat right, lift weights, all that.

Every summer's a hay-day. They think they're going on vacation! I do the job on, say, one a month. That keeps me satisfied. I mean, they're all over the place, thousands of them, all trim and slim, all suntanned, all beautiful.

I just…

I just can't help it.

«« —»»

They never find the bodies. Hell, I'm not stupid. I got a nice inboard Sea-Ray, a twenty-four footer. After I do one, the next morning I just go out for a cruise a couple miles out, and dump the body parts out in weighted lobster pots.

The lobsters eat good around here.

«« —»»

Sometimes it's like a dream. Late evening's the best time. I'll cruise the beach bars—shit, there are probably a hundred of them— and check out the tush. You wouldn't believe how stupid they are. Buy them a few drinks, flatter them, then make the move and that's that. My place or yours, you know? I always insist on my place.

Then, of course, we get it on. Mongo sex, bigtime. I fuck their brains out. I give it to 'em like you wouldn't believe. And I always serve champagne afterwards. They all like that, it's a classy touch.

Their glass, of course, is spiked with sodium amobarbitol.

And by the time they wake up, I've got them in the basement, shackled down but good…

«« —»»

Peerless detention cuffs, they're the best brand. Shackles for the ankles, cuffs for the wrists. I work on them long and slow. Christ, it's so much fun! The *snap! snap! snap!* of the cuffs as they jerk on the table. The way their long, tan, beautiful legs tense each time I stick another needle in. Sometimes their eyeballs hemorrhage from the pain, and turn this weird tomato-juice bright red. I love to hear their brittle, beautiful screams. I love the way they plead and whine, the way they *beg* me, the way they *promise* they'll do *anything* I want if I let them go.

SHIVERS

Some of the things they promise to do—
Christ. It's downright sick.

«« — »»

Yeah, that's the best thing about the world today. Things aren't always as they seem. Just ask any of them.

God, it's *so* easy.

Once they get a look at me, in my Bill Blass string bikini, my 36 C-cups, and my nut-brown tan and long blond hair...

These fuckin' guys are all mine.

The Other Man

Ray Garton

M y wife's body was empty again.

She lay beside me in bed, eyes closed, breathing so shallowly that when I placed a mirror beneath her nose only the faintest vapor appeared on the glass. Even the small twitches and tics her body usually went through during sleep were absent. The muscles of her face were so flaccid that her cheeks seemed to sag, as if about to run fluidly off her skull.

I lifted her arm, then let go; it dropped heavily to the mattress like the arm of a corpse and she did not stir.

I pinched the back of her hand. No response.

I clutched her shoulders, shook her violently and shouted her name. Nothing.

Sharon was not there.

I sat on the edge of the bed for a while, holding my head in my hands, thinking thoughts that made me doubt my sanity, absurd thoughts that had haunted me for weeks, seeming less and less absurd as time passed.

Putting on my bathrobe, I left the bedroom, made myself a drink and started a fire in the den's fireplace. With only the light of the small lamp beside my chair and the flickering glow of the flames, the den became a ballroom where shadows danced with light all around me, mocking me, making light of the cold fear that grew in my gut.

There were three books stacked on the lamp table. They were *her* books. There were others like them scattered all over the house. I reached for one, stopped, then jerked my hand back as if burned. I stared at the book warily, as I might have stared at a poisonous snake coiled to strike. To open one of those books and begin reading would be to admit that my idea might not be absurd at all. I wasn't sure I was ready to admit that yet.

The room grew cool as the fire waned and I finished three drinks, all the while sitting in my chair staring at the top book on the stack. The liquor made me tired, but I knew I wouldn't be able to sleep. Finally, I opened the book and began to read....

«« —»»

The first change I noticed in my wife was her silence in the evenings. After twelve years of marriage, I had grown fond of our conversations at the end of the day, our dinner table banter and discussions of the day's events. But eight months ago, I ate dinner alone for the first time I could remember. When I asked Sharon why there was only one place set at the table, she said she'd already eaten and left the dining room. After dinner, I found her in the den curled up with a book before the fire. I asked her what she was reading, but had to repeat my question again before she was even aware of my presence.

"Oh, I'm sorry, Jim," she said, distracted. "Just a book I picked up." She continued reading.

She picked up a lot of books over the next few weeks, some of them dusty and dog-eared used copies, others brand new and all of them about the same thing: astral projection.

I had always known Sharon to be an extraordinarily rational, level-headed person who was so uninterested in sensationalism that she didn't even glance at the tabloids at the supermarket check-out stands. Even more odd than her new interest was the growing distance between us. There was less and less conversation; we never made love anymore; and when she was reading one of her books—which she seemed to be doing all the time—I felt completely alone in the house.

When I tried to get her to talk about whatever was wrong, she would only smile, maybe laugh and swipe a hand through the air gently, and assure me that *nothing* was wrong, she was just *reading,* that was all.

"But why are you reading *that?*" I asked one evening.

"This? Because it's interesting."

"But you've never been interested in that sort of thing before. People floating around outside of their bodies? Come *on,* Sharon."

"So I'm interested now. What's wrong with that? I had no idea there was so much written about the subject, that there was such a large pool of knowledge. It really is fascinating, Jim. You oughtta give it a chance."

She went back to her book and I walked away frowning.

I finally decided it was nothing more than a passing preoccupation and tried to bury myself in my work...until she started talking in her sleep.

I began to wake up in the early hours of the morning to the sound of Sharon's voice. I couldn't understand her words the first time, but she spoke urgently. Then, after a few moments, she sighed, rolled over and was still.

It happened again the next night. And several nights after that. And it was always at about the same time—shortly before four a.m.—and only for a few moments. Then she would roll over and fall silent. Sometimes I was able to make out a few words—"It's coming...I'll help you...I promise...it's coming...hurry, hurry...it's coming..." But nothing that made any sense to me. And always, even in the grogginess of sleep, her voice sounded so urgent and passionate and...so very secret...

On one of those dark early mornings as I listened to Sharon's unconscious ramblings, it struck me: she was talking to another man in her sleep...a man she'd no doubt been seeing for some time...the man who had put such a chill in my once warm life...

I was unable to face her the next day and was grateful, for once, that she was somewhere in the house reading when I got home. The day had been long and painful; unable to work, I'd agonized over my suspicion, wondering what I might have done—or might *not* have done—that would turn Sharon's eyes to another man. Was I boring? Had I grown stagnant? Did she even *love* me any more? I even found myself wondering if I loved *her* any more. I was unable to eat dinner and instead, vegetated in front of the television. I waited until long after I knew she was asleep before I went to bed—in fact, it was about three-thirty in the morning, maybe a little later—knowing that I wouldn't sleep but willing to try. I slid carefully into bed, not wanting to wake her and reached for the light when I noticed something...*different*.

The room was completely, utterly silent.

My hand froze halfway to the lamp and I listened. Nothing.

Sharon had never been a silent sleeper—who is?—and I had spent twelve years falling asleep to the rhythmic sounds of her slumber: the throaty breathing, the occasional snore, the sniff or cough that was usually followed by a change of position under the covers. I heard none of those sounds as I sat up beside her, arm outstretched toward the bedside lamp.

I turned, leaned toward her.

She lay on her back, arms outside the covers, hands resting atop the other on her abdomen. Her lips were parted slightly, her hair pooled about her head. But her breasts did not rise and fall as she breathed; there were no facial tics, no sleepy stirrings. Even her eyes did not move beneath her eyelids, subtly shifting the thin flaps of skin as they usually do during deep sleep.

I felt a jolt of panic and touched her hand.

Her skin was cool. *Too* cool.

"Oh, God," I hissed, leaning down and pulling the covers back so I could put my ear to her breast. I heard nothing. And when I pressed two fingers to her throat, I felt no pulse. "Oh, my God, Sharon? *Sharon!*" I clutched her shoulders and began to shake her vigorously; I lifted her into a sitting position and shook her some more, making her head loll back and forth like that of a rag doll.

I dropped her back onto the mattress and stared at her stupidly; I found myself unable to breathe, to move for a moment. Then I bounded for the telephone to dial 911. My fingers suddenly had no feeling and punched the wrong buttons repeatedly. I don't know how many times I hung up and tried again before I finally made the connection. The *burrrr* of the phone ringing at the other end seemed eternal and I felt myself beginning to hyperventilate, suddenly having forgotten the possibility of Sharon's infidelity, and—

—I heard a sound and stiffened, spun around.

Sharon's head was rolling back and forth slowly on the pillow. Her mouth was moving. She began to speak very softly.

"...coming...it's coming...I'll...be back...promise...I'll help you..."

I dropped the receiver back in its cradle as I stared at her, dumbfounded.

After a few moments, she smacked her lips a few times, then rolled over and began to snore softly.

I plopped onto the bed, jaw slack, my body weak with sudden exhaustion. "Sharon?" I asked, my voice hoarse. I touched her shoulder. "Sharon? Are...are you all right? Sharon?"

She stirred, muttered, "Fum? Shebble carf?"

"Are you all right, Sharon?"

Her eyes opened slightly. "Corsham. Gosuhleep."

I did not sleep, though. As I sat there, I found myself staring at the book on Sharon's nightstand. It was a new one. The title was written in shimmering gold letters on the cover: *Going Solo: Adventures Out of the Body.* For the rest of the night, I couldn't get that title out of my mind.

It happened again the following night, but I was waiting for it. When all signs of life left her at about one-thirty a.m., I began trying to wake her. I shook her, I shouted at her, I pinched her—*hard*—and even, much to my shame, gave her a solid slap across the face. Nothing worked. I finally gave up and just watched her until, shortly before four o'clock, she began to stir, mumble and then snore.

The next day, I noticed her books around the house more than ever before. They were on the coffee table, in the kitchen, in the dining room, the bedroom, the sewing room…there was even one in the bathroom. The titles caught my attention, held it, and wouldn't let go: *Astral Travel…Leaving the Body: A Personal Memoir…Outside the Earthbound Carriage*…and more…so many more…

With each book I saw, I remembered Sharon lying in bed, still, lifeless, cold, *empty*, and I began to think thoughts…consider possibilities…that made me ashamed of myself, that even made me doubt the state of my mind.

That night it happened again, at the same time, in the same way. Except on this night, I got out of bed, went to the living room, opened the closest book and, against my better judgment, began to read.

«« — »»

I was still reading when it came time to go to work and found it difficult to put the book down. Not because it was such a great book, but because I was finally getting a glimpse of what had been holding Sharon's attention in such an iron grip, and it read like a long, elaborate gag. And yet, after my initial reaction, I began to realize that there was a certain kind of logic to it all—a bizarre kind of logic, granted, the kind of logic one might find between the covers of a complex, well-thought-out fantasy novel, but logic nonetheless—and I began to play a sort of connect-the-dots game with it all, connecting the bits of information I found in that book and the others on the lamp table with the strange things I'd witnessed over the past several nights.

I put two of the books I hadn't opened yet into my briefcase and took them to work with me, leaving shortly before I knew Sharon would be waking up.

With the help of a lot of coffee and a couple No-Doz, I managed to stay awake that day, but I got little work done. I worked in a small tax-consulting firm but did not hold a terribly important position, so I was able to postpone my one appointment, lock myself in my little office and read.

I read until my eyes watered. I read until I'd finished both books, then went back and read over sections that were particularly interesting.

According to the books, the best time for a beginner to try leaving his or her body was during sleep. In fact, the author claimed that many dreams were not dreams at all but memories of out-of-the-body journeys experienced during sleep; the sensation of "falling awake," as the author called it—the sudden feeling that one is falling, and then waking abruptly, startlingly—was actually caused by the spirit "falling" back into the body of the sleeping traveler. Both of the books I'd taken from the house included long chapters giving explicit instructions for preparing oneself, before going to sleep, to leave one's body during the night. It read like self-hypnosis to me, but neither book used that term.

The most disturbing thing I found was a single paragraph under the heading, *Soulmates:*

> *It is almost unheard of for one to find one's true soul-mate in the physical plane, but not so on the non-physical planes, although it is rare. There have been passionate romances between out-of-the-body travelers who have never met physically, in the physical plane, both parties have been involved with other people. According to those who have experienced them, out-of-the-body soulmate romances eclipse anything they've experienced in the flesh, but, in the end, they remain unconsummated and, therefore, they remain unfulfilling.*

That single paragraph gave me a flesh-crawling chill and made me want to read more on that particular aspect of out-of-the-body travel. Unfortunately, that was all I could find in the two books I had. So...

When I went home that night, I avoided Sharon—which, of course, was easy—and gathered a few more books together, took them to the den, locked myself in and began poring over them like an adolescent hunched over his father's girlie magazines.

I found little more information on soulmates meeting outside their bodies...just enough to feed my suspicions that perhaps I'd found the man to whom Sharon had been speaking in her sleep for a few minutes each morning.

I was shocked by my own thoughts, shocked to learn that I was even capable of taking such a fanciful idea seriously. But somehow, it felt right. The idea that Sharon had been seeing another man—actually having an *affair*—simply did not ring true to me; but the idea that she was meeting with someone *outside* her body...

I was growing so tired that I was unable to continue reading. Sharon was fast asleep in bed. Before joining her, I read once again the instructions for preparing for out-of-the-body travel during sleep and, once I'd committed them to memory, went to bed.

As I lay in the dark staring at the ceiling, unable to sleep at first despite my wariness, I felt a bit nervous, like a schoolboy about to give an oral report in front of the whole class, a report for which he was not prepared.

Part of my unrest was due to the stillness of what I was about to try. But when my hesitation went on too long, I turned to my right and watched Sharon for a moment as she slept, her head tilted toward me, lips almost but not quite smiling. I wondered if that look was caused by some whimsical dream she was having or the knowledge that she would soon be with her ethereal lover...if in fact he existed. As I watched her, I felt a jealous ache in my chest and found myself unable to doubt the existence of the other man.

I looked up at the ceiling again, closed my eyes and began taking the slow deep breaths that the book said were necessary to start my journey. I relaxed each and every part of my body, felt myself sink into the mattress as if it were shifting sand.

Following the book's instruction, I visualized a gentle blue light glowing softly inside my body from head to foot. When the image was clear in my mind, I began to concentrate on the very center of my body, pulling that blue light into a single throbbing globe in the pit of my abdomen.

As I continued breathing deeply, slowly, eyes closed, body limp, I began to drift off.

The last image I remember before falling asleep was that of the blue globe rising slowly out of my body.

«« — »»

I awoke suddenly with my body stiff, hands clutching the mattress.

I'd been startled from my sleep by a falling sensation, as if I'd been thrown from the bed.

Almost ninety minutes had passed, barely enough time for me to dream. But I *had* dreamed. I remembered a vague but unsettling image from my sleep; I'd seen *myself* from above—my body lying beneath the covers, lifeless—as if part of me were hovering over the bed...

«« —»»

The next morning I awoke with unexpected enthusiasm. I left the house as if to go to work but called in sick and rented a cheap motel room.

Not wanting to raise Sharon's suspicions, I didn't take any of her books from the house. Instead, I went to a local bookstore and bought half a dozen books on astral projection.

In my motel room, with the DO NOT DISTURB sign on the door, I spread the books out on the bed, opened them and went from book to book, reading them urgently, like a knowledge-hungry student. In fact, I was exactly that.

I read and meditated, as the book directed; I underlined and took notes, memorized and recited. I hadn't worked so hard since my last college final exams.

As the shadows lengthened in the late afternoon, I grew tired and hungry, but couldn't bring myself to stop yet. I hadn't really done anything; so far, I'd just studied the books, inhaling information like fresh air.

Finally, I stacked the books on the floor, took off my shoes and lay down on the bed. It felt good; my neck was stiff and my shoulders ached. It would have been so easy simply to go to sleep, but I couldn't.

I closed my eyes and breathed deeply.

I visualized the cool blue light inside me and willed it to merge into a fist-sized sphere in my center.

As the sphere began to rise from my body, I allowed myself to drift off...

Soon I began to dream of floating. I was floating above my body, watching it lie motionless in bed. I moved around the motel room, inspected the dirty corners where the walls met the ceiling, saw the dead insects that lay inside the opaque cover on the overhead light.

When I woke later, rather suddenly, I tried to tell myself that it had not been a dream, but I couldn't. It had possessed the vague soft-focus of images that came during sleep and had looked no different from any other dream I'd ever had.

I'd slept for less than an hour and decided to take advantage of the fact that I was awake. I got up, opened the books again and continued reading.

It was getting late and I knew I would be getting home much later than usual, but couldn't stop yet. I continued studying…underlining…reading aloud to myself…memorizing.

I skipped the sections of the books that seemed irrelevant or silly, but absorbed everything else.

Soon I was nodding off even as I read.

I put the books aside once again.

I went through the steps once again.

And, once again, I slept…

«« — »»

In the dream that wasn't really a dream, I opened my eyes and saw the motel room's stained ceiling. The ceiling began to lower and the stains grew larger as the room seemed to tilt back and forth. But the room wasn't moving at all and the ceiling was where it had always been.

I was rising.

I could feel nothing; I was weightless and no longer felt my own body. Slowly, unsure of myself, I turned over. Normally, what I saw would have made me gasp, but I no longer had breath.

About four feet below, I saw my body lying on the bed. It was exactly like the dream I'd had the night before, but much more vivid.

I continued to rise; my body grew smaller and smaller until—

—I felt an odd feathery tingling sensation and—

—I was outside, rising above the motel. I saw my car in the parking lot, the 7-11 across the street, the mini-mall on the corner, all of them shrinking until they looked like toys.

My first reaction was one of amazement and wonder but it was quickly replaced by fear as I passed up through vaporous clouds, higher and higher until the evening light began to fade and I was moving through a vast, utterly empty blackness. When I began to shoot through the darkness at lightning speeds, I tried to control my direction, hoping to turn back, but failed. I wanted to scream, but had no voice.

Specks of light began to rip silently past me like tracer bullets trailing iridescent streaks that lingered for a few seconds before fading. More and more passed by me—or was *I* passing by *them?*—and the blackness around me began to dissolve slowly. I sensed that I was approaching something and, for no reason I could see, I began to slow down.

There was light ahead…no, *below*…the light was *below* me. Was I…*landing?* Once again, I passed through clouds but they were unlike any clouds I'd seen before; there were layers and layers of them, each layer a different color from the last, and tiny pinpricks of blue light—like small jolts of electricity—shimmered through them this way and that, crisscrossing and zigzagging.

I knew, although I'm not sure how, that I was suddenly no longer alone. Somehow, I sensed the presence of others. A moment later, I sensed the *communication* of others. And shortly after that, I sensed an end to it as something else approached. Whatever it was, it was not yet in sight, but there was a new feeling in the atmosphere...a throbbing feeling...a distant pulse that was growing rapidly...growing more intense and closer...closer...

The sparkling pinpricks of energy in the multicolored clouds around me stopped, remained still a moment, and I felt a final communication. It was not in the form of words, it was literally a *feeling*, but unmistakable in its urgency. Had words been spoken, they would have been, *it's coming...it's COMING!*

I remembered what I'd heard Sharon say in her sleep: It's coming...I'll help you...I promise...hurry, hurry...it's coming...

What's coming? I thought as the shimmering clouds around me began to disperse as if blown away on a strong wind.

The throbbing grew louder. I could somehow feel it now. And it felt...bad. Wrong. *Malignant.*

Without having seen the source of the sound, I sensed its strength and enormity, and suddenly I feared that an arm—perhaps a long, tentacle-like arm ending in a hideous claw—might shoot from the surrounding darkness, perhaps *several* arms, all of them attached to the same black, throbbing mass of a body. I willed myself away from the approaching entity and found myself moving suddenly back the way I had come. In a blurred rush, I passed back through the darkness, down through the clouds and toward the small buildings below, which grew larger and larger as I fell toward my motel, down...down...until—

—I sat up in bed with a startled yelp.

I sat there for a long time, staring at the opposite wall, holding my breath and listening to my heart. It throbbed loudly in my ears, making a sound not unlike the one from which I'd just fled in my—

"No," I said to myself, getting off the bed. "That was no dream."

I searched through the stack of books until I found one in which I'd skipped over a section titled, *Dangers of the Non-Physical Planes.* I'd skipped it because it seemed unimportant; I did not yet believe in a non-physical plane, so how could I possibly feel threatened by the dangers to be found there?

Now I felt differently. Whatever it was I had fled in that strange cloudy place, it had been dangerous...malicious.

I flipped through the pages until I found the section I wanted.

Just as it is in our physical existence, the astral planes hold their share of evil. However, there are two differences. First of all, the evil is far more powerful, infinitely more consuming than any evil we know. Secondly, it cannot be hidden; if an evil entity is nearby, it will not—it cannot—hide its intentions, and you will know that you are in danger. In such a case, it is essential that you flee, and the only safe place to which you can flee is the physical plane— your own body. Waste no time in doing this, because if you are taken by such an entity, you will NOT return to your body.

There was more but I read no further. What else did I need to know? My body chilled for a moment at the thought of what I'd just done, at the realization of how much danger I'd been in, however briefly. But more than that, I realized that Sharon was exposing herself to that same danger every night.

I thought of her sleepy words once again: *It's coming...I'll help you...I promise...hurry, hurry, it's coming...*

What was coming? And who had she promised to help again and again every night?

Whatever it was that had been rushing toward me in that dark place, it was something so evil, so unimaginably deadly, that its malevolence had preceded it. I shuddered at the thought of it, and I groaned at the thought of Sharon being taken by it.

I couldn't let that happen. To prevent it, I might have to face that thing again, but even so...

...I could *not* let that happen.

It was dark outside. Dusk had come and gone long ago. I gathered up the books, checked out of the room and hurried home.

«« —»»

When I got home, Sharon was busy writing letters—or so she said as she sat at the desk in the kitchen—and did not even ask why I was nearly four hours late from work.

I made a sandwich in the kitchen and ate it quickly as I continued reading in the den. I learned nothing new, but reviewed everything I had learned.

I did not look forward to repeating the experience I'd gone through earlier; my skin crawled at the very thought of coming within range of whatever hideous, filthy thing had been pulsing its way through the darkness.

It's coming...

But I knew it was necessary.

...I'll help you...I promise...

I was willing, if necessary, to meet it face to face in order to keep it from Sharon.

...hurry, hurry...it's coming...

I read late into the night.

Sharon went to bed without saying goodnight.

I joined her later, hoping I would be able to leave my body at, or close to, the same time she left hers.

I slid under the covers and visualized, once again, the soft blue light...

«« — »»

When I left my body for the third time that day, I felt no amazement or wonder as before; instead, I focused my attention on Sharon to see if she was still there. Her body did not move; there was no sign of life; I knew she had gone before me.

I rose from the room, out of the house, above my darkened neighborhood and into the black sky. I passed quickly through the darkness that had so frightened me before, until pencil-thin streaks of light were shooting by me, until I found the shimmering clouds I'd seen earlier.

I moved among them, sensing the wordless conversations that passed between them, listening without ears, eavesdropping not on conversations but on feelings, until I picked up something that made me stop. There were no words as such, but I recognized the emotion, the sensations that passed through my non-physical body.

I'll help you, I promise. It's only a matter of time. Just a matter of time.

It was Sharon. But there was someone else, someone whose emotion was just as strong...

But how can you be sure it will work?

Because I know. Trust *me!*

Trust you? I love you!

When that sensation reached me, I ached. Although I had no blood, I bled.

The sensations were strong and I searched for the closest entities. I found them: two nebulous clouds shimmering with energy, both of them a soft yellowish-green.

The unfamiliar entity continued:

And even if I didn't love you, I have to trust you. I have no other choice. I've been here so long. I've been running for so long! I can't run any longer.

I love you, too. And don't worry. I'll help you.

I was devastated. But I had no fists to clench, no teeth to grind, and no voice with which to protest.

How did they communicate? There had been nothing in the books about communicating on the astral planes. I was mute, a helpless observer. I waited for more, bracing myself for something even more painful.

Then it happened.

The throbbing.

It was distant at first, even more distant than before, but coming closer. I sensed Sharon then; had she been speaking, she would have recited the words I'd heard her speak in her sleep so many times.

It's coming. It's coming!

Yes, coming again, I know. But we've had so little time.

You have to go. I'll help you. I promise! It won't be long now.

The two yellowish-green clouds began to move along with all the others. They were whisked away from me as if blown on a breeze.

I followed.

The throbbing grew louder, closer.

Hurry, hurry, please...it's coming closer...

I followed them into the darkness, deep into the black nothingness that lay between me and my body. I waited for the familiar sight of clouds, of my neighborhood far below...

But it did not come.

Instead, a vast, unfamiliar landscape appeared below. I followed them downward. The ground below began to take on shape. It was clay-red, the flat ground webbed with great jagged cracks from which rose tall peaks of all heights—some short and stubby, others tall and needle-like.

The two clouds before me moved low to the ground and headed for a dense group of peaks and hills. I tried to follow them closely—

all the while trying to ignore the horrendous pulsing behind us—but they increased their speed and began to zigzag between the hills and mountains, moving so quickly that, in a short while, they were nothing more than green streaks ahead of me that appeared in flashes as they shot out from behind the mountains ahead of me, moving back and forth, back and forth, until...until—

—they were gone.

I stopped, positioned between two towering mountains that rose high above the others on the alien landscape. Below, I no longer saw the dry, cracked ground I'd seen before; there was only darkness, as if the mountains rose up from endless nothingness.

And somewhere behind me, the throbbing continued. It grew closer, louder...

If my voice had been with me, my scream would have echoed through the darkness, bouncing off the dry clay walls of the peaks and hills, continuing endlessly downward in the depths that fell below me.

I fled.

Behind me the evil drew closer.

I tried to move faster through the blackness, but wasn't sure if I was successful. In the darkness, it was impossible to tell.

For a short time, I passed through familiar surroundings; once again, the specks of light shot past me, leaving behind their colorful tails.

Then they were gone and I was once again blind.

Until I found the clouds.

Although the throbbing continued behind me, I felt relieved. It wasn't long before I saw the familiar sight of lights below.

Streets.

Houses.

My house.

I moved faster.

The throbbing grew more and more distant. The feeling of danger—the sensation of being pursued by a black, cancerous mass—subsided.

I was in my bedroom.

I saw my bed. I saw my body, lying peacefully beside Sharon, who was equally motionless.

I fell as fast as I could, unable to re-enter my body quick enough. But something made me freeze.

Sharon moved. She jerked, stiffened beneath the covers, then sat up, her eyes wide. Her head turned and she stared at my body with an odd expression on her face.

I dropped lower and lower until I was mere inches from my body and—

—I froze once again.

My heart would have stopped if I'd had one.

I saw my eyes open. I watched my shoulders jerk. I saw my body sit up. Its head turned to face Sharon.

She seemed tense for a moment, squinting as she asked, in a breathy voice, "Is...is it *you?*"

My face smiled. My head nodded. My voice said, "Yes. It's me. I'm here."

Sharon's face split into a grin and she shrieked like a happy child. "It worked! It worked, just like I thought! Just like I promised!"

My arms lifted slowly and my hands touched her shoulders.

Sharon's arms embraced my body and she laughed, "My God, we're finally together!"

My own laugh filled the room, deep and heartfelt.

They kissed passionately, hands moving intimately over one another's bodies.

"I told you," Sharon said, kissing her way down my neck, "I *told* you it would work." Kissing...kissing...like she hadn't kissed me since the early years of our marriage. "I knew if I left the books around the house...he'd read them sooner or later." They disappeared beneath the covers, their bodies nothing more than jostling lumps. "I knew he'd get suspicious," she went on, her words interrupted by loud wet kisses. "I *knew* he'd try it after a while...I *knew* he'd follow me...you're safe my love...*safe*...it can't find you here...it can't chase you any more."

It...

There were no more voices for a while. Only labored breathing and squeaking bedsprings...moans of pleasure and wet smacking sounds...

The movement of their bodies became very familiar; they were moving in ways that Sharon and I had not moved for a long time.

They were making love.

Her moans and sighs stabbed me like hot knives.

I watched helplessly, hovering above them, as Sharon began to speak, her voice growing louder and louder.

"Yes...oh, God, *yes*...don't stop...more...*more*..."

The sounds that came from beneath those covers were wet and rhythmic. I wanted to be sick...but, of course, I couldn't.

Then I heard it.

The throbbing.

SHIVERS

It was far above me at first, nothing more than a *feeling*. But it was growing closer, growing louder, more intense.

"Oh my *Gawwwd*," Sharon hissed.

It came closer, that malignant thing that had pursued me through places known only to the disembodied spirits of the living and the lost souls of the dead. The throbbing became louder and louder, as if it might surround the entire house and swallow it whole.

"I'm coming," Sharon whispered, "my God, I'm *coming!* I'm—"

—coming, it's coming, it's—

"—*coming*, I'm, I'm, oh God, I'm—"

—coming, it's coming, hurry, hurry, it's—

"—*coming*, I'm *coming!*"

There was nothing to do but go. I rose from the bedroom, up and up until I could see the entire house below me. And yet I could still hear her.

"I'm *coming*, my *God*, I'm—"

—coming, it's coming, it's—

"—*coming*, I'm *coming!*"

It was close, so close that I could sense its form, the lumpy pustulous surface of its massive flesh, and I fled. I shot upward into the darkness as the throbbing grew louder behind me. I envisioned its limbs—numerous and writhing, reaching outward for the nearest life force, the closest source of energy to feed its insatiable hunger—and I continued upward.

My cry, if I'd had voice, would have been endless. My fear was beyond description.

I fled, screaming silently, into the vast and endless blackness...

The Sympathy Society

Graham Masterton

T he phone rang just as Martin was cracking the second egg into the frying pan. He wedged the receiver under his chin and said, "Sarah! Hi, sweetheart! You're calling early!"

There was an uncomfortable pause. Then, "Sorry, Martin. This is John—John Newcome, from Lazarus."

"John? What can I do for you? Don't tell me Sarah's left some more documents at home."

"No, no, nothing like that. Listen, Martin, there's no easy way of saying this. We've just had a call from the British Embassy in Athens. I'm afraid there's been an accident."

Martin suddenly found himself short of breath. "Accident? What kind of accident? Sarah's all right, isn't she?"

"I'm sorry, Martin. We're all devastated. She's dead."

Martin turned off the gas. It was all he could think of to do. Whatever John Newcome said next, he wasn't going to be eating the full English breakfast that he had planned for himself. The flat was silent now. The television had switched itself off. The birds had suddenly stopped chirruping.

"You're going to hear this sooner or later," said John Newcome. He was obviously trying to be stable but his words came out like a bagful of Scrabble tiles. "The press will be onto you. You know. Sarah had an accident on a jet-ski, late yesterday afternoon. It seems as if she went between two boats. There was a line between them. The chap from the Embassy said that she probably didn't see it. Only a thin line. Braided steel."

"No," said Martin.

"I'm sorry, Martin. But it's probably better that you hear it from me. She went straight into it and it cut her—"

259

SHIVERS

Martin could never tell afterward if he had actually heard the words, or if he had imagined hearing them, or seen what had happened to Sarah in his mind's eye, as if she had sent him a Polaroid snap of it. Full color, blue sky, blue sea, yachts as white as starched collars.

"Head—"

No this can't be true. This is Thursday morning and as soon as I've finished my job in Fulham I'm flying out to Rhodes to spend the next ten days with her, swimming and snorkeling and going to discos. Not Sarah. Not Sarah with her long blonde hair and her bright gray oyster-shell eyes and her Finnish-looking face. And the way she laughed— wild exaggerated laughter, falling backward on the futon. And those toes of hers, kicking in the sunlight. And she hated fat, she used to take her ham sandwiches apart and put on her reading glasses and search for fat like a gold prospector.

And her kisses, clicking on his shoulder, in the darkest moments of the night. And suggestive little whispers.

"Off."

《《——》》

His mother said that he was very brave. His father stood with his hands deep in the pockets of his brown corduroy trousers and looked as if he had just heard that interest rates had gone down again. He spent most of the weekend in his old room, lying on his candlewick bed-spread, facing the wall. He saw so many faces in the floral wallpaper. Devils, imps, demons and fairies. But he couldn't clearly remember what Sarah had looked like. He didn't want to remind himself by looking at photographs. If he looked at photographs, he would remember only the photographs, and not the real Sarah. The real Sarah who had touched him and kissed him and waved him goodbye at Stansted Airport. Turning the corner. The sun, catching her hair. Then, gone.

After the funeral, he went for a long walk on the Downs, on the bony prehistoric back of Sussex, where the wind constantly blew and the sea always glittered in the distance. But no matter how often you walked up there, you always had to return. And, as evening turned the sky into veils of blue, he came down the narrow chalk path, clinging on to the hawthorn bushes to keep his balance, and he knew that he was going to go mad without her. He was going to kill himself, take an overdose, cut his wrists, fill his car with carbon monoxide. She was gone, and she had left him all alone in this world, and he didn't want to be here any longer. Not alone. What was the point? What was the purpose? His whole life from the moment he was born had been leading him toward her, by all kinds of devious paths and diversions. They had given him her jewelry. Her necklace, her watch. What was the point of them, if she wasn't alive to wear them?

And more than anything, he kept imagining what it must have been like for her, rounding the prow of that yacht, laughing, revving up her jet-ski, only to see that steel cable stretched in front of her, far too late. Maybe she hadn't seen it at all. But what had she *felt*, when she hit it, and her head came flying off? Don't tell me she felt nothing. Don't tell me she wouldn't have suffered. Don't tell me that for one split-second she wouldn't have realized what had happened to her?

Nobody had any proof, of course, but didn't they always say that when they guillotined the nobles in the French Revolution, and their heads had tumbled into the basket, some of them had cried out in shock?

«« — »»

In their flat, two weeks later, he stood in front of the bathroom mirror and tried to cut his throat with the steak knife that he had stolen from a Berni Inn the previous summer. Because Sarah had dared him to. Now he believed that he knew why she had dared him. She wanted him to have a way of joining him, when she died. It was drizzling outside. One of the gutters was blocked with leaves and water was clattering intermittently into the basement area outside.

He drew the serrated blade across his neck. It tugged at his skin and blood suddenly poured onto his shirt. It didn't hurt, but the tugging was deeply unpleasant, and the knife obviously wasn't sharp enough. He had expected to cut through his carotid artery and send spurts of blood all over the bathroom, up the walls, over the mirror.

Sarah's neck must have pumped blood, when her head was cut off. He remembered reading about the beheading of a British soldier in a Japanese POW camp. His commanding officer said that blood jumped out of his neck like a red walking-stick.

He lifted the knife again. His hand was already slippery and his fingers were sticking together. He tried to cut again, but his neck was so messy that he couldn't see what he was doing, and he was beginning to tremble.

He slowly dropped to his knees onto the floor. The knife fell in the washbasin. He stayed where he was, his head bowed, his eyes streaming with tears, his mouth dragged down in a silent howl of loneliness and agony.

«« — »»

Jenny came to see him in the hospital. Jenny was plump and pale with scraped-back hair. She worked in the accounts department at Hiya Intelligence, but ever since he had started working there, she had made excuses to come up and see him in software. She had brought him a box of Milk Tray chocolates and a John Grisham novel.

"You've lost an awful lot of weight, Martin," she said, laying her little nail-bitten hand on top of his.

He tried to smile. "Throat's still sore. Besides, I haven't got much of an appetite."

"How long have you got to stay in here?"

"I don't know. The psychotherapist said he wasn't very happy with me. I said, 'What's happiness got to do with anything?'"

"So what did he say?"

"He said, 'If you don't know, you ought to stay in the hospital.'"

Jenny reached down and fumbled in her big woven bag. She produced a folded copy of the *Evening Standard* and handed it to him. "There," she said. "Read that ad I've circled. I don't know if it'll help, but you never know."

It was a small display advertisement in the classified section, under Personal Services. It read: "Grieving? Suicidal? When you've lost a loved one, The Sympathy Society understands how you feel. Unlike all other counselors, we can offer you what you're really looking for." Underneath, there was a telephone number in Buckinghamshire.

Martin dropped the paper onto the floor. "I don't think so, Jenny. The last thing I need is even more sympathy. I've had so much sympathy I've been feeling sympathy-sick. Like eating a whole box of chocolates at one sitting.

"By the way—" he said, handing her back the box of Milk Tray, "I don't like milk chocolate. You eat them."

"It's all right. Give them to the nurses."

She looked so disappointed that he took hold of her hand and squeezed it. "I'm just pleased that you came, that's all. I can't expect you to understand how I feel. Nobody can. Sarah was everything to me. Everything. I'm not making a song and dance about it. I simply don't see the point of living without her."

"What about your family? Your mum and dad? What about all of your friends?"

"They'll get over me."

"You really think so?" she challenged him, with tears in her eyes, and her lower lip quivering. "You're hurt, of course you are. You're absolutely devastated. But why should even more people have to suffer?"

"I'm sorry, Jenny. It's my life and I have the right to do what I want with it. And that includes ending it."

Jenny stood up, and sniffed, and picked up her bag. "If that's the way you feel, I hope you make a better job of it next time."

Martin gave a painful cough and held out his hand to her. "Don't be angry with me, Jenny. Please."

"I'm not. I just can't stand to see you giving in. I'd give my life for you, you know that."

He looked into her eyes and he could see how much she loved him. He had the dreadful, unforgivable thought that if only *she* had died, instead of Sarah. Hadn't she offered her life? And if it could make any difference, would he have taken it?

"Thanks for the book, and the chocolates," he said.

She didn't answer, but she leaned forward and kissed him on the forehead. Then she left the ward, dancing awkwardly in the doorway with a man on crutches.

Martin lay back on the bed. The sun crossed the ceiling like the spokes of a broken wheel. He dozed for a while, and when he opened his eyes it was almost four o'clock.

"You've been sleeping," said a soft voice, very close to his ear.

"Mmm," he said. Then he suddenly opened his eyes wider. That was Sarah's voice. He was sure that it was Sarah's voice. He turned sideways and she was lying right next to him, her eyes bright, her blonde hair spread across the pillow. She was smiling at him in that gently mocking way she had, when she caught him doing something embarrassing.

"Sarah," he whispered, reaching up and touching her hair. "I had this nightmare that you were dead. It seemed completely real. You don't have any idea."

She didn't reply, but very, very slowly closed her eyes.

"Sarah, talk to me. Don't go to sleep. I have to tell you all about this dream."

Her eyes remained closed. The color gradually began to seep out of her cheeks. Her lips were almost turquoise.

"Sarah—listen to me—Sarah!"

He tried to take hold of her shoulder to shake her, but his hand seized nothing but blanket. He sat up, shocked, and it was then that he realized that only her head was lying next to him. Her severed neck was encrusted with dried blood and part of her windpipe was protruding onto the sheet.

He made an awful moaning noise and half-jumped, half-fell out of the bed, tangling his feet in the sheets. His head struck the edge of his bedside table and his plastic water-jug dropped to the floor, along with his book and his chocolates and his wristwatch.

A nurse came hurrying over. "Martin! Martin, what's the matter?"

She helped him up. He tilted onto his feet, and twisted around to stare at the bed. Sarah's head had vanished, and he knew that it hadn't really been there at all. It had been nothing more than a nightmare. He sat down on the side of the bed, feeling shocked and bruised. The trouble was, it was worse being awake. Sarah was dead and he was alone, and he could never wake up from that, ever.

«« ——»»

Back at the flat, with the blinds and the curtains drawn, he sat at the kitchen table and smoothed out the page from the *Evening Standard* that Jenny had given him. He had read the advertisement for The Sympathy Society again and again, and every time he read it he had been left with an odd feeling of unease. "Unlike all other counselors, we can offer you what you're really looking for." How did they know what he was looking for? How did they know what *anybody* was looking for?

He ate another spoonful of cold spaghetti out of the can. That was all he had eaten since he came out of the hospital. He didn't have to cook it, he barely had to chew it, and it kept him alive. It seemed absurd, to keep yourself alive when you wanted so much to die, but he didn't want to die a lingering death, through starvation and dehydration; and there was always a chance that somebody would find you, and resuscitate you, and feed you with drips and tubes. He wanted to die instantly, the way that Sarah had died.

After almost an hour, he picked up the phone and dialed the number in Buckinghamshire. It rang for a long time, with an echoing, old-fashioned ringing tone. Eventually, it was picked up. There was a moment's breathy pause, and then a clear voice said, "Miller."

"I'm sorry. I think I must have the wrong number. I wanted The Sympathy Society."

"You've reached The Sympathy Society. How can I help you?"

"I've, er—I saw your ad in the *Standard*."

"I see. And may I ask if you have recently been bereaved?"

"About six weeks ago. I lost my partner. She—" He found that he couldn't get the words out.

Mr. Miller waited for a while, and then he asked, with extreme delicacy, "Was it *sudden*, may I ask? Or an illness?"

"Sudden. It was very sudden. An accident, while she was on holiday."

"I see. Well, that means you're very suitable for Sympathy Society counseling. We don't counsel for illness."

"I've had some psychiatric counseling on the NHS. It hasn't made me feel any better, to tell you the truth."

"That doesn't surprise me. Psychiatrists, on the whole, have a very conventional view of what it is to be 'better.'"

"I don't quite understand what you mean."

"Well, if you're interested in us, why don't you come to see us? It never did anybody any harm to talk."

"How much do you charge?"

"Financially, nothing."

"You mean there are no fees at all?"

"Let me put it to you this way. I do expect some output from all of the people we help. I'll explain it when you come to see us."

"You sound pretty confident that I will."

"We word our advertisement very carefully. It appeals only to those who we can genuinely help."

It started to rain again. Martin couldn't see it through the blind, but he could hear the castanet-clatter of water on the concrete outside.

"Tell me how to reach you," he said.

«« — »»

The taxi dropped him off by a sagging green-painted gate, at the end of a driveway that was made almost impassable to motor vehicles by its overgrown laurel-bushes. His feet crunched up the wet pea-shingle until eventually a redbrick Victorian house came into view. Its windows were black and empty, and one of its sidewalls was streaked green with lichen. Three enormous ravens were strutting on the lawn, but they flapped away when they saw him coming, and settled on the roof instead, like three bad omens.

Martin went to the front door and rang the bell. He waited for two or three minutes but nobody answered, so he rang it again. He couldn't hear it ringing anywhere in the house. A corroded brass knocker hung in the center of the door, with the face of a hooded monk. He banged it twice, and waited some more.

At last the door opened. Martin was confronted by a white-faced young woman with her hair twisted on top of her head in a messy but elaborate bun. She wore a simple gray smock and grubby white socks.

"You must be Martin," she said. She held out her hand. "I'm Sylvia."

"Hello, Sylvia. I wasn't sure I'd come to the right house."

"Oh, you have, Martin. Believe me, you have. Come inside."

Martin followed her into a huge gloomy hallway that smelled of frying onions and lavender floor-polish. On the right-hand side of the hallway, a wide staircase ran up to a galleried landing, where there was a high stained-glass window in ambers and browns and muted blues. It depicted two hooded monks in prayer and a third figure in a thick coat that looked as if it were made of dead stoats and weasels and water-rats, all sewn together, their mouths open, their legs lolling. This figure had its back turned, so that it was impossible to see who it was meant to be.

Sylvia led Martin along the hallway until they reached a large sitting-room at the back of the house. It was wallpapered and furnished in brown, with two dull landscapes on the walls. Here sat three others—two men and a woman. They turned around as Martin came in, and one of them, a silver-haired man in a baggy brown cardigan, stood up and held out his hand. The other man remained where he was, black-haired, with deep black rings under his eyes, hunched in his big worn-out armchair. The woman was standing by the window with a cup of milky coffee in her hand. She was so thin that she was almost transparent.

"Geoffrey," said the silver-haired man, shaking Martin's hand. "But you can call me Sticky, my dear Mary always did. Ardent stamp-collector, that's why."

"Sticky—the stamp-collector who came unhinged," put in the black-haired man, in a West Country accent.

Sticky gave Martin a tight little smile. "This is Terence. Sometimes Terence is extremely cordial but most of the time Terence is extremely offensive. Still, we've learned to take him as he comes."

"What he means is, they've learned to keep their gobs shut," said Terence.

Sticky ignored him. "Over there—this is Theresa. She used to be a very fine singer, you know. Cheltenham Ladies' Chorus."

Theresa gave Martin an almost imperceptible nod of her head.

"It's a pity," said Sticky. "She hasn't sung a single note since she lost her family."

Terence said, "Where's the pity in that? I haven't plowed a single furrow and you haven't stuck in a single stamp, and Sylvia hasn't strung together a single necklace. There has to be a reason for doing things, doesn't there? A reason. And none of us here has a single reason for breathing, let alone singing."

"Come on, Terence," Sticky chided him. "You know we do. You know what we're here for, all of us."

At that moment another door opened on the opposite side of the sitting-room, and a very tall man entered, leaning on a walking-stick. He was very thin, almost emaciated, with steel-gray hair scraped back from his forehead, and a nose as sharp as an ax. His eyes were so pale that they looked as if all of the color had been leached out of them by experience and pain. A triangular scar ran across his left cheek and disappeared into his hairline.

He wore a black double-breasted suit with unfashionably flappy lapels. As he walked into the room, Martin had the impression that beneath his clothes, his body was all broken and dislocated. It was the way he balanced and swiveled as he made his way across the carpet.

"Martin," he said, in a voice like glasspaper. "You'll forgive me for not shaking hands."

"Mr. Miller," said Martin.

"Tybalt, please. Ridiculously affected name, I know; but my father was an English teacher at a very pretentious boys' primary."

He eased himself into one of the armchairs and propped his stick between his knees. "You must tell us who you have lost, Martin; and how. But before you do, your fellow-sufferers here will tell you why *they* sought the help of The Sympathy Society. Sticky—why don't you start?"

"Silly thing, really," said Sticky, as if he were talking about nothing more traumatic than allowing himself to be bowled in a local cricket match. "I was looking after my grandson for the day. Beautiful little chap. Blond hair. Sturdy little legs. We were going to go down to the beach and look for crabs. I went to get the car out of the garage, and I didn't realize that I'd left the front door open. Little chap followed me, you see. I reversed out of the garage and he was so small that I didn't see him standing behind me. I ran him over. Slowly. And stopped, with the wheel resting on his stomach."

He paused for a moment and took out a clean, neatly pressed

handkerchief. "He was lying on the concrete looking up at me. There was blood coming out of his ears but he was still alive. I'll never forget the expression on his face as long as I live. He was so *bewildered*, as if he couldn't understand why this had happened to him. I moved the car off him, but that might have been the wrong thing to do. He died almost at once.

He smiled, but tears were filling his eyes. "Of course, that was the end of everything. My marriage; my family. Do you think my daughter could ever look me in the eye again? I thought of killing myself by putting a plastic bag over my head. I nearly succeeded, but a friend of mine stopped me just in time. And I was glad. Suffocating like that— that was the coward's way out."

"Sylvia?" said Tybalt.

Sylvia stared at the floor and spoke in a hurried monotone. "My husband Ron was all I ever wanted in the whole world. He was loving and kind and generous and he was always bringing me flowers. He was a firefighter. About nine weeks ago he went out on a shout in Bromley. Paint factory on fire. He was the first in, as usual. His nickname was Bonkers because he was always rushing into things without thinking.

"He kicked open a door just as a tank of paint-stripping gel blew up. He was covered in it, from head to foot. The coroner said it had the same effect as napalm. It stuck to him, and it cremated him alive. He was screaming and screaming and trying to get it off him, but there was nothing that any of his mates could do. Two of them had to take early retirement with post-traumatic stress disorder. And me? I missed Ron so much that it was like a physical pain. I wandered around like a zombie for the first few weeks. I walked in front of buses, hoping that they wouldn't stop. I thought of pills. I bought two hundred paracetamol from different chemists. But then I thought, no. That's not the way. That's when I saw the ad for The Sympathy Society. And rang. And here I am."

"Your turn, Terence," said Tybalt.

Terence didn't say anything at first, but cracked his knuckles one by one. Theresa, at the window, winced with exaggerated sensitivity at every crack.

"Come on, Terence," Tybalt coaxed him. "Martin needs to know what happened to you."

"Farming accident," said Terence, at last. "There's a kind of plow called a disk plow. It's got steel disks instead of shares. Ours got jammed last year, and my sister tried to fix it. It decided to unjam itself when she was right underneath. Dragged her halfway through it. She called for help for two hours before she died. I was plowing in the next field and I couldn't hear her. The doctor said he'd never seen anybody suffer such terrible injuries and stay alive for so long. Half her face was torn off and one of her legs was twisted around backward, so that the foot was pointing the other way.

"After the funeral I went home and I took out my shotgun. I sat in the parlor for nearly an hour with the barrel in my mouth. But I think I knew all the time that I wasn't going to do it."

There was another long pause and it became obvious that Terence wasn't going to say anymore than that. "Theresa?" said Tybalt.

Theresa gave a wan smile. Without turning away from the window, she said, "It's extraordinary how your life can be heaven one second and hell the next. Just like that, without any warning at all. We were on holiday in Cornwall, my husband Tom and I and our daughter Emma. It was a beautiful, beautiful day. The sun was shining. The breeze was blowing off the sea. We went for a walk on the cliffs. Tom and I were holding hands and Emma was running all around us. Then suddenly she was gone. Vanished. We were frantic. We thought she'd fallen over the cliff, and we searched and searched but there was no sign of her anywhere. Not on the rocks. Not on the beach. It was just as if she'd vaporized; as if she'd never existed.

"I can't describe the panic I felt. Tom called the police and the coastguard, and they searched, too.

"They had tracker dogs out, helicopters, everything. I overheard them saying things like, 'She'll probably be back on the five o'clock tide, three miles down the coast.' Tom was wonderful. He kept telling me that she was probably playing some silly game, and that she'd soon turn up, teasing us for being so worried.

"But she wasn't playing some silly game, and she didn't turn up. We did an appeal on television. You might even remember it. Somebody said they had seen her in Fowey, with a strange man in a raincoat. But that was all a mistake.

"A little Jack Russell terrier found Emma, in the end. She had fallen down a natural chimney in the ground, nearly sixty feet down, and so narrow that she was completely wedged, and scarcely able to breathe. The post-mortem showed that it had taken her five days to die.

"Tom went out the next day and it was only when I was putting away the ironing that I found the letter he had left me. It was too late by then. He had hanged himself in a lock-up garage in Ealing.

"Everybody was so kind. Once or twice my sister nearly per-suaded me that it was worth going on, that life could still be worth living. I took too many pills, but I washed them down with vodka, and I was sick. I thought of cutting my wrists, they say you have to do it from wrist to elbow, don't they, so that nobody can stop the bleeding before you die. But what happens when you take pills? You fall asleep, and that's it. And what happens when you cut your wrists? You gradually lose consciousness. You don't stay wedged in a hole in the ground for five days, slowly dying of thirst and starvation, looking at the little circle of daylight sixty feet above you and wondering why your parents haven't come to rescue you. You don't suffer, as Emma must have suffered. You don't lose your faith in the people who are supposed to be taking care of you."

She stopped in mid-flow, and lifted one hand, as if she were trying to attract the attention of somebody in the garden. But there was nobody there. Only the overgrown bushes, and the apple trees heavy with half-rotten Worcesters.

Martin turned to Tybalt, and Tybalt raised one eyebrow, as if he were asking him if he was beginning to understand what was happening here, at The Sympathy Society. Martin looked from Theresa to Sylvia, and then at Sticky, who was making a show of folding up his handkerchief again.

"Martin?" said Tybalt. "Why don't you tell us *your* story?"

«« — »»

Later in the evening, they sat in the kitchen and ate a supper of chicken casserole with green peppers, and home-made bread—prepared, said Tybalt, by "Mrs. Pearce…such a dear person…she comes up from the village." The atmosphere at dinner was strained. Terence was twitchy and obnoxious. Sylvia couldn't stop dabbing her eyes and her nose with her paper napkin. Theresa wouldn't eat anything, except for a tiny nibble of bread, and Sticky was deeply distracted, as if he were thinking about something else altogether.

During the cheese course (when the table was messy with crumbs and stripped-off sticks of celery) Tybalt scraped back his chair and said, "Martin—you've realized by now what we're doing here, haven't you?"

"I'm not sure," said Martin. "I think perhaps I'm missing something."

"Understatement of the year," said Terence.

Tybalt ignored him. "We're not here to cry for you, Martin; or mollycoddle you; or make you believe that life has to go on. What a fallacy that is! Life doesn't have to go on, if you don't want it to. Where were you, before you were born? You weren't anywhere. You didn't exist. In the same way, you won't exist after you're dead. There's no heaven, Martin. There isn't any hell. But there is one thing: in the instant when you die, there's *revelation*."

"Revelation?" Martin was used to being the center of attention, and he didn't like the way that Tybalt dominated the whole room, and everybody in it.

"Revelation like the Book of Revelations," said Terence. "Revelation like the scales falling from your eyes."

Tybalt smiled. "When you're dead, you're dead. That's all there is to it. Blackness, nothingness, that's it. We all know it, even if we're scared to admit it. But I believe there's a split-second, when you die, that you see the world as it really is. We probably see it when we're born, too. Why do you think babies cry, when they first come out of the womb? But babies forget; and babies can't tell us what they've seen."

"Neither can dead people," said Martin.

"Well, you're right there. Nobody comes back. But these days, there is a way to record what people are seeing, in their mind's eye. When people think, electrical impulses jump from one synapse to the other, inside of the brain. And we can catch those electrical impulses and record them, just like a DVD disk."

"What are you trying to tell me? That you can record what's happening inside of other people's brains?"

Tybalt nodded; and nodded. "You've got it, Martin. That's exactly what we can do. The technology is still in its infancy, but we've managed to recover five or six minutes of footage of living brain activity; and at least six seconds of post-mortem activity. We can see what people are thinking about, when they die."

He stopped for a moment, to light up a cigarette. Then he waved away the smoke, and said, "We can record those last split-seconds of human life. We can record it in pictures and sound, DVD no problem. The entire technology has been in place since 1996. What it needed was the will to make it work."

"And you think that you have that will?" asked Martin.

"Not me, you. You're the only one who can show us what happens when you go to meet your Maker. You and Terence, and Sylvia, and Sticky, and Theresa. You're the only people who can make this work."

Martin said nothing. He was beginning to grasp the enormity of what Tybalt was saying, but he needed to hear it spelled out. Tybalt said, "I have my suits tailored, but I'm a physical mess. When I was twenty-four, I borrowed my friend's motorcycle and took my girlfriend for a ride along the Kingston bypass. We went through the New Malden underpass at 125mph, and then I lost it. She came off the pillion and flew right over the central reservation, straight into the front of a Securicor van. I tumbled nearly half-a-mile down the road in front of me, and smashed up everything that was smashable. Ribs, pelvis, arms, legs, ankles. I was like a jelly filled with bits of bone. And I died. I lay there on the road, dead. And when I was dead, I saw something. Only for a few seconds. But I saw the world as it really was. Not the way we imagine it, when we're alive. I *saw the world as it really was.*"

"But you survived," said Martin.

Tybalt shrugged, and tapped his stick. "Yes, I survived. By good or bad fortune, an ambulance was passing, and they took me straight to Kingston Hospital. They thought I was past saving. They gave me so many electric shocks that they burned my nipples off. But after the seventh shock, I started to breathe; and I have never stopped breathing since.

"All the same, I know what I saw, after that accident, and I don't believe that it was shock that caused me to see it, or concussion, or psychological trauma. As I lay in the road, Martin, I saw things that would make your hair stand on end."

"So what are you saying to me?" asked Martin.

"I'm saying nothing. But you listened to all of your fellow society members this afternoon, didn't you? They're all bereaved, just as you are. None of them want to carry on without their family or their partners. They all want to die. But none of them want to kill themselves with tablets, or exhaust fumes, or by cutting their wrists. When they die, they want to feel what their loved ones felt. They want to suffer in the same way. Sylvia wants to burn; Sticky wants to be crushed; Theresa wants to be trapped below ground. This will be their redemption.

"You know what I'm talking about, Martin. How many mornings have you lain awake and thought about Sarah, and what she felt like, when that steel wire cut off her head? You want to experience that too, don't you, Martin?—or else you wouldn't have answered my advertisement. The Sympathy Society isn't the Samaritans. The Sympathy Society *really* sympathizes. We'll give you what you're craving for. The same death that your loved one suffered."

Martin's mouth was totally dry. "You'll do that—you'll burn Sylvia? You'll trap Theresa under the ground?"

Tybalt nodded. "Nobody else understands, Martin, but I do. You want to die. But trying to cut your throat with a steak knife...that doesn't even compare, does it? What did Sarah feel? After her head was cut off, did she still *think* for a second or two? Did she see her body, still speeding along on that jet-ski, with blood pumping out of her neck? You want to know that, don't you, Martin?"

Martin cleared his throat, and nodded.

Tybalt leaned forward and touched his knee with chalky finger-nails. "The Sympathy Society can arrange for you to be killed in any way you choose. There's only one thing we ask in return. We need to record your impressions with synaptic monitors...we need to see what you see, think what you think, the instant you die. I saw something terrible when I lay on the road after my motorcycle accident, and I need to know whether I was hallucinating or not."

"What did you see?" asked Martin.

Tybalt shook his head. "I don't want to put any ideas in your head. Besides, if I tell you, you won't want to be killed at all."

"I want to die," said Martin. "I want you to cut off my head, and kill me. I need to know what Sarah went through. I need to know exactly what she felt like."

"There you are," said Tybalt, with unexpected gentleness. "That's why we call ourselves The Sympathy Society."

«« —— »»

The following morning was chilly and overcast, and inside the house it was so gloomy that they had to switch the lights on. They gathered for breakfast in the kitchen, although Martin couldn't manage anything more than a cup of coffee. Sylvia sat at the head of the table, her hair all pinned up. She looked even paler than usual, and there were dark circles under her eyes. Around her neck hung a small silver cru-cifix.

At half past eight, Tybalt came through the garden door. He was wearing a long black overcoat with the collar turned up. "Well," he said, chafing his hands together. "Everything's ready, Sylvia, if you are."

Sylvia set down her teacup. She looked around the table, at each of them, although she didn't smile. "I don't like goodbyes," she said. "Anyway, we're all going to meet again, aren't we?"

Theresa reached across the table and took hold of her hand. There were tears in her eyes. "I envy you," she said. "You don't know how much I envy you."

Tybalt said, "None of you have to come out and watch. This is Sylvia's moment, after all. But if you want to be with her, I'm sure she'll appreciate it."

Sylvia stood up. She was wearing a plain green linen dress, and she was barefoot. Tybalt went back out into the garden and she followed him, leaving the door ajar.

Theresa said, "I'm not going. I can't."

Terence didn't say anything, but made no move to get up from the table.

Sticky went through to the hallway and came back with his brown tweed overcoat and his checkered scarf. "I'm going. Poor girl deserves somebody there. Terrible thing, to die on your own."

"*Don't*," said Theresa.

Sticky laid an apologetic hand on her shoulder. "Sorry…didn't mean it like that."

Martin didn't know whether he wanted to witness Sylvia's death or not; but Sticky said, "Come on, old boy. You never know. When you see this, you might change your mind."

They went out into the garden. The grass was wet underfoot and dew was clinging to the branches of the apple-trees. Martin was shivering, and it wasn't because of the cold. In the far corner of the garden stood a dilapidated shed with broken windows, and just in front of it, Sylvia was already kneeling on the ground. Tybalt was standing over her, taping electrodes to her temples with silver fireproof tape. A little distance away stood an old metal table with a PC standing on it, and a collection of equipment for recording Sylvia's heart-rate and brain activity.

Martin and Sticky stopped and stood at the respectful distance, close to one of the trees. A robin perched on the fence close by, beadily watching them. Sylvia looked so plain and pale she reminded Martin of St. Joan, about to be burned at the stake. But her expression was completely calm, and her eyes were lifted toward the sky, as if she were quietly looking forward to it.

It took nearly ten minutes for Tybalt to fix the last electrode, and Martin was beginning to lose his nerve. "I think I'll go back inside," he told Sticky.

But Sticky took hold of his hand, and gripped it tight, and wouldn't let it go. "You're best staying," he said.

Tybalt went across to the metal table and switched on his PC and his recording equipment. Then he went to the shed and came back with a large blue petrol-can. He told Sylvia to cover her face with her hands, and then he unscrewed the lid and poured the contents all over the top of her head. Sylvia shuddered, and let out a muffled, high-pitched *ah!* It wasn't petrol. It was a thick, greenish gel, which dripped slowly down her neck and over her shoulders. Martin could smell it, even from twenty feet away. It was paint-stripper, and it must have been searing the exposed skin on Sylvia's hands and neck already.

Tybalt's expression was grim, and he worked as quickly as he could. He picked up a large paintbrush and smeared the gel all down Sylvia's dress, back and front, and over her legs. She was trembling in agony already, but she kept her hands pressed over her face, and the only sound she made was a thin, repetitive *"eeeshh—eeeshh—eeeshh—"* But the pain that she was suffering was nothing to the pain she would be suffering next.

Without any hesitation, Tybalt took a cigarette lighter out of his pocket, and snapped it into flame.

"Are you absolutely sure you want to do this?" he asked her, in a voice so quiet that Martin could scarcely hear him.

With her hands still clamped over her face, Sylvia nodded. Tybalt lit the top of her piled-up hair, and instantly her head burst into flame. Martin jolted with shock, but Sticky kept gripping his hand. He had never seen anybody burn before, and it was so horrific that he couldn't believe what he was looking at. Sylvia's hair caught fire in a whirl of tiny sparks, and then her ears shriveled and curled over like blackened bacon-rinds. She kept her hands over her face even though the tips of her fingers were alight. But then the fumes from the paint-stripper exploded with the softest *whoomph* and she was completely buried in flames.

Martin couldn't understand how she could bear the pain without moving. The flames were so fierce that he could hardly see her, only her blackening elbows and her scarlet-charred feet. But then she threw open her hands and screamed the most terrible scream that he had ever heard in his life. It wasn't just a scream of agony, it was a scream of total despair.

Sylvia tried to stagger onto her feet. Martin instinctively tried to move forward to help her, but Sticky held him back. "It's what she wants, man! It's what she came here for!"

Sylvia toppled sideways onto the grass, with flames literally pouring out of her face. She opened and closed her mouth two or three times, but her lungs were too burned for her to scream again. The flames ate through her dress and turned the flesh on her thighs into charcoal. She quivered, as her nerve-endings were burned, but eventually she stopped quivering and it was clear that she was dead. Thick smoke rose into the gray morning sky, and the smell of roasted meat brought a surge of bile into Martin's throat.

Tybalt switched off his equipment and approached them gravely. "I think she understood what her husband went through. I hope so."

"Did you record anything?" asked Martin.

"I won't know until later, when I analyze all of the images."

"I wouldn't like to think she died for nothing."

"She didn't die for nothing. She died because she's a human being, and human beings should have the choice to die in any way they want to. You haven't changed your mind, have you?"

Martin thought about Sarah speeding toward the cable. "No," he said. "I haven't changed my mind. But I wouldn't want to burn, like Sylvia did."

They went back into the house. Theresa was sitting in the corner, in tears. Terence was hunched in his chair, saying nothing.

"She's gone," said Sticky, unnecessarily. "A good girl, a very brave ending."

《《———》》

Later that evening, Martin knocked on the door of Tybalt's study. Tybalt was sitting in front of his PC, frowning at the blurry, silvery gray images that danced on the screen. As soon as Martin came in, he switched it off.

"Anything?" asked Martin.

Tybalt shook his head. "Not so far. It's too soon to tell. There's a lot of filtering to do, a lot of enhancing. But I think I caught something today."

Martin hesitated. Tybalt appeared tense, and anxious for him to go, as if he had recorded some images from Sylvia's last agonized seconds of life that he didn't want to discuss.

"Of course—as soon as I come up with anything…" Tybalt began.

Martin nodded. Then he said, "Who's next?"

"Theresa. Hers will take the longest, of course. There's an old dry well, right at the end of the garden, beyond the orchard. I had it bored deeper, fifty feet or so. She's going to go down tomorrow morning."

"Isn't anybody going to miss us? What about our bodies? Aren't you worried about the police?"

Tybalt gave a small, secretive smile. "By the time the police come looking, The Sympathy Society will have moved to pastures new. And everyone here has written a letter explaining that they have taken their own lives. As will you, when your turn comes."

"Yes," said Martin, at last.

«« —»»

Theresa dropped herself down the dry well at the end of the garden just after dawn the following day. It was drizzling slightly, and her hair was stuck wetly to her forehead. They kissed her, each of them, before she went. She was obviously frightened, but she was smiling.

Tybalt attached the last electrodes to her forehead, with reels of cable so that he could monitor her alpha-rhythms right down at the bottom of the well. She knelt down in the brambly grass, and then, quite abruptly, she slithered out of sight.

They heard her cry out. "My leg! I think I've broken my leg!" But they didn't answer, and she didn't cry out again. She had chosen to suffer the same death as her daughter, and her daughter had broken her left wrist and her collarbone, when she fell.

There was nothing more to do. They walked through the orchard and back to the house.

«« —»»

Three days later, it was Terence's turn. Tybalt had arranged to hire a tractor fitted with a disk plow. It was delivered to the top of the lane that ran down to the paddock past the orchard. He whistled as he steered it onto the grass. For the first time since Martin had met him, he seemed cheerful and contented.

This was one death that Martin really didn't want to witness. But, again, Sticky insisted. They walked to the paddock by way of the orchard, and Martin stood for a while by the well, listening. Theresa had insisted that nobody should peer down the well to see how she was, because that would mean that she wasn't completely forgotten, the way her daughter had been forgotten.

He listened, but he heard nothing. Tybalt had checked this morning and said that she was still alive, but "very, very weak."

The tractor was parked beside the paddock gate, with its engine chugging over. Terence was already lying underneath the plow, between its shining circular disks. He was stripped to the waist, with Tybalt's electrodes fastened to his forehead. He caught sight of Martin and Sticky making their way across the grass, and he gave them an elated thumb's up.

Martin went up and hunkered down next to him. "Are you all right?" he asked.

"Couldn't be better. I've been looking forward to this. You don't know how much."

"Aren't you frightened at all?"

"Frightened? What of? Pain? Dying? If we were all frightened of pain and dying, we'd all sit at home with a blanket over our heads, wouldn't we?"

Tybalt came over. "Are you ready, Terence? This is what you really want?"

Terence's eyes were bright. "Come on, Mr. Miller. Let's get this over with. The sooner the better."

Tybalt reached out and touched Terence's lips with the tops of his fingers, as if he were a cardinal giving benediction. Then he stood up and said, "Better stand clear, Martin."

He went to the tractor and climbed into the cab. He revved the engine two or three times, and each time Terence grinned in anticipation. Then, with no further warning, he engaged the plow.

"*Oh, Christ!*" shrieked Terence. The shining steel disks dragged him in like gristle into an old-fashioned meat mincer. His right arm was crushed into a bloody rope of bones and thin white tendons, and twisted around the spindle. Another disk cut diagonally into his shoulder and opened up his chest, so that one of his lungs blew out like a balloon. His groin was minced into bloody rags, and his legs were twisted in opposite directions.

The plow-blades stopped. Martin could see Terence's head wedged against one of the disks. His eyes were wide with exhilaration.

He tried to say something, but all that came out from between his lips was a large bubble of blood, which wetly burst. His eyes slowly lost their focus, and he died.

Although Terence's death was so grisly, Martin was strangely elated by it. It was the expression on his face, as if he had found at last what he had always been looking for—as if he would have laughed, if he had been able to.

«« —»»

The following Saturday, inside the garage, Tybalt slowly reversed a Mercedes saloon over Sticky's stomach. Martin stayed outside, but he heard Sticky sobbing in pain for almost twenty minutes, and a single runnel of blood crept out from underneath the closed garage doors, and soaked into the pea-shingle.

"Have you seen anything yet?" he asked Tybalt, as the two of them sat over supper the following evening.

Tybalt poured himself another glass of Fleurie. "Not yet," he said evasively. "But you will, won't you? It's your turn tomorrow."

«« —»»

Martin didn't sleep that night. He sat on the end of the bed staring at his reflection in the dressing-room mirror and wondering if he were mad. Yet somehow, it seemed the most perfect and logical way to go. Even if he didn't meet Sarah in the afterlife, at least he would have shared the same death.

At seven o'clock, Tybalt knocked discreetly on his bedroom door and asked him if he were ready.

«« —»»

It had been impossible to find a lake or reservoir where they could moor two boats close together and stretch a steel line between them. So Tybalt had devised a substitute: a motorcycle, and a wire tied at neck level between two substantial horse-chestnut trees.

It was a sharp, sunny morning. They walked together down to the paddock, with Martin pushing the motorcycle.

"I haven't been on a bike in years," he told Tybalt. What he was trying to say was: I hope I don't make a mess of this, and blind myself, or cut half my face off, instead of dying instantly.

Tybalt said, "You'll be fine. Just make sure you're going full-throttle."

He sat patiently in the saddle while Tybalt attached the electrodes. "It's funny," he said. "I really feel at peace."

"Yes," said Tybalt. "Death is a good place to go to, when you understand what life really is."

"So what is life, really?"

"Life is mostly imaginary. That's what I saw when I nearly died, coming off that motorbike. Our imagination always protects us from ugliness, and unhappiness, and fear. We have a gift for rationalizing our existence, to make it seem bearable. We're always looking on the bright side."

"It's human nature," said Martin.

"No, no. You don't realize what I'm talking about when I say 'imaginary.' I mean that our lives as we know them and recognize them are mostly in our minds. You'll see, believe me. Beauty is imaginary. Happiness is imaginary."

"I was happy with Sarah."

"You *imagined* you were happy with Sarah."

"I just don't follow."

Tybalt stuck on the last electrode. "I can't explain it any more clearly than that. You'll just have to experience it for yourself."

"No—tell me!"

Tybalt shook his head. "If I told you, Martin, you wouldn't believe me. This is something you have to witness for yourself. Now, start up your engine, and think of Sarah. Think of how *she* felt."

Martin took a deep breath. It was plain that Tybalt wasn't going to explain himself any further. All the same, what he had said had given Martin a strange feeling of dread, as if there were something far worse beyond those horse-chestnut trees than instant oblivion.

He pressed the self-starter, and the motorcycle whined into life. Tybalt leaned close to him and said, "You're still sure about this? You can change your mind...go home, build a new life. I won't think any the less of you."

Go home to what? A silent flat, with Sarah's clothes still hanging in the closet? Years of grief, and loneliness.

"The recording wires will play out behind you," said Tybalt. "Don't worry about them. Go as fast as you can. And keep your chin up." Martin revved the motorcycle again and again. The sun began to come out from behind the trees, and the morning looked almost heavenly. At last he thought: this is the moment. This is it. The dew was glittering and a flight of starlings came bursting past. You couldn't leave the world at a better time.

The motorcycle sped across the paddock. Martin thought of Sarah, on her jet-ski. He could see the two horse-chestnuts but he couldn't even see the wire yet. It must have been the same for Sarah. Perhaps she didn't see it at all. He opened the throttle wider and the motorcycle bucked and jostled over the grass at more than fifty miles an hour. The breeze fluffed in his ears; the sun shone in his eyes. Chin up, remember.

He felt the blow. It was like a tremendous karate-chop to the adams' apple. He heard the motorcycle roaring off-key, and then suddenly everything was spinning out of control. His head hit the grass, and bounced, and he *saw*, he could actually *see*.

And he understood then what Tybalt had been trying to tell him, and why Tybalt had been trying so hard to see what only the dying can see.

He couldn't scream, because he was decapitated, and his brain was a split-second instant away from total death. But he could scream inside his mind. And that was how he died, screaming.

《《——》》

Tybalt sat alone in the house in front of his computer, running the recordings again and again. Martin's was one of the clearest. He could see him approaching the horse-chestnut trees. At the last second, he could see the wire.

Then—as Martin's head flew from his body—he saw what he himself had seen when he nearly died on the Kingston bypass.

He saw the polluted yellow sky, with tattered rooks circling every-where. He saw gnarled and shriveled trees, and grass as slimy as sea-weed. He saw a distant house with a sagging roof, and fires burning in the distance. He saw hideous, hunched creatures running along the lane. He even glimpsed a brief blurred image of himself, the way he really was.

A tall, white-faced figure, distant and sinister, with frightening deformities.

He switched off the computer and went downstairs. He opened the back door and stepped out into the garden. The sun was still shining—or, at least, it was still shining in his imagination. He lit a cigarette.

A cat came stalking through the grass. It stopped for a moment, and stared at him, almost as if it instinctively knew what he had dis-covered with technology: that it was not a tortoiseshell with gray eyes and gleaming fur, but something grotesque, like he was, and that both of them were living in a hell on earth.

About the Editor

RICHARD CHIZMAR is the founder and publisher/editor of *Cemetery Dance* magazine and the Cemetery Dance Publications book imprint. He has won two World Fantasy Awards, four International Horror Guild Awards, and the HWA Board of Trustees Award. Two collections of his short fiction will see print in 2003, as well as several more anthologies. Chizmar lives just north of Baltimore, Maryland.